BLACK
IRON
MERCY

BLACK IRON MERCY

a novel by ERIC SCHLEHLEIN

Best wishes!

Eric Schlehlein

8 / '16

Deeds Publishing | Atlanta

Published by Deeds Publishing in Athens, GA
www.deedspublishing.com

Printed in The United States of America

Library of Congress Cataloging-in-Publications Data is available upon request.

ISBN 978-1-944193-18-8

Books are available in quantity for promotional or premium use. For information, email info@deedspublishing.com.

Cover design by Mark Babcock and Matt King. Book design by Mark Babcock.

First Edition, 2016

10 9 8 7 6 5 4 3 2 1

ACKNOWLEDGEMENTS

This novel would not have been possible without the hard work and support of many people. I owe my thanks to generations of historians and experts who devoted their entire adult lives to learning and recording the events of the American Civil War. I couldn't possibly name all of those authors that stirred in me fervor for the topic. Instead, I'll credit Mr. H. Derus, my 8th grade social studies teacher, with instilling in me a passion for learning all I could about our nation's most tumultuous time.

One of my greatest debts is to Mr. Lance J. Herdegen, this generation's foremost Iron Brigade Scholar, who has done more to preserve the memory of the brigade than anyone else in history. I can count every one of his books among the many resources I used in researching the wartime events—and some of the post-war ones, too—that are in this book. For this reason alone, I would have adequate motivation for including his name in this section, but there's more… Mr. Herdegen, having no knowledge of me or my ability to write, agreed to read a very raw manuscript, which he did in four days, before writing a very favorable endorsement. I shall be forever grateful to him for this incredible act of magnanimity.

A similar debt is owed to Mr. Phil Spaugy, a true-life "Black Hatter," who has lived the life of an Iron Brigade Soldier in the form of advocate, writer, and reenactor. Mr. Spaugy is a walking encyclopedia on anything and everything pertaining to our Civil War. Without his patience and corrective guidance this book would be a lot less accurate. His level of knowledge puts mine to shame.

A special mention of gratitude is required for Mr. Frank P. Marrone Jr. Mr. Marrone is a Gettysburg resident and battlefield expert who walked the battlefield in the Sixth's footsteps for me, allowing me to see the field through his eyes (and video camera), so that I might better understand the terrain.

Even after ten months of research and a lot of help from the people I've mentioned above, there is still the possibility of factual errors appearing in this book. Let it be known that any mistakes are mine and mine alone.

To all who read and/or edited my manuscript—Deb Johnson, Scott Hickok, Erin Griffith, Tanya Little, Frank Frascello Sr., and Angela Higbee—thank you for your time, talents, and efforts. If not for all of you, this project never comes to fruition.

Thanks to Mr. Chad Harvey of Blazingtundra Artistic Solutions, Inc. for his artistic talent in the form of the illustration of Arlis tending to the wounded Rebel. Your ability matches your character, Chad.

I must mention that the staff of the Hartland Public Library—notably Jan, Sue, Heidi, Charlie, Paula, Ryan, Pam, Claudia, Catherine, Jill, and a pair of Nancy's—spent countless hours tolerating my presence in their presence. Thank you, all. I'll give you some time away from me as a reward for putting up with me. Okay, time's up. The Hartland Public Library is my favorite place in the world. Well, besides Disney World, anyway.

I'm so very grateful to Mr. Bob Babcock, the CEO of Deeds Publishing LLC, who spent an entire holiday weekend reading my manuscript before changing my life forever. No one I've encountered in the world of publishing is better at communication and follow-through than Bob. His company is aptly named.

To my friend, Andy Fallon: Those tiny moments of encouragement often came during my darkest hours. Thank you for that. You'll never know the impact.

Mom and Dad, thank you for inspiring in me a fervor for the patriotic and a love for the written word. I owe all I am to the two of you.

And finally, I'm grateful to my family for supporting me throughout this five-year project, allowing me to live the eclectic life of a writer while putting up with my lengthy absences, even when I never left the house. Brenda, Tyler, Bailey, and Lindsay... I love you all so very much.

TO THE READER

THE MAJOR EVENTS OCCURRING IN THIS STORY ARE REAL. MY sole intention at the beginning of this project was to convey the truth about the Civil War experience through the eyes of a soldier of the Iron Brigade. And although I hope that the story I've developed surrounding those events - which is also dipped in fact – will entertain and invoke an emotional response, I have held true to my conviction of telling the real story of the boys of the Sixth Wisconsin Volunteer Infantry Regiment.

That said, this is a work of fiction. The protagonist, Arlis Jenkins, his family, and the civilians scattered among the plotline are fictitious, although all are modeled in the style and attitudes of the antebellum period. As for the boys in uniform: Every soldier who is named in this novel was a real person, excepting Arlis and a recruit named David Bath, whom I used to convey a story without changing the personal history of a real soldier. The commands given by officers during the battle scenes are real. The dialogue and banter between the men is fictitious.

This book was inspired by the post-war experiences of James "Mickey" Sullivan, who spent much of his later life correcting false histories. Mickey advocated long and hard for the Sixth Wisconsin's reputation, writing letters and making appearances with his brethren on behalf of the regiment. In the end, history did get the story correct. Even so, many of the exploits of the Sixth Wisconsin and their Iron Brigade comrades have been shoved aside, moved to a back burner by other events. A typical example of this is the brigade's actions on the first day of the Battle of Gettysburg, which are often overlooked because of the actions of the 20th Maine on the next day, and the charge of Pickett's Division on the last. It is my hope that this novel will bring the achievements of the Iron Brigade, at Gettysburg and elsewhere, back to the forefront of the minds of historians and novices alike.

It should be known that I have taken liberties with the layouts of a few Wisconsin towns, most notably Hillsboro and Wonewoc, in that I have added stores and scenery which hadn't existed. These modifications had no bearing, however, on my original goal of telling the factual events of the Sixth Wisconsin Regiment. I hope the citizens of these communities will forgive me, as I hold them and their respective communities in high esteem.

Thank you for reading.

Eric Schlehlein
Hartland, Wisconsin
January, 2016

For Mickey and the rest of the Calico Boys.
We remember.

"Loss is nothing else but change, and change is nature's delight."

—Marcus Aurelius

"Grief is the agony of an instant; the indulgence of grief the blunder of a life."

—Benjamin Disraeli

"…and where are the comrades, so kind and so brave,
Who proudly left Mauston, the Union to save?
The death roll, so lengthy, does mournfully say,
How foremost in battle was Company K."

—James P. "Mickey" Sullivan, "Old Company K"

1

Hillsboro, Wisconsin
July 15, 1881
Afternoon

HE HEARD THE TOWN BEFORE HE COULD SEE IT. A LOUD
mechanical whine shot through the silence; Arlis wasn't sure
how close he was, but he knew he would soon come upon the
landmark he was looking for. Beads of sweat appeared on his
arms and forehead as the sun reached its apex in the sky and
he assured his mount, Nelda, that he'd find a drink for her
soon. He'd been on her back for nearly three hours. The road
had twisted, climbed, and receded through the hills of Juneau
County, entertaining the rider—and perhaps the horse, too—
with all of the beauty that western Wisconsin has to offer.
Now, as the sound of the Hillsboro sawmill reached him, the
road straightened, the landscape flattened, and Arlis felt the
anticipation as the end of his journey neared.

"We're almost there, ol' girl," he said, caressing her crest,
and the Florida Cracker mare snorted her approval. At twelve
and a half hands, she was a bit small for her breed, but Arlis
had never seen (much less owned) a more magnificent animal. Having run a livery for nearly eighteen years, Arlis had
known a lot of horses. This one was intelligent, charming, and
more patient with Arlis' physical difficulties and limitations
than any other he'd owned. Arlis loved her, and she loved him
in return.

He thought again of the reason for this journey and turned
his head to glance at his saddlebag, eyeing the satchel hiding the cause of a week's worth of fitful sleep. He fought the
urge to scour through the bag and search for the newspaper;
though he knew full well it would still be in there, he felt the

anger rising in his chest again. *Scoundrel,* he thought, shaking his head.

Seemingly from everywhere, the mechanical whine came again…and then, again. He could smell the mill now, a light breeze carrying the scent of freshly cut lumber to his nose. Arlis took it in deeply. For now, the anger abated.

Ahead, Hillsboro came into view. Arlis could see the dirt road widen into a street, and soon the buildings came into view, lining both sides of the rutted road. Nelda sped up the pace slightly, knowing relief was ahead, and Arlis didn't disappoint her. They rode into Hillsboro, and horse and rider stopped before a full trough on the left side of the street, just two buildings into town. Arlis groaned audibly as he slowly dismounted, pulling his prosthetic leg, the left one, over the top of Nelda's back and ensuring it was planted firmly on the ground before allowing the right leg to leave the stirrup. He stood in the street, slightly bent; making sure the blood was flowing correctly before letting go of the mare. Nelda waited patiently. Then, with access to the trough at the edge of the street, she drank heartily.

Arlis pulled his canteen from the saddlebag, took a long drink of water, then wiped his mouth with the back of his sleeve. He slowly elevated his five foot nine inch frame to its full height and stretched. Drawing his handkerchief from his back pocket, he removed the black slouch hat to wipe his brow. Short, brown hair covered the top of his head, with the exception of the small round bald spot that had started to appear as it did for most men. His eyes matched his hair in color. A scar he'd carried for the last eighteen years began under the outer corner of his right eye; the long half-inch wide line carved by a minie ball stretched from his cheek bone through the center of his ear, forever marking one of his several close calls with death. His cheeks were worn and weathered, much like the saddle on Nelda's back, and though he'd been good looking in youth, he hadn't turned the ladies' heads for a long time now. Carrying two days of stubble, Arlis had never been able to grow facial hair consistently enough to grow a moustache or a beard, something that had caused him great frustration in his younger days. Now, at thirty-eight, he found it to be one of the few blessings he could count on. Unsure of how time contrived to rob a man of his youth, Arlis often felt like he should just now be about twenty. His body, however, told a much different story; it insisted it was much, much older. He took another drink from the canteen before returning it to the saddlebag and had a look around.

"Milner's Hotel and Saloon" was printed neatly in large, white letters upon a sign board on the front of the building before him. It was a two-story structure with newly painted yellow siding and handsome, white trim. Arlis gave Nelda a pat on the neck and walked out into the street with a mild limp to get a better view of the town.

Sharing a wall with the hotel on the left was a small, one story structure. "Lawrence Nixon, Esq," was written on the sign that hung from two eyelets on the post out front. A pair of half-barrels guarded the front door, each the home of tulips and some other flower Arlis didn't recognize. Peering down the street, the buildings continued on for perhaps a couple hundred feet. Signs, decent and crude, adorned each establishment; one each for a seamstress, who kept shop above the bank, a newspaper office, a butcher, an eatery, another saloon. On the other side were the post office and a mercantile with an adjacent open lot. Arlis could smell the fires of a blacksmith, the scents of burning wood and molten metal easily recognizable on the breeze. Most of the buildings in the town appeared to have living quarters on the second level. A man leaned against the wall of one of the shops. If it wasn't for this man, the town would have appeared uninhabited. Another whine came screaming down the street. And another. Then, a third time. Arlis gritted his teeth. *Couldn't live here with all of that racket,* he thought.

The door to Milner's opened and a couple walked out, laughing and talking. Like Arlis, both wore calico, the man in plain brown pants and a lighter brown shirt, and the woman in an off-white dress that tapered into an attractive red petticoat. They turned away from Arlis at first, walking along the wooden planks that ran along the buildings, then descended a staircase and entered the street. Arlis watched the woman carefully lift her petticoat to descend the steps, never allowing the lace fringes to touch dirt, and never once exposing her feet.

"Calico," Arlis muttered under his breath, grinning. "Huckleberry," he answered.

The couple turned and headed further into the town. Either they hadn't seen Arlis or they'd ignored him. He didn't mind.

Nelda had gotten her fill of water and was looking at Arlis out of one eye. He laughed.

"Come on, then," he said, and they walked together side by side, Arlis limping slightly. Both were taking in the sights of Hillsboro for the first time.

"Much like home, Nelly…except a bit bigger, maybe. Not too much, though."

Passing the bank, the door opened and a stout gentleman dressed in a black suit, complete with a vest, came outside. He eyed Arlis, raising an eyebrow, curious.

"Beautiful Friday, isn't it?" he asked, lighting a cigar.

"It is, at that," Arlis said. The mechanical whine sounded, coming from the other end of the street. Arlis grimaced and looked that way, trying to locate it. The noise made his teeth hurt.

"Sawmill. You get used to it once you're around it enough," the man volunteered, matching Arlis' gait and direction.

"Name's Travis. George Travis. I'm the banker here in Hills-boro. Passing through?" He pulled on the cigar while offering his hand. Arlis shook it, reluctantly surrendering to civility. Affability and sociability were not his strong suits; they hadn't been for a very long time now. Generally, this wasn't out of meanness or disrespect for people, nor was it because of an inability to act agreeably in a social situation. He could offer a tepid warmth to anyone, even sell it as genuine if he tried, but it often wouldn't last long, ending with Arlis either going silent or exiting the scene altogether. Those who didn't know him well thought him chilly, disaffected, spiteful, and surly. Those who *did* know him thought differently, although he'd only allowed a select few to get close enough to truly under-stand. On the whole, Arlis was a good man of sound character with honorable intentions, though he'd been slowly hardened by difficulty, distress, anguish, loss, and war. No one subjugat-ed him to more scrutiny and mental dissection than himself. He struggled against himself every day.

To Travis, he responded, "Arlis Jenkins. Yes…uh, no. Well, sort of, Mr. Travis. I have some business with a man on the other side of Hillsboro. Mr. James Sullivan." He immediately felt silly. No one, especially Arlis, had ever referred to Sullivan as "James." He knew what was coming next.

"Mickey, you mean?" Travis tilted his head slightly and went on. "Don't call him James to his face unless you want to hear a ten minute diatribe…" He trailed off and stopped walking, realization taking hold. Nelda noticed the hesitation and halted, causing Arlis to stop and turn around. Travis was gaping, open-mouthed, as if he were singing "oooohhhhh," but no sound escaped him. He was round all over, Arlis no-ticed, in his face, chest, belly, and even his legs. He thought him to be about 28.

"Mr. Jenkins, it's a pleasure to meet you." He caught up to Arlis, who waited for Nelda, and all three began walking again. The sawmill screamed around them. "I assume you and Mr. Sullivan served together." Travis had found the scar on the right side of Jenkin's face and was now staring at it.

"Yes, you assume correctly," Arlis answered, shifting a bit to hide the scar.

"'The Iron Brigade,'" Travis said, bowing grandly. "Your reputation, the Sixth's reputation, precedes you to Hillsboro, sir. Will you allow me to buy you dinner before you conduct your business with Mr. Sullivan? Please!" He smiled brightly. "Ms. Norton cooks up a mean bacon sandwich at the eatery, best you'll ever eat. I promise!"

Arlis felt his face flush. He'd dealt with some Iron Brigade admirers occasionally, especially when he'd first returned from the war, but not often. Never a boaster, he was not comfortable in these situations. Long ago, he'd learned not to offer any information about his service unless asked.

He looked hard at the banker, trying to picture him in a blue suit, the uniform of the union soldier. He couldn't see it. "Uh, no…please. I mean," he paused and stopped walking, turning to face Travis. "Thank you, Mr. Travis, but I'll have to decline your invitation. I've come from Wonewoc with some urgent business for Mickey. I am hard pressed to see that business through."

Travis looked a bit like a scolded child. "Oh, I see," he said, slowly. "I can certainly understand, Mr. Jenkins. I'm a businessman myself." He laughed, half-heartedly. "Perhaps you'll look in on me on the way home, then." It was more a question than a statement.

Arlis looked hard at Travis. He saw blood soaking through the man's shirt and vest. A wound, not there a moment ago, opened deep and long on the banker's neck. Blood began pouring out, soaking his suit coat through. Now, Mr. Travis had just one leg, and suddenly the man was hopping up and down on it, searching for balance. Arlis looked at Nelda, then back to Mr. Travis, who was now clothed in a federally issued, blue woolen suit complete with leather accoutrements. It was resplendent except for the blood that was quickly soaking through. Arlis could smell the wool and leather. Now, his nose filled with the odor of blood, hot, salty, and sweet. He could feel his stomach beginning to rise.

"Mr. Jenkins," the banker was saying. He was staring at Arlis now. "Are you alright, sir? We could get out of this heat if you're not well."

Arlis shook his head and closed his eyes. He shut them tight, keeping them closed for a few seconds. When he opened them again, the banker was just a businessman again, with two legs, dressed in business attire, smelling of tobacco and sweat. Just as quickly as they had appeared, the wounds and blood had gone.

Arlis smiled politely. "I'll stop by and see you on my way back through town, if time permits," he said, knowing he had no intention of allowing Mr. Travis to buy him anything. A gratuitous gesture like that would end up with lots of back slapping and calls for stories of glory and grandeur. Arlis was sure that his host would suddenly act as if he had known Arlis all his life once his friends were around, and he had no stomach for any of it. He and Nelda began walking toward the sawmill again.

Travis walked alongside, "Well then, I shall look forward to seeing you pass through town again," the banker said, dragging on his cigar.

"I appreciate your hospitality, Mr. Travis," putting his hand out. Travis took it and shook vigorously. Pain shot up Arlis' arm, causing him to wince noticeably. Travis recoiled in horror.

"I'm terribly sorry, sir," he lamented. "I was unaware your wound still troubles you."

"*Wounds*," Arlis corrected. He stopped walking to lift his

left pant leg, revealing the wooden ankle, then took the few remaining steps to put him directly before the sawmill, Travis tagged along. "I have scars all over this old body," he said, looking at the mill. Through an immense, open set of double doors he and Travis watched two men adjust a large oak log, or perhaps it was maple, onto a platform. This platform was attached to a huge steam powered machine that resembled a hollow locomotive and had the name "Merlin" die-cast into the front. Merlin was belching smoke and cranking a wheel that turned a belt which, in turn, rotated the saw. With the log in place, one of the men pulled a lever, activating the saw blade, and the men plied their trade. The saw screamed as it pierced through the log, dropping a well-cut section of wood on the side platform. The saw operator pulled back on the lever, drawing the log back toward him again, and the process was repeated.

"It saddens me that you suffer so severely on account of your service, Mr. Jenkins."

Arlis turned again to the banker and found his eyes. "Thank you," he replied, looking to the saw as it finished another cut. He waited for silence. "But I'm better off than so very many, Mr. Travis."

2 Mineral Point, Wisconsin
July 20, 1853
Morning

THE DAY THAT CHANGED MAMA FOREVER, THAT CHANGED all of them forever, had dawned cloudless, warm, seemingly as normal as any other Wednesday. Papa was at the mine by six o'clock, well before the kids were awake. Mama roused Arlis and Rachel and the daily ritual of breakfast and chores began. The eggs were on the table before the toddler, Ezra, awoke. Once he was awake and freshly diapered, the four of them sat and ate breakfast together, mostly in silence. There'd be plenty of talking after the chores were completed, when Mama began today's lessons.

Arlis finished his breakfast before the others and went outside to fetch the water for the dishes and the baby. It was bath day for two-year old Ezra, and Mama had ordered an extra bucket of water drawn up for this task. As he drew the water from the well, Arlis remembered that Ezra meant "helper" in Hebrew, one of the many biblical lessons that Mama had taught during their home schooling. Silently, he wondered just when Ezra was actually going to start helping.

When the water had been drawn and brought to Mama, Arlis went to the little structure behind the main house, the 2-room "mother-in-law" cabin, as Papa called it. Grandpa Jenkins had lived in it before he'd set off for California with Mr. Evans back when Arlis was five, exactly half a life ago. Six-year old Rachel tagged along with him. They swept the floor, then Arlis knocked down a cobweb or two with his broom before they went back outside.

Next, the children began their daily rounds of tending to the animals. They fed the chickens, the goat, and the cow. As Rachel collected the eggs from under the hens, Arlis milked the cow and the goat. They cleaned the barn and the coop together, singing *Amazing Grace, Jimmy Crack Corn,* and *Walk-Along John.*

"Is Papa comin' home for dinner at noon?" Rachel asked as they were finishing the coop. She popped her thumb in her mouth.

"No. Mama packed some vittles for him early this morning. You know how Mr. Gregory and Mr. Baker have been ill. Pa's got more work ta do than he wants ta." Arlis put the broom in the corner of the coop. He looked down at his sister. "And get yer fingers outta yer mouth, girl. You ain't washed up, yet."

Rachel obeyed. "He ain't come home fer dinner fer a year," she protested.

"Well, it ain't been that long. Maybe a fortnight or so, though." Arlis looked in the direction of the mine, which lay directly southwest of the house. "C'mon, Rache," he said, "maybe Mama'll let us get some play time in before our schoolin'. Who knows, if she's still doin' the washin' then mebbe she'll let us go up to the mine and see Papa awhile. Let's go and wash up, now."

They found Mama behind the house near the well, sitting on a stool with her bucket, her washboard, and her dirty laundry spread around her. Ezra wasn't far away, playing with a whirligig in the form of a retriever, its front paws spinning wildly around its head.

"Kin we go an' see Papa, please?" Rachel blurted out. Arlis gave her a glare. He was wise enough to know that sometimes you had to work a bit to get a "yes" out of Mama.

Mama looked up at her little girl, smiled, and asked, "All of your chores are done already?" She dried her hands on her apron and pulled Rachel to her lap.

"Yes," the siblings sang in unison. Arlis bit his lip in anticipation.

"I wanna have dinner with Papa," Rachel said, throwing her arms around Mama. "We never git to anymore."

Mama squeezed her daughter and set her on her feet. She stood, pulling the first clean shirt out of the rinse water and walked to the clothesline. She was facing the direction of the mine, pinning the garment to the line when she saw the clouds. Covering the horizon were tall, black, threatening storm clouds. Arlis noticed a hitch in Mama's breath and he knew she was about to disappoint them.

She pointed to the clouds and looked to Arlis, then Rachel, whose fingers had again found her mouth. "Not today, children, I'm sorry." She looked back at the thunderheads. "There's a storm brewing."

Mama, or Abigail Mary Fields, was born to Jeremiah and Mary Fields in Cuyahoga County, Ohio. She took her first breath on the fifteenth anniversary of the seating of that county, which was June 7, 1822. Her father had attempted to farm nine acres of land outside the township of Strongsville. Through either his ineptness or the lack of decent planting soil, Mr. Fields pulled up stakes and moved his family of three to Prairie Du Chien, Wisconsin in 1830 to make a go at trapping for a living. This endeavor went about as well as the farming, and, after several other failures, he moved to Mineral Point in 1837 to try his hand at mining after hearing a trader speak of the town and surrounding area as "the land of gray gold."

Rather than use their scant resources to build a house or cabin, Jeremiah dug a "Badger hole" into the bluff above Mineral Point, which was a common practice in the 1830's mining town. After the Fields family moved into the hillside, Abigail's mother died in early December as the result of a ripe fever. Though Abigail was devastated, her father didn't seem to mind much.

After obtaining the proper permit for a few dollars and staking a claim, Jeremiah bought some basic supplies and began mining a 200 square yard plot of land. For nearly six months, he never even dug into the soil. Lead ore was everywhere, sitting right out in the open in plain sight.

"That ol' crazy sum-bitch was right," he'd say to everybody, smiling. "The laaannnd of the graaaay gold." Jeremiah would just pick it up and haul it in a wheelbarrow down to Benjamin Smith, who operated a smelter in the creek bed. Mr. Smith was paying a handsome three cents per pound for the ore.

Once the ground was picked clean of the loose ore, Jeremiah learned that wherever Masonic Weed grew, ore was underneath. For three years he never once dug deeper than you'd dig a grave, and he prospered.

Life wasn't easy, but by age fifteen, Abigail was spending nearly all of her free time reading and writing. She attended a local school run by Mr. Thompson, a rather brash but dedicated teacher that encouraged Abigail to learn everything she could about the world around her. He acquired books through acquaintances in Galena and Chicago for his students to read, and he taught them to speak rudimentary French and Latin. Abigail devoted much of her free time to Bible study, and could recite the Psalms, Proverbs, and most of the New Testament before age sixteen. When the First Methodist Church opened in 1839, Abigail spent her Sunday mornings in worship, enjoying and nurturing a deep, loving relationship with God; the type of relationship she'd had with her mother, and had often longed for with her father.

Throughout the 1830's Mineral Point thrived and grew. Word of the rich lead deposits had travelled far and wide, even as far as Europe, drawing workers from everywhere, including Cornwall, England. The Cornish immigrants were experienced and knowledgeable in mining and masonry, and added to the overall success of the booming mining town. In 1836, Henry Dodge, a miner himself, had been inaugurated as Wisconsin's first territorial governor in Mineral Point, paving the way for politics and lead mining to enjoy a mutual partnership in Wisconsin, each rubbing the other's back for the next fifteen years.

Jeremiah Fields ignored most of what was happening around him. He continued to mine his claim, taking on a hired hand and digging shafts as deep as 20 feet. Following a relatively harsh winter where life in the Badger hole was excruciatingly difficult, Fields paid some Cornish immigrants in the spring of 1840 to build a proper house of stone in town. Completed in late May and finished with luxuries like a brand new, Majestic wood burning stove, a kitchen table, two feather beds, and a "necessary" out back, father and daughter moved in. Abigail felt like a queen. Oh, how she wished Mother had lived to enjoy this, too.

Suddenly comfortable in her home and heart, Abigail found little want for anything outside of her small world—except for books. It seemed that Mr. Thompson just couldn't supply her with enough of them. Her illiterate father saw no need for books himself, but was willing to supply his daughter with all the reading material that she could find in the frontier town. She often would visit the docks and make trade agreements with those going downriver to Galena, asking them to bring back any books they could get their hands on. She would trade homemade shirts, trousers, dresses, petticoats, apple butter, applesauce, buckwheat cakes, fresh baked bread—anything, essentially—for reading materials. Once, she even obtained a cookbook from which she prepared recipes in order to trade for more books.

By all accounts, Abigail Mary Fields was one of the most refined, if not *the* most, refined young woman in all of Mineral Point. Her physical beauty would have singled her out even in the largest of cities. Here in Mineral Point, she couldn't leave her house without attracting a longing look from the men, both young and old. She was articulate and charming, well educated, a fine seamstress, a great cook. Since Jeremiah was now bringing in some decent money, she was well dressed, also. There was a lot of talk in Mineral Point about the availability of Miss Fields, though Jeremiah didn't hear of it. If he did, he paid little attention to it. Occasionally, a suitor would appear at the door of the Field's residence. These occurrences would invariably end in one of two ways: Mr. Fields would slam the door, or Miss Fields would slam the door, albeit met-aphorically.

So in May of 1841, when the widower Thomas Adam Jen-kins arrived in Mineral Point with his twenty-year-old son, Thomas Jr., Abigail didn't even notice. The rest of Mineral Point, however, did. Supposedly, Thomas senior had pur-chased twenty acres, and had given bond for five thousand dollars in order to mine 320 acres. Since the town had been settled, farmers and miners hadn't seen eye to eye, and few, if any, attempted to do both. Abigail thought this was silly, considering miners needed farmers for sustenance and the farmers needed the miners to buy their produce. They need each other like bread needs butter, she'd say.

Abigail eventually learned of the Jenkins' plan to over-throw convention through word of mouth, but actual contact with a Jenkins wouldn't occur until July. She was down at the docks with three jars of black butter and an equal amount of apple butter, which she'd made for Dr. Anderson, the Mineral Point physician who had family in Galena. Abigail had a run-ning agreement with Dr. Anderson that anytime he traveled to Galena and had some extra time he'd visit the bookseller there. He'd make a list of available titles, returning with it and any titles Abigail had selected from the previous list. Abigail would then barter food for them or, sometimes, pay out of the allowance that Jeremiah provided her for her housekeeping duties.

Last week, she'd selected three from the list, hoping that when Dr. Anderson returned today he would come back with all of them. "Democracy in America, Volume 2" by Alexis de Tocqueville was chief on her list, since she had just finished the first volume the month before. Washington Irving's "The Life and Voyages of Christopher Columbus" was next, closely followed by "Oliver Twist" by Charles Dickens. Okay, perhaps she wanted the Dickens novel more than the others, but she wasn't willing to admit that to the doctor.

It was a partly cloudy and seasonally warm July day when Abigail headed down to the docks to await the arrival of the doctor. She'd left just before noon, bringing along some buttered bread to eat while she waited. Dr. Anderson was expected at one o'clock.

She passed the time by sitting on a bench and watching some men unload farm implements and mining equipment from a Natchez Flatboat. She didn't recognize all of the tools, but realized soon enough that someone had quite a big operation in mind judging by the amount of hardware being unloaded from the flatboat and into the wagons…and there were several wagons. She saw spools for mine windlasses, counting at least four of them and enough rope for twice as many. She saw parts for multiple smelters, bricks for furnaces, and molds suitable for making "pigs" from lead ore. There were axes, shovels, picks, lanterns, hammers, Argand lamps, Carcel lamps, torches, and many unmarked crates that could have held just about anything, Abigail figured. And the barrels! There were barrels that were marked "whale oil," "colza," and "whiskey."

It was all very entertaining if not a bit intimidating, and when the sun was suddenly darkened by storm clouds it took Abigail by surprise. Her umbrella was at home, as she'd not expected rain, but rain was certainly coming. She'd asked a passerby the time, nearly one-thirty, but Dr. Anderson's steamer was nowhere in sight. She decided on waiting a bit longer. Certainly the doctor would arrive soon.

There was little warning. When the rain came, it didn't mist or sprinkle, it hammered. Air to ground lightning exploded all around, and large, intricate streaks spider-webbed across the sky. Abigail suddenly wished she'd gone home instead; in hindsight, the books could have waited. As she was scolding herself for lacking the foresight to have gone home, a man suddenly appeared next to her. It wasn't the doctor, but rather, one of the young men she'd been watching unload the flatboat. Abigail stood in the rain holding her crate of butter.

"My name's Tom," he said. His umbrella was open and welcoming; the two of them sat down on the bench together to wait out the storm.

"I'm Abigail," the grateful girl replied. "Thank you."

An hour or so later, the rain had stopped and Abigail had learned all about this young man. His father, who was also Tom, but went by "Thomas," worked for a Mr. James Evans, a Cornish immigrant who had brought his wealth to America with the intention of increasing it. Mr. Evans had found Thomas running a successful lead mine outside of Galena, and, as Tom put it, was so impressed with his work that he hired him on the spot to supervise his operations in Mineral Point. These operations were just now getting underway, of course. Mr. Evans had stayed on in Galena, running an even bigger mining operation there.

So the rumors about the Jenkins' mixing farming and mining were only partly true, Abigail reasoned. Mr. Jenkins owned the farmland, but was working for Mr. Evans. *Blessed small town gossip*, she thought.

"We arrived too late to plant this season," Tom explained, "so as soon as the mules arrive I intend to give winter wheat a go. Our plow is on one of those wagons. I'll plant as soon as I can. We're gonna get some cattle, too, I reckon. And chickens, too, of course."

By the time the steamer arrived Abigail had all but forgotten about the doctor and her books, and young Tom had already decided he'd attempt to court this young lady.

"I've got two of the three, Miss Fields," Dr. Anderson announced, when he had arrived, "The one written by the Frenchman and the other by Mr. Dickens." She hardly cared anymore. It was funny how much things can change in one short hour.

Eleven months later, Tom and Abigail were married at the First Methodist Church.

3 Mineral Point, Wisconsin
July 20, 1853
Noon

EVERY DAY MAMA STARTED THE LESSONS OFF WITH AT LEAST one Bible verse. Today had been no exception and Arlis was trying as hard as he could to remember which passage they had studied this morning. He was sure that it had been from the New Testament, but he'd already passed through his mind all of the books from Matthew to Revelation and hadn't been able to come up with it. Now, as he rattled off the Epistles again, he grew more frustrated…and the water drip, drip, dripping on the back of his neck wasn't helping.

The Jenkins, Tom and Abigail, had decided their children would be educated at home following the death of their third child, Mary, after pneumonia had ravaged her frail, one year old body in the spring of 1850. After Mary had passed, Abigail had gone through a period of months where even rising from bed had been difficult. Tom recognized that an undertaking such as educating Arlis and Rachel would help to busy Abigail, allowing her to better handle her grief. Additionally, Abigail's former teacher, Mr. Thompson, had passed on in December of 1846, leaving the town of Mineral Point to hire, fire, and lose several teachers in rapid succession. One had seemed interested only in imposing discipline on the children rather than educating them. Another drank in the schoolhouse. It had become obvious to both parents that Arlis wasn't in the best of hands at the schoolhouse. And so, after

Tom proposed the idea to Abigail, they decided to keep both children at home for their lessons, especially since Rachel was now approaching school age by this time as well.

While teaching her children, Abigail was in her element. *Her* classroom, unlike the school's classroom, was open year round, albeit part-time during planting season and harvest time. Providing routine, structure, and a loving, nurturing environment, Abigail took tremendous pride in her own education and her ability to project it onto her children. She taught the basics; reading, writing, spelling, and arithmetic, of course, but she also included a heavy dose of religion, common sense, logic, and basic living skills, such as how to properly fold a tablecloth, blacken a pair of boots, make a bed, etc. Then in July of last year, just after Arlis had turned nine years old, Abigail had begun a regimen of rhetoric. She knew no boy should go too long without learning to speak properly, lest his bad habits embed too deeply. Even now, she would catch him using the word "ain't" far too often. Next year, she planned on adding some rudimentary French and Latin to her curriculum, just as Mr. Thompson had done with her.

"It doesn't matter how you obtain it," she had said recently, "In America, any man that has been educated can go as far as any other man. It is my intention that you, Arlis, go all the way."

Arlis hadn't been sure just what "all the way" meant, but he certainly didn't want to let Mama down. Now, as he tried in vain to remember a specific Bible passage, he feared that he couldn't possibly live up to Mama's expectations even if he had a thousand years.

Lying on his stomach with his head turned to the right, he abandoned his attempt to remember anything, pouring all of his energy into an attempt of shifting to his left side. He failed. Above him, water dripped repeatedly from a piece of destroyed timber onto his neck, keeping perfect rhythm. *Drip, drip, drip, drip.* His right arm was completely numb now, which was okay with Arlis since it had caused him so much pain earlier.

Rachel screamed. She'd been quiet for a long time and the suddenness of it terrified Arlis. The scream mutated into a long wail. When it ended, she cried, sobbing uncontrollably. Arlis thought again that he should be able to see his sister, as she seemed so close. *She can't be all that far from me, anyway,* he thought, *the house ain't that big.*

"Rache!" Arlis yelled, trying to get her attention over her sobs. His throat and lips were dry and his voice cracked. He wanted water badly. "You gotta try and settle, Rache. Can you move at all?"

Sobs came in response, then: "I caaann't," followed by another wail, long and angry. When it was over, it was followed by more sobbing.

"Do you hurt, Rache?" he asked, licking his lips.

"Yeah."

"Where do you hurt?" Arlis tried raising his head to see her. He could only raise it about an inch off of the floor.

"I hurt all over!" she yelled, and started crying again. "Mama, where are you, Mama? Papa!" There was more wailing.

Arlis looked up through the debris and at the sky. He saw three layers of blue, accented by puffy white clouds floating by slowly. They were moving in the same direction the storm had been earlier. He thought now that it was almost as if the storm had never even happened, except for the mess they were in. Looking back on that morning, after she had told them that they couldn't go and see Papa, Mama had had the foresight to know they needed to quickly put everything in the yard away that couldn't hold itself down. For safe measure, she'd barred the doors to the chicken coop and the barn. After checking the cabin out back to make sure it was shut up tight, they'd all gone inside and started their lessons for the day.

Following the Bible lesson, they'd worked on arithmetic. Mama had given Rachel some simple, single digit numbers to add. Arlis was solving multiplication problems. Mama was holding Ezra, looking out the window as the storm moved in overhead. It rained hard. Arlis could hear the wind whistle and rattle through the timbers of the house. He remembered how scared he became when Mama had set Ezra down on the floor and started racing back and forth through each of the rooms of the house. She was trying to see through the windows, gauging what was happening outside. When Rachel had asked her why she was moving about like that, she had replied that she had never heard such wind before. After seeing the fear etch across Rachel's face, she told her daughter that it would be okay and not to worry. That was merely seconds before the loud *POP, POP, CRACK* noises filled the air, and the house had suddenly leaned, all in one direction, before toppling down upon them all.

For a long time Rachel had cried, screamed, and yelled for Mama, who hadn't answered her calls. Arlis, too, had cried. First from the severe pain in his arm, then in fear, then in anger from being trapped under a bunch of debris, and finally, out of the intense loneliness that had engulfed him. He, too, had repeatedly called for Mama. The wind had continued to howl and blow, and the rain pelted Arlis hard on the side of his face and the small of his back for some time. He assumed that he had been buried under timber, wooden shingles, and part of the table he'd been sitting at. His right arm felt as if it were on fire, his legs wet and numb. He was broken, wet, miserable, and scared, and Mama wouldn't answer his cries. He hadn't heard anything out of little Ezra, either.

Time passed, though Arlis had no idea how much. The rain stopped. The wind stopped. He could hear the birds singing close by, yet so far away. And the water dripped slowly downward from the top of whatever was above him, drip, drip, dripping in perfect tempo onto Arlis' neck. He had timed the rhythm of *Yankee Doodle* and sang it in his head until the ritual annoyed him enough to make him think about something else.

Now, Arlis thought again about the Bible passage he couldn't remember and had an idea. Rachel's crying had slowed again to occasional sobs.

"Rachel."

"Hmm?" she squeaked.

"Do you remember our Bible learnin' from this morning?" he asked. Before she could answer, he continued, "Remember what book of the Bible it was from?"

"Phillipuns," she said. "Be careful 'bout nothin' an' God'll take care of you," she paused, a sob escaping her, "so long as you talk to 'im," she finished.

"*Philippians,*" Arlis corrected, the verse coming back to him. "It was Philippians: four…six and seven. 'Be careful fer nothing; but in everything by prayer an' supplication with thanksgivin' let yer requests be made known unto God. An' the peace of God, which passeth all understandin', shall keep yer hearts and minds through Christ Jesus.'"

Silence passed between them. *Drip…drip…drip.* Rachel's breath hitched with a sob.

After a minute Arlis spoke again. "Rachel?"

"What?"

"Talk to God, Rache," he said, his eyes tearing up again. "God loves you…an' I love you, too."

4 Hillsboro, Wisconsin
July 15, 1881
Afternoon

ARLIS STOOD IN FRONT OF THE SAWMILL LOOKING FOR A date on the letter from Mickey Sullivan. Mickey had sent it to him awhile back, perhaps as far back as two years ago, to let him know that he'd moved to Hillsboro with his wife and children to give farming a go. Arlis glanced to his right and saw the banker, Mr. Travis, walking back toward the bank. The round little man stopped short of the bank and walked into the mercantile as the saw screamed through another log.

Turning his attention back to the letter, Arlis realized that Mickey hadn't dated it. He scanned the letter again. Mickey loved to write in rhyme and nearly always wrote with the same cadence. Where one poem ended, another, unrelated poem, could begin and not seem out of place. The last lines, written in prose, were the words that drew his attention:

> With nigh nothing left there, we've left old poor Mauston,
> Yet with what's here in Hillsboro, We should've chose Boston.
> Veer north at the sawmill if ye venture to visit us,
> Forty acres hardscrabble sourly marks our business.

Arlis chuckled and looked up. He found himself looking directly into the eyes of one of the millers, who, seeing Arlis there paper in hand, cocked his head slightly. Arlis realized that the worker was thinking that this stranger standing in front of the mill might have business with him. Arlis smiled politely, tipped his cap and turned away, walking in the direction Mickey's letter had instructed him.

He opened the saddlebag and removed the jar of jerky he'd brought along. He pulled out two pieces, replaced the jar, and found an apple in the bag. He looked his horse in her left eye.

"Just a few more miles, I think, Nelda," he said, giving her the apple. "You ready now?"

He stepped around to the right side of the mare, planted his right foot firmly in the stirrup, and swung his other leg over the top. Settled in, he clicked his tongue twice and they moved beyond the mill, turning right and following the road beyond the mill's left wall.

On his left was an apothecary, the final shop he'd see as he left Hillsboro. Just like the other end of town, the street narrowed into a road, which was really more of a bridal path, and soon the terrain became a hilly frontier again.

Arlis chewed on the jerky…just another thing that seemed to get harder to do with each passing day. His teeth, those that were left anyway, ached a little with each bite. At least it made the jerky go farther. The road twisted and turned, climbed and receded again as he left the sounds of the mill behind him. Soon, he couldn't hear the saw anymore. He was entering wilderness. The vegetation and trees were thickening with branches that groped one another across the road, which was becoming more grass and weed than dirt. Arlis briefly wondered whether or not he'd taken a wrong turn, but once he crested another hill he could see the land below him flatten out into farm and grazing land, the terrain lusciously green with cornstalks and amber with ripening summer wheat. Prairie grass grew tall to his left.

The sun was beating down through a clear sky and there was no hope of reprieve through cloud cover. Arlis found his handkerchief, removed the soft hat, and wiped his brow. Below him to the right was a field of corn.

"Knee high by the fourth of July," he said. He glared at the stalks and the open rows between them, silently contemplating, analyzing, evaluating. Gaping hard into the corn, his mind slipped back to another field, this one far away in time and distance, on a farm alongside the Antietam Creek near a small town in Maryland.

5 Miller's Farm, north of Sharpsburg, Maryland
September 17, 1862
7:15am

COMPANY K HAD BEEN ORDERED INTO THE CORNFIELD. THE corn stalks were tall, the produce ready for harvest. Just a few steps into the field, Arlis was already growing wary of the lack of visibility. He could see no more than ten feet or so to the front, as the position of the line had them all moving at an angle to the rows. He turned his head to the left and found Billy Harrison next to him.

"Not too fond o' this, Billy. Feels all closed up in here. The Rebs might be on top of us before we see 'em."

"Can't be too far ta the other side," Billy answered.

"Wonder what's waitin' for us there, though," Arlis countered, squinting and trying to see beyond the field.

"Don't worry so much, Badger. Do yer job an' we'll all be fine," Billy said, calmly. Billy had a knack for repose in situations that would rile most men, but Arlis wasn't always sure whether it was blind courage or general blindness to the situation that caused such repose. He looked to his right. There, looking nervous as a cat in a dog pen, was Danny Cummings.

The regiment was straddling the Hagerstown Pike. There were three companies in the open field to the west of the road, one in it, and the rest—including Company K—sat to the east. They hadn't gone far when the Rebel batteries opened up, sending solid shot through the corn and into their lines. Men shattered like corn stalks, corn stalks shattered like men. To the right, a great volley of musketry could be heard, and Arlis immediately felt sympathy for the companies that had been deployed there. He looked in that direction, seeing only three or four men in blue in a sea of corn, including Danny, and then looked to his front again. The boys kept moving, stepping around the stalks as they advanced further into the cornfield. Another volley crashed, this one close, tight, and loud, sounding like one giant 100 barrel gun going off. Arlis knew it was his brethren answering in kind.

The regiment was suddenly halted and ordered to lie down in the cornfield. They had just begun to comply when a battery opened up on them from the right. *I think that's our artillery*, Arlis thought, moving into a position between stalks to lie down. He had turned to tell Danny this very thought when the battery opened up again. Danny was sent flying directly into him, knocking him sideways and backward, and then Arlis was on the ground with the wind knocked out of him, struggling for breath. He was flat on his back with his knees bent, gasping for air, his body too stunned to react to his brain, which was begging him to assess how badly he was hurt. *We ain't been in this fight but ten minutes*, he thought, and lay as flat as he could as canister and solid shot flew overhead. The lead and iron blasting through the cornstalks sounded to Arlis like someone was whipping a chopping block with a belt. He realized that whatever had struck Danny had also struck him. Lead, or perhaps iron, had embedded in his right side. It felt like he'd lain upon a hot iron.

He lifted his head and looked around. His shattered friend Danny, no doubt dead and nearly unrecognizable, lay close by on his right. Blood soaked the ground near and around the torso, and pieces of flesh were strewn about. An arm— the right one, Arlis noted—lay detached a few feet away, its palm facing skyward, as if it were in the act of praising God. *Christ…Danny*, Arlis tried to say, but no sound came out. Looking to his left, Arlis saw Billy Harrison clutching his shoulder. Evidently he'd also suffered a wound. Arlis found his tall black hat, complete with the large capital "K" and the numeral 6 inside the horn on the front, within reach. He grabbed it and dragged it near him, leaving it on the ground near his head. He saw his musket lying beyond his reach, the stock shattered, rendering the weapon useless.

From the left came the loud, booming voice of Lieutenant Ticknor. "Up men, up!" it said. Arlis still hadn't taken a breath since being knocked on his back. Suddenly the men of Company K were standing in line all around him, including Billy Harrison, who was still clutching his shoulder with one hand, his musket in the other. Arlis was relieved to see that the entire company hadn't been swept away by the blast from the cannon.

"Forward, guide left, men. March!" Ticknor shouted, and the company began advancing. Now, with the exception of Danny's corpse lying near him, Arlis was all alone.

Oh please, no, don't leave me, Arlis' mind screamed, and then he began breathing again. The first breath entered in a great rush, like that of a child who had been sobbing so hard they had failed or forgotten to breathe. He allowed his head to fall back to the ground and he lay there panting, staring at the morning sky. In the distance he heard a volley of musketry, and buck and ball flew past from the direction of the Rebel line, cutting through the cornstalks.

He felt wetness on his cheek and forehead, and wiped his left sleeve across his brow. It came away dark and bloody. For a few panic-filled seconds, Arlis searched his head and face for holes, wondering how he could have sustained a head wound without feeling pain. Then it dawned on him: This wasn't his blood at all. This blood belonged to Danny Cummings. He found more blood on the left shoulder of his frock coat. Even though he knew that this, too, was Danny's, he rifled his hand inside his coat and over his shoulder. Everything appeared to be intact. A shell exploded to the left and rear, then another, and Arlis wondered for whom those shells were intended.

He closed his eyes for a few moments, then lifted his head and looked at his wrecked uniform. The right side of his coat was riddled with holes under his arm, in the area below his ribcage. Arlis counted three of them. There was another hole in his sleeve just above the right elbow.

"I gotta sit up," Arlis said, surprised and grateful that he could speak. He fumbled with the buttons of his coat, unfastening each of them while still prone, so he wouldn't expose his head and body to the stray gunfire quite so long. Then he turned slightly to the left and planted his left hand firmly onto an ear of corn, pushing and twisting his body to a seated position. He had been prepared for failure and excruciating pain, and was astonished by how little the maneuver had antagonized him. He grabbed the strap of his canteen and removed it from around his neck, laying it on the ground next to him. Next, he blew out hard through his nose, and took off the heavy, wool coat. The battle ahead of him intensified, with multiple, large scale volleys being unleashed. Minie balls, lots of them, zipped past him with a *THWAP, THWAP, THWAP* thundering through the cornstalks, making Arlis work with a greater sense of urgency.

"Damn," he whispered, as he lifted the white shirt to have a look. Sure enough, there were three large and jagged holes in his right side, between the hip and the ribcage. He wiped the blood from the area with the coat to better see the damage. The wounds were about a half-inch in diameter. Arlis noticed if they had been connected by lines, they would form an almost perfect equilateral triangle, with each side being nearly three inches apart. Blood was slowly ebbing out of all three. Peering closer, Arlis could see that dozens, perhaps as many as fifty tiny holes, some no bigger than a pin point, others three or four times that size, lay between and around the more serious wounds, each one marking the entrance of a tiny piece of metal.

"Jeez," he panted.

He tore a section of cotton from the left side of the shirt and folded it in half, then folded it again, creating a makeshift bandage. He placed it over the wounds and held it there for a time, then remembered that he was hit in the arm as well. He let go of the bandage slowly, finding that it stuck to the wound. Hopefully it would do so long enough to accomplish what he needed done. He found his coat and wrapped it around his mid-section as another volley of musket fire zipped by, one ball buzzing in his ear. He tied a knot in the coat directly over the bandage and then examined his arm.

"Okay, a flesh wound," he said, relieved. Whatever had torn through his arm had only nicked the flesh, the wound had nearly stopped bleeding. He ripped another piece of cotton from his shirt, wrapped it around his arm, and did his best with one hand to put a knot in it.

"Good enough," he said, pulling the section of the coat that was behind his back downward so it wouldn't cause discomfort, and he lay back down.

He closed his eyes and allowed the battle to fade from his mind as best he could. *THWAP, THWAP!* The bullets continued to rip through the cornstalks, still wet with the dampness of the morning dew. The long, sharp leaves and stalks lay in great numbers upon the ground. *Some farmer is gonna be right pissed,* Arlis thought, opening his eyes and examining the corn around him. *This keeps up and there'll be* nothing *left of the harvest.*

He was acutely aware of movement to his left. He froze; ready to play dead and more than a little aware that he had no weapon with which to defend himself. He shifted his eyes to the right, searching the ground for Danny's musket. It was nowhere to be found.

Men were moving through the corn from his rear, traveling in the same direction Company K had gone, but these men had red pantaloons on their legs. He wondered if maybe the Rebs had somehow gotten behind the sixth, but then dismissed that thought as a flag bearer came into view, displaying the colors of the Fourteenth Brooklyn. Soon, the men of this regiment were moving past him, one man from each of three ranks having to either step over or go around Arlis as he lay on the ground.

Have at 'em now, you Devils, Arlis thought.

A sergeant, never losing stride, said to Arlis, "Ya rest easy, boy. Once we've thrown 'em in the Potomac we'll be back ta take care o' you."

Arlis lay down. Now, he had no doubt of the outcome. Once reinforced with the New Yorkers, the Sixth would take the field for sure.

He found his canteen now. It was blessedly full, and he took a long drink from it. Ahead, a volley was fired, then a return volley. The balls that missed their targets tore through the corn around Arlis. He capped the canteen and put the strap around his neck again. Now, he found his hat, placing it on his chest, and then looked toward Danny, trying not to really see him. He pushed hard toward the rear with his feet, scooting perhaps four or five feet through fallen cornstalks, and then turned to the west, scooting again. He grabbed Danny's mangled body and pulled it up onto its armless side and then lay back down flat behind it. This put Arlis in a position behind Danny's corpse, so that any errant shots low enough to hit him would strike Danny instead.

More musket volleys- three of them- sounded in addition to all of the individual firing going on. Then a distant battery containing at least four guns opened up, firing in rapid succession—*BOOM, BOOM, BOOM, BOOM*—on unseen targets. He looked at Danny again, laying there facing the front. He couldn't bear to look at his face, let alone see the damage that had been done to it.

"I'm sorry, Danny." Tears welled up in his eyes as his bottom lip started to tremble.

There was movement to the front, and lots of it. All at once, men were coming back through the corn from the way they had gone, Red-Legged Devils and Black Hats mixed together. At first the retreat was orderly, the officers calling for the men to maintain their lines and fall back, but then the men began moving with more haste, as the Rebel gunfire had increased again. Now, some of the men were moving at a full run.

Arlis sat up, looking wide-eyed at the men coming straight for him. One man from the fourteenth stepped directly on the hand of Danny's unattached arm before bounding directly over the top of Arlis, causing him to flinch and fall back down. He sat up again and watched as a line of Wisconsinites formed a line and fired a volley through the corn at the pursuing enemy, which Arlis could not yet see.

"Now, save who can!" someone yelled, and the line broke and the men raced for the rear again.

Wide eyed, Arlis couldn't believe it, and panic quickly overcame him. He attempted to stand up. As he did, a man ran directly into him and they both went toppling to the ground, the man turning a somersault over the top of Arlis.

"Badger! That you?" the soldier asked.

"Yeah Talty," Arlis managed, in nigh a whisper. He was looking into a face blackened from gunpowder. Obviously, Talty had gotten off quite a few shots this morning. He looked as if he'd been eating shoe polish.

Talty was known as Private Hugh Talty of Company K. In addition to being an uncle of Mickey Sullivan, he was well known in the Sixth for being the smallest man in the regiment at just five feet two inches, if he stood up well and straight.

"O' cripes, me boy! Are ye hurt bad?" he asked, in his distinct Irish accent. Without waiting for an answer he stole a glance behind them and then asked, "Kin ye walk, Badger? Ah, sure ye can, be gob! I'll help ya!"

Talty got to his feet and found his musket, then discarded it, "Bugger's empty, anyhoo!" He didn't hesitate. He stepped behind Arlis and grabbed him under the arms, pulling him up to his feet. Then he stepped to the right and threw an arm around the taller man's waist, grabbing Arlis' right hand in his own, planting it on his own right shoulder and then holding it there.

"Move!" Talty said, and they didn't look back.

6 Hillsboro, Wisconsin
July 15, 1881
Afternoon

NELDA, WITH ARLIS ABOARD, WAS APPROACHING AN intersection now, with a road going off to the left and a very old and tall oak tree hovering over the junction. High up in the tree a crow sounded an alarm, scolding horse and rider for their invasion into these parts. The sound brought Arlis out of the memory of Talty and the cornfield battle.

Arlis looked up into the tree now, finding the bird with his eyes, and said, "We're gettin' now. You've gone and scared us off." They continued down the road, leaving the crow to guard his tree and boast of his victory.

Talty, he thought, going back in time again. Arlis knew there was zero chance of his survival had he not gotten out of that cornfield when he did. It was estimated that the cornfield had changed hands twelve times throughout that day. Following the battle, General Hooker would describe the scene in detail, writing, "Every stalk in the northern and greater part of the field was cut as closely as could have been done with a knife."

"Make a hole and let them through," Major Dawes ordered to the reformed company as Arlis and Talty had come back down the hill. The line opened up briefly, allowing the men to pass along with a couple of other walking wounded. Fifty yards later they were approaching a makeshift hospital. Talty had helped Arlis gently to the ground, and then he had sat with him for a few minutes, both men silently taking turns at pulling swigs from Talty's canteen.

"Alright then, Badger," Talty finally said. "I best be gettin' on. There's hell ta pay, now, be gob. Hell ta pay! Imma gonna whip them Rebs and then I'll be back to get on yer arse 'bout loafin' around on a workday."

"Thank you, Tall-Teee," Arlis said, mustering a smile. Tall-T was the ironic nickname that the boys of Company K had given the shortest man in the regiment. "You get a few for me, too, oh...and for Danny Cummings, too. Danny's dead, Talty."

Talty frowned, adjusted his hat, and threw his canteen strap over his shoulder.

"Doncha worry 'bout that none, now. I've already bled enough of 'em fer the three of us," he said, and was gone.

Arlis let the memory linger a few moments longer, and then patted Nelda on the neck. "I'm thinkin' that once we're around that bend up there we'll be where we need to be," he told her. She snorted.

He chanced one more visit to his Antietam memory vault, this time ruminating on those men that had died in Maryland: Captains Brown and Von Bachelle, the brave commanders of Companies E and F, respectively, and First Lieutenant Bode, also of Company F. Private Atwood of Company K, whom Arlis hadn't know well, but was famous in the regiment for his rowdy disposition and keen sense of humor. Private Billy Harrison who, after clutching his wounded shoulder, had decided to advance with the company anyway only to take a minie ball in the spine and die in a hospital at Boonsboro three days later. Looking at the sky now, he thought of Danny. Danny, who couldn't read or write but could drop a squirrel at a hundred yards; Danny, who had always been so protective of the younger men, including Arlis; Danny, who had been milled right along with the corn. Maybe a meat grinder would be a better descriptor for it, but Danny hadn't been walking through a cattle pasture or slaughterhouse. He shook these thoughts out of his head, silently admonishing himself for such weakness.

He and Nelda were around the bend in the road now. Golden fields of wheat bordered the road on both sides. Arlis noticed an unusual amount of fieldstone that had been discarded in the grass along the roadside. He smiled. *Hardscrabble,* he thought, gnawing his jerky. *It won't be long now.*

He batted at a swarm of gnats. His thoughts shifted to drilling along the Potomac River with Mickey and all of the others, when Nelda suddenly halted without warning. Arlis snapped back into the present and looked ahead for what might have startled her. To the front and left, at least 150 yards ahead of him, were two men standing just off the road, a horse hitched to a wagon behind them. One of the men appeared to be working a shovel, digging something out of the ground on the edge of a field of summer wheat. Two children darted in and out of the rows of wheat, one chasing the other.

Arlis squinted, then smiled. Nelda sure was a cautious girl. She'd swung her head around to the right, waiting for instructions from Arlis.

"You're a good girl, Nelly. We've made it, meaning fresh water and a bushel of oats for you." He looked again to the people in the field and chuckled, shifting a bit in the saddle. "Nope, even at this distance there could be no mistaking Mickey."

"Gee-yup," he told the mare, and they began closing the

distance. Soon, it was time for the men in the field to do the staring, looking in wonderment at the stranger approaching on the horse. Arlis could see Mickey place a flat hand over his eyes, attempting to shield the sun in an effort to better see who was coming down the road.

"Whoa," Arlis said, bringing Nelda to a stop. Mickey and the other man, much younger, stood about fifteen feet to the west of the road. There was no recognition in Mickey's face.

"Hi fellas," Arlis said, "I'm looking for an Irishman with a square head and a mean temperament. One that goes around talking in prose all the time, bragging about his exploits with some brigade, one supposedly made of metal."

"Well, I'm not sure on the rest of it," the older of the two men replied, flatly, shuffling a few steps toward Arlis. "But you've certainly found an Irishman with a hot temper." The younger man shifted his weight, his face showing discomfort.

"The man I'm lookin' for," Arlis continued, "looks a bit like you old man, only he's about three feet taller and he's a lot better lookin'." He smiled a crooked smile and pointed at Mickey. "He'd never grow those pesky whiskers on the side of his face neither. People might get to thinkin' wrong and mistake him for General Burnside. No, sir, the Irishman I'm lookin' for was a pretty boy, not some ol' codger with a leather face."

"Mister, who the hell are you to –," the younger man started. Mickey raised a hand, cutting him off.

"Hmm…seems to me, stranger, that I once knew a Calico boy that had the look of you, too," Mickey said, limping slightly while closing the distance between himself and the horse. "Now if I get to rememberin' right, somebody done found that *Badger* in a hole somewhere west o' here diggin' rocks outta the ground. We felt sorry enough fer the bastard ta feed him an' take care o' him fer a few years." He was directly next to Nelda now, and he grabbed the reins, rubbing her on the nose. He squinted at Arlis.

"Nah, you ain't him. That boy was tough. You look like a slight wind'll knock ya off this mare."

Arlis chuckled and dismounted, and then he stretched and walked up to Mickey.

"How are ya, Mick?" he asked, offering a hand.

"Fair to middlin', Badger. How the heck are ye, besides ugly?" Mickey ignored the hand, instead opting to grab Arlis around the midsection, and the two men embraced. The young man behind Mickey let his guard down, looking relieved.

"Well, to be honest, Mickey, I hurt, and you're squeezing the shit outta me...but I guess I had that comin', giving you all that grief about your square head and all."

Mickey laughed and let Arlis go. "Well mebbe you had it comin' and mebbe not, but ya know it's never been a difficult thing to hurt *you*," he chided. Then, leaning in close, he added softly, "I hurt all the damn time, Badger. None of us had it comin'. Never in a lifetime, not even for a minute. You still carryin' that metal in yer side?"

"Reckon I am, every day since the cornfield," Arlis answered. "This your boy?" he asked, pointing to the other man, who was ignoring them now and heading for the wagon.

"It is," Mickey said. He gestured to the wagon. "Come on, I need some water." Pointing at his son, he said, "I think ya mighta met him once when he was a wee lad. Now, he's 17. I've got a couple o' younger ones runnin' through my field, no doubt doin' their best to wreck this bumper crop I've got goin' this year," he said, sarcastically.

Arlis grabbed Nelda's reins and led her to the wagon, looking around the wheat field. There were large patches of barren earth. He tried to think of something positive to say, but couldn't.

"George, this is Mr. Jenkins of ol' Company K," Mickey said, "Arlis, this is my son, George."

George stuck his hand out, "Pleased to meet you, Mr. Jenkins. You sure had me going for a minute there," he chuckled, then added, "My Pa here has spoken of you often, and fondly, too."

"It's nice meeting you, too, George," Arlis replied, shaking his hand. He winked at the young man. "Later I'll tell you some stories about your Pa that I guarantee you *haven't* heard."

Arlis looked in the wagon. A wooden bucket half full of water, two shovels, a pick, and several large rocks were strewn about the back.

Mickey and George pulled a couple of tin cups from a bucket of water in the back of the wagon. George offered his to Arlis, who declined and got his canteen out of the saddlebag. The three of them stood silently for a minute or so, drinking water and wiping the sweat from their eyes and faces in the hot sun.

"You still run that livery in Wonewoc?" Mickey asked.

"Yup," Arlis said.

Mickey set his cup back in the bucket and pulled one of the shovels out of the wagon. As if on cue, George figured out that the break was over and he, too, returned his cup to the bucket. The two of them, with Arlis trailing, went back to where they'd been when he rode up. Mickey waddled like a man whose feet were always troubling him. George picked up the shovel that he'd left on the ground.

"Just let us git this bugger outta the ground and we'll take a ride up ta the house, Badger," Mickey said, placing the tip of his shovel under an exposed section of a large piece of fieldstone. The stone was on the very edge of the wheat field, using up space where seed might otherwise take hold. "We'll git your horse watered and fed…and then we'll grab some grub and talk about whatever it is that would make a farrier with a wooden leg ride twelve miles to visit with a failin' farmer. I don't s'pose you brought any of that new fangled dynamite with ya now, did ya?" Mickey asked.

"No," Arlis laughed, limping off toward the wagon, "But I can work a shovel a bit. Heh heh, look who's diggin' rocks out of the dirt now! Least the ones I used to pull out had some value. Looks to me like you're just dressing up the side of the road with 'em." He pulled the remaining shovel from the wagon and returned to the others.

Mickey gawked at him, "One of these suckers will surely be made of gold," he quipped.

"See, you were expecting *somebody*," Arlis said, smiling at Mickey's joke, "Plenty of shovels to go around." Mickey and George were taking turns stabbing and lifting at the stone. Arlis joined them on an open side.

Mickey grunted, said, "Ah, me boy, John, was diggin' for a time with us. Truth be told, we're a lot faster without him, but helpin' is the expectation, at least til he grows tired of the helpin' an' goes off gallivantin' with his sister. Never hurts ta have an extra shovel 'round, seein' as we're breakin' 'em all the time. Blasted land." He pulled the shovel out and stuck it in the ground near his feet. "This is really all George and I've been up ta all summer. Every summer, actually, since we moved here. Diggin' the damn rocks outta the ground and movin' em to the road so I can plant a bit more seed next season. Seed that probably won't grow anyway." He pulled a handkerchief from his pocket and wiped his face, then retrieved the shovel again.

The stone began to give way with the trio working at it, and as Arlis and George finished freeing it from the ground Mickey maneuvered the wagon into a position to receive it. The three men worked together to get the rock into the wagon.

"A hunnert pounds if she's ten," Mickey said.

They threw the tools into the wagon and then George negotiated it through the ditch and onto the road. Working together, they hoisted each of the rocks over the side and into the ditch, moving the wagon each time to spread them out.

"Why doncha ride up with me, Badger," Mickey said. "George'll take care of the mare, if she's alright with it. What's 'er name?"

"Nelda," Arlis answered, looking at her. She had been grazing on the roadside, picking through the long grass. "She'll be fine. I imagine she's quite hungry, now. She'd probably even let *you* ride her, Mick. She's my favorite mount, ever. She's found a lot of favor with Mrs. Jenkins, too."

Mickey looked at Arlis, blankly, looking as if he'd forgotten something. "How's she doin'?" he asked, finally.

"Feisty," Arlis came back with, quickly. "She nips at me every time I get up on her."

Mickey howled. "I meant your wife, ya dolt," he said at last, and laughed again.

"So did I," Arlis said, and then they both laughed.

"Nah, she's good, Mickey," Arlis said. "You know, when things don't change, they're good. She's still teaching when school's in session…and she's running the livery, so to speak, until I get back. We're paying a kid to take care of the horses, actually."

Mickey nodded to Arlis and then told George to go ahead and ride Nelda back to the barn.

"Feed and water her," Mickey instructed.

George looked to Arlis, silently, and Arlis nodded his approval. Mickey stepped down carefully from the wagon, put two fingers into his mouth and let go a long, ear piercing whistle. Half a minute later, two children, a boy and a girl, came bounding out of the wheat, headed for Mickey.

"Come over here an' meet my ol' pard, kids," Mickey said.

The children ran over, racing the whole way. It wasn't much of a contest, though. The girl won by nearly eight steps.

"Fannie an' Johnny, this here is Mr. Jenkins. You remember that name from my storytellin'?" Mickey asked, scooping up Fannie. She had a round face like a porcelain doll, Arlis thought, with gorgeous blue eyes and straight strawberry blond hair that went nearly to her hips. She was wearing a brown calico dress, or at least it looked brown, could've been yellow, or even white, but Fanny looked like she was wearing an acre's worth of dirt. One thing Arlis knew: This girl knew how to play hard.

"Sure do...You called 'im Badger," Fanny answered, looking at Arlis bashfully. Johnny nodded along, eagerly. He had a square head and a feminine face, with the same blue eyes as his sister. Arlis recognized those eyes as belonging to Angeline, Mickey's wife, whom he had met years before. Johnny wore denim overalls, "Levi's" it said on the butt, and he was even dirtier than his sister.

"Pleasure meeting you, Mr. Jenkins," Johnny said, and his sister echoed him. Arlis returned the greeting, thinking that both of these kids would one day break hearts with their handsome faces.

"You kids ridin' or walkin'?" Mickey asked, putting Fannie down.

The kids looked at each other, then at their father. "Runnin'!" they yelled in unison, and bolted off after George and Nelda.

"Whoa, HOLD ON!" Mickey bellowed, and the children stopped in their tracks and turned around. "You both wash up and brush off yer clothes before goin' inside. No, make that brush off yer clothes and then wash up."

"Yes, sir," they answered, again in unison, before turning around.

"Wait, I ain't finished with ya yet. Tell yer Ma that we have a guest and that he'll be arrivin' right soon," he said. He hesitated, then added, "not so soon that she'll be interrupted in her activities, mind ya. Tell her that she'll have ample time for completin' those. Also, ask her to put the stew on the fire if it isn't already."

Johnny and Fannie looked at their Pa, waiting for more.

"Well okay then, *now's* the time to git," Mickey said, and then they were gone. Turning to Arlis, he said, "I've got another boy, too. Jimmy. He's back at the house with his Ma. Never shoulda named him after me. The little buck is turnin' out just like his old man."

The men watched the children go for a moment longer and then climbed onto the driver's bench, Mickey taking the reins. He hesitated, looking at his feet. Arlis looked at him curiously.

Mickey shot a look at Arlis, "You really think I got a hot temper, Badger?" he asked, releasing the brake.

Arlis laughed, quick and loud. "I'm beyond thinking on it, Sullivan. I'm *counting* on it."

Mickey stared at him, blank faced. Arlis smiled back at him. Mickey snapped the reins.

"Ha!" he said to the horse, which Arlis figured to be a young colt, and they were rolling again.

They were silent for a couple of minutes. Arlis watched as the creamy wheat winked and glinted in the sun as they rolled past.

Mickey broke the silence, "Your wife and kid are doin' alright, I presume. You just got the one boy, right? What's his name again? Somethin' Irish, as I remember." He watched the road.

"Yes," Arlis said, "His name's Rhys. And they're both doing well. I've got nothing to complain about at home." He looked hard at Mickey, now, noticing the age and the weathering. Mickey still had a full head of hair, which Arlis could not boast, but he'd begun to gray around the edges. His eyes were deeper set than they used to be, giving his leathery nose the appearance of being bigger than it actually was. Like Arlis, his cheeks and neck had the look of aged parchment. *We're the same age*, he thought. *Do I look as old to him as he does to me?*

"Is it your house then?" Mickey asked. "Maybe you're losin' the livery?"

Arlis realized that Mickey was fishing for the reason he'd come. "No, Mick. It's nothing like that. Frankly, I'm here because there's a man marching around New England spreading lies and half-truths, stealing the Sixth's glory and giving it to others. You'll be interested in reading something that's in my saddlebag."

"I see," Mickey said. "Gonna get my blood up, are ya? Ya know I don't need much help with that, doncha?" They were approaching the road that would lead to the house, which forked to the left, heading due west. Ten feet or so off of the road, alongside the new path, was a fairly large maple. A crude shingle was nailed to the trunk, about six feet up. "Sullivan," it read in jagged black block letters.

"You hear 'bout the President?" Mickey changed the subject.

Arlis nodded, "Yeah, shot by an office seeker's the word."

"Damn shame, Badger. Garfield's a good man and a fine Republican," Mickey lamented.

"Agreed," Arlis said, shifting on the wooden seat. "Hopefully he'll pull through. I can't say that I think all that highly of the Vice President. I've heard that Mr. Arthur was given a commission, a generalship, no less, and served during the war as a quartermaster outfitting New Yorkers. Once the politics changed and the guy who gave him his star was voted out, he lost his post. Rather than request a field commission, the man went home."

"I'm thinkin' the President's a goner," Mickey said, removing his hat and running his hands through his hair. "The latest word is that his docs can't find the bullet and he just a lies there all day, never wakin'."

To the left and off the road sat a small hog parlor with an attached pen, pigs lolling about inside. One in particular grew excited as the wagon passed, squealing in delight to see people nearby. They went on by, leaving the hog disappointed. Beyond the sty stood the barn, gray and worn and in need of a new coat of paint. The house sat across the drive from the barn, looking to be in similar shape. Both were sturdy, well-built dwellings, Arlis noted. Other than being in need of paint, they had been well maintained.

"If that's the case, and President Garfield dies, then I'd sooner want Hancock as President than that 'masquerader,' Chester Arthur," said Mickey, coldly. He was speaking of Winfield Scott Hancock, another former general, who had run on the Democratic ticket in the 1880 election. He had lost to Garfield handily in electoral votes, but by less than 10,000 popular votes nationwide.

"I don't know, Mick," Arlis replied, "Regardless of the man's past, whether he's a fighter or not, once we're discussing running the country from the big chair it's the man's politics that interest me, and I find Mr. Hancock's politics to be downright disturbing." He looked at Mickey, who raised his eyebrows, and smiled.

"Of course," Mickey laughed. "Mr. Hancock is one fine lookin' Irishman, indeed. Ha! Yes, sir, it's hard to find fault with that."

"No such thing," Arlis retorted.

Mickey pulled the wagon up to the barn and halted the horse. George walked out of the barn, carrying Arlis' saddlebag, and grabbed the reins, as the men stepped down out of the wagon.

"Nelda's all taken care of, Mr. Jenkins," George said, handing Arlis the bag. "I removed her saddle and gave her a quick brush down, too. She's a wonderful girl."

"You have no idea," Arlis said, smiling and stretching. "Thank you, George. I'm grateful."

"My pleasure," replied George, unhitching the horse from the wagon. He led the colt into the barn.

Arlis turned to Mickey, said, "What you said before, you know, about Chester Arthur masquerading…" he scratched his nose, and then walked with Mickey to the back of the wagon, reaching for the tools. "I think we had enough of those types of leaders during the war." Mickey handed him a pair of shovels and then grabbed the remaining shovel and the pick, and both men walked toward the barn. After a moment Arlis said, "I'd like to think that maybe the reason the Vice President went home after losing his post was because he had enough sense to know that he had no business on the battlefield."

Mickey looked at his shoes and thought on that.

"That's a fine point," he said, and thought on it some more. "Badger, you've always had a way of making me see things in a new light."

Stepping through the open double doors of the barn, Arlis was impressed by what he saw inside. The barn was immaculate, the tools stored neatly along the wall to the left where a ladder led to the loft, which ran for the entire left half of the barn. An empty but recently occupied enclosure for goats or sheep lay straight ahead, and then there was the finest feature, which pulled at Arlis like a toddler pulling his mama's apron. Stables, eight of them, stood against the wall to the right. Wooden gates with bolt action locks kept mules and horses, including Nelda, enclosed inside. Spacious quarters lay beyond, providing ample room for the animals to move about in their enclosures, with a half-wall on the other side so that they could enjoy fresh air and a view of the hills in the distance, should equidae be interested in that sort of thing. Arlis noticed, looking through the stall Nelda was occupying, that an awning along the outside wall provided relief from the sun and protection from the rain even if the animals chose to stick their necks outside. It was a smart, luxurious arrangement, allowing for feeding to transpire at either end of each stall, depending on the season and the weather. George was in the stall in the back corner, brushing the colt he'd just unhitched from the wagon. Arlis walked over to Nelda, his boots making sharp reports on the wooden floor. He rubbed his mare between the eyes, looking at the construction of her stall.

"Like our setup?" Mickey asked, noticing Arlis' interest in the stables. "It's the only feature of the farm worth braggin' on. It took some doin', and I've gotta give my neighbor to the north a lot of the credit. His name's Edwards. Those slidin,' pull down doors were his contraption. Check 'em out." He set the shovel and the pick against the wall of Nelda's stall and then slid the bolt back on the stall next to Nelda's, where a mule stood looking at him, a look of curiosity on its face. He walked to the back corner. A rope was looped around a hook at about eye level, leading to another hook set in the wall at a height of about twelve feet. From there, the rope led to a panel of sorts that was about five feet high and as wide as the stall. Mickey loosened the rope, allowing the panel to drop the necessary distance to sit on the edge of the half-wall, shutting the outside world off from the enclosure.

"It's amazing, Mickey…genius really," Arlis said, and he meant it. "I've never seen anything like it. I just might have to steal this idea for my place, you know."

"Go ahead. Like I said, it wasn't my idea to begin with," Mickey replied. Then, pointing to the metal hardware on the panel, he said, "There's more, though, Badger. Ya just slide these bolts on the panels into the augured holes and it's good to go fer the winter," he explained, proudly. He gave the rope a tug and the panel rose back to the position it had been in, and then he wound the rope around the hook again, securing it in place. "The same kinda doors are on the goat pen o'er there." He pointed to the back of the barn, opposite the door they'd come through when they'd entered. They exited the stall, and Mickey closed the door and latched it again. He grabbed up the pick and shovel again. "Here, bring those shovels over here."

They walked to the far end of the barn, the sound of their boots echoing. Mickey placed each of the tools in their proper place neatly against the wall. Here was a plow, along with two extra plow points, two broken ones, wedges, more shovels, another pick, axes, and hoes. On the wall, neatly arranged in rows of nails and screws, were every sort of hand tool, a drill, hammers, saws, hatchets, and more.

George had finished grooming the horse and called to Mickey, "I'm done in here, Pa. Need anything else?"

Mickey turned to face him, "Nah. Ya done good today, George. Wash up an' get some grub. The rest of today's yours."

George smiled. "Thanks, Pa. See you in the house, Mr. Jenkins."

"Few minutes, I'm sure," Arlis replied. He squatted, looking at one of the broken plow points.

"Yeah," Mickey said as if Arlis had spoken. "Damn fieldstone busts 'em. I broke half a dozen in my first plantin' season here. Then we were usin' the plow to get the rocks outta the ground. Not the best of ideas I've had, I gather. Busted my points and confused the hell out of my beasts. They're used to plowing in a straight line, not backin' up and goin' forth again all day long. Finally jus' gave up and started diggin' 'em out myself, well, usin' the power of George's back, too."

From outside of the barn, George called, "Pa, are you gonna use anymore of this water here in the wagon?"

Mickey sauntered back to the door so he could look at his

son, outside. "Just leave it there," he said. "We'll use it to wash up." He motioned with his head for Arlis to come with him. "Hey George, did ya wash up in the bucket?"

George stopped near the house and turned. "Nah. I'm gonna wash up at the well, Pa." He walked to the corner of the house and disappeared, heading for the back of the house.

They walked back outside and stopped at the back of the wagon, filling the tin cups from the bucket before silently downing another drink of water. The water was warm and tepid, but the day was hot and dry, and the water felt refreshing nonetheless.

Mickey sat on the tailboard of the wagon and refilled his cup.

"Sit a moment with me," he said, and Arlis hopped up on the wagon with him and sat to the left of him. He reached down, grabbed his right leg and pulled it up onto the wagon so that the entire leg from the ankle up was on the tail end. In doing this, he'd turned his body nearly ninety degrees so as to face Mickey. He too, finished his water and reached into the bucket, refilling the cup.

"Ya know," Mickey said, looking toward the house, "When we moved down here ta take on this farm, I felt a lot younger and lot more able-bodied than I do now. Damned if ain't growin' old fast." He shook his head and then took another drink, let out a silent belch. "This is the toughest piece o' land I ever did attempt to grow a crop on, Badger."

Arlis reached in his pocket and retrieved the letter. He unfolded it and held it out for Mickey, who furrowed his brow and took it. A look of recollection crossed his face.

"Hmmm," Mickey said.

"'Forty acres hardscrabble', you wrote," Arlis said, pointing to the words on the page.

Mickey set the cup down and scratched his chin with his left hand, "I tell everybody that, too! There's no exaggeration," he said, looking at the letter. "We dig them rocks outta the ground and I swear, the same ones, maybe even bigger ones, grow back the next day. Sometimes I think this land musta been used as a burial grounds by some Indians. Maybe each of those rocks was a marker fer one of 'em." He drank, swishing the water around in his mouth before swallowing. "Come ta think of it, maybe I could get me a few more dead Indians and plant 'em in the ground. I'm sure they'd make a fine fertilizer. We might actually grow somethin' that ain't made of stone." He handed the letter back to Arlis, who folded it up and returned it to the pocket he'd retrieved it from.

"Looks to me like you're doing alright here," Arlis said. "Yes, I saw bare patches, but there seems to be plenty of wheat growing in that field back there. What else are you growing?"

Mickey gestured to the west, "There's corn out that way... well, a lot of it planted anyway, less of it growin'. I've got a field of beans on about the same scale." Pointing behind the house, he said, "I'm growin' tomatoes and cabbage and lettuce out yonder. There's also pumpkins, rhubarb, eggplant, squash—there's a couple a kinds of squash—and rutabagas. The wife says that rutabagas are the only thing on this earth that are uglier than my feet. With my missin' toes an' all, well, I'll give her that one. Anyway, all of those things are growin' out back in what I'd call an oversized garden." He stopped for a moment, thinking. "Did I say tomatoes? There's tomatoes planted back there, too. I'm still tryin' to find out what grows in this devil dirt and what don't." Mickey turned and spat over the side of the wagon. He pointed a weathered finger past the barn, and said, "There's an apple orchard in the valley a few acres over. Apples are always wormy, though. As far as this summer's cash crops, it's pretty much corn and wheat. Next year it'll be the same 'cept I'll rotate the fields. Maybe I'll give somethin' else a go on a grander scale if it shows me somethin' out back." He finished his water and threw the cup back in the bucket, hopping off of the wagon. Pointing north, he said, "Mr. Edwards' property borders alongside mine up that way. He's been farmin' here fer nearly twenty years now and he does okay, I reckon." He pulled the bucket to the edge of the tailboard. "Ya want any more of this water, Badger?"

Arlis shook his head. Mickey took off his hat and placed it in the wagon before shoving his hands into the bucket, washing them, and then splashing water over his face and neck.

"Aaahhh," he said, "That's right better." He let the water run down his face and the front of his clothes. "Sometimes I think that the fella that sold me this land *knew* that it wasn't worth a lick as farmin' land. Don't know fer sure, of course, but when I get to thinkin' like that, the thought really sticks in my craw. Gives me a bit more…" he paused, searching for words, and said, "motivation. Gives me motivation for makin' this land work."

Arlis pushed himself off of the wagon, throwing his empty tin cup into the bucket. "Know what I think?" he asked, not waiting for an answer. "I think that you just plain think too much."

The door of the house opened and Johnny came running out, turning toward the road Arlis had come in on.

"Johnny!" Mickey hollered, stopping the boy in his tracks. Mickey thought for a moment and then asked, "What's your mother up to?"

"Well, she's done with her bathin', if that's what's worryin' ya," Johnny answered. Fannie burst through the door and joined him.

Mickey chuckled, "It was, me boy. Off with ya now." He turned to Arlis. "Well, so much fer bein' discreet about it, then. As you can see, I've been stallin' ya out here fer good reason. Friday is Angeline's bathin' day, and she don't take too kindly to bein' rushed through it." He frowned. "What are yer plans for the night, Badger? I hope you're not planning on headin' back today."

"No, sir. If you all don't mind the intrusion, Mickey, I'd like to spend the night. It'll give us time to hash out on the reason I'm here. The wife's not expecting me home again until tomorrow, anyway. Plus it'll give Nelda's legs a rest. She's good and strong and all, but she is definitely not used to traveling for three hours in one day. If Mrs. Sullivan objects, then I can certainly stay at the hotel in town."

Mickey frowned. "Nonsense. You're welcome to stay the night." He pointed at the sky to the southwest, where the blue sky faded into pink and lavender fluffy clouds. Beyond, giant, black and blue thunderheads were rolling in. The horizon looked as if someone had beaten it, resulting in a massive bruise. "You might not have a choice in stayin', anyway," he said. "Looks like there's a storm brewin'."

7 Mineral Point, Wisconsin
July 20, 1853
Afternoon

ARLIS JOLTED AWAKE TO THE SOUND OF SOMEONE YELLING HIS name, slamming the side of his face on the broken timber above him. Pain shot from his cheek to his neck and down through the rest of his body. He tried to sit up again and failed, angry and scared. It took him a second to remember where he was, trapped inside this fortress of debris. *Oh, God, no,* he thought, the memory of the day coming back to him. His right arm felt as if it were on fire again and he was acutely aware of the burning sensation coming from the scratches and abrasions all over his body.

Then, "ARLISSSSS!" came from beyond his feet, perhaps ten or twelve feet from where he lay on the floor of the destroyed house. It was Mama!

"I'm here, Mama, I'm here!" he yelled. "Can you see me, Mama?" He lifted his head as best as he could, trying to look down the length of his own body, and saw nothing except broken timber and shingles.

"Arlis, oh thank God! Arlis," Mama cried, "I'm stuck, baby. Can you help me?" She grunted, as if trying to lift something, and then groaned, softly. "Oh, my head."

Rachel spoke now, "Mama, oh Mama. I thought ya left me. Where'd ya go, Mama? Where *were* you?"

"I'm stuck too, Mama," Arlis interrupted. "We're all stuck." He looked up at the sky. It was still light outside, the sky blue and vibrant, with no clouds visible to Arlis at the moment. He didn't remember falling asleep. He had no idea how long he'd been sleeping.

"I'm right here, darling," Mama said to Rachel. "I didn't go anywhere. I was…I was just sleeping, baby. Are you alright, Rachel? Are you hurt? Are *you*, Arlis? Oh dear God, what… what happened?"

Rachel told Mama that yes, she was hurt, and that she hurt all over, which led to her crying again. Arlis told Mama that the storm had knocked the house down and that his arm hurt really, really badly, and that he couldn't even lift his head off the ground because so much wood was piled on top of him.

"Mama, I was *so* worried about you," Arlis explained, the tears coming again. "I called for you so many times and you didn't answer. I thought…I thought you were—" he couldn't say the rest.

"I'm here, Arlis," Mama replied firmly. "Rachel, everything's going to be fine. Just give me a minute to get my head together, honey. Oh my God. EZRAAAA! Where's Ezra, Arlis? EZRAAAA!"

Arlis tried to swallow and couldn't. His lips and mouth were unbearably dry. *Water, please God, oh just some water,* he prayed, and remembered the water that had been dripping onto his neck earlier in the day. It wasn't dripping anymore, but there was a little bit on the floor beneath his face. He tried desperately to slurp at it. He was left wanting. Across the room, Rachel sobbed.

"EZRA!" yelled Mama, short and angry this time, like she'd caught him sneaking into the cupboard. "You answer me *now*, Ezra!"

Arlis felt his stomach tighten. He didn't want to tell Mama what he knew about Ezra, which was simply that he hadn't been heard from since the house toppled over.

"Ezra…Oh, Ezra, where are you, baby?" Mama asked, softly this time. Then, after receiving no answer, she began to cry too.

8 Mineral Point, Wisconsin
July 23, 1853
Morning

THE DAY, A SATURDAY, HAD DAWNED COOL AND RAINY, AND Arlis had tramped alone through the mud to complete his chores. His right arm in a sling and swath, he was learning to get things done using just one arm. Being naturally right handed, the learning was taking a little longer than expected. The combination of learning a new way of doing things and the constant, gnawing pain in his arm caused him to grow frustrated easily. The milking and collecting of eggs was easy enough, just set the bucket or basket on the ground and use one hand, but tasks such as sweeping the barn out and collecting the water took longer to get the hang of. Worse, Rachel was laid up in the house with her legs broken, so Arlis didn't have his usual tag-a-long helper to ease the burden of the chores that usually required two hands.

He was trying to sweep the coop out, tucking the top of

the broom under his right arm pit and dragging the broom across the floor with his left hand, when Pa walked into the coop.

"Let me give you a hand with that, Arl," he said, taking the broom. "You get the pan and we'll do it together."

These two sentences comprised more conversation than Arlis had heard out of his father since he'd come home from the mine three days before. Like the rest of the family, Tom Jenkins had found himself trapped after the storm came through Mineral Point. Working in the mine was something that Tom hadn't done for a long time. He'd been supervising since his father had gone west five years before. His time was spent on the surface, and his day usually consisted of travelling between the seven mine shafts the company was now operating. His duties included running the books, purchasing, payroll, providing support, ensuring efficiency, and promoting safety for his workers.

Recently, however, the town was experiencing a fever epidemic and many of the workers were out with the sickness. Beginning the week before, Tom had gone back into the holes to keep production at an acceptable level.

Last Wednesday, he had been in one of those holes at a depth of forty-five feet with four other workers. The man working the windlass at the top of the shaft that day had been John Johnson, a forty-three year old family man that had once worked with Henry Dodge himself. Mr. Johnson had been in Mineral Point since the city was founded; few knew more about mining than Johnson.

When the storm came through (a twister, most were calling it now, though nobody had actually seen it), the windlass had broken from its moorings and Johnson, in an attempt to avoid disaster, gave his best effort to stop it from falling into the mineshaft. He had failed. Both the windlass and the miner tumbled to the bottom of the vertical shaft, breaking Johnson's neck and killing him instantly. The miners at the bottom had spent the rest of the day in the mine, unable to climb out because the windlass had destroyed much of the safety ladder that lined the shaft of the mine on its way down.

Another miner, from another shaft, discovered the trapped miners while walking past, carrying a wheelbarrow full of ore ready for the smelter. It took an additional hour to forge a plan and collect the tools to get a rescue operation under way. After the four other living miners ascended the shaft to safety, Tom secured the deceased John Johnson to a board and stood to the side, just in case, while the men above lifted the dead man out. Only then was Tom pulled from the mineshaft.

Instead of heading home right away, Tom had taken on the burden of going and telling Johnson's widow, Martha, and their two children, of the horrible accident. They had not taken the news well.

By the time Tom was in a position to set his eyes upon his own destroyed house the sun was near the horizon. He'd found his entire family buried in the rubble; his elder son's arm broken; his daughter's legs broken; his wife, with a head injury, so hysterical that he worried for her very sanity, and his baby boy…

All of the other buildings, the barn, the coop, and especially, the mother-in-law cabin, had gone undamaged. For a while, Tom had dwelled on that, but then realized that having that second house at least allowed them shelter for the time being.

"Thank you, Papa," Arlis said, holding the pan with the flattened side so that Papa could sweep the dirt into it.

"Anytime," he replied.

Arlis stood up and took the pan outside, dumping it on the pile behind the coop. Papa followed him.

"You all done, son?" Papa asked, squinting in the light rain.

"Yes, sir," Arlis said. He took the pan back into the coop

and placed it on the floor by the broom, then came back outside.

They stood in the rain looking at each other. Arlis thought for a moment that maybe Papa had something he wanted to say, but maybe he couldn't find the words. Instead, he turned and looked at the destroyed house, saying nothing. He took a few steps in that direction and stopped.

Arlis walked up and took Papa's hand, surprising him. He looked down at the boy, then back at the rubble. Tears welled up in his eyes as he sat down in the soft mud, and Arlis sat down with him. He had never seen his pa cry before, but now Papa began to sob, and Arlis threw his arms around his neck, squeezing him hard.

"Papa," Arlis said, quietly.

Papa continued to sob, an occasional high-pitched sound coming from his throat, and Arlis waited, his arms around Papa, while the tears came down.

Minutes passed. The rain lightened into a mist. Papa regained control, wiped tears and rain from his eyes and face.

"Papa," Arlis tried again.

"What?"

"Papa, what Mama said to you about the baby the other night…" Arlis hesitated now, thinking of the proper words. "Mama was wrong to say that. There was nothing you coulda done about it." He wiped the rain from his own face now, and looked toward the house that still stood. "Papa, Ezra never once made a sound after the house came down. I was callin' for him the whole day. There's no way you gettin' here sooner woulda changed anything fer him. That stuff that Mama said 'bout Mr. Johnson bein' more important than us…she didn't mean it, Papa."

Papa tenderly grabbed Arlis' face with both hands, looked him in the eyes, and forced a smile through closed lips.

"Arlis, you're incredibly wise for your age. I can't remember ever knowing a smarter, more compassionate boy of just ten years. I am incredibly proud to be your papa." He let his hands slip down around the boy's shoulders and pulled him close, embracing him. "I love you, Arl'."

"I love you, too, Papa."

To say that Abigail had lost her faith as she had cradled her broken and lifeless two-year-old son would not be entirely correct. She still *believed* in God, and she would continue to believe in God until the very hour that she died. But after God had taken this child—the second child that He had taken prematurely from the Jenkins family—she'd decided that she would no longer serve him.

The funeral began at eleven o'clock in the Mineral Point Cemetery. Tom hadn't discussed the funeral with his wife except to tell her where and when it was going to transpire. Prone to long, loud bouts of sobbing, Abigail had seldom talked to anyone since she'd gone off on Tom last Wednesday night. Occasionally, she had given Rachel some attention, her motherly bearing returning for short periods in attempts at soothing the girl who was delirious from pain and the small dosages of Laudanum that Tom had administered. But her unpredictability in mood and behavior had affected Tom in such a way that he neither encouraged nor discouraged Abigail to attend Ezra's funeral.

Rachel would not be attending the funeral. Instead, she remained in bed while a friend of the family, Betty Wilkins, stayed at her bedside. Arlis, however, had put on his Sunday best after Tom had found the clothes in the rubble and cleaned them up. He looked sharp as Mama surprised them both and climbed into the wagon with a fine mourning dress on, complete with hoop and bustle, her hair finely combed and put up in a bun.

Tom had prearranged the service with Pastor Martin. This was to be a quick, graveside service, with the Pastor saying a few words and then reading a few bible passages. The service would conclude with Olga Meyers, a woman who arguably had the best singing voice of anyone in the church, singing a few hymns.

The Jenkins arrived at twenty minutes to eleven. The rain had stopped but the cloud cover remained, leaving a ghostly haze that allowed the sun to be looked at without irritation to the eyes. Pastor Martin was already there with the casket, a simple pine box barely larger than Abigail's wicker picnic basket, sitting astride two poles over Ezra's final resting place. Abigail, upon seeing such a sight, placed the fingertips of her right hand over her closed mouth and sobbed gently for a few minutes while Tom held her other hand. Arlis expected his mother to lose control at any second but, to his relief, she kept her composure.

They spent several minutes just sitting in the wagon, silently looking upon the grave, the pastor and the cemetery in general, before a few of the other attendees started to appear. There was Doctor Anderson, who'd taken care of Arlis' arm and had set Rachel's legs a few days prior. A few of Tom's co-workers who'd been close to Tom also showed, and the entire Rhys family, the immediate neighbors of the Jenkins', Bob, Florence, and their three kids, Violet, who was about four months older than Arlis; Bobby, who was the same age as Rachel; and Andrew, the infant.

Arlis would remember what happened next for the rest of his life. After joining the guests near the grave, each attendee had offered their sympathies along with some kind but futile words of encouragement. The pastor spoke to each member of the Jenkins family as well, but when Arlis later attempted to recall what the preacher had said to him he would come up blank, remembering only that the man had placed his hand on his left shoulder and squeezed, causing annoyance that Arlis had not made known to the preacher.

The funeral began on time and as scheduled. Pastor Martin opened with a prayer that had something to do with God providing comfort to the Jenkins family. He followed this with some words about how this young boy is in Paradise with Jesus, and then said something about the Lord's plan for us here on Earth, and that once our duty to God was complete, he would call on us to carry out his duty in Heaven.

Arlis knew his mother as well as anyone, save perhaps his father, and he instantly discerned that the Pastor's words would not sit well with her. He looked up at Mama and watched her transform from a gentle, grieving woman into something he'd never seen before.

Abigail Jenkins had been staring at the ground near her feet. Now, she looked up, finding Pastor Martin in her gaze, and snapped.

"I beg your pardon," she interrupted him, quietly. "'Once our duty completed here on Earth', you said? Just what was the duty that my boy was sent here to complete?"

"Abi, please," Tom said now, taking her hand in his. She pulled away, and took a step toward the preacher, who stood there open-mouthed, his glasses on his nose.

"What was the duty that my baby girl, Mary, was sent here to do?" she asked, and then, not waiting for an answer, she went on, louder, "What, in God's name, could either of them have done in service to *Him*, except to be taken from us? What have I done to God, besides praise his name—and his son's name, too—and learn his ways, teach his ways, and be kind and faithful and *Christian* in everything I've done in my life?" she paused then, breathing heavily. She looked away from Pastor Martin, now, trying to find the eyes of the guests, who were all looking either at the ground or at their feet.

"Abigail." Tom said, quietly. "Please, let—"

"What in *GOD'S NAME*," she interrupted again, shouting now, "have I done to deserve having my children's *duty to God* be completed at such a tender age. Have I not studied His word to His contentment? Am I to be a modern-day 'Job,' being as I just didn't get the message he was trying to convey?" She was crying now; her eyes on Pastor Martin, who, if he had known any words to say at the moment, he certainly didn't have the courage or audacity to say them. Instead, this gentleman of the cloth, who had helped bring Abigail into her relationship with God, who had joined her and her husband in matrimony, then baptized their children, stood there, silently taking it.

Arlis had heard the "F-word" before. What child living in a mining town hadn't? He'd even liked to say it when he was alone or with the Rhys kids. But from this day forward he would forever associate that word with his mother and this day, at this time, at this location, at this event. He would never, ever say that word out loud again, for each time he'd hear that word, he would come back to this moment.

"Has my fucking faith not been strong enough for God?" Abigail yelled, a gasp coming from the guests. Arlis saw that Mrs. Rhys, who was standing behind her boy, Bobby, was trying to put a hand over each of his young ears while still holding the baby.

"Have I been so weak that he needs to send children to me so that they can die and teach me a lesson?" she screamed at the pastor with her eyes blazing, pointing a long index finger at him. *"I'll tell you what! God is nothing more than a fucking murderer. He's just a common, no good, fucking murderer!"*

"Alright Abigail, we're leaving," Tom said, springing into action. "I'm sorry, Pastor Martin." He reached for Abigail, and as she tried to pull away, he grabbed her tight around the waist, and lifted her, carrying her in the direction of the wagon. "Arlis, you're gonna have to drive the team," he said calmly.

"Lemme give you a hand, Tom," Bob Rhys said, stepping toward the couple.

"I'll handle this, Bob," Tom replied harshly, and Bob froze. Tom stopped and set Abigail on her feet momentarily to adjust his hold. Then he scooped her up, one arm under her knees, the other behind her back.

"Don't you apologize for me, Tommy. I don't owe anybody an apology," Abigail screamed at her husband. Then, looking back toward the casket, she wailed, *"He murdered my children! Where the fuck is* my *apology?"* as she was carried away like a bride in black being carried over a threshold. She no longer fought her husband's efforts to take her from the gravesite, but continued to yell and scream at the preacher, who calmly waited for peace to transpire before continuing again. *"I loved him with all of my heart, all of my soul, and he killed my babies. You hear me? He killed them. FUCK Him!"*

Tom all but threw her into the back of the open wagon as she landed on her backside with a thump. As he climbed into the wagon and sat beside her, Arlis leapt onto the driver's bench, ignoring the pain in his arm and shoulder, and grabbed hold of the reins. He'd driven before, but never before had he been alone on the driver's bench. He could feel his heart racing. He remembered the brake now and grabbed the lever, releasing the wheel.

"Geeyup!" he said to the horses, lightly slapping the reins. The animals knew their duty and started forward. Arlis allowed them to pass by the headstones on the left, then circled around them and headed for home. Had he not been so worried and embarrassed about his mother, Arlis might have enjoyed the drive home. He looked at the funeral goers, who were all watching him and the wagon as it rolled out of the cemetery. He peeked behind him, seeing his father holding his mother tightly in the back of the wagon, softly caressing her hair like Mama had done so often for Arlis throughout his ten years.

An hour and a half later, with the horses put away and Abigail in the bed, lying next to Rachel and nearly catatonic from Laudanum, Doctor Anderson had stopped by the homestead. He brought with him his medical bag and copies of Webster's latest dictionary and the Farmer's Almanac, gifts he had planned on presenting to Abigail earlier but hadn't found the opportunity.

"Plans change as events unfold," he told Arlis at the door. "If you don't mind, son, I'd like to have a look at your mother and have a talk with her. That's in a medical sense."

Arlis hesitated, saying nothing, knowing that Mama was in no condition to sit up, let alone engage in conversation.

"Best to let him in, Arl'," Papa said, from a corner chair. "Some doctoring just might do her some good."

The doctor went into the bedroom alone, and there he spent nearly a quarter hour. Finally, he stepped from the room, took his glasses off, and opened his bag on the meal table. From it he took a small glass vial that looked to Arlis to contain a number of small pellets which resembled the feces of rabbits. Then he pulled out a small mortar and a matching pestle, using them to grind the pellets, black as night and dry as bone, into a fine powder.

"Those peppercorns, Doctor?" Arlis asked, examining the stone-like pellets from across the table.

Dr. Anderson looked up briefly, said, "Frontier medicine is all, son." He mashed and ground the remaining pellets. "Got a drinking cup handy, Master Jenkins?"

"Yes, sir." Arlis went and found a clay cup, made sure it was dry, and then handed it to the doctor.

Pouring the powder into the cup, Dr. Anderson turned his focus on Tom, saying, "Now tonight, Mr. Jenkins," he started, then paused to find his glasses and put them on his face. He looked at Tom, ensuring that he had his attention. "Tonight when your wife rouses from her sleep, should she revert back to where she was at the cemetery today, you take three pinches of this powder and add it to a cup of water. You *make* her drink it if necessary. Now, don't use this cup. There's enough of this powder in here for a week or more. You put the water in a different cup and add the powder to it. You understand?"

Tom stared at the doctor.

"Mr. Jenkins, did you hear my instructions?" Dr. Anderson asked patiently.

"I did," Tom answered, looking at the floor. "Put water in a different cup, add three pinches of powder," he repeated.

Arlis spoke up, "What's it for, doctor?"

"It's a sleep aid that'll help her sleep dreamless," he answered, looking at Arlis. Then, facing Tom once again, he said, "She's so full of Laudanum right now that I'd initially feared for her life, Mr. Jenkins. The powder will suffice. No more Laudanum for a couple of days or more." He turned the mortar upside down over the cup and used his fingers to loosen the remaining powder. Then he did the same with the pestle, tapping it on the cup. "Your daughter seems in good order, although I'd recommend that you come out of the shell you're in and pay her some mind…read to her or whatnot." He looked at Arlis and said, "You listen to me, too, son. Spend some time with your sister." He turned back to Tom, "Maybe you could play a game with her, when you're feeling up to it. She is gonna be in that bed a great deal longer than your wife will, sir. The inactivity alone could open the door to insanity." He placed the mortar, pestle, and the vial back in the bag, then closed and fastened it.

"I'll read to her, Dr. Anderson," Arlis said. "She likes to sing, too. I can take care of her."

"You're a good brother, then," the doctor said, flashing Arlis a smile. He picked up the bag and walked to the door, then turned around and addressed Tom one last time.

"Mr. Jenkins, I have been a doctor for much of my life." He

took his glasses from his face and wiped them on his shirt. "Never have I claimed to know much about ailments of the mind…In this instance, though, it is obvious that this family has reached a crossroads." He paused, thinking, and then cleared his throat, "I know not where all the roads will lead to, Mr. Jenkins. What I do know is that *right now* matters. This time, this very moment in your lives is crucial to the future of all of you." He trailed off, pointing with his glasses to Arlis and to the bedroom. Looking again at Tom, he said, "Your family requires *you*, sir, to be strong. They will require *you* to bring them out on the sunny side of this terrible, terrible ordeal." He stood there at the door, silently waiting to see if Tom would react. After nearly ten seconds of silence, he put his glasses on and said, "Good day to the both of you," and out he went.

9 Mineral Point, Wisconsin
March 4, 1857
Afternoon

MARCH FOURTH FELL ON A WEDNESDAY. ARLIS HAD MARKED it on the calendar in the loft way back in January. Today was inauguration day, and nearly 900 miles to the east, in Washington City, James Buchanan was being sworn in as the fifteenth President of the United States. This event, as well as the actions and inactions of the Buchanan administration, would have long-term effects on Arlis and the rest of America's thirty-one million inhabitants in the years to come. But Arlis had no interest in Mr. Buchanan, his policies, his abilities, or even in the fact that he was being inaugurated. March fourth of this year had even bigger implications to Arlis. March fourth of this year was Violet Rhys' fourteenth birthday.

Arlis was excited. All winter he had anticipated this day,

going so far as to spend his entire savings on things that Violet liked best: Half a jar of peppermint twists, fishing line, two floats, and the granddaddy of all gifts…an original J.A. Bailey 1856 model fishing reel attached to a first-rate fishing pole. He'd needed to borrow a little money from his pa for that last item, after spending nearly a month of that winter attempting to talk his parents into allowing him to shower such lavishness upon the neighbor girl.

"You don't even give your own sister such consideration on her birthday," Mama had argued back in January.

"I don't intend to marry my sister one day," the thirteen-year-old had blurted out, his face flushing.

"Does Miss Rhys know that you have such intentions?" Mama had asked.

"Certainly not," he had answered. "But when I present a brand new fishing reel to her on her birthday she might come to some realizations."

"You're both just thirteen years, Arlis. She's just a girl… she's a girl that is going to receive fishing tackle as a birthday gift, if you get your way. She still runs around playing with the boys and spends her weekends fishing. Ladies don't do that, girls do. The last thing that she's thinking about is getting married."

"What's your argument, Mama? I'm not asking the girl to marry me now, you know. I'm wanting to give her some decent fishing equipment so that she'll have an easier time this summer. Her stuff is rubbish, pure rubbish."

Mama smiled, tilting her head. "*I want* to give, Arlis…not 'I'm wanting to give,'" she corrected. The grammar lessons in this house were relentless.

Arlis retrieved the newspaper from his knapsack and showed it to Mama again, pointing to the fishing reel in question. "See, patent number 15,466," he said, pitching the idea again. "It's a fine piece of equipment, Mama."

"I've no doubt of that," Mama replied. "My worry is that you will just be wasting your money on something…on some-one that will fail to show you appreciation for your efforts."

Arlis was convinced that Mama was wrong and he thought about saying just that, but didn't. Instead, he tilted his head forward, looking at the floor, and then quietly said, "Mama, besides the people that live in this house, she's my favorite person in the entire world."

This had not been the first time that Arlis had pitched this idea to a parent, nor would it be the last. But with each en-suing sales pitch Arlis had chipped away at the edges of his parents' resistance, and eventually Tom and Arlis had taken the wagon through two feet of snow to the Mineral Point Post Office, mailing payment and a request for shipment of one authentic J.A. Bailey fishing reel.

"You know you're gonna take one look at it and decide to keep it for yourself, don't you?" Tom had asked on the way home, giving Arlis a wink.

Arlis hadn't offered an answer.

Now, with the peppermint twists and the smaller fishing tackle boxed and wrapped with a pretty bow on top, Arlis stared at the rod and reel wishing he had a way to conceal it while in the act of presenting it to Violet. Even had he wrapped it in plain butcher's paper it would still appear to be what it is.

Finally giving up on concealment, he again grew excited with anticipation, and thought back to last summer's fishing adventures. Of course, last spring had begun in an entirely different fashion, with warm sunny weather already the norm by the time of Violet's thirteenth birthday. It had been un-seasonably warm when the kids had first drowned a worm on the first of March, a Saturday, and even if the day's catch had been a disappointment, the opportunity itself had invigorat-ed Arlis. Bobby, Violet's little brother, had tagged along that day and several other days until the middle of May, when he had lost all interest in fishing and all the other things associated with the pond or the creek. The rest of the summer found Violet and Arlis alone together on Saturdays to pull fish out of one body of water or the other. They were getting good at the trade, working together and helping each other out when one of them tangled a line or set their hook tight in a weed or a tree. Mostly, they talked. They learned about each other, their likes, their dislikes, their wants, their hopes, their families.

"Mrs. Newhouse said that yer Mama was possessed by the devil at yer brother's funeral," Violet said one Saturday in April.

Arlis was taken completely off his guard. He turned and looked at her, and she must have seen the shock in his face.

"I know it ain't true," Violet added. "I get why yer Ma went off on Pastor Martin that day. *My* Ma even talked ta us about it. She said that she mighta said something like that too, had our ol' preacher gone and said anything like that when my brother died. Ma says the world gets dark on ya, even in the sunlight, when you lose a child, and that you're apt ta say an' do a lot of things ya might regret later on if someone gets yer blood up at the wrong time."

"I didn't know you had a brother that died," Arlis admitted.

"T'was before we moved here from Indiana. I wasn't even walkin' yet, Mama says. His name was Benjamin, after my granddad. He fell into a bucket of washin' water and didn't come out. Let's see," she paused, looking up at the sky. "He'd be about fifteen now." Attempting to set the hook, she jerked her fishing pole. "Ah, dangit. I lost 'im," she said. Looking at Arlis, she continued, "I don't 'member Benjamin. Sometimes I think 'bout what it would be like havin' an older brother. If I think on it like that, well, that's when I miss 'im."

They were silent for a while, each lost in their own thoughts.

Arlis brought his line in, checked the bait, and then recast. Violet sat quietly, keeping an eye on her float.

Arlis flopped backward, lying on the bank of the pond. "When I think about Ezra and what happened to him, I don't really think about how he died. I think about the funeral and what happened to Mama," he said, suddenly sitting up as his float disappeared. He went to set the hook and then, just like Violet, lost the fish. He brought his line in to replace the worm and then sat back down next to her. "It's hard to believe that it's been nearly three years now," he said, reflecting. He put a dirty hand to the back of his neck, scratching. "Mama was sick for a while after she said all of those nasty things. She lay in bed and wouldn't get up for weeks. Then all of a sudden everything went back to normal. Well, kind of, anyway. Mama's a lot quieter now…and something's different about the way she treats God."

Violet absorbed that, staring at the side of Arlis' face. "She's mean to God?" Her eyebrows fell into a frown. "How so?"

"No. She's not really mean to him, she just treats him differently." He looked at Violet now. "See, before Ezra died we always used to start our school lessons with Bible passages. We'd have to study a passage, memorize it, and then show Mama that we knew what it meant. Mama used to always say that the most important thing we'll ever do in life is serve God. But now, Mama says we need to learn the Bible so that we can use it as a point of reference in life. So we can show that we're educated biblically to people who might ask later on. She says that knowing the verses is a sure sign of a good education. Instead of preaching to us every day about the importance of serving God, she'll tell us every so often that all we need to do to get into Heaven is believe that Jesus Christ is the Son of God and that he died for our sins. Rachel and I usually only study Bible verses one day a week now."

He pulled his line from the water again, baitless. He re-armed the hook and turned it loose. "Mama doesn't talk to God like she used to. She used to praise him for everything; for a nice day, for a rainy day, for having a roof over our heads on a rainy day, for teaching her humility…for everything. Now, she'll say Grace when we eat and that's about it. She doesn't praise him and she doesn't ask him for anything either."

Violet had a fish on. She tugged and pulled in the line, revealing a nice rock bass. It was a keeper. She took the hook out and handed the fish to Arlis, who pulled the metal end of the homemade stringer from the ground, ran the twine through the fish's mouth and out its gill, and pushed the fish down the string and into the water with the two fish they'd caught earlier. Then he pushed the metal end of the stringer back into the earth.

"Nice one," Arlis said.

"Thanks," Violet replied. She put fresh bait on her hook and returned the line to the pond. "What do you study instead of the Bible, then, if you're only takin' to it once a week now?"

Arlis allowed a chuckle to escape his lips. "That's the strange thing. We study 'America.' She's turned all of that religious devoutness into some kind of patriotic heat. She bought or borrowed every American history book she could find. Now, we study the Presidents, all fourteen of them. She made me learn all about them; where they're from, what party they belong to, what their politics are, their wives' names, that sort of thing. Then she made me rank them by how well they filled their position. Rachel and I have studied the Senators, the Congressmen, and all of the forefathers that don't fit into those offices, like Ben Franklin and Samuel Adams. We learn about the branches of government, the Constitution, and the Declaration of Independence. Lately, we've been studying about the great military leaders we've had and what made them so great. We're getting to know all of the important generals, like Washington, Morgan, Greene," he paused for a breath, "Harrison, Dearborn, Taylor, and Scott. We learned all about how Henry Dodge led troops in the Blackhawk War in the '30s. We learn about the Revolution, the War of 1812, and the Mexican War. We study the battles, the soldiers, the causes, and the everyday lives of those who experienced it." Arlis checked his line. Everything seemed okay. He thought momentarily about how to wrap it all up. "I guess you could say that we study everything that can be called 'patriotic.'"

"So who's the best?" Violet asked.

"Huh?" Arlis replied.

"Who's the best President, Arlis?" She asked again, pulling her line in a little.

"Oh, that's easy. Washington is, of course. The worst one's easy, too. Harrison only lasted a month before giving up his ghost. It's silly, really. He got sick because he gave a long speech in a hard, cold rain. He didn't get anything done. The rest of them are harder to judge. I don't include President Pierce, yet. Hard to tell how good they are when they're still doing the deed. Mama likes Jackson a lot, but Papa's a Whig, seeing as they're for internal improvements, like the new railroad that everyone's all in a froth over here in Mineral Point. Papa says he might vote for Fillmore, who was a Whig when he was President, but now belongs to the American Party. The Whigs are falling apart, Papa says, over all of this state's rights stuff. Papa says he doesn't know what to think anymore. He says the American Party hates people because of their religion and the Republicans are too worried about slavery for their own good."

"I think ya spend too much time with yer nose in a book, if ya ask me," she said, looking at him out of one eye, "But I like hearin' ya talk smart like."

"Me too…I mean," he was suddenly embarrassed. "I mean I've got my nose in a book too much." He grinned, "Try convincing my mama of that would ya? Imagine if you went home with your teacher after school every day and the lessons just never stopped coming."

He looked up at the sky. Cottony cumulous clouds floated underneath hazy cirrus clouds. "You're smarter than me, Violet. You just don't get your schooling poured down your throat like herb bitters as I do. Shoot, Mama's got me studying grammar like I'll die if I say something in the wrong way. I find myself wanting to correct adults when they speak out of line. Anyway, Pa says once I turn fourteen I can go and work the mine in the afternoons. That'll get my nose out of the books for a while."

"I reckon if I started goin' home with my teacher every day it would be right scand'lous," she joked. "And if you start correctin' my grammar then I'll have ta bash ya a time or two, Arlis Jenkins."

They smiled at one another and went quiet while each checked their hooks for bait and then returned them to the water. The sun was high overhead now as it peeked through the scant cloud cover, feeling warm on the skin in contrast to the breeze, which kept the air mildly cool.

"That old Mrs. Newhouse wasn't even at Ezra's funeral, you know." Arlis said, suddenly angry. "Funny how those having the weakest ties to you form the strongest opinions."

"Yup, funny." Violet agreed.

The conversation ended when Arlis said, "Mrs. Newhouse can go and suck eggs."

Spring turned into summer. Every Saturday found Arlis and Violet together, either near the stream or next to the pond, socializing and maximizing their fishing skills.

Then, on the twenty-third day of August, Arlis had stolen his first kiss from the neighbor girl. She hadn't resisted, had even kissed him in return, and soon it was something they were doing on every fishing excursion. Things had suddenly changed, although they hadn't really changed at all, as the kids continued to make fishing the priority any time they were together. Kissing was secondary, and Violet had even made rules about it. No more than three kisses per Saturday. No kisses whatsoever until they had both caught at least one fish. Lips couldn't touch for longer than five seconds during any one kiss. No one was to know about the kissing. Lastly, if anyone else was around, or if Arlis and Violet could see anyone else from where they were fishing, there would be no kissing.

September sure went by quickly, according to Arlis anyway, and October blew by even faster. November brought snow with its arrival, and the fishing excursions stopped altogether after November first.

Winter set in. The temperature dropped and then dropped some more. Come mid-January, reports of temperatures as low as -30°F had been reported by weather observers all over the area. By February, folks all around the state of Wisconsin were already calling the winter of '56 and '57 "The Hard Winter," or "The Winter of Crust," as people would often be able to walk on top of sixteen or twenty inches of snow without leaving behind a dent. There had never been a harsher winter in both temperature and snowfall in the short recorded history of Wisconsin.

Arlis had still seen Violet from time to time. They'd played together plenty of times when the air had not been quite so bitter, building snowmen and throwing snowballs, and sometimes riding on Tom's ninety inch work sled that he often used to pull lead ore down to the smelter. But during these times, there were always other children around and sometimes adults, too. Arlis agonized, but he didn't make any attempts to kiss the Rhys girl.

Now, on the fourth of March, the weather had still not relented. With near freezing temperatures and plenty of snow on the ground, Arlis grew frustrated with spring for choosing to remain dormant longer than Arlis had wanted it to. He had prayed for good fishing weather by the time of Violet's birthday so that she could put her gift to good use on the first Saturday following her birthday. That would not be the case, and Arlis was filled to the brim with disappointment.

"You could wait until the weather's warmer," Pa teased him. Arlis just stared at him blankly.

When Arlis had found out that his father's pomade was made primarily from the fat of a bear, he'd shunned it. *Animal fat…in your hair? Yuck!* Today, however, his hair was slicked back in style with the substance and he checked himself in the mirror to make sure he was presentable before gathering his wits and telling his folks he'd be back before dark. He put on his woolen coat and threw his slouch hat on his head, being careful not to muss up his hair. He found his mittens in his coat pocket and, once they were on his hands, he carried his parcels outside and took about twenty steps, trudging through eight inches of sloppy, wet snow that remained, and then stopped to consider his options. Although winter was still lingering, the "winter of crust" had softened. The Rhys' homestead lay nearly a full mile to the east. If he took the road, he'd be walking through several inches of dark mud. If he walked alongside the road he'd be walking through more than a half foot of slippery, miserable snow. Either way, he risked falling or possibly dropping the neatly wrapped gift into something wet, wrecking the precious and vulnerable paper.

He turned and looked back to the farmhouse, rebuilt by a group of generous miners in the fall of 1853, replacing the house that had been destroyed by the twister. Finding no solutions there, he turned to the barn, and, finding the work sled from the mine still inside along with a coil of strong twine, he fastened the rod and the box to the sled, making certain it was held in place snugly, and then headed out. He decided not to muddy up his boots so he stayed off the road, pulling the sled alongside it instead.

The sky was cloudless and the air seemed bitterly cold. It was frostier than yesterday, Arlis realized, and he wondered silently why a day like today, when the sun is shining brightly down on the earth, could be so much colder than yesterday, when the sun hadn't come out from behind the clouds all day. He walked carefully, watching his foot placement and stepping deliberately, his mission being to stay upright for the entire distance.

He pulled his watch from his pocket and checked the time. Nearly 2:30. *She should be home by now,* he thought, knowing that she and her brother would be attending school in town until two o'clock. He felt panic rising as he thought of all the reasons she might not be home. In all of his planning and preparation for this day he'd never really considered the possibility that she might be somewhere other than at home on her birthday. He had surely not wanted to give up his secret by announcing ahead of time that he wanted to visit her. What if her family had been planning something all of this time, too? Maybe they were all in Mineral Point, celebrating with a feast at the eatery. Perhaps the entire Rhys family had gone to Indiana to avoid this wretched winter. His mind raced to think back on the last time he had seen her. When was the last time that he had seen any of them? Early February, maybe? His heart rate increased and he breathed a little heavier now as the anxiety pushed its way into his throat. Each breath was a visible cloud as it was expelled and turned to vapor in the cold Wisconsin air.

"Silly boy, just settle," he said as he stopped walking. He adjusted his hat and pulled his mittens on tighter. Then he took off his right mitten and retrieved his watch again. The watch, a gift he had received from his parents for his thirteenth birthday last July the second, had fogged up a bit since the last time he'd checked it three whole minutes ago. He wiped the condensation from the glass and carefully returned the watch to his pocket, then pulled his mitten on again.

Arlis stood still and listened to the silence. He held his breath and concentrated. The loudness of the dormancy seemed deafening. He had often done this, especially in the winter, when the inactivity of everything was total. The calming affectation was profound and immediate, and he relaxed, his heart rate returning to normal. He closed his eyes and raised his face to the sky, absorbing what little heat the sun offered and breathed again, listening to the din of his own respiration.

"Hiya, Arlis."

He nearly jumped out of his skin and whirled around. There she was, standing in the snow near the edge of the woods. She was carrying a book and her slate.

"Darn it all, girl! You scared me out of my wits," he said, his heart rate elevating right back to the level it had been before.

"Didn't mean ta, surely," Violet said, sounding concerned but looking amused. "You scare easy is all. It's not like I'm out here sneakin' 'round. You're the one outta place. I come home this way every day." She walked over and stood near him, eyes on the sled.

Arlis smiled. She looked beautiful. Her eyes were as green as ever against this colorless backdrop. She had her hair tucked up under her bonnet and her red scarf pulled tight around her neck. Her cheeks matched her scarf in rosiness.

"Whatcha doin' out here all by yerself, fisherman?" she asked, eyeing the fishing pole. "Can't wait for spring to try out your new tackle?"

Arlis glanced at the sled and felt the panic coming back again. "Oh darn it all, Violet. You had to go and... and...You ain't supposed to see this yet. Aren't. You aren't supposed to see this, yet."

"Well, that's a terrible way to talk to a girl on her birthday," she said, scolding him and smiling. She seemed to be enjoying his discomfort.

"Aw, heck," Arlis said, surrendering to the hopelessness of this encounter going anything like he'd imagined it. "Happy birthday, Violet. These gifts are for you. The wrapped box *and* the fishing gear, too."

She went to the sled and set her school things on it. Then, untying the rod and holding it in her hands, she examined the reel.

"I've never seen one of these before, Arlis. I reckon it's right nice. I'm not sure I'd know how ta use it." She ran her hand down the pole. "One problem."

Arlis gaped at her. *Oh, oh,* he thought. "What?" he asked, his head tilted like a dog trying to comprehend.

"I can't accept it," she said, setting it back on the sled and standing up straight.

"What?" he asked, dumbfounded. "Whatta you mean, 'can't accept it?'" His heart was breaking. "You have any idea what I had to go through to get that reel?"

Violet smiled, looked around, and then stepped forward and kissed him, firm and long, surely longer than the five-second rule allowed. After a short while she backed off a little, and he felt the softness of her lush lips on his. Their tongues touched briefly, light and exquisite, another new experience, and then she withdrew, keeping her face just inches from his, the smile returning to her face.

Her mittened hand found his and held it gently. "You gotta come to the house and give it to me, Arlis, or my Pa will ask me a lot of questions. He'll probably wonder who I been sneakin' off with ta get such a gift. Wait five minutes and then follow me home. I'll say 'thank you' to you proper-like then." She picked up her book and slate and turned, walking toward her house.

"I thought you just did," he mumbled, tasting her on his lips. He was suddenly aware of how tall she was, no doubt the result of a winter growth spurt. She towered nearly half a head over him now. "Okay," he said, relieved, and then he realized something was amiss. "Hey, where's Bobby?"

Violet spun around to face him, walking backwards. "He's already at home," she said, "The younger ones get out at noon on Wednesdays an' Fridays." She pointed at Arlis and smiled again, her teeth white as the snow. "Five minutes," she reminded him, and then turned around again.

"I'll be counting the seconds," he said to himself, and then bent over and retied the fishing pole to the sled.

Five minutes. That was a long time. Arlis didn't really count the seconds, but after checking his watch again he knew exactly when five minutes was up. Well, almost exactly. Once two minutes had passed, he thought that maybe five minutes wasn't enough time and decided to give Violet ten minutes before setting out after her. Then he thought that she might be timing him and that she might get mad at him for taking too long, so he'd just give her six minutes instead. He got to five minutes and twenty seconds before he picked up the towrope for the sled and started toward the Rhys' farm again.

"Boy, something's wrong with you," he told himself.

He walked on. He decided to worry about his footing again, rather than what Violet was thinking. There were two sets of established footprints he could use now. The Rhys kids had made these tracks walking to school and back over a period of a couple of weeks now, as there had been no fresh snowfall since the middle of February. Arlis found that he could step easily in the set to the right, allowing the sled to drift out away from the road, giving Violet's birthday presents a smoother ride than if he pulled the sled over the footprints.

Ahead, the terrain sloped downhill and the road curved to the left slightly, giving Arlis a rather majestic view of the

Rhys' farmland butting up against the woods nearly a half mile off to the right. Acre after acre of unmolested snow was visible, beautiful but blinding, and Arlis found himself looking to the trees to keep his balance after losing his bearings while awing at the snowy landscape.

He followed the road downward and to the left. After negotiating the curve, he could see Violet's house. The nervousness slammed back into him, hard…and he suddenly felt nauseous, and then foolish. *What the heck is happening to me?* But he knew.

He stopped walking and sat down on the front edge of the sled, allowing the nausea to pass. In short time, it did, but he remained on the sled awhile longer as he was abruptly unsure of himself. Minutes passed, though Arlis wasn't sure how many as he refused to bring the watch out again. *How many? Five more? Ten more?*

"This is lunacy," he said aloud. "You're gonna make a fool of yourself."

He stood up again and checked the sled. Satisfied, he started off again. In short time he was standing in front of the door to the Rhys' house, hesitating and listening again to the silence, trying to get lost in it. He couldn't. He could hear movement and talking inside the house, though he couldn't make out what was being said. From the barn, maybe fifty rods to the right, he could hear noises as well. *Oh well, let's get this over with,* he thought.

He untied the rod and the wrapped gift from the sled, picked them up, and then changed his mind, setting them back on the sled. Seconds passed… then a minute. He silently scolded himself again for his indecisiveness, closed his eyes and then rapped on the door.

10 Mineral Point, Wisconsin
March 4, 1857
Afternoon

MOVEMENT...AND THEN A VOICE—A MAN'S VOICE—AND suddenly Arlis realized that he needn't have been so nervous about seeing Violet today. *I should've been thinking about what I'm gonna say to Mister—*

The door opened. In the doorway stood Robert Rhys, tall and grim faced. The smell of smoked bacon or ham or some other wonderful edible wafted through the doorway, and Arlis felt his stomach pang with hunger in addition to his anxiety.

"Why, Arlis Jenkins," Mr. Rhys said, "What a surprise! You brought a gift for me?" he asked. His face revealed no emotion. With a large head, round face, and a bald pate, Mr. Rhys reminded Arlis of those pictures of the full moon with faces drawn on them in "*The Farmer's Almanac.*" Now, it appeared as if the moon had just stepped through the door and had closed it behind him.

"Hello, Mr. Rhys," Arlis said. He removed his hat, holding it against his chest in his left hand. "No, sir," he went on, "I understand that today is Violet's birthday. I've come bearing these gifts for that occasion," he said, pointing to the sled. He swallowed. He was suddenly very thirsty. "May I see her, please?"

Robert Rhys looked at Arlis, revealing nothing through his body language. "Well, I don't rightly know," he said, eyeing the sled behind Arlis. "I was just thinkin' about takin' a little walk," he said, and then took Arlis by the left arm, walking him along the front of the house toward the barn. "Why don't you just leave that here?" he asked, letting go of Arlis and pointing to the sled. "No harm'll come to any of it, I assure you."

"Yes, sir," Arlis said, weakly. He pushed the sled up against the wall of the house and out of the way.

"Good, good. Now walk with me," he said, retaking Arlis'

arm and heading toward the barn again. He didn't smile. He didn't look at Arlis.

Arlis was sure that he was either going to explode from fear or retch at any minute. He had seen Mr. Rhys at a rare barn dance (usually one of those held by the Brown family on the edge of town) and had had a few conversations with him in passing, like when he and his father had run into him at the mercantile. Once, the December before Ezra died, the entire Rhys family had come to the Jenkins' house for Christmas cheer, and there had been talk of making it a yearly tradition. Evidently that tradition had died with Ezra. Occasionally Mr. Rhys had come over at Tom's request to help with a project that required the strength of two grown men. Tom had likewise gone to the Rhys' house when their household required similar attention, with Arlis tagging along. Arlis couldn't remember speaking to Mr. Rhys in any of these situations, except in greeting or farewell. He'd certainly never set foot inside the Rhys' house.

"How did you know that it's Violet's birthday today?" Mr. Rhys asked, flatly. He was still not looking at Arlis.

"She told me last fall, sir, when we were fishing together at the stream," he lied. Violet had actually told him about it on the first day of March of last year, when they'd gone fishing for the first time that season. Arlis knew it was not in his best interest to tell Violet's pa that he had looked forward to this day since last April.

Mr. Rhys stopped walking but his hand remained on Arlis' arm, just above the elbow. He looked skyward at the weathervane that sat atop the barn. "What's in the box?"

"I got her some fishing line for the new reel. It's top-notch line, Mr. Rhys. There are also two floats in there, along with a good number of peppermint twists. She told me she likes them." Arlis realized he was still holding his hat and that he had been wringing it harshly. Now, he quieted his hands.

"I see," said Mr. Rhys. He turned and looked directly at Arlis for the first time since coming outside. "That fishing pole is something special isn't it. It would seem that a reel like that one would cause a boy to part with a whole lot of coin," he said.

Arlis said nothing. He wasn't quite sure if there had been a question asked, anyway. If he wasn't asked then he wouldn't offer. He looked at his boots.

"What are your intentions here, Arlis?" Mr. Rhys asked.

"Huh?" Arlis replied, wringing the hat between his hands again. "I'm not sure—"

"You've come to my house looking for my daughter. You've got your hair slicked up and you're bearing gifts…one *very* expensive gift, mind you. Are you planning on courting my daughter, Arlis?"

Arlis knew that this was an important moment and he raised his eyes to meet the eyes of his elder. He cleared his throat and said, "Sir, I have but few friends in the world. I play fairly often with the Johnson boy, Teddy, and sometimes I play games with Jimmy White and his little brother Sammy. But those boys are usually looking for mischief and sometimes, well, they're just plain up to no good. The time I spend with them is short. Violet is my best good friend in the entire world and I can think of no one I'd rather spend my time with outside of my family."

He glanced at the house. He could see Violet, obscured by glare, watching the two of them through the closed window. He looked at Mr. Rhys again. "I'm just now thirteen, Mr. Rhys. I have neither interest in nor experience in courting girls. My interest in your daughter comes out of her kindness to me. She doesn't expect anything from me and she doesn't ask me for anything…except to go fishing with her." He paused and stopped twisting the hat again. "We both like to fish and I just wanted her to have a better tool to that end is all."

Mr. Rhys sniffed and turned his head away from Arlis, looking at some point in the distance that Arlis couldn't discern. "You speak pretty good for a boy of thirteen, Arlis."

Pretty well, Arlis thought. *I speak pretty well.* He said, "Thank you, sir. My mama sees to that."

Mr. Rhys turned, took a step back toward the house, and looked down at Arlis, his head in perfect position to block the sun from Arlis' view. *An eclipse…a full solar eclipse,* Arlis thought, stifling a laugh.

"One more question now," Mr. Rhys said, placing his hand on the back of Arlis' neck and guiding him past the woodpile and toward the front door where the gifts lay on the sled.

"Yes, sir?" Arlis said, bracing himself.

"Have you ever tried a 'potato crisp' before?" Mr. Rhys asked, smiling now for the first time.

Arlis laughed, more out of relief than anything else. "No, sir."

"Well, you've arrived at a good time for that, then. Mrs. Rhys has been busy today. We're gonna have scotch pie and bacon and some greens, too. You come on inside with me. And you're welcome to give your gifts to Violet now, too."

"Thank you, sir," Arlis said. He suddenly felt exhausted, like those times he'd spent cleaning the hay out of the loft, or stacking the harvest in piles for transport to the markets. He removed his mittens and put them in his pockets, retrieved Violet's gifts from where he placed them, and approached the door.

Arlis entered the house before the elder man, as Mr. Rhys held the door open for him. Again, the boy was assailed by the smell of a wood fire and pork, lavender, and something else; wonderful but unrecognizable to Arlis. He stood in a fairly large room, at least ten by fifteen, with the length being toward the back of the house. Two Howard style chairs the color of wood ash sat adjacent to the fireplace, which was lit, the fire close to death from lack of attention. The main attraction of the room was a long, oaken dining table, complete with six Portuguese Baroque-style chairs, a very impressive ensemble for a Wisconsin farming family. The table was set, Arlis noted, for six. Since there were five people in the Rhys family, Arlis realized that Violet's mother had anticipated an approval of Arlis by Mr. Rhys ahead of time.

The boys were on the floor on the opposite side of the table, Bobby seated and Andrew lying on his stomach, each interested in a picture book that was open in front of them. They didn't look up. To the rear of the room was a door leading to the kitchen where Violet stood in the doorway, dressed in an elaborate red calico dress, resplendent with a repeating, white maple leaf pattern running from the shoulders to the waist. Her chestnut hair was down and at a much longer length than Arlis had ever seen it, as it passed over the front of her shoulders and flowed nearly to her waist. He noticed her height again; the girl had begun to bud and sprout over the winter like plants in the springtime. She was beautiful and it was obvious to the boy that she was so much closer in body to becoming a woman than Arlis was to becoming a man. He suddenly understood the concerns of Violet's father. He swallowed hard.

Arlis stood the fishing rod up in the corner, behind the door, and then balanced the wrapped gift on one hand while he removed his boots, wet from the snow. He took a couple of steps in, allowing Mr. Rhys to accomplish the same task, and his eyes met Violet's eyes, which suddenly grew round and big…maybe a sign of worry for the unheard conversation between this boy and her father, or, more likely, a silent apology for what had transpired outside.

"We've got a guest in the house," Mr. Rhys dryly announced. "Master Jenkins has blessed us with his presence, and he's about to bless Violet with his presents," he said, chuckling at his own pun.

"Happy birthday, Violet," Arlis said, holding the wrapped gift in both hands, arms extended as if she'd just reach across the entire room and take it from him. Feeling foolish, he allowed his hands to drop again.

The boys looked up at Arlis now, Andrew leaning to one side to see past one of the chairs. Seeing the wrapped box, they stared silently, more than a little interested in their guest and the gift he came bearing.

Violet made the journey across the room. She gave him a warm, closed mouth smile, very unlike the one she'd given him less than a half-hour before. This smile said, "*My father is in the room.*" She locked her eyes with his, and her eyes gave him a very different smile, however. Arlis smiled back.

"This is for you. It was all I could do not to slip and fall on the way over here in that snow. It's really a wonder it got here intact."

"Thank you," she said, her eyes shifting to the box. "My ma will be out shortly. I'll wait til then ta open it." She set it on the table. "How do you like my dress, Arlis?" she asked, holding her arms out and spinning 180 degrees, then reversing and spinning a full 360 degrees, before reversing again and facing him. "Ma and Pa gave it ta me before school. I just put it on fer the first time when I got home. It's the finest garment I've ever owned."

"It's beautiful," he said, and thought, *you're beautiful,* but knew he shouldn't say it. "I don't suppose you could go fishing in a dress like that, though," he added, nervously glancing at Mr. Rhys, who by now had added logs to the fire and was stoking it to life.

Violet laughed, "I reckon not!"

Mrs. Rhys stepped through the doorway from the kitchen with a platter full of single serving scotch pies, placing one of them on each plate at the table.

"Welcome, Arlis," Mrs. Rhys said, her green eyes shining

in the firelight. Nearly as wide as she was tall, Mrs. Rhys was as short as any grown woman Arlis had seen, failing to reach five feet in height by at least three inches. The contrast in height between her and her husband was startling. He towered over her by nearly a head and a half. Violet was already an inch taller than her mother.

"I'll help ya, Ma," Violet said, moving to the kitchen.

"Just the cabbage, Vi, and bring the coffee out and fill the cups," Mrs. Rhys called, "Leave the crisps in the kitchen until supper's finished."

"Thank you, ma'am," Arlis said. "If I had known you were planning on such a fine meal to celebrate Violet's day, I surely wouldn't have interrupted." He shifted his weight from his left foot to the right, suddenly nervous again.

"Nonsense, Arlis, it's so nice of you to come by to mark the occasion, and bearing gifts no less! I trust that my husband didn't rile ya up too much outside?" she said, looking sideways at Mr. Rhys.

"No, ma'am," he answered, also glancing at Mr. Rhys, who was taking his place at the head of the table. "I can understand Mr. Rhys' concern. Should a boy come looking to shower my little sister with gifts, I'd have a right mind to ask questions, too."

"Ha!" Mr. Rhys said, not really laughing. "This boy is a master of the proper answer. Someday he'll make a fine politician! Boys," he said, addressing his sons, "Put it away now and find yer chairs."

Mrs. Rhys smiled politely at Arlis as she sat down. "Do you think your folks would mind if you joined us for supper?"

"No, ma'am."

To Violet, Mrs. Rhys said, "Open your gift now, Vi. Arlis, you come and sit next to me."

Arlis sat in the last chair on the fireplace side of the table, Mrs. Rhys to his left and Mr. Rhys to his right, at the head of the table. Violet sat across from Arlis, the gift in front of her. The boys sat across from each other, the elder one next to Violet and young Andrew, sitting on a small wood crate, to the left of Mrs. Rhys.

Violet carefully and daintily removed the paper from the square, paperboard box, being careful not to wreck either in the process. "It's a nice little box. I've seen these in Mr. Nelson's shop from time to time. He says they're imported from London." Inside, she found the floats and the line, examined them, and then removed the jar containing the peppermint twists, which was enough to finally get the boys interested in the goings on in the room.

"Ooohhh," Bobby said, reaching for the jar. "Can I have one, too?"

"Simmer, Bobby," Violet answered. "There'll be plenty for all of us. You have ta eat yer pie first, though." Facing Arlis, she said, "Thank you, Arlis. You're very kind."

The politeness was killing him. "Wait until you've cast your first line from your new pole," Arlis said, pointing to the rod in the corner, "After supper, and with your parents' permission, of course, I'll string the reel and you can have a go at it in the yard."

"There'll be a round of chores first. There's work to be done even on birthdays. There's plenty of time left in the day, though." Mr. Rhys said.

They ate. The scotch pie was of the mincemeat variety, and Arlis had never tasted one quite like it. They talked of weather and schooling, the mine, and current events, including the fact that today was inauguration day. Arlis commented that President should be lucky to have a feast such as this, drawing a smile and a thank you from Mrs. Rhys. Mr. Rhys, an ardent new Republican and a radical abolitionist, spoke out against the new President so strongly that it drew a hushing from his wife.

Once the meal was finished and the coffee cups refilled, Mrs. Rhys brought out the potato crisps, explaining that all one needed for this amazing treat was a few potatoes, some butter and salt, and since today was a special occasion, she'd added a bit of sugar to the mix, making a fine treat into one fit for nobility. "Perhaps even the President," she teased, looking directly at her husband.

"The President isn't welcome in this house," Mr. Rhys chided in return.

Three quarters of an hour later, the dishes were cleared and being washed by Violet's parents. Her father had volunteered to help in the kitchen so that Violet could get right to tending the animals, therefore getting to the casting practice sooner. Arlis followed her outside, eager to help, and they headed for the stable to retrieve the buckets for watering the horses, while Bobby pulled firewood from the cord next to the house and took it inside for stacking near the fireplace.

"What did Pa say to ya?" Violet asked when they'd put some distance between themselves and the house. Arlis regaled her with the gist of the conversation. They retrieved the buckets and headed back outside, aiming for the well.

"He's not as harsh a man as he acts sometimes," she said.

"Nah, I don't blame him for worrying after you like that. Then I go and convince him that I'm not going to court you and you walk out of the kitchen looking finer than I've ever seen you look before." Violet smiled and blushed, pushing the hair back from her face with a free hand. "Well, I couldn't get home fast 'nough after runnin' into you like I did. I wanted…" she trailed off and took the bucket with her other hand. "I wanted ta look pretty for you, Arlis. That's the real reason I made ya wait afore comin' over." She looked at him, light beaming from her green eyes. "I had to make the family think I was dressin' up for *them*."

They were at the well now. Violet worked the rope and

bucket, pulling water out and transferring it to one of the other buckets.

"Got your mittens?" Arlis asked.

Violet shook her head.

"Here, use mine," he said, holding his out for her.

"No, Arlis. You gotta stop bein' such a gentleman 'round me. Won't make a diff'rence what ya tell my Pa if he sees ya fussin' so much. If he sees that yer sweet on me, well, then we'll never be alone together, even ta do chores."

"Oh," Arlis said, putting his mittens back on. He took the full bucket from her and watched as she filled the other one.

They walked back to the stables silently this time. Arlis stole a glance at the house, expecting to see Mr. Rhys watching them, but the window was vacant. Violet punched through a thin layer of ice that had formed in the trough water with a hoe that lay strategically placed for just that purpose, and then they both poured the water into the trough and returned to the well, repeating the entire process over again. She fed the horses and began the process of straightening up the stalls, the two of them replenishing the supply of straw in each partition.

"Wait here," she ordered in a loud whisper. She walked to the door with the pitchfork and pretended to gather the loose straw, stealing a look outside. Then she set the tool against the wall and returned, offering a smile. It was the good smile, like the one she'd given him after the kiss earlier in the day.

He took his mittens off and put them back in his pocket as she threw her arms around his neck. He placed his hands gently on her waist, as if she would break if he touched her too hard, and she kissed him like she had before, but softer. Then she pulled away a little and laid her head on his shoulder and they embraced, holding each other like that for a couple of minutes. He absorbed her and pulled her hair to his face. It was recently washed, no more than a day ago he knew, and had a hint of lavender in it. He stood there, taking her in, knowing he was in too far, too deeply, too soon. There'd be no going back.

"Violet, I thought about this day all winter long," he told her. She lifted her head and they looked at each other, still embracing. "I missed you terribly, and when I get to thinking about you, I get all messed up and start acting the fool, like today when I ran into you on your walk home."

"I missed ya too, Arlis," she replied, gently touching his cheek. "C'mon," she said abruptly, taking his hands, "I've gotta tend the goats, too."

11 Hillsboro, Wisconsin
July 15, 1881
Late Afternoon

OUTSIDE, LIGHTNING FLASHED. ARLIS SILENTLY COUNTED the seconds before the thunder. *One, two, three, four*…Boom! Another flash, another boom. He took a sip from the cup. The coffee, strong and bitter, burned his tongue. Another flash, *one, two, three, four*…Boom!

"Can't stand the thunder, ever since the war," Mickey said, breaking four or five minutes of silence. "Just seems to be randomly placed artillery. God's artillery, that is. I reckon He's right better at his aim than the Rebs, too."

"Yeah? Tell that to my missing leg, Mick," Arlis said, feigning offense.

After washing up an hour before, the two old soldiers had come into the house together. Arlis had been hit with a collection of odors; the wood fire, the stew that was simmering over it, the smell of dampness and mold, body odor, dust, dirty feet, and various toilet waters. To Arlis, it all reminded him of one thing in particular: Home.

Mickey's wife, Angeline, wearing a plain yellow dress, stood there as if she'd been there all day waiting for them without annoyance. Arlis immediately felt a pang of guilt, although he wasn't sure why. "Mr. Jenkins," she had said enthusiastically, "It is a joy to see you again." She reached out with both hands and took his hands in them as he kissed her cheek.

"Thank you, Mrs. Sullivan," he replied, silently scorning the formality. "It's good to see you as well." He closed his eyes and absorbed her scent, "I detect violet water, ma'am. May I admit, here and now, that violets are one of my favorite things on Earth?"

She smiled, "You may, indeed."

"And please, Mrs. Sullivan. Call me Arlis. I am but a humble guest in your home."

She agreed to do so, as long as he agreed to call her "Angeline," or "Angel," whichever he preferred, as it didn't matter to her. He had resolved to use both.

"How's your family, Arlis?" she'd later asked him over a bowl of stew.

Arlis blew on a spoonful, "They're healthy, Angel. My wife sends her regards to all of you. My boy is rambunctious, as all seven year olds are. I've been blessed."

With the meal over and the dishes removed, the youngest boys had been sent to the loft to find something to do, and George had gone outside, taking care of what needed doing. Fannie was helping her mother in the kitchen.

Though the sun wouldn't set for hours yet, the sky had darkened and forced the lighting of oil lamps in the house, which consisted of four rooms; the kitchen, the dining area, a bedroom off of the living room, no doubt occupied at night by the adults, and a loft, which was accessible by ladder only. This house was nearly identical in Arlis' memory to the one in Mineral Point that was destroyed in 1853. Arlis had mentioned this fact to Mickey over the bowl of stew, omitting the part about the twister leveling the house, and the Irishman had responded by saying that this type of architecture was common in Wisconsin farmhouses.

Lightning flashed again, and Arlis realized that Mickey was staring at him. "What?" Arlis asked.

"How long are you gonna make me wait? Yer gonna wanna tell me 'bout this feller that's spreadin' lies before I slap it outta ya! Now, I don't mind doin' *that*, but I sure as hell ain't gonna beg." He slurped at the coffee. In the kitchen, dishes clinked together as Angeline and Fannie washed and dried them.

Arlis stood and found his saddlebag, sitting near the door. From it, he pulled a newspaper, returned to the table, and sat. He threw the paper on the table in front of Mickey.

"Reckon I need to get my eyes on," Mickey said. He stood and walked to the fireplace where he retrieved a pair of smoked glasses, the lenses round and thick, and put them on his face. Before coming back to the table, he grabbed a clay pipe and a leather pouch from the mantle. Then, limping mildly, he returned to his seat and looked at the newspaper, setting the empty pipe and the pouch in his lap.

"The Oswego Daily Palladium, Sunday, May 29, 1881," Mickey read aloud. He picked up the paper and scanned the front page, then opened it and ran his eyes over pages two and three.

Arlis looked on silently, calmly sipping his coffee.

"Well," Mickey said, not looking up, "should I want to get a good deal on 'French Yoke Shirts,' whatever the hell they are, all I need ta do is write a letter ta Mrs. Kate Arden of..." he trailed off, looking for information, "ah, Oswego." He looked up at Arlis. "Where the hell is Oswego?"

From the kitchen came Angeline's voice, "Three times, now, James...That's enough cussin'."

"Oooh," Mickey said quietly, grimacing as if he'd been shot. "When she calls me James, I know it's time to mind her."

"Oswego is in New York State," Arlis said. "It's a ways north of Syracuse and lies on the bank of Lake Ontario." He pointed to the newspaper, said, "You're looking for the letter to the editor on page three. It says, 'New York Glory at Gettysburg.'" He pointed at the type. "Right here, below the advertisement for Waldridge and Morton Furniture." He sipped his coffee again and said with disdain, "The letter is written by an M.W. Taylor of Trenton, New Jersey. Mr. Taylor is a book writer and professional speaker. Earns his living writing books, then touring from town to town, speaking about and selling his work."

"Mmm," Mickey grunted, finding the material. He sipped from his cup and read.

Arlis watched as Mickey wrinkled his nose here, dropped his eyebrows in a frown there.

Then, "Oh, you lying son of a bitch!" Mickey yelled, drawing censure from the kitchen again. "Who the…what the…" Looking into the kitchen, he said "Oh, for goodness sake, woman!" Angeline turned and looked at Mickey.

"There are times when a man cussin' in his own home is not only allowable, my wife, but downright necessary!" he said through gritted teeth. "There is a son of a…a son of a *gun* that is tootin' his horn all over the East Coast that needs to have his head shoved up his *arse!*" He banged an open palm on the table. The coffee cups jumped.

Arlis smiled at Angeline. "I'm sorry Angel, for bringing something so worthy of Mickey's wrath into your home. I'm afraid I behaved in much the same way." He paused and looked at Mickey, who was holding his forehead in one hand and glaring at the newspaper. "Have you ever noticed that your husband speaks with more Irish in his voice when he's angry?" he asked, smiling.

"Oh? You think he's angry?" she asked, "He's just getting warmed up!"

Arlis laughed and held his coffee cup above his head in a silent toast.

"Who was the 147th with? Cutler's Brigade?" Mickey asked, ignoring the both of them.

"Cutler's Brigade," Arlis echoed. "They were one of the regiments being driven by Davis' Rebs."

"This makes me skin crawl," Mickey said, slowly and angrily. "Nothing in this letter is even close to bein' truth." He skimmed through the columns again, and read out loud:

The gallant boys of the 147th held firm, repulsing charge after charge of the maniacal Rebels belonging to General Harry Heth. Many a brave New Yorker would never leave the field, being buried where they fell by those that were fortunate enough to call themselves survivors. The last brave man being deposited to God's earth, the brave remnants of our good regiment left the field of glory honorably, only to have the ground given up by soldiers of a lesser quality, those belonging to the XI Corps of O.O. Howard."

He stopped and looked at Arlis. His red, square face looked bulky, swollen even, and sweaty in the lamplight. His eyes flashed anger. "He doesn't even mention the Sixth Wisconsin, or the Iron Brigade, or even the 14th Brooklyn."

"The 95th New York is omitted, too," Arlis said.

Mickey seemed to study the table next to the paper, said, "That's right. It's rubbish, all of it." Looking at the paper again, he pointed at some text and said, "And I don't recall *anyone* havin' any time a'tall to bury any of the fallen on that day," he said, his voice rising again. "The dead lay in the field fer weeks. Some, fer months! They were still buryin''em when Lincoln gave his little speech. When was that? November?" He paused, reaching under his glasses to rub the corners of his eyes with two fingers. "That last part, about Howard's Corps losin' the ground, well that's the only truthful matter of this here letter." Looking again at Arlis, he added, "And I'm no expert on the 147th, but I'd hazard a guess that as far as quality fightin' went, they weren't any better quality of regiment than General Howard had led out onto that field... at least on that particular day."

Arlis drank his coffee and said nothing. Lightning flashed outside the window again, and Arlis counted the seconds, *one, two, three, four, five* this time. *Good, it's moving on,* he thought.

Mickey looked up abrubtly, "How'd you get this paper?" he asked. "New York's a ways away."

"The wife's got family in upstate New York, Arlis said. "They found it. A few of them know more about the war than I do. Her brother figured something wasn't right." He finished his coffee and set the cup down near the end of the table. "They're in Fulton, a few miles from Oswego. Fulton and Oswego are roughly the same distance from each other as Hillsboro and Wonewoc, I gather. Did ya see the bottom of the letter? The part not written by Mr. Taylor, I mean."

Mickey searched for the text to which Arlis was referring to. After a moment, he read out loud, " 'Mr. Taylor is making appearances throughout the state all next month. See him speak in Buffalo on June 4th, Oswego on June 8th, Fulton on June 10th, Syracuse on June 13th, Schenectady on June 15th, Albany on June 16th, Poughkeepsie on June 21st, and in White Plains on June 25th. He'll be giving two speeches in New York City as well, on Long Island on June 29th, and Manhattan on June 30th. Mr. Taylor will have ample copies of his book, '*Pennsylvania Thunder*' on sale at each location.' " Mickey frowned and looked out the window. He ran the fingernails of his hands through the sideburns on his face, producing a sound very much like sandpaper on wood. After a moment, he returned his gaze to the newspaper. "Any inquiries regarding speaking engagements can be made directly to the editor of this publication," he finished.

They sat in silence, rain falling hard on the wooden shingles. To Arlis, it sounded like bacon frying. In the kitchen, the lamp went dim as mother and daughter finished cleaning up. Angeline brought the coffee pot out and refilled both cups.

"Thank you," Arlis said.

Angeline nodded, "C'mon little one," she said to Fannie, "You and I'll get something done in the bedroom while these two men solve the world's problems by cussin' in my house."

Fannie laughed and Arlis did, too, and he watched as Angeline picked up a basket filled with knitting needles and yarn and other things that Arlis knew little to nothing about, and mother and daughter went into the bedroom.

Arlis tried to sip his coffee, found it too hot, and set the cup down in front of him, cupping his hands around it. Mickey sat across from him, in serious thought, his square cheeks flushed with obvious anger. They sat that way for several minutes, the rain rattling on the roof and occasional lightning bursts flashing, now far off on the horizon.

Mickey spoke at long last, quietly, succinctly, "The winners don't always write history."

Arlis pondered this for a few seconds, and said, "Hard to say the 147th were losers."

"They ain't the ones writin' this history. This Taylor character is certainly a loser," Mickey retorted. "What exactly do you have in mind to do about this, Badger? You come all this way just ta get my ire up?"

"Heh heh," Arlis chuckled, "Of course not…but if I had, you surely didn't let me down."

"No, I reckon not." Mickey said, sipping coffee. "It's time for a smoke, now." He lifted the pipe from his lap and set it on the table. Then, untying the drawstrings from the tobacco pouch, he packed the bowl, pulled the strings tight, and then tossed the pouch to Arlis, who threw it back, unwanted.

"I can't say anyone in the regiment ever had more power behind his words than you, Mickey," Arlis said. "Most of the boys love you…all of them listen to you, even the officers. Hell, Dawes himself practically put you in his pocket."

Mickey grunted and struck a match on the underside of the table. It flared to life and then calmed. He held it to the tobacco, puffing away with a "puh, puh, puh," until it caught.

Arlis went on, "You're the first one that gets excited about reuniting the company or the regiment. Pretty much need to reunite the whole regiment for a company's worth of men, come to think about it. You're a leader in veteran's affairs and veteran's rights and disability—"

"Quit yer ringin' my bell," Mickey said, clearly embarrassed. "Ya don't have ta tell me what I do fer the regiment."

Arlis didn't hesitate. "You asked me what I have in mind. I'm stating my case for it before I explain what that is, is all." He went silent, reloading his arguments in his mind. Tobacco smoke floated up and across the room, leaving its dank, sweet scent behind as it crept away from the pipe.

"I know what yer gettin' at anyhow, Badger," Mickey said. "Why not you, though? You write better than me. Yer always so proper with yer speech and yer grammar."

"I *speak* better than you, Mick. You *write* as well as any-one…and people love it when you put things in prose. You have more charisma than anyone I've ever met. You speak. Even if the grammar isn't up to standard, people listen." He sipped from the coffee cup. "I used to think that our perfor-mance on the battlefield would speak for itself, resonating through history with little to no maintenance. I know better, now…It falls to us to write our history. The winners *have* to write the history, Mick, or someone else will."

Mickey puffed on his pipe.

Arlis continued, "You're the man who knows who to contact about issues like this. Because of your activities with the veteran's affairs committees and such, you have the contacts and the resources to stop these lies from spreading. This clown, this Mr. Taylor, is gonna speak—excuse me -" he corrected himself, "has *already* spoken all over the Empire State, bragging on a battle and a regiment of which he knows little or nothing. He's stealing our 'Pennsylvania thunder.' It's our job to discredit him. It's our job to tell our story." He paused, sipping coffee, and looked out the window.

"Why not me?" Arlis suddenly mimicked, "because I'm not one to go hanging around with old soldiers, Mick...and quite frankly, you're a better man for the job. I'll help you, though. Anything you need." His words were left hanging in the air, mingling with the smoke from the pipe. "Besides, you're friendly with Jerome Watrous. He doesn't know me from Adam, I don't think," he added. Watrous was a veteran of the Sixth Wisconsin and was currently a newspaper reporter. Arlis turned sideways in the chair, watching out the window. The rain had slowed, and more sunlight was getting through the clouds, brightening the view a bit.

From the bedroom, Angeline's voice rang into the room. "Husband, you open a window if yer gonna smoke in the house. The rain's a trickle now, and Fannie's eyes are waterfalls."

Mickey stood and walked to the window to the left of the door. After pushing it open, he walked to the other window on the same wall and opened it as well.

Sitting down, Mickey said, "Last I knew, Watrous was with a paper called 'The Sunday Telegraph' in Milwaukee, and he's got power in the press, far as I can tell. Dawes is back in Ohio. Has been fer a long time." He drew from the pipe. "Former Governor Fairchild would be one ta turn this matter's attention ta, but last I knew he was counsel general ta Paris or something like that." He walked back to his chair and sat down across from Arlis again. "I think the first thing ta do, though, is ta send Mister, what's his name?" he asked, spinning to look at Arlis.

"Taylor, like the President," Arlis clarified.

Mickey looked at him quizzically, appearing to Arlis as if he'd acquired a sudden belly ache. His head tilted slightly left, and he said, "I'm surprised yer so up in arms about this, Badger. Yer usually pretty low key on these things."

Arlis was thoughtful. "I know, Mickey. I'm not looking to take the lead on anything here. I've got the money, though. I'll foot the bill for whatever it takes to quell things like this." He hesitated, reflecting. "The more time that passes, the more important that railroad cut becomes…at least to me, anyway. We charged, boys died, we won. Doesn't matter what happened afterward. We can't let the people that know forget. We can't let the people that don't know go on *not* knowing, or believing something else entirely. That was *our* day. It was my day."

Mickey sat silently, nodding in agreement. He puffed on the pipe, the stem locked between his teeth.

After half a minute or so, Mickey said, "The first thing ta do is ta send Mr. Taylor a kind letter of congratulations on his speaking tour, complete with our intentions to not only discredit his entire platform, but also to give him our guarantee to embarrass him ta the point of becoming a recluse."

Arlis grinned. "Well, I knew I came to the right place."

12 Mineral Point, Wisconsin
March 4, 1857
Late Afternoon

THEY HAD TENDED TO THE GOATS QUICKLY SO AS TO HAVE A few moments to hold hands and bask in each other's warmth, sitting in the fresh hay in the corner where no one would easily see them. Arlis sat with his back against the wall, legs splayed out before him. Violet's hand was in his, no mittens to interfere with the intimacy. She sat as he did, except that her head was on his shoulder and she had one leg crossed under the other in a position that was as lady like as the situation would allow.

"Five minutes, Arlis," she'd said as they sat down. "No more."

At least two minutes of silence had ensued, and Arlis thought about how much had changed since they'd first kissed.

"We never did anything like this while we were fishing," he told her now. "Even when we would kiss each other, by the pond or down at the stream, it was just that, kissing."

She lifted her head off of his shoulder, looking at him. "What're you gettin' at, boy?"

He wished for a moment he hadn't said anything, not in regret for what he'd said, but because it had made her move her head off of his shoulder. "There's more in it now, I mean. This isn't two kids seeing what kissing's like anymore. There's more in it now," he said again.

"Now yer talkin' in doublespeak, Arlis," she said, one eyebrow raised. "Say what you mean outright."

He thought for a moment, realized he never heard Violet talk about the Bible. "Do you read the Bible, Violet?"

"Some," she answered. "We're as religious as a few, not so much as most. Nobody makes me learn it by heart."

"First Corinthians, in the New Testament," he said, pausing to see if she'd acknowledge knowing of it or not. She didn't, so he continued, "Verses four through seven read 'charity suffereth long, and is kind; charity envieth not; charity vaunteth not itself, is not puffed up, doth not behave itself unseemly, seeketh not her own, is not easily provoked, thinketh no evil; rejoiceth not in iniquity, but rejoiceth in the truth; Beareth all things, believeth all things, hopeth all things, endureth all things.'"

"I'm not rightly followin' what all of that means, Arlis," Violet said. "We've got about a minute before I get nervous 'bout someone walkin' in here."

"I know...and I know," he said, glancing at the door. "I don't get the Bible easily, either. Mama always had to explain it to me." He shifted to the right so as to face her and took her left hand in his right, holding both of her hands now.

"What it means is that if you care about somebody, you'll never do them harm. You'll be patient and humble, never boasting or misbehaving." He hesitated, the words not so forthcoming. "What it means, is that if you care about someone, you'll trust them, you'll protect them, you'll pray for them, and you'll always feel that way. That's how I've been feeling about you, Violet. All these long, cold months, I've been missing you and thinking about you."

She smiled shyly, blushing. "But what's this 'bout charity an' all. That passage mentioned 'charity' three or four times. Who needs charity? You? Me? I don't need any charity, Arlis."

"No, you don't," he said, squeezing her hands lightly. "Charity in the Bible doesn't mean the same as it does today. See, when the Bible says 'charity,' it's really talking about love."

The smile vanished from her face. She pulled her hands away and stood up. "Love? *Love?* Arlis Jenkins, I do a little hand holdin' with you and ya go and start talkin' 'bout *love?*" She walked toward the door.

Arlis stood, horrified. He followed her. "Wait!" he said, "Why are you—"

She turned and faced him, interrupting him. "You gotta get that manure outta yo—" she exclaimed, nearly shouting. Realizing her volume was excessive, she paused and turned toward the door. "Wait here!" she said in a harsh whisper. She walked to the door of the barn and opened it a crack, looking outside. After a moment she pushed it closed again and walked the six paces back to Arlis, putting her hands on her waist. "I'll betcha if Martha Tubbs had enjoyed fishin' as much as I do, and she had planted a kiss on ya down at the pond, you'd be in her barn instead of mine, talkin' 'bout love."

Arlis squirmed. "Hey! If my memory serves me right it was I that kissed you, not you that kissed me. What makes you think I even wanna kiss ol' Martha anyway?"

"You boys will kiss anything that's willing to kiss ya back," she said, adding, "an' you'll claim ta fall in love with anyone that's in front a ya that's paid a mind to ya."

Arlis steamed. He could hardly think straight now. If coming here hadn't been a mistake, opening his mouth surely had. He walked to the barn door and opened it wide. Seeing no one outside, he turned, standing directly in the doorway, and said, "You don't rightly get it. Did you not hear what I was saying? What I was confessing to you? Heck, I hadn't even said it yet, had I? Well, if you're gonna be awful to me for it I might as well get it out, then. I...love...you," he purposely paused between the words. "There!" He mocked her now, hands on his waist in mirrored impression of her.

She walked slowly toward him now, her hands dropping to her sides. In a harsh whisper, she said, "You stupid, stupid boy." She raised one arm, pointing an index finger at him. "You might have that head of yours filled with Bible verses, and the Presidents, and math, and grammar, and all that. You might have more knowledge stacked up like ginger cakes in there than I've seen ginger cakes. But really, as smart as ya are, ya got no common sense, boy, ya hear me? This is how it is: I just now turned fourteen, somethin' you ain't gonna do until July the second. There ain't gonna be any way fer you to be courtin' me til we're both rightly sixteen, as my Daddy's said many a time. 'No boys til yer sixteen,'" she said, impersonating her pa.

Arlis studied his boots, saying nothing. Violet turned, inspecting the barn. She walked across the room and picked up a hay fork, standing it in its place in the corner, before returning to the doorway.

Softly now, she spoke, "You listen to me now, Arlis. If you wanna be with me next summer…if you wanna kiss on me and hold my hand and sit nice and close like, then you better get all yer ideas 'bout love outta yer head. There's to be no more talk 'bout love 'til my Pa says it's okay for ya to court me." She paused and Arlis looked up at her, finding her eyes. "Don't get any ideas 'bout talkin' to my Pa, neither," she said, sternly. "Two years, Arlis."

Arlis nodded, kicked sideways at a fallen icicle just outside the barn. "I'll go home, then. I'm sorry I angered you on your birthday, Violet."

She tilted her head and frowned. "Things are goin' too fast is all, Arlis, and you ain't leavin' yet. You ain't strung up my new reel an' showed me how ta use it yet."

He smiled at her, and she smiled back. Quietly, he said, "Two years isn't that long, Violet. It's just over seven hundred days, is all. I'd wait ten thousand for you."

She shut the door to the barn and locked it with the worn wooden bar. Grinning, she turned and said, "Ya better. I'll be holdin' ya to it, now. Let's go," she said, leading him toward the house. "Can't wait ta try an' cast that thing, even in the snow."

They walked together back to the house.

"Hey," Arlis said, "I didn't know you even knew when my birthday was."

13 Mineral Point, Wisconsin
December 1, 1857
Near Midnight

HE WAS FEELING AS SICK AS HE'D EVER FELT IN HIS FOURTEEN plus years. The sniffles that had invaded his body two nights ago had mutated into heavy congestion, the bulk of which had settled deep in his chest. His body wanted desperately to cough it out, but the ensuing pain induced Arlis to stifling the fits as best he could. Now, with his head throbbing and his body ripe with fever, new symptoms had arrived. Arlis was sure that all of the fluids his young body held were determined to exit his body.

The night was cold and bitter. A light snow was falling that wouldn't stick yet, as winter had delayed its arrival to southwestern Wisconsin and the ground was still unyielding in its efforts to absorb the precipitation. Arlis thought, between retches, that perhaps the winter was delayed because it felt culpable for its transgressions last year. The previous winter had burdened its victims with hardships innumerable, the kind that wouldn't be forgotten for generations to come, but rather spoken about in front of fireplaces well into the next century. He threw up again, kneeling in his night clothes, barefoot, alongside the privy, which his family often referred to as the "necessary." He had pulled his bottoms up from the ankles to a position above the knees so as not to get the garment wet while his body disgorged whatever poisons were afflicting it. He had suffered from the gripes as well, his real reason for being out here in the cold. After spending several minutes relieving himself of diarrhea, he spent a few minutes throwing up in the privy before exiting to complete that task outside. Retching in such proximity to the vile contents of the necessary could go on eternally.

It's over, he thought, attempting to push off on the cold, wet ground. He was wrong. Halfway to a standing position he felt the heaves coming on again and returned to his former position, vomiting until he was empty, and then vomiting some more. Loud belches ensued, his stomach able to offer the ground nothing but bile and air now. His belly pained him fiercely, feeling as if someone had stabbed him in the lower abdomen. "Burrrrrp! Burrrrrp! Burrrrrrp!"

"Oh God, why?" he asked between belches. When the air stopped coming, the heaving continued, silent yet violent, and had anyone witnessed him at that moment they might have compared him to a house cat, heaving silently in the night until a hairball was finally produced.

Arlis stayed there, kneeling upon the ground, waiting, sweating, shivering, and wondering whether he was done or not. His head throbbed with his heartbeat. Panting, his breath was raspy and noisy. He struggled to regain control of his breathing, worried that another attack of retching would cause his breathing to cease altogether.

He glanced at the sky, the full moon visible through the cloud cover as if it were lurking behind a sheer curtain. He looked to the house and saw a light in the window. He blinked twice, wondering if he was seeing things, and then watched as the light moved across the wall, the door opened, and a lit lantern, held by someone, came toward him through the moonlit night. He squinted. *Mama.*

She came to him. "Arlis, baby, are you poorly?" she asked. Then, when no answer came, she asked, "Have you taken ill, my boy?"

Arlis gasped, weak from the episode, his breath turning

to clouds in the lamplight. "Yes, Mama. I've got the liquids from both ends," he said quickly, worried that if he paused he wouldn't get it all out.

"Can you walk? We've got to get you inside, Darling. You'll catch your death out here dressed as you are."

I already have, he thought. "Give me a bit more, Mama. I'm sure I'll come around, alright?"

"Alright, then," she said, squatting down next to him. She was wearing her night clothes, including her winter bonnet, and had put Arlis' boots on over her bare feet.

Arlis laughed when he realized that Mama had his boots on, as he had no idea that his feet had reached hers in size. Looking now, it appeared as if Mama had huge feet, causing him to laugh harder.

"What's gotten into you, child?" Mama asked, concerned.

"Nothing, Mama," he answered, not having the strength to explain it to her. He returned his thoughts to his sickness to put the laughter down. "I'm just laughing at the ridiculousness of it all." He stood, Mama's arm around his waist to steady him. They walked together into the house, Mama following him up the ladder to the loft, ensuring he made it to his bed safely.

"I'll be right back, Arlis. You lay still," Mama said, retreating back down the ladder.

He lay on his back in his bed, looking sideways at Rachel, who lay sleeping in her own bed alongside his. He peered at her angelic face in the moonlight, which shone on her like a beacon through the small round window above the foot of his bed. *Glad it's me and not her,* he thought. *God, please don't make her feel like this.* He felt the nausea returning, and rolled to his right, preparing for the heaves. He timed his breathing in a rhythmic attempt to delay the inevitable, succeeding long enough for his mother to return to his side.

She sat now on the edge of his bed and placed a lit oil lamp on the small nightstand next to the bed. In her other hand was her washing bucket, which she placed on the floor alongside him. From this, she withdrew a chamber pot. "You may use this as you see fit, Arlis," she said, gesturing to the bucket. "I brought you a chamber pot, too, should the necessity for it arise." She placed it next to the bucket. Then feeling his forehead, damp with sweat and cold from the outside air, she said, "Oh my, you're feverish, too."

He was still concentrating on his breathing, which he interrupted now to say, "I think it's best if I'm not in the same room with Rache, Mama. I'm so poorly that I fear for her health."

"Shhh," she soothed, pushing his hair from his forehead softly with her hand. She looked at Rachel and then to the window, as if looking for an answer to an unasked question there. "Don't worry now, son. Sleep."

Arlis let the exhaustion take hold. The tiredness was stronger than the nausea at the moment, and he closed his eyes and allowed the cobwebs to creep into his head. He was soon half-asleep, only taking partial notice when Mama said something about setting up a bed somewhere.

When he awoke again time had passed, though he had no worldly notion if it had been minutes or hours, and Mama was standing over him, asking if he felt able to descend the ladder.

Why he needed to descend the ladder eluded his mind, but he answered dutifully, "Yes, Mama," and sat up. She helped him to his feet, explaining that she'd lit a fire in the mother-in-law cabin's fireplace and that she had made up the bed in there with fresh linen, and Arlis realized what her intentions were. He felt relief. Perhaps whatever ailed him would not take hold of his sister as well.

Once Mama was sure Arlis could stand on his own she descended the ladder, ahead of him, and then waited while he followed her down, ready to react if he should fall, which he didn't. She'd found her own footwear, and wrapped a blanket around Arlis while he fumbled with the chore of putting his boots on. Then, the two of them went outside, trekking through the yard toward the cabin.

"To the privy," Arlis said abruptly, as a low pain and a sudden need overtook him. "I'll be a few minutes in here, Mama," he said, closing the door.

"I'll watch from the window," she told him, and gave him leave.

His bowels unloaded as his bottom made contact with the seat, the cold wood acting as a catalyst. The liquid ran from him in such a fine stream that for a few moments he didn't even know he was going. The realization of this, however, was sobering and shocking, and he jerked full awake with fear, wondering just what was happening to his insides. *Was it something I ate?* His stomach pained again, as if stabbed by a sharp metal object.

Nausea returned now with such suddenness and fury that he hadn't sensed it coming on until the retching began. He spread his legs, making room to throw up directly in front of the privy hole, but these were dry heaves, resulting in little substance other than a little bile, which lay in small amounts on the privy floor and on his nightshirt. Now, it was more heaves and then more liquid hell from behind. He wondered if this would stop or if it was possible for it to continue on for the rest of the night.

The heaving over with, he restarted his breathing regimen, pacing himself. He tried breathing in through the nose, out through the mouth…in through the nose, out through the mouth, but the congestion in his nose was too thick, and he burst into a coughing fit, his chest burning badly with each purge. He moaned, low and deep, reminding himself of a birthing cow. The chills hit him hard now as his hot, feverish, and overworked body vented sweat into the cold air, steam rising from his arms and his forehead. His entire body began shivering, his teeth chattering, and he did his best now to perform his post-privy hygiene before opening the door, the silent signal to his mother that he was ready to resume the trip to the cabin. She was there before he was all the way out.

"Come on, then," she said softly, placing her arm around his waist. She held him like this all the way to the cabin door.

"Did I wake Pa, Mama?" he asked, leaning on her. "Or Rache?"

"No, Honey. Pa sleeps like a stone," she said, her eyes on their feet as she watched their footing on the frosty ground outside the cabin door. She pushed open the door and they entered the cabin, already warm from the fire she'd started in the fireplace.

Minutes later, Arlis was covered up with three blankets in the double bed, which Mama had pulled from the wall to the center of the room, allowing the warmth of the fire to better reach him. She sat in the rocker next to him, calmly assuring him that he'd feel better after getting plenty of rest.

"Papa's gonna be right sore at me, Mama." Arlis said, thinking of the morrow. "I was supposed to be at the mine early tomorrow. We're doin' rope testing, and I'm supposed to train the Gardner kid and a couple of other new miners."

"Your Pa won't pay any mind to you other than being concerned for your well-being, child," she reassured him. "You relax now. Think about good things, like fishing, or Christmas, or your beautiful mother…"

Arlis managed a laugh. "Thank you, Mama. You *are* beautiful…" he said, half smiling. He closed his eyes again, shifting his thoughts to fishing with Violet. He thought about her hair, long and perfect. It was longer than ever now, and thought back on her fishing with the new reel at the pond, her hair blowing in the breeze. *'Long as we're on the subject of beautiful,'* he thought of telling Mama, but didn't.

Violet had taken to the new reel like a duck to water, and before long she had perfected its use. Arlis had found casting it to be an odd and clumsy task, but as Violet had explained once in late April, a proper cast took a gentle, feminine touch. She claimed that boys were altogether too violent and stubborn to handle such a precise task correctly. Arlis figured there was some truth to what she said, and stuck to his own fishing pole, crude as it was.

They'd settled into their regular summer routine. Saturdays were fishing days once the chores were completed. Violet had been adamant: the kissing rules would be in affect again all summer long. Arlis, though disappointed, understood, knowing that he'd hardly get any fishing done without such limits. Occasionally though, while fishing the stream, they'd sit close and hold hands for a while. The pond made such behavior unwise, as the hills and terrain surrounding the pond made viewing anyone who might be approaching the couple difficult. Someone could be ten paces away and still not be seen.

Arlis had to constantly fight his urges to tell Violet how he felt about her. The kissing grew more intimate, more meaningful, as the couple got better at the practice. Soon, all awkwardness disappeared with the kissing, as their lips and tongues reacted to the movements of each other. Arlis was very aware of this phenomenon. He compared their skill at predicting each other's maneuvers to kissing one's self in the mirror. While in the act of kissing they were one being...a single, affectionate entity.

Then, in late May, Mr. Rhys had interrogated his daughter about the nature of her relationship with Arlis. Someone, most likely young Bobby, had reported seeing the two of them holding hands while fishing together at the stream.

"He wouldn't tell me who said it though," she'd told Arlis

the following Saturday. "I denied it, Arlis, and I told Pa that whoever would say such a thing must not want us fishin' together. I said they must be jealous of what good friends we are or somethin'." She was pretty sure that she had convinced her father that the hand holding incident was a farce, but Arlis wasn't sure…especially since Bobby had been made to tag along on Saturdays for more than a month following the alleged incident. There had been no kissing or hand holding throughout the entire month of June.

Fishing aside, June had been an important month for the Jenkins family. On the eighth, a hearing was held at the courthouse in regard to the estate of Thomas Jenkins, Tom's father, who had left Mineral Point with his boss, James Evans, and a small party of miners during the mad rush to California after gold had been found there, nine years prior. They intended on claiming a large stake of land and using their experience in lead mining to make a fortune in gold mining. They had a good plan, a solid wagon train with healthy animals, plenty of muskets and tools, and had hired a guide to get them there. None of them had ever been heard from again.

All inquiries sent westward had turned up nothing. It was as if the party had fallen off the face of the earth. Tom Jr. went through a series of emotions, from worry to the agony of not knowing what had become of his father, to the dreadful knowledge that he was most certainly dead but without having any real proof of the matter. Months went by, and the focus turned from finding Tom Sr. to attempting to obtain the legal right to his property and assets which, thanks to the generosity of Mr. Evans over the years, had grown considerably. Tom Jr. soon found himself embattled with banks, attorneys, and all sorts of folks that wore suits and fancy hats, and years of court hearings and meetings ensued.

Then on June eighth, a Monday, a judge had ruled that Tom Jr. had a legal right to all of Tom Sr.'s property, cash, and holdings. All in all, it added up to a pretty penny, though Arlis knew not to ask his parents about the details regarding the true value.

But there was more. On the exact same day, the exact same judge had ruled that any and all of the wills of those who had vanished on the trip westward back in 1848 should be opened and honored per the writers' wishes. Now, the Jenkins had paid little attention to this other ruling, but a little more than a week later, on Wednesday the seventeenth, Tom Jr. had been summoned to appear at the Mineral Point office of Jacob H. Starling, Esq., "on the morrow, if practicable." It had been practicable, and upon meeting with Mr. Starling, he found out that Mr. James Evans, having no surviving family in these United States, had bequeathed all of his holdings to Thomas Jenkins Sr., who, being declared legally dead, had left all of his holdings to Thomas Jenkins Jr.

Tom was suddenly the sole owner not only of his father's farmland, but also the mining company that he had been running in the absence of the owner and his father for the last nine years. He also had access to all of the profits that had sat, untouched, in Cadwallader C. Washburn's Mineral Point Bank all of these years. These profits had undoubtedly had much to do with the success of the bank, success which Mr. Washburn had used in a successful bid for Congress on the Republican ticket in 1855.

Arlis didn't know much about how the fortunes of his family had changed overnight, but within days of the inheritance, he had witnessed his parents arguing over his future. It seemed that Mama was suddenly in complete opposition of Arlis working the mines, claiming that he should instead get into a decent college prep school and prepare for getting a good secondary education. Papa had claimed that Arlis should learn the value of hard, physical work, learning the mining industry from the ground up—*from below ground up*—Arlis had joked to himself, overhearing this argument. Mama had countered with her best argument, the safety factor, which eclipsed the whole education issue anyway, she'd said. What it really came down to was this: Arlis didn't need to go into the mines now that his financial future was in order. He could get hurt or killed in the mines, she said.

With Mama gaining the upper hand, Arlis suddenly grew wide-eyed with fear. If Mama won her case, he'd be sent to some private school far away, and his days of fishing with Violet every spring and fall would be over. Violet might even find someone else to fish with, a horrifying possibility to Arlis. He had no intention of leaving Mineral Point. Not now, anyway.

"I'll work the mines," he interrupted. "Please," he added, looking at Mama. "I've been waiting a long time for a chance at the mines, and I'll be fourteen in just two weeks now. I'll learn the business. I'll learn how to do everything Papa's workers know how to do. *Then* I'll go to school. In the meantime, Mama, you can continue to school me here at home. The extra money will help you to buy better books and such. I'll have no problem getting into any school we choose. You've said so yourself, Mama." He paused, scratching a mosquito bite. Looking at his father now, he said, "Then I'll use my experience and what I learn in college to run the mines when it's my turn to do so."

Mama had just stared at him; Arlis had seldom been so bold. Papa had looked at him too, then smiled and looked at Mama, and when they didn't yell at him for butting in or for speaking out of turn, Arlis turned and walked outside, taking his time grooming the stock. When he returned to the house later, the matter had apparently been settled as Mama hadn't brought it up again. Beginning July third, Arlis had spent his weekday afternoons in the mines, digging lead ore out of the holes and placing it in the basket for extraction.

Now, as Arlis' thoughts shifted from Violet to mining, mining to schooling, and then schooling back to Violet, his chattering teeth jolted him back to reality. He rolled to his side, silencing his teeth and stopping the shivers. He looked at Mama, who had taken to reading in the rocker in the low lamplight.

"What are ya reading, Mama," he managed, closing his eyes again as the nausea threatened.

She removed her reading glasses and used a finger to mark her page, closing the book around it. "Grandpa's Bible was on the mantle," she said, looking at Arlis. "How're you feeling now?"

"Comes and goes," he said. He felt warmth at the thought of Mama reading the Bible. He couldn't remember the last time he'd seen her reading her own copy, other than during their schooling. Perhaps it was the only thing to pass the time at the moment, but at least she was reading it again. "What book are you reading?" he asked.

"Revelation," she said.

The chills returned.

14 Mineral Point, Wisconsin
December 2, 1857
Midday

LYING ON HIS LEFT SIDE, HE AWOKE WITH A START. THE PAIN in his lower abdomen became acutely unbearable, making him swing his right arm wildly as he rolled to his back. *Thump!* His balled fist slammed into the flesh of another being, who grunted in return. The feverish Arlis realized that he was no longer alone in the bed, but sharing it with his father. He tried to think on that but the fever wouldn't allow it. He rolled back to his left side, hung his head over the edge of the bed, and dry heaved. Suddenly his mother was sitting at his hip, holding his shoulder and saying the things that mothers say in times like these. Arlis barely heard her. As he finished the silent retching, he rolled to his back again and passed out as Mama laid a cold, wet rag upon his feverish forehead.

He slept.

15 Mineral Point, Wisconsin
December 3, 1857
Night

"ARLIS, BABY…YOU NEED TO DRINK THIS."

He stirred, the words reaching him, the meaning of them not. He groaned, feeling the burn of the sickness in his chest.

"Arlis," the word came sharper now, more urgency behind it. The boy attempted to roll to his right and couldn't. He remembered his father, sharing the sick bed with him. He opened one eye; saw a hand on his arm.

"Doctor Anderson says it's imperative you get some fluids into you, Arlis." It was Mama. She sighed, looked at the floor, appearing hopeless. One tallow candle lit the room from the end table, throwing shadows across the wall.

"Mama," Arlis croaked. "I'll try." He fought against an urge to cough and lost, barking several times. With each cough, the pain intensified, and he felt as if someone had placed hot coals on his chest. After the fourth or fifth hack he felt the congestion loosen, relieved that the spell was over.

"Can you sit up?" Mama asked. She slid toward the foot of the bed, allowing him room for the effort.

Arlis tried to sit up but had no strength. He attempted to prop himself on his left elbow. It gave out, and he fell back on the pillow. Mama was suddenly there again, her hand under his neck.

"It's okay, I'll help," she said softly. "Let's just get your head off the pillow a little." He lifted his head, feeling every muscle in his neck straining, and she held his head in that position while bringing the clay cup to his lips. He drank, staring at the mantle above the fireplace on the opposite wall. The water was cold and wonderful, and he felt the thirst overtake him, his body demanding the wetness, and he wondered how long he'd been lying in this bed now. He brought his right hand to the cup, trying to pour the water in faster, needing every drop in his mouth right now.

"Easy, Arlis," Mama said, not allowing the boy to gain control of the cup. He hadn't the strength to fight her. "Slowly, child, slowly. If you drink too much too quickly it'll all come up again."

He obeyed, letting her handle the cup. Slowly, patiently, he was given every drop. When the cup was empty, Mama laid his head back on the pillow and stood, returning the cup to the table.

"What day is it?" Arlis asked. He could remember waking fitfully from time to time, tossing and writhing, but hadn't attempted to discern between day and night. He had no idea how much time had passed since he'd taken ill, and wouldn't have been surprised if Mama had told him that it was just one day or seven.

Mama was wringing out a washcloth over the bucket. The sound of the water exiting the rag and returning brought back the thirst in Arlis. He licked his lips. They were cracked.

"It's Thursday," Mama said, sitting next to him again. She placed the cool, wet washcloth on his forehead. "Don't worry about what day it is, Arlis. You just think about getting better. This whole town is sick, including your Papa. Although he was spared the gripes and the vomiting, he's been coughing continuously since the morning after you took to this bed. Seems his whole body is filled with water. Yours too. Doctor

Anderson says its influenza. It's spreading throughout all of Wisconsin, and it's our turn to bear it."

"Are you sick too, Mama?"

"No," she answered. "Not yet, anyway... and neither is your sister. I am *worried* sick, though. You and Papa are still feverish, and neither of you has eaten for days. It's time for this nonsense to pass." She smiled at him. "You look a little better, but you're still burning up." She flipped the washcloth over onto its other side. "I'm never sure whether you and your father are hot or cold. When I think you're cold you throw your covers off, and when I think you're too warm you start shivering."

He fought another urge to cough. "I'm okay now, Mama," he said.

"That's good. Anyway, I've decided that I'll keep the house at a level of warmth that *I'm* comfortable with." She withdrew the washcloth, dunked it in the bucket, and then squeezed most of the moisture back into the bucket. Placing the cloth back on his head, she grinned and said, "Time to stoke the fire now. I'm a bit chilled."

He reciprocated the smile best he could, and when he tried to prop up on one elbow this time, he succeeded. "Can I have a bit more water first, Mama?"

"Of course," she said, and refilled the cup.

16
Excerpt from the Democrat Tribune
Mineral Point, Wisconsin
Sunday, December 20, 1857

INFLUENZA EPIDEMIC RUNS RAMPANT
ALL OF IOWA COUNTY AFFECTED

OVER ONE THOUSAND ILL, HUNDREDS PERISH
MINERAL POINT HIT PARTICULARLY HARD
FEW FAMILIES UNAFFECTED
REGISTER OF THE DECEASED OF MINERAL POINT

MINERAL POINT, WISCONSIN—The great influenza epidemic of 1857 has found its way into every nook of the county, leaving few homes untouched in its path. The result has been devastating, especially in areas of great congregation, such as the mining camps and urban centers.

Dr. David Stevens of Dodgeville believes the death count in Iowa County to be over 200 as of Friday. "The disease seems to have come into the area via the riverboats, catching all by surprise. We were not even aware of an outbreak before there were hundreds stricken. Now, thanks to the good Lord, it seems to have tempered. Still, we're asking everyone to remain in their homes as much as humanly possible."

The following is a partial list of those in our great city who have succumbed to the sickness.

The deceased are alphabetized by last name.

Allen—Joseph

Anderson—Dr. Charles, Elizabeth, Claire

Bielefeld—Horst

Bowe—Robert

Cook—David, Mark

Davis—George, George Jr

Donner—Sarah, Nan

Dunning—Luke, Sarah

Fleming—Ralph

Fletcher—Harriet

Gold—Sally, Stephen

Harris—Thomas, Marla, Bertha

Jackson—Mark

Jackson—Christopher, Steven
Jessup—Abigail
Johnson—Martha, Mary
Jones—James, Violet
Land—Jeremiah
Long—Victor, Martin, Lydia
Martin—Paul, Jonathan
Mellon—Harriet
Meyers—Olga
Middleton—Frederick
Nichols—Earl, Eliza, Earl Jr
Peale—Samuel, Ruth
Petry—Dr Peter
Rhys—Robert, Andrew, Robert Jr, Violet
Roberts—William, Horace, Mildred
Romer—Godfred
Sampson—Craig
Sayles—Mary
Schultz—Hans, Gretchen, Bruno
Smith—Adam, Jacob, Mary, Nathaniel,
Smith—Gwendolyn, John, Arthur, Ann
Travis—John, Matthew
Tubbs—Alonzo, Martha
Wallace—John, Evan
Williams—Theodore, Lettie
Wilmot—Alexander

17
Mineral Point, Wisconsin
May 8, 1858
Afternoon

IT WAS A SATURDAY, SO IT WAS A FISHING DAY. ALTHOUGH starting late in the morning, Arlis had finished his chores quickly. A rather heavy rain had been falling when he began his tasks, forcing him to move quickly between jobs. Besides avoiding the wetness, he had no motivation to hurry. He had left the farm just before noon, strapping his leather galoshes over his shoes to avoid mucking them up too badly. The rain had slowed to a drizzle, but had picked up again as he left and headed off down the road toward the pond.

He hadn't planned on fishing at all. Spring had come late again this year, waiting until mid-April to melt the ice and bring the people out of their houses, their cabins, and their depression. Still reeling from sickness and loss, "Pointers," as the residents of Mineral Point had started to call themselves, slowly got back to their routines; working, planting, socializing, living. Arlis was no exception. Since the first truly warm Saturday, he had made the weekly treks to the fishing holes as usual. Around sundown, he'd return home, sauntering down the road empty handed, his stringer void of fish.

"No fish today?" Mama would ask the first couple of weeks.

"Nah. They weren't biting," Arlis would say, going to the well to wash up. Mama would stare after him, obviously worried. Arlis could feel her looking, her disquiet slowly burning a hole through the back of his shirt. He felt her concern as he could every other day, and he'd quickly put some distance between her and himself, avoiding the awkward silence and possibility of a question pertaining to his feelings, his health, his well-being. He'd just lie to her anyway, and she would know he was lying to her, making the silence following the questions even more awkward than the silence before.

Mama had been thankful and openly grateful to God for the complete recovery of her husband and son. She'd praised Jesus for sparing Rachel from the sickness altogether. When the sickness passed, and as Arlis had spent hours staring at the text in the newspaper that reported the extent of the pestilence, Mama had tried to soothe him. She was never able to do for Arlis what she hadn't been able to do for herself. Providing solace, reason, comfort, and acceptance was no longer a talent that she possessed. Mama was very good at providing physical comforts, such as warmth, a soothing touch, nourishment, and routine; providing the right words when necessary was a different story.

Of course, Mama had no inkling of the real truth, anyway. Although Arlis had previously stated his intention to marry the neighbor girl one day, he'd never again mentioned his feelings for her to them or anyone else. Being thirteen at the time, and now fourteen, he was old enough to know that his folks would say that he was too young to know what real love felt like. Telling either of them about what had really been going on during their Saturday fishing outings had been out of the question last summer, as that sort of behavior would have been considered taboo in their eyes. Violet's passing had changed nothing in respect to this. If Mama found out now, Arlis knew, she'd take it personally that Arlis had hidden the truth from her and Arlis would find his leash on the world at a considerably shorter reach. Besides, Mama would insist that proper girls didn't kiss boys, especially at fourteen, and there was no way that Arlis would allow the reputation of the girl he cared so much about to be forever ruined in anybody's eyes, especially the people he was closest to. So he kept his real agony inside; the agony of knowing that he'd never again feel about someone else in the way he had felt about Violet. He'd never lose the memory of how she made him feel. He'd never go a day the rest of his life without thinking of her, and whether she was watching him at that moment, judging his every move; if what he was doing right now would affect Violet, had she lived to be by his side. No, Mama would never understand how he felt about Violet. Without understanding, she could offer no help, no counsel, and no hope.

Papa provided no help, either. Many families experiencing close calls with death become closer, thankful for a second chance at life, cherishing their time together in ways they hadn't appreciated before. Arlis knew that the relationship between his parents hadn't been the same since Ezra died; any intimacy and displays of affection being all but extinct between the two. Papa seemed to be embarrassed by his contraction of influenza, perhaps thinking it as a weakness, and upon feeling well again poured even more time into running the mine. When he heard about the deaths of the four Rhys family members, he'd said, "Oh, my," and then had gone out to the barn to do some menial task or another. He'd never once offered any sort of advice or counseling to his son over the matter. Thus, Arlis took his sole consolation from his Saturday "fishing" excursions.

After every week of daily schooling, afternoon mining, and silent, awkward nights on the farm, he'd again head off to go "fishing" on Saturday afternoon, only to come home without any fish again. It didn't take long for Mama to stop asking about the lack of fish, but the staring and the concern remained. Last week, Arlis had cut the pretense altogether, leaving his fishing pole and tackle at home even after announcing to Mama that he was going fishing. She had noticed, but said nothing.

Today, the same routine was the plan. He'd head to the pond and then sit at its edge all afternoon, getting lost in the unfairness of life...the cruelty of sickness, loss, death. He'd hold one-sided conversations with God while throwing rocks into the pond, where he'd long for death, pray for Violet's earthly resurrection, beg for forgiveness, and shout angry accusations similar to those his Mama had shouted nearly five years prior, minus the cuss words. He'd fantasize about a life with a grown up Violet, one with marriage and a family and a huge pond where they could fish and hold hands and kiss each other, openly, all day long. Then, his eyes would well up with tears, leaving him longing for the hard cry that might allow him to finally release some of the pain. Frustrated, he'd begin the whole regimen again.

Now, as he meandered along the road toward the pond into a headwind, the rain picked up in intensity, forcing him to shut his eyes as it punished his face. He'd take about twenty blind steps before opening his eyes again, verifying that he was still on the road.

"You're gonna try and take this away from me too, are ya God?" he mumbled, turning his face to the sky, his eyes still closed. "We'll just see about that now. I'd sit in the mud thinkin' on that girl 'til the four horsemen come." He opened his eyes to the sky and the rain pelted them, forcing him to close them again. He lowered his head. "Bugger," he said, quietly.

He picked up the pace, showing God that he was resolute and wouldn't be deterred from his routine. After a few minutes, however, with the rain coming as hard as any he could remember, he began to second-guess his afternoon activities. He quickly shut any thoughts of changing them out of his mind, determined to not allow God any knowledge of his weakness. He marched onward toward the pond.

"*Old Dan Tucker was a fine old man,*" Arlis sang. "*He washed his face in the frying pan. He combed his hair with a wagon wheel, and died of the toothache in his heel.*" He opened one eye, peering at the road, and saw he was only a few rods from the path that cut from the road to the pond. "*Get out the way,*" he continued, "*fer ol' Dan Tucker, as he's too late to git his supper. Supper's over and dishes washed, ain't nothin' left but a piece of squash.*"

The rain continued. Arlis approached the path, ready to make the turn off the road and the final footslog through the mud to the pond. Instead, he hesitated, stopping at the edge of the road, staring down the path, looking at nothing. He shivered, his eyes slits in the rain, barely open.

"Don't you get any ideas that you mighta changed my mind now, God," he said, lifting his face to the heavens and shutting his eyes. "I'm not gonna go home, you know. I've just now decided on a better place to be today." He looked back down the path, then to the road. After a moment, he continued down the road in the direction he'd been heading, singing, "*I come to town the other night, I hear the noise and saw the fight. The watchman was runnin' around, cryin' 'old Dan Tucker's come to town.'*"

18 Mineral Point, Wisconsin
May 8, 1858
Afternoon

THE SHINGLE WAS STILL IN PLACE, SET BY TWO HOOKS holding fast to two eyelets, which were attached to a strong, whitewashed post on the edge of the property. It sat at the junction of the dirt road and the path that led to the farmhouse and the buildings beyond. "Rhys," it announced in a thick, dark blue block lettering style. Below it was a hand-drawn, black and white Holstein cow with "you're home now" written in a fine cursive script. Oddly, it seemed to give any visitor the immediate impression of farm elegance, if there is such a thing, allowing him or her to feel welcome as they set foot onto the property. On the other side of the path, a less homey sign reading "FOR SALE, See James Barrington, High Street, Mineral Point" stood facing the road, perpendicular to the other sign. Arlis' detour had taken him here. The pond and his one-sided argument with God forgotten now, Arlis stood in the rain, which had slowed again to a drizzle, squinting at the newer of the two signs. He had known of Mr. Barrington and his responsibility to the farm, but was somehow surprised by the existence of the sign and its intrusion on the Rhys' property. He felt immediate indignation.

"No memorial…no funeral," he hissed, through gritted teeth. "I didn't even get to say 'goodbye!'" The rising anger burned through his body, warming his face and extremities, even as the cool rain continued to fall. He allowed the emotion to fill his mind and body, every pore and crevice, until he could no longer contain it. A scream came from his lips, and he lashed out at Mr. Barrington's sign, grabbing it and ripping it from its moorings. Grunting, he tried desperately to break it in half, and, having failed to be able to crack the solid, half-inch thick slab of wood, he instead threw it into the mud in one of the wheel tracks of the path, and then jumped up and down on it repeatedly. He continued until it was buried in the soft, wet mud and barely visible to the eye. Then he turned his wrath upon the post that the shingle had been attached to, pushing and pulling the tall, rectangular piece of wood back and forth, back and forth, until it had given enough to be yanked from the ground. He tossed it into the weeds alongside the road.

His wrath not nearly extinguished, he searched the area for something else to destroy…something else to blame for the pestilence that had taken Violet from him. He saw the Rhys' sign again, stepped toward it, and then swiftly sat down in front of it, knowing full well he couldn't bring harm to *that* sign. His anger quickly diminished, turning to despair, and very suddenly he began to cry hard. Knowing he was all alone, the only person for nearly a mile, he allowed himself to wail, long and loud, the tears falling down his cheeks, mixing with the rain and tasting salty on his tongue. For more than a minute, perhaps as many as two, he cried. He became aware of how good it felt to let it all out, then he suddenly felt guilty for feeling good about anything. He began wailing hard again, crying as hard as was possible until he was spent. He crossed his legs, Indian style, and propped himself up with his arms behind him. He raised his face to the sky, allowing the drizzle to wash his face, his body, his soul. There he sat, allowing his breathing to return to normal as the uncontrollable sobbing diminished and his strength began to return. He let out three consecutive long sighs through pursed lips, his cheeks puffed out like a bugler without an instrument, and then sat upright, looking at the Rhys' farmstead, which lay some 100 yards or so to his left.

The driveway that led from the road to the farm buildings was nothing more than a path through the prairie grass, with two dirt paths where the wheels of the Rhys' wagon and carriage had cut through. The grass between the wheel marks, normally kept short by the tramping of beasts of burden or through contact with the underside of vehicles, was now nigh knee deep. The wheel marks themselves were no longer solid dirt tracks. Grass and wild vegetation could now be seen poking from the ground, proving beyond debate that the farm was abandoned. Arlis was amazed at how quickly the earth had regained control of the terrain, realizing that in just a few short years, there'd be no sign whatsoever of the wheel marks should the farm remain uninhabited.

Now, sitting in the mud and grass, Arlis became cognizant of the wetness on his legs and bottom, the moisture causing him to feel cold all over and shiver a little. He stood up, his shirt causing a hitch in his breath as it stretched to its full length and the cold wetness contacted his back. He could feel the exhaustion from the crying episode in his knees, which buckled a bit before he locked them in place.

The drizzle had faded to a fine mist as Arlis walked down the driveway, staying in the left wheel mark, until he'd reached the well which was situated neatly between the house on his left and the barn, stables and the glaringly empty chicken coop on his right. The retrieving bucket was perched on the edge of the stone well, as if it had been used only minutes before, or perhaps, waiting with eager anticipation to be needed again. Arlis peered down into the blackness of the well. Seeing nothing, he turned his attention to the house.

He'd expected to see it boarded up, or if not, to at least see a shingle with the words "KEEP OUT" nailed to the door. He saw neither. He walked to the porch, climbed the steps, and reached for the lever of the door handle before hesitating, his hand an inch from the lever. He cocked his head, listening for any sound coming from within. Though he heard nothing, he decided to knock first instead.

Knock, knock, knock. "Hello?" he said, realizing the word was useless at the volume he'd uttered it. He cocked his head again, listening for movement in the house. Nothing.

He tried the door, knowing that either the lever wouldn't give or that the door would be barred from the other side. He was sure that Mr. Barrington wouldn't want intruders in the house, and that he'd go to some effort to keep kids or squatters out. To Arlis' surprise, however, the lever gave a soft "pop" and the door creaked open.

He stood there, open-mouthed with the door open perhaps two inches. Finally, he gave the door a push, opening it nearly half-way. The top hinge, in need of lubricant, scolded him with a loud shriek, making Arlis wince.

"Hello?" he said again, this time loud enough to be heard anywhere in the house. "Is anyone here?" Receiving no answer, he pushed the door open the rest of the way and stepped in the room, surprised now to find that it wasn't empty, but was instead furnished and decorated in nearly the same manner as when he'd been here for Violet's birthday more than a year before. The smell of wood smoke lingered.

Arlis had read the *Democrat Tribune's* announcement in mid-January that told of Florence Rhys' move back to Indiana following the epidemic. The article had been short and vague and had angered Arlis for its coldness. It had not even mentioned Violet and her siblings by name.

> Mrs. Robert Rhys of Mineral Point has moved back to her home town of Terre Haute, Indiana, having lost her husband and three children to the recent Influenza epidemic. The Rhys' property has been placed under the care of Mister James Barrington and is for sale. Interested parties should call upon him at his office on High Street.

Had Arlis given any thought to Mrs. Rhys and her move back to Indiana, he would have assumed that she had either packed up and taken the furnishings with her or sent for them soon after the move. This room gave evidence to the opposite, and as Arlis stepped into the room, closing the door behind him, he was overcome with the feeling that Mrs. Rhys—or perhaps any of her deceased family members—might walk through the door at any moment, admonishing him for being in their home without their consent. Perhaps Mrs. Rhys still planned to send for her furnishings. Perhaps this was why the house was left unsecured. Then again, perhaps Mrs. Rhys wanted nothing to do with anything in this house, knowing that she'd forever associate the objects with disease, death, and loss.

Goose bumps rose on his arms. He felt the hair stand up on the back of his neck, causing him to call out again.

"Mrs. Rhys? Are you here?" He felt silly now, but nevertheless went to the window that offered the view of the barn, peering outside to make sure that no one would surprise him by walking into the house. Satisfied yet uneasy, he turned and crossed the room, passing the oaken table and the Baroque chairs. He entered the kitchen, his galoshes quietly squishing with every step. He paused in the doorway. This room appeared untouched, too, although Arlis hadn't seen it up close before. Cast iron pots and pans lay against the wall above the stove. A door to his left led outside to the back yard. Arlis, less concerned with the contents of the kitchen than the fact that no one occupied it, turned back toward the fireplace. After a brief sweep on the area, his attention fell on the short hallway to his right. He stood, transfixed on the three closed doors the hall offered to him. Two of the doors were directly opposite of each other, on each side of the hall, and the other was opposite of where he now stood.

He looked from side to side again, lingering in the large room, silently contemplating what might lie beyond those doors. He was sure that visiting any of those rooms might be an invasion of the former occupants' privacy, even more so than entering their home in the first place. He thought briefly about the possibility of angering their spirits, who might lash out from beyond the grave at him for being where no boy ought to be.

The silence in the room was obvious. Arlis didn't believe in ghosts, but he didn't necessarily doubt their existence, either. Unquestioningly, he did not want Violet angry with him in the afterlife any more than he had wanted it in this life.

The air felt stuffy. Arlis reckoned that the house could benefit from the opening of a window, something which probably hadn't been done since the previous fall, when the house still flourished with the occupation of a family. Knowing he'd only be here a short time, he quickly dismissed the thought of airing the place out. He was acutely aware that his clothes were still dripping, causing a puddle to appear on the floor beneath his feet. Looking at the fireplace, he saw that there was still plenty of firewood stacked nearby, and for a few moments he contemplated the idea of finding the means to start a fire so that he might dry himself out. He let this thought drift away as well, and then headed down the hallway.

Without any real purpose or intention, Arlis chose the door to the left. The door opened inward, creaking much like the front door had, and the boy felt a chill go through him again. Two straw mattresses, one against the wall to the right, the other at a perpendicular angle to it against the far wall, sat unmade in the perfectly square room. *The boys' room*, Arlis thought, deducing from the multiple beds. He was surprised by the relief he felt at not having randomly chosen Violet's room. Apparently he wasn't quite ready for that yet. A curtained window was centered in the far wall, and Arlis ascertained that this window was the one that looked out upon the yard in front of the house. A dresser and wooden toy box, the latter open and full of toys fit for use by young boys, lay against the wall to the left. Arlis went to the dresser and slowly pulled open each drawer, one by one, until all five lay open. Each contained various garments belonging to the boys. He touched a pair of gray trousers, took out what he thought was a shirt but turned out to be a pair of bedclothes, then neatly folded them and returned them to the drawer. Not sure what he was looking for, he rummaged through the toy box. Finding nothing that drew his interest, he returned his attention to the dresser, closing the drawers as he had opened them...one by one. He turned in a circle, examining the room again, searching himself for emotion, for *something*. He felt nothing.

Returning to the hall, Arlis hesitated again. When he opened the next door, he would surely be in Violet's room. He was struck by his lack of courage, yet astonished that such a simple task required courage in the first place. Realizing that with each passing second he was adding more thought to the process, he jolted forward and turned the knob, opening the door wide. The hinges screamed at him through the silence, catching Arlis off his guard and paralyzing him with fear.

"Dammit," he whispered at the door, admonishing himself for not realizing that this door should be no different than the others.

Ahead lay Violet's bed chamber. Arlis took two steps forward and paused, taking in the visuals. Her bed, also straw, was in the same linen free condition that her brothers' beds had been. The bed was centered in the room with the foot near where Arlis stood inside the doorway, and the head of it stood against the far wall directly under a curtained window. To the right of the bed an oil lamp, half-full with oil, sat on an end table, which had a closed drawer in it. To the left of the bed, a mirrored, three drawer bureau stood. Arlis remained still for a moment, and then he turned and slowly closed the door, minimizing the creak. He turned and surveyed Violet's room, waiting for her spirit to appear and chastise him for his boldness, but he remained alone in the room. Again, that feeling of invasion came over him. Instead of immediately going through her things, he sat on her bed, glad for the moment that it was unmade and therefore in no danger of being spoiled by his wet clothing. There, he closed his eyes and quieted his breathing, listening and absorbing the silence of the room. He imagined Violet in this room, adorned in her beautiful red dress, fussing over herself for him. He imagined her smiling at him, turning around and around, showing off the maple leaf pattern that was hand sewn into the calico. He tried to smell her lavender scent but couldn't, his imagination only being capable of so much.

He was just about to kiss her when a crow cawed from outside the window, bringing him back to the present and causing him to open his eyes. Crows seldom raise a fuss without a good reason, Arlis knew, and he rose and went to the head of the bed, where he drew back the curtain slightly to peer through the window. No crow was visible. The only thing he could see was an unoccupied pig sty, beyond which lay a field of winter wheat that Mr. Rhys must have planted last year. The field would be ready for harvest soon. Arlis wondered if anyone had plans to harvest the field. It would certainly be a waste if all of that wheat was left to wither away.

Satisfied that the crow was not announcing the arrival of an unknown person, Arlis turned his attention to the bureau, opening the top drawer. There, he found Violet's unmentionables and quickly looked away; not out of embarrassment as much as out of respect for the girl's intimacy. Looking at the chamber door, he ran his hands underneath the garments, searching for any baubles or trinkets that she might have hidden there. After a couple of passes through the drawer, he closed it and moved on to the next one.

There, in the middle drawer, he found her everyday dresses and skirts, along with some long pants that he'd often seen her wear during their fishing excursions. Again, he searched with his hands, and this time his eyes too, for something hidden underneath the clothing. Again, he came up empty.

After rifling through the final drawer's contents, producing nothing but bedclothes and bonnets and the like, he sat again upon the bed in disappointment. He suddenly remembered the drawer in the end table and rolled backward, turning a somersault upon the bed. Upon opening the drawer, he found nothing inside. Again, he sat upon the straw, feeling crushed and disappointed. He'd come into the house thinking it would be completely empty, but after finding it was still furnished he was hopeful of at least finding something of Violet's to take with him. He'd thought there'd be something more sentimental—something he could hold, save, keep.

Once again, he felt the guilt overcome him. Why had the sickness taken Violet's life—and the lives of her father and brothers—and not the life of Arlis or the lives of his family, even though the disease had been in their house, in their bodies? If Pastor Martin had been right when he had said that God only took those who had completed his work, then how was it that nearly an entire town had all completed their duties at the same time? What exactly had Violet's part in all of it been? None of it made any sense to him.

Furthermore, what right did he have to assume that Violet's death had anything to do with him? How selfish of him to think that the death of hundreds of people had been staged by God only to…only to…what? To hurt Arlis? To teach him a lesson? A lesson like the ones that God had attempted to drive into Mama by dropping a house on her baby boy and filling her baby girl's lungs with water? Did he really think he was important enough to warrant all of that attention from God? Did he think the whole world was about him? What a selfish thing it was to put himself at the center of Violet's death, when Mrs. Rhys had lost so much more.

"You stupid, stupid boy," he remembered Violet saying when he had told her that he loved her.

"Yeah," he agreed now. "Stupid and selfish."

He felt the tears coming again, but this time denied them. If God had created the world for people to experience loss, then he'd have to live with it. *Everybody experiences loss,* he thought. *Some more than others. Most more than me.* He'd have to learn not to dwell on it so much.

Arlis sneezed. Feeling the cold moisture in his clothing, he suddenly longed for dry garments. Through the curtains he could see that the sky had brightened, and he went to the window. Peering outside, he saw that the rain had stopped and the sun was peeking through the cloud cover, reflecting off of the waves of wheat in the field.

Then, abruptly, a thought occurred to him. "Where's the red dress?" he asked the empty room. "Even her dress is gone."

"It's the finest garment I've ever owned," she'd said to him through a smile on her fourteenth birthday…and then Arlis knew.

"She's wearing it," he whispered.

19 Mineral Point, Wisconsin
May 8, 1858
Late Afternoon

ARLIS STOOD SHIRTLESS AND BAREFOOT IN THE FARMYARD, basking in the warmth of the sunshine on his back as it dried his body. The wind had died with the rainstorm, and when the sun peeked out from behind the clouds, the air felt warm on his clammy skin. Before exiting the house, he'd gone into the bedroom at the end of the hall, finding nothing but another unmade mattress and a few drawers containing Mr. Rhys' clothing. Apparently, Mrs. Rhys had taken her own clothing along with her to Indiana. Arlis felt some relief at this, as he'd begun to imagine that she'd fled the house all at once, in an out of control, insane state. He could sympathize with her if that had been the case.

He'd found the clothesline behind the house, just outside the door that led to the kitchen. The bucket of clothespins was still where Mrs. Rhys had last set it down, and soon Arlis' shirt, trousers, and stockings were dangling from the line. His shoes and leather galoshes sat side by side on a tree stump between the barn and the coop. He'd removed everything except his undergarments, not willing to risk being caught on the Rhys' property in his birthday suit. He could explain away being dressed in his underwear…he'd been stuck out here in the rain for goodness sake. But getting caught running around on abandoned property wearing nothing but what God gave you might get you locked up, no matter your reasons. Besides, Arlis wasn't totally convinced that he wasn't being watched by members of the Rhys family, living or dead.

He stood, absorbing the sun for several minutes until he was dry enough to forget about his clothes and the rain. He then went to the barn, where he removed the wooden bar from the doors before pulling the left door open. Like the doors in the house, it opened with a loud groan. Although he expected this, Arlis still felt a chill go down his spine.

The barn remained as he remembered, minus the livestock. Arlis had no idea where the animals had gone, but he was pretty certain that they hadn't made the trip to Indiana with Florence Rhys. He hadn't heard of any conversation between Mrs. Rhys and Papa about the Jenkins family taking on the animals, either. He was pretty sure that his father would have purchased them from the widow if she had asked, and he would have offered a generous price too, just to release that particular burden from the lady's shoulders.

The sunlight infiltrated the slats of the wooden walls of the western side, projecting an angelic light into the barn at a forty-five degree angle. Dirt and dust, disturbed when the door of the barn was opened, floated visibly through the beacons. Arlis stepped inside, noticing the stack of tools in the corner to his left containing various hoes, forks, shovels, and other everyday farming implements. The plow sat nearby, dirty and well used, an extra plow point propped against it. He walked past the plow to the tool stack, not interested in the tools themselves, but rather in Violet's fishing gear, which lay on the floor next to them. Her old pole, with fixed line attached, lay underneath her new one, which sat next to her bait bucket and tackle box.

At once, Arlis felt nauseous. He turned toward the door, ready to retreat if his stomach decided to come up. He squatted, placing a hand on the floorboards to steady himself. He stayed this way for half a minute or so, until he lost patience with the position, finally convinced that the feeling would pass anyway. He stood and walked the remaining steps to the fishing gear, picking up the rod and reel he had gifted her the previous year.

He ran his fingers along the length of the pole, feeling the knuckles of the wood, the smoothness of the sanded and lacquered rod. He touched the reel; the line ready for casting, a hook tied to the end, the float attached a foot away. Perhaps this was what he'd been looking for all along. Perhaps this was the keepsake he'd been seeking. He could take Violet's rod and reel home and keep it, hold it, cast it, cherish it, forever.

He suddenly felt sick again…but this time he knew there would be no retching. This sickness was in his mind, his brain forcing the stomach to turn at the idea of the fishing pole coming home with him. He knew then that he'd never, ever want to fish again; not with his own pole or Violet's pole or anybody else's pole for that matter. Not without Violet. The pole would stay here in the barn until someone came and took it to Indiana, or until someone bought the property or until someone came here and stole it. Gently, Arlis placed the fishing pole on the floor where he'd found it. He scratched an itch on his shoulder, staring at the pole. Then he turned away from it forever.

Turning his attention to the rest of the barn, Arlis crossed to the other side, glancing up at the loft as he walked under it. He thought about going up the ladder, but instead went to the corner where he and Violet had sat in the straw cuddling and holding hands on her birthday. He sighed and sat down with his back to the wall, his legs splayed out before him, as he had before. There he sat. He allowed his mind to wander where it wanted, and he recalled, conceived, conjured, and considered all sorts of things as he lost track of the time. The sun, as it approached the horizon over the hills to the west, changed its position minute by minute, casting shadows throughout the barn that danced and dodged across the floorboards and the wall above the boy, who pulled his legs up and hugged his knees while studying his bare toes in the straw. He wiggled them, aware of the sensation of the straw on his bare feet.

Now, he began purposely sliding his feet back and forth through the straw, enjoying the stimulation as each piece either slid along or rolled underneath each foot. Moving faster and faster now, one foot moving away from his body as the other returned, he soon kicked nearly all of the straw from underneath himself, exposing two bare strips on the floorboard. He slowed his kicking now, as the friction on the bare floor was beginning to make his feet hot, and as he did he realized that the floor under his left foot was not as smooth as it felt under his right foot. In fact, it felt...grooved.

Curious, Arlis leaned forward. Indeed, there was a groove in the floor...no, not a groove, but a letter V, obscurely carved into the wood. Pushing the remaining straw away, he gasped audibly, amazed at what he'd found. His eyes again welled up with tears, and he was overcome with sudden gratitude to Violet, and God, that he'd been led to this spot.

"Thank you, Lord," he praised. "Thank you, Violet." The tears were falling freely now. They were tears of joy and bliss, relief and validation. Then, sorrow. In the end, always the sorrow.

Carefully yet crudely carved into the floorboard, in letters barely larger than Arlis' thumbnail, was a three-word message:

VIOLET
LOVES
ARLIS

Tracing the letters with the tip of his index finger, Arlis

laughed through a sob and used his free hand to wipe the moisture from the tip of his nose. His voice cracking with emotion, he said, "I love you too, Violet."

20 Camp Randall, Madison, Wisconsin
July 8, 1861
Late Afternoon

ARLIS SAT ON A WOODEN CRATE INSIDE THE TENT, TRYING not to fidget. He'd been on the crate long enough to make his tailbone ache. Directly in front of him was a small rectangular table, serving as a crude desk. The captain dipped the pen into the inkwell for the umpteenth time, then returned it to the paper, taking notes about the eighteen-year-old man that sat before him. Arlis hadn't been nervous when he'd entered the tent, which was actually more of a square, open-sided canopy, offering no privacy or shelter from the wind. It did offer shade, however, and Arlis was grateful to be out of the sun in the heat of the late afternoon, especially now that Dawes was seemingly writing a biography of him.

He'd been invited into the tent for an "informal interview," a mandatory occurrence if he was going to become a member of this officer's company. Nearly an hour later, he was still sitting across from the captain, feeling more and more nervous with every word that the man put to paper.

The man asking the questions was Captain Rufus R. Dawes. He was young for a company commander, Arlis thought, thinking the man to be between twenty-one and twenty-five years of age. Dawes was a slight, handsome man, with a narrow face and high cheekbones. His eyes were light and compassionate, his brown hair short, well-groomed, and parted to the left. He sported a smart moustache above his lip. The man exuded confidence and, Arlis thought, competence, too. Yet to be issued an official uniform, Dawes appeared splendid in a quality white button-down shirt under a sharp, black vest and black, woolen trousers. Uniformed or not, to Arlis, the man radiated leadership.

"So," Dawes said, looking up from the desk, "you're an abolitionist, then?"

"No, sir," Arlis said immediately. "I'm rather indifferent to slavery on the whole... although it's not for me. I could never *own* anyone. I don't approve of how southern slaveholders treat their slaves. It's wretched. The south should look to the Greeks as a model for how to treat their slaves. Except for those that worked the mines, Greek slaves were well treated and sometimes respected by those who held them in bondage."

"You seem very well-educated, Mr. Jenkins," the captain said, studying Arlis' face, "For a man with so little formal education. In level of interest, I'm more of a 'Roman' man, myself." He raised an eyebrow. "You have a preference between the two? Rome and Greece, that is?"

"Not really a preference, sir. Both have given much to the world. Most notably, the Romans gave us law; the Greeks, art and philosophy." He chose his words carefully. "When all is considered, however, I don't find either of them to be ideal role models. The British, the French...all of Europe has been idolizing the Romans and Greeks for two thousand years. In all of that time, the thing that has remained constant is war. England and France haven't been able to go more than a half century, until now, without attempting to conquer each other."

The captain nodded at him, offered a smile. "You're a philosopher?"

"No, sir, I'm just opinionated. I'm not nearly wise enough to be a real thinker. But I do think that the world could use a little *new* philosophy...one that didn't involve killing each other over ideas, land, and profit. We humans have a hard enough time surviving disease and pestilence. We needn't work so hard to find ways to kill one another." He paused, waiting to see if the captain would interject. When he didn't, Arlis continued, "Perhaps one day we can find a way to settle our differences without gun powder."

"Huzzah!" Dawes said excitedly, finding the inkwell with the tip of his pen again, "But until then, I need to know if you're willing to fire a musket at another man."

Arlis had arrived in Madison that very morning, Camp Randall being his destination. He'd turned 18 six days before and had made the journey by foot and wagon, with the intention of signing a roll and being mustered into the army. He'd checked his pocket watch upon arriving at the east gate of the camp, eighteen minutes until eleven o'clock. He remained outside the camp, sitting on a nearby bluff roughly 150 yards from the gate, trying to appear inconspicuous as he watched the goings on of the camp and those who came and went. No one paid him any mind. A solitary guard, armed with a pike, protected the whole of the camp from an attack from the east. He halted all of those who wished to enter, demanding to know their business, and then let them pass without further issue. At eleven o'clock, another soldier relieved the guard, taking over the business of camp security.

Inside the camp, soldiers drilled. Arlis watched as men in groups as large as 100, and as small as ten or twelve marched, counter-marched, turned, about-faced, wheeled, and stood at attention. Some of the groups were dressed in gray uniforms while others wore the fancy Zouave uniforms, their pants striped in splendid bright colors. Most wore homespun clothing, yet to be issued an official federal uniform. All were busy, the camp giving Arlis the impression of a beehive, with each bee doing his duty and working hard to make the collective productive.

He was in no hurry. He sat watching, mesmerized by the drills. A light breeze blew directly into Arlis' face, carrying the voices of the captains and sergeants giving the commands to Arlis' ears, allowing him to get an idea of what he could expect on the drilling ground. Occasionally, the sound of musketry would erupt deep in the camp as one unit or another practiced live firing. He absorbed it all, noting in his mind which units were more practiced than others, even if he had no name by which to label them.

By one o'clock he'd grown hungry, and had reached into his knapsack for the bread and apple butter his mother had given him for the trip. He'd eaten sparingly the last few days, not knowing exactly how long he'd be on his own. Now, however, he filled his gullet until satisfied, eating the last of the bread and using his finger to extract the last of the apple butter from the jar. He washed it down with water from his canteen.

Another hour passed, and Arlis had watched how groups of soldiers, in numbers of about 100 men, had passed into and out of two long wooden buildings in twenty-minute intervals. A dinner rotation, he guessed. When the last of the groups had come out, returning to the drilling field, Arlis reckoned it was time for him to become a soldier. Throwing his knapsack over his shoulder, he rose from his comfortable viewing position and walked down the hill to the camp entrance, the guard watching him as he approached.

"State your business," the guard barked as Arlis walked up. The guard was a rugged looking man of perhaps thirty years. He was dressed in a frumpy blue federal uniform, the brim of his leather kepi reflecting the sunlight. Three chevrons on the sleeve identified him as a sergeant.

"I'm looking to sign up," Arlis said.

"You're not with a company?" the soldier asked. The pike he was holding was actually no pike at all. It was basically nothing more than a long, round dowel, about eight feet in length and perhaps an inch in diameter.

"No, sir. I'm here to join the army."

The soldier eyed Arlis, looking him up and down. He turned his head and spat a wad of chaw into the dirt. "Don't call me 'sir,' boy. I work for a living," he said.

Arlis stood motionless and said nothing, confused by what the man meant by this.

After a moment, the soldier said, "Take a seat on the ground here by the fence. We'll find a company that's looking for another kid."

Arlis obeyed. The sergeant turned and walked about twenty feet into the camp, never taking his eyes off Arlis or the gate he was charged with guarding for more than a second. Then, he put his fingers to his mouth and let out a whistle, short and sharp, which brought another soldier running to him like an obedient hunting dog. The two soldiers talked for a moment before the new man scurried off to the right, and the sergeant walked back to his post. He had nothing to say to Arlis, who turned his attention to a group of men that were drilling about fifty or sixty yards away.

With his back to Arlis, a sergeant with a heavy German accent was standing in front of two lines of soldiers, each containing about fifteen men. Although a couple tents and a small, square building obscured Arlis' view of some of the men, he could see that they all wore short gray jackets and lighter gray pants, with a black welt running down the leg on the outside seam. Their hats were linen and glaze cloth caps, resplendent with patent leather trimmings. These uniforms were obviously new.

"Support...arms!" the sergeant ordered, the word "arms" sounding like "aahmz." The soldiers fumbled with their weapons, which appeared to be real muskets, leaving Arlis wondering why the sergeant at the gate was guarding the camp with a wooden pole. Lifting their weapons and pushing them away from their bodies, they grasped the lower band with their left hands, raised them until the hand was at neck level, then seized the weapon with their right hands a few inches below the cock.

"Halt!" the sergeant shouted, and the men froze in their current positions. "Now is ven you rotate ze musket. Rotate ze barrel to ze front, und place ze weapon on yer left shoulder," he explained. "Begin again, from ze rest position!" The men placed the butt ends of their muskets on the ground, their right hands grasping the muzzles above the upper band, their left hands grasping their right wrists.

"Support…aahmz!" the sergeant said again, and the men went through the motions again, only this time without interruption from the non-commissioned officer. Once they had completed the maneuver, each arriving at completion at a different moment, each was holding their musket on the left shoulder, perpendicular to the ground, supporting it with the cock against the left forearm, the left hand resting on the right breast.

"Sehr gut!" the sergeant said, "You must remembah ta roll ze weapon after you've placed ze right hand on ze stock. You vill not usually go to ze support position from ze rest position. Most often, it'll come from ze shoulder ahmz position." He pulled a watch from his pocket and looked at it. "It's time fer rotation." Pointing south, he said, "Stack yer muskets ver you found zem und report to Sergeant Schreiber. Dizmissed!"

The men did as ordered. Arlis watched as the soldiers stacked the muskets neatly, barrels up, against each other in two neat circles. As the soldiers walked away, realization came over him: There were but few muskets in the camp. These men were sharing weapons while learning to become soldiers. He wondered how long they'd have to wait before the government would issue each of the soldiers in the camp their own musket. There had to be thousands of men here. All of those arms would add up to a hefty bill for somebody.

"You!" a voice snapped, and Arlis whirled his head to the right. About ten feet away and approaching was a man in civilian clothing, wearing a finely tailored red shirt and black trousers. Arlis quickly jumped to his feet.

"Yes, sir," Arlis said quickly. He worried he might have called this man "sir" by mistake, too. Rising to his feet, he braced for a smart retort.

"I'm Lieutenant Crane," the man said in a heavy, Irish accent. Arlis noticed that *lieutenant* sounded like *"leftenant."* "I hear you're interested in soldiering."

"Yes, sir." Arlis said again. "My name's Arlis. Arlis Jenkins." Aware now that Crane was an officer, he straightened up and saluted.

The lieutenant smiled. "No need for that, laddie. Not yet, anyhoo. No saluting until you've signed a roster sheet, now. Come with me, Mr. Jenkins."

Arlis followed the man, who led him past several buildings and an assortment of tents. Crane moved quickly, forcing Arlis to pay more attention to his footing than his surroundings. After a minute or so, they approached a group of men, all wearing homespun, calico clothing. Each of them was unloading large burlap bags labeled "flour" from the back of a flat-bed wagon, then stacking them on a platform outside one of the buildings that Arlis had earlier identified as a mess hall.

"Sergeant Westcott," Lieutenant Crane said.

A stocky man with a large head and an angular chin stepped forward, and immediately snapped to attention.

"Sir!" he said, sharply, firing off a salute.

The lieutenant returned it, said, "This is Mr. Jenkins, Sergeant. Put him to work." Turning to Arlis, Crane said, "The captain will want to meet with ya, son. He'll need ta have a talk with ya before ya sign the muster. In the meantime, help these men get these supplies into storage. I'll be back fer ya shortly."

"Yes, sir," Arlis said, moving to the back of the wagon. One man was in the wagon, passing the goods off to another, who passed it on again. Arlis counted six more, seven, including the sergeant, handing off the bags to each other as a fire brigade would pass buckets at a house fire. All were sweating in the day's heat.

"Mickey," the sergeant said to the man in the wagon, who stopped and looked down at him. "Come on down. Let's have the recruit have a go at it."

The man jumped down from the wagon while the rest of them gathered around Arlis, who was suddenly uncomfortable with the attention. Arlis was taller, at five foot, nine inches, than all of them.

"Ah, so yer joinin' up with the Lemonweir Minutemen, are ye?" the man called Mickey asked. Like Lieutenant Crane, he also spoke in an Irish accent. Without allowing Arlis to answer, he added, "That's a damn fine decision, as the Minutemen are the finest and toughest company of men from here ta Washington. What's yer name?"

"Uh, Arlis…Arlis Jenkins."

"Well, Arlis Arlis Jenkins," Mickey said. He paused, pulling a handkerchief from his pocket. He wiped his hands and then his brow. "Arlis is a downright unusual name. Are ye from Mauston?"

"Uh, no," Arlis answered, puzzled by the question. "Mineral Point." He shifted his weight from his left foot to his right.

"I see," Mickey said, returning the handkerchief to his pocket. He looked sideways at Arlis, glaring at him with one eye. "I knew ye weren't a Mauston lad. If ye were, I'd already know ya." Looking away from Arlis and making eye contact with several of the other men, he said, "And jus' what would be the reason that our beloved little company, containing ninety-four fine Mauston men, would require the services of a lad from Mineral Point?"

Arlis nervously shifted his weight back to his left foot.

"Look at 'im, he's a pack mule," the shortest man said, drawing snorts and laughs from the others.

Great, Arlis thought. *Yet* another *Irishman!* Although he had no issues with the Irish, he did have difficulty understanding their English.

"Ha, a pack mule," Mickey repeated. "Is that the sort of work ye did back in…*Mineral Point?*" he asked, the last two words coming out with obvious derision.

Arlis ignored the insult, and instead kept his voice steady. "Mining. I was a lead miner."

Another man, silent until now, took a step forward and spoke up. "He's a badger!" He smiled broadly. "Did ya live in a cave in the hillside?"

"Ha, no," Arlis said, relieved that someone else was talking now, and in a voice without a foreign accent. "No one in the Point's lived like that for a long time now. My Grandfather was a badger, though. He lived in a badger hole up on the bluff for a while." He cleared his throat. "I've never seen a real badger hole. Well, one that's occupied, anyway."

"Well," Mickey said with a snort, "You're goin' from being a badger to a pack mule. What d'ya say we load our packs on yer back and ya can carry 'em all the way ta Richmond?"

Without hesitation, Arlis quipped, "Alright, but I'm gonna need to take a rest sometime around Chicago." This drew laughter from all of them, and Arlis drew a breath of relief, his unease abating.

"Boys," Mickey said loudly, "This here is Badger Jenkins!"

They took turns introducing themselves to Arlis. Sergeant Westcott was officially known as Sergeant Linneus Westcott. The rest were private soldiers: James "Mickey" Sullivan, Ira Butterfield, George Chamberlain, James Scoville, and Billy

Harrison. The short man, who'd called Arlis a pack mule, was Hugh Talty. The last man, the one who'd asked him about badger holes and labeled him "Badger," was Albert Tarbox.

With the introductions complete, Arlis leapt up onto the back of the wagon, eager to show the boys that a badger could handle the work of a pack mule. The work was quickly accomplished. Within minutes of completion, as the men were replenishing their fluids from a large barrel of water nearby, Lieutenant Crane returned.

"The captain is ready ta meet with ya now, Mr. Jenkins."

The captain stood waiting, watching as Lieutenant Crane led Arlis past the storage shed adjacent to the tent under which he stood. Arlis felt the man's eyes upon him, already measuring, already judging. As Arlis approached, he saw that he and the captain were the same height.

"Captain Dawes," Crane said, snapping to attention and saluting. "This is Arlis Jenkins. He's lookin' for a company ta call home."

Dawes returned the salute, said, "Very well. Thank you, lieutenant. You may leave us." Looking at Arlis, now, he gestured to a wooden crate on the opposite side of a small table. "Have a seat, Mr. Jenkins."

Arlis moved to the crate, stumbling over a stake the tent was tied to. Sitting down, he was relieved that his mistake hadn't brought the tent down.

"Don't be nervous," the captain said. He sat on his own crate, on the opposite side of the table from Arlis. "I promise not to bite you. This interview will be informal. As the commanding officer of nearly one hundred men, it is my responsibility to get to know each of them. I've done similar interviews with all of the men under my command."

"I'm alright, sir," Arlis said.

Dawes smiled broadly, adjusting his belt and pulling the sides of his vest down. His smile was as white as ivory, the teeth straight and perfect. Arlis found it comforting, reassuring, and he felt at ease.

"Arlis, is it?" Dawes asked, "A-R-L-I-S?"

"Yes, sir."

"Jenkins is spelled in the usual way, I presume. J-E-N-K-I-N-S?"

Again, Arlis said, "Yes, sir."

"How old are you, Jenkins?" the captain asked, looking hard into Arlis' eyes.

"I'm eighteen, sir...and I've brought paperwork to show it."

Dawes found his pen, dipped it in ink, and put the pen to a piece of parchment. "I'll have a look later. Arlis is an unusual name. Don't think I've ever met an 'Arlis' before."

"It's Hebrew." Arlis said. "It means 'Pledge'."

"How appropriate, then," the captain said, smiling again. "You're going to have to make an 'Arlis' to the company before the end of the day." They both laughed at the joke. "Unusual or not, the boys of the company have all given each other nicknames, anyway. Chances are, you'll have one before the week is out."

Arlis leaned forward, "Oh, they've already stamped me with one, sir. Before coming in here I was given over to a work detail by Lieutenant Crane. A wagon full of flour required unloading. Sullivan, Tarbox, Talty, let's see, uh, Harrison, Butterfield, uhh," he paused in an attempt to recollect the rest. "Can't rightly remember the other three. One of them is a sergeant."

"Sergeant Westcott would have been with that group," Dawes offered.

"Yes, Sergeant Westcott," Arlis agreed. "Anyway, they're already calling me 'badger.'"

"I'll be..." Dawes said, smiling again. "You must have made an impression, Mr. Jenkins." He winked at Arlis. "Nicknames are the first real initiation into a company, you know." He paused to write something down. "Badger, huh?" he went on, "I'm an Ohioan by birth, but I've spent more than a few good years here in 'the Badger State.' In all my time here, however, I've never once seen one of the large rodents. It's puzzling to me how Wisconsin decided upon the badger to be its representative from all of the choices available in the animal kingdom."

Arlis shifted on the crate.

"I can shed some light on that, captain." He paused, not wanting to give him the impression that he was showing off. "Badger isn't really a representation of the animal. Rather, it's a representation of the lead miners from the southwestern portion of the state, who, early on, used to live in holes, or man-made caves, that were burrowed into the sides of the hills near the mines they worked in. These holes were called 'badger holes.'"

A group of soldiers, wearing the dark blue federal suit that Arlis admired, marched past, a non-commissioned officer barking out the cadence. Arlis again noticed an Irish accent... or perhaps English.

"I mentioned to Mickey and the others that I'm a lead miner...well, I was a lead miner until a week ago, and one of the boys slapped the nickname of 'Badger' on me." He *hoped* he was correct in making this assumption, as there was still a good chance they'd label him "Pack Mule."

"'Badger' is a fine nickname," Dawes said. "You got lucky... wait'll you hear some of the names the boys call each other. Where are you from, then?"

"Mineral Point, sir."

"Well, other than mining, spin me a yarn about what your life is like and what you've done with it up until now."

Arlis, feeling like his life had been mundane and monotonous, had difficulty in figuring out where to begin his story. Dawes, sensing this, threw him a bone.

"Tell me about your schooling," he said.

Arlis started with his early years, his days in the Mineral Point schoolhouse, and how they hadn't lasted long due to the high turnover of teachers. He told Dawes about his chief educator, his mother, and how for nearly ten years she had taught him and his sister in their home. His story included his mother's passion for books, religion, etiquette, language, and patriotism. He explained his daily schedule of farming, schooling, and mining. Dawes listened respectfully throughout, asking questions about Arlis' curriculum of rhetoric, Greek, and Latin.

"I'd had plans to attend college when I'd turned eighteen," Arlis continued. "But last year my mother had decided that she'd done all she could for me. She insisted it was time I enrolled in college, so we wrote letters to nearly twenty schools. Some showed interest, some even as far as sending someone out to Mineral Point to meet me and to give me an entrance exam in person. I had a few offers."

Arlis had chosen Carroll College, a school affiliated with the Presbyterian Church, after much discussion with his mother in the kitchen of their home. Arlis had wanted to attend the University of Wisconsin at Madison, but his mother was adamant that a school with Christian guidance was the best option, and Carroll was the only religious school that had accepted him. Mama's willingness to overlook the fact that Carroll was not a Methodist school surprised Arlis.

"Your savior is not a Methodist, Arlis," she'd said. "Presbyterians are Christians, too."

So Arlis had gone off to attend school in Waukesha, a town in southeastern Wisconsin. It had once been named "Prairieville," but was renamed in the mid-1840s in honor of the local Potawatomi leader, Wau-Tsha (or Wauk-Tsha, depending on who you asked). Arlis noticed a trend lately that white people had been naming their towns after Indian words or chiefs. *We'll take your land, and then we'll name it after you,* he'd been known to quip. Carroll College was nearly twice as far from Mineral Point as the University of Wisconsin at Madison, but he doubted that the distance had any effect on how deeply he felt the homesickness during his first semester. It was devastating, the loneliness, and Arlis was shocked by how much he could miss people that seldom had anything to say to one another. He'd missed the daily routine. There was comfort in going through the same motions day after day.

At first he struggled, not actually having been in a classroom since he was little. He found himself ruffled by the new schedule, the different meal times, the strangers he interacted with every day, including his roommate, Fred, who seemed aloof and distant. Before long, he found a new routine, all his own, and he learned to move along with the rhythm of everyone else. His work improved noticeably.

But soon arrived the election of 1860 and with the election of Abraham Lincoln, the State of South Carolina had decided to form its own republic. The topic on everyone's tongue that winter was war, and shortly most of the students were having difficulty with distraction. Every day, the favorite sport was seeing who could get to the newspapers first, scanning the pages of The Milwaukee Sentinel and the local abolitionist circulation, The Waukesha Freeman, to see which state had seceded from the Union.

"Around the time that spring began," Arlis told Dawes, "even the faculty had their heads in the south. Then the President called for volunteers, and within days the classrooms were half-empty. Everybody was signing up. Of course, I was still seventeen, so I had to sit and watch with the others as the exodus turned into a mad frenzy. By the time I'd gone home for the summer, some classrooms were at one-third capacity. Even a few of the faculty left to sign up. By the time I'd made it back to the Point, the place looked like a ghost town, as the majority of the boys had already mustered up and left." He looked around the tent, as if he were looking for people he knew. "I'm sure that most of them are probably here."

Dawes set his pen down and said, "I saw some of that *frenzy*, too. I imagine the whole country went through it. There's plenty of it still going on." He looked in his lap, as if he held his memories there. "Truth be told, I got caught up in it myself." He looked at Arlis again. "As I mentioned, I'm from Ohio. I attended the University of Wisconsin for a time, and then went home, earning my degree at Marietta College. I came back to Wisconsin with my father, conducting business with him up in Mauston. When I heard the call I put out a call for volunteers right in Mauston. There was no way I was gonna go back to Ohio." He looked to his right, gesturing in that direction with the pen. "This company was put together back on the thirtieth of April, at Mauston's Langworthy's Hall. We elected officers that very night." He paused in reflection, staring at something outside the tent. "We adopted the name 'Lemonweir Minute Men' that night, too. The boys will tell you, it's been a challenge to get this company into the army. We were forced to wait so long that many of our boys left to join other companies. We actually had to hold another recruitment rally in mid-June." Looking again at Arlis, he continued, "It's taken a lot of letter writing on my part to get us where we are right now, which is without uniforms and weapons. You've arrived at a good time, Mr. Jenkins. The company arrived here just yesterday. We came with orders to report to the Sixth Regiment, and we only received those because of the failure of several other companies to report here on time. When we began, we had hoped to get into the First or Second. So you see, even the company commander was guilty of being caught up in the frenzy of it all. We were all in a great big rush and ended up going nowhere."

From somewhere far across the camp, a volley of musketry

sounded, ragged and sloppy. Arlis turned his head in the direction of the sound. The captain didn't seem to notice.

"The boys are antsy." Dawes said. "They're worried they're going to miss the fighting and the war will end before they're out of Wisconsin."

Arlis shook his head. "There's little chance of that," he said.

The captain cocked his head, raising an eyebrow. "How's that?"

"Well, sir, few wars end after a single battle. Looking at our own history, General Washington got his tail whipped time and time again, retreating after each loss. When he crossed the Delaware to attack Trenton, he could muster only about two thousand soldiers. The fate of the Patriot cause was in the hands of two thousand men."

Another volley, as uneven as the first one, exploded far off in the camp.

Arlis continued, "If our side should lose the first battle of this war, the rest of us aren't going to go home. The President won't give up that easily. On the contrary, if the Rebels massing in Virginia are whipped, I find it hard to believe that Texas and Mississippi are going to capitulate."

Dawes put the pen back in the ink and then dabbed the excess away. He wrote, the tip of his tongue poking out of the corner of his mouth. Finally, he said, "Taking Richmond will certainly help…and what if the Rebels capture Washington?"

Arlis considered this while rubbing his chin. "I doubt they'll take Washington, sir, but if they do, we'll take it back. On the same note, if we capture Richmond, there'll still be plenty of fight in the South. Remember, the Brits occupied Philadelphia and still lost the war."

Dawes studied the young man, smiling with his eyes. Writing again, he said, "You're very astute for only eighteen, Mr. Jenkins. Your mother seems to have applied her trade well."

"Thank you, sir," he said, leaning forward and trying discreetly to see what Dawes had written. The writing was small, cursive, and upside down, making it difficult to decipher the words. It was hard to imagine what he'd said to motivate so much use of ink. He was becoming uneasy again.

"On the subject of your mother, how is she with the idea of you soldiering?"

Arlis thought back on the conversations he'd had with Mama. She'd not wanted him to go, as she knew as well as Arlis about the dangers he'd be facing. But her years of preaching about patriotism, duty, and her ardent fervor for everything Americana was ammunition enough for Arlis to force her into eventual surrender.

"She took a bit of convincing, sir, but not much. She was always worried that I'd get killed in the mine, which is a daily possibility. Trading a living of mining for one of soldiering is a pretty fair transaction in her mind. Besides, she believes in the cause…in saving the Union." He paused, watching as two soldiers uniformed in gray walked past carrying a fairly large crate. He found the eyes of the officer again, and said, "My father was a tougher sell. With all of the boys leaving the mine for the army, he wanted me to stay to help with the work. Truth is, after spending a year at Carroll it was hard to go back into the holes. I really don't want anything to do with mining anymore. Don't get me wrong, it's not because I want to be a soldier. I think the schooling itself spoiled it out of me."

"So," the captain said, "Why are you here, Mr. Jenkins?"

"I'm sorry, sir?" Arlis said, more nervous now. He fidgeted.

Dawes put the pen down and folded his hands on the table. "Why are you signing up, Arlis?" he asked gently, using the young man's first name for the first time.

"Because everyone else is, sir," Arlis said. "I can't imagine this thing being settled and not having been a part of it. It seems like…well, it seems like I'd be less of a man than I want folks to consider me." He hesitated. "Plus, being here gets me out of the holes."

More musket fire sounded. Dawes, smiling, picked up the pen again and wrote something down.

"Besides," Arlis continued, "We need to teach the slave-holders that they can't just up and leave because they don't like the results of an election."

More note taking from Dawes, then he asked, "So, you're an abolitionist, then?"

The conversation turned from slavery to philosophy to war, and Arlis was amazed that the commander of the company was so interested in the opinions of a lowly recruit.

Later that night, between his nervousness about what to-morrow would bring and his apprehension of looking foolish in front of his new comrades, Arlis would think back on this conversation with Captain Dawes. He'd marvel at how he'd not mentioned the things that might have given Dawes the most insight into who he was, those things that had had the most impact on molding him into the person that he was right now.

He hadn't spoken of his family's acquired wealth, or how he could probably live comfortably on that income for the rest of his life, never having to work again. Not once during the interview had he mentioned the losses of his baby sister to pneumonia or his brother to a storm. Both events had had a profound effect on Arlis, if for no other reason than they had markedly changed the personalities of both of his par-ents. They had altered not only his education, but his upbring-ing. Additionally, he'd omitted the loss of Violet, his eternal paramour, to a disease that he himself had also struggled to survive. It was a calamity that had certainly affected his dai-ly thoughts and actions more than anything else; the conse-quences of which were still reverberating, still molding him into the man he would eventually become.

But here and now, after Arlis had commented on the world needing to find a better way of solving their differences than by killing each other, Dawes responded by insisting that he needed to know if Arlis was capable of firing a musket at another man.

"I'll do my duty, sir," he answered confidently. Dawes continued to study him.

"How do you think you'll stand up to being shot at?" the captain asked, fidgeting in discomfort on his own crate now.

"I won't know until it happens, sir. I mean, I could boast about my courage like boys always do…and I'll definitely boast in front of those boys out there. It's what they'll expect. I reckon that you know better, though. The truth be told, sir, there's plenty of things that military life will throw at me that I'm more afraid of than getting shot at."

Dawes' eyes were looking over Arlis' shoulder at something, and Arlis realized that someone was approaching the tent from behind him.

"Captain," the voice said in full Irish accent. "Please forgive the interruption. A message." It was Lieutenant Crane again.

Waving a hand in indifference, Dawes took a folded piece of paper from Crane, returned a smart salute, and dismissed him back to whatever duties awaited. Unfolding the message, he quickly read it before placing it in his pocket.

"Have a quick stretch, Mr. Jenkins. Lord knows I need one." He stood, and Arlis did as well.

"Thank you, sir."

As Dawes left the tent, Arlis was left wondering what he should do. Before he decided on a course, however, the captain returned carrying two tin cups. He offered one to Arlis, who took it.

"Water, Arlis," Dawes said. "This heat is something."

"Thank you, sir," Arlis said again.

Dawes sat down again on his crate, motioning for Arlis to

do the same. Once he did, the captain said, "Lieutenant Crane informs me that there's another boy at the gate looking to join a company." He pulled the folded paper from his pocket, unfolded it, and said, "William Anderson's his name." He cocked his head, "Is he with you?"

"No, sir," Arlis said. "I came alone."

Dawes returned the paper to his pocket, said, "You were talking about things that are worse than getting shot at. Just what things did you have in mind?"

Arlis took a pull from the cup, amazed at how cool the water was. He swallowed and said, "Disease, sir. Measles, small pox, typhoid, typhus, cholera, influenza." He paused after influenza, and then went on, "Yellow fever, chicken pox, malaria. Disease kills more soldiers than bullets in every war, sir. Put a bunch of men together and one of them gets sick, then many of them get sick. I'd rather take a bullet than lie in a bed with the likes of cholera. I'm also wary of things like shoes, sir, and food, or the lack of it. Winter quarters, too, like Valley Forge and Morristown. We've heard nightmares about all of these things. During the Revolution, soldiers in the Continental Army resorted to eating things like fire cakes and boiling their shoes..." he trailed off, and his eyes moved to the floor. "Anyway, these are the things that scare me the most about soldiering."

Both men fell silent; the captain's pen was quiet as well. Arlis, still not looking up, felt the eyes of Dawes upon him. They both drank from their cups.

"Do you aspire to becoming an officer, Mr. Jenkins?" the captain asked.

Arlis looked up, wide-eyed, and found the man's eyes. Realizing that Dawes was serious he said, "No, sir."

"Well, this isn't a formal offer, Arlis, but you know as much about warfare as any man in this company. A commission would not be out of the question." He finished his water and set the cup down on the desk.

Arlis, horrified at the prospect of leadership, said, "No, sir...and if I'm elected or commissioned I'll refuse it. I know a lot about American military history, dates and battles and such, but I know absolutely nothing about tactics and drill and whatnot. Please, sir, I'm interested only in doing my duty as a private soldier."

Without argument, Dawes reached down next to his crate and pulled a leather-bound book from a brown leather satchel. Opening it, he laid it on the table in front of Arlis. Dipping the pen in ink, he turned it 180 degrees, offering it to the recruit. Pointing to a line on the page, he said "Sign here then, Mr. Jenkins."

Arlis accepted the pen and signed the page where Dawes had indicated.

"Congratulations, Private Jenkins. You're officially mustered into the Lemonweir Minutemen," Dawes said, smiling as he stood. Arlis followed suit.

"Thank you, sir," he said, and saluted.

21 Camp Randall, Madison, Wisconsin
July 22, 1861
12:40pm

THE COMPANY HAD FORMED IN A LIGHT RAIN ON THE PARADE ground and marched into the mess hall, the ranks on each side of two long wooden tables. When every man had reached his place, all stood at attention, their supper upon a tin plate in their left hand, waiting on the order from the company commander.

"Company K, inward face!" Captain Dawes ordered loudly. The men turned ninety degrees, facing their seat, which was upon a long bench alongside their table. "Uncover!" he said, and the men removed their gray cloth caps. "Seats!" The men took their places at the table.

"Father in Heaven," the captain offered, his head bowed, standing at the head of one of the tables, "We thank you for this bounty and for your continued blessings in becoming better men, better soldiers, better souls. We ask that you persist in nourishing our minds as you nourish our bodies, so that we may better complete your work. We hold you with affection in our hearts as you hold us in your hands, and we pray for your enduring guidance as we progress in our trade. Through thy providence and that of your son, Jesus Christ, we pray..."

"Amen," the company said as one.

They ate.

Until the sixteenth of July, the captain had begun his mealtime orders by addressing the company as "Lemonweir Minute Men." But upon that day, they'd officially been assigned as Company K of the Sixth Wisconsin Volunteer Infantry Regiment. Each had signed a roster sheet indicating that they'd serve for three years or for the duration of the war, should it end sooner.

A lot had occurred in the previous fortnight. The men of the Sixth had been issued their first official clothing in the form of the typical gray uniform, which was issued to all of the volunteers from Wisconsin. The jacket was short, reaching to the hips, with black facing at the ends of the collar, the upper side of the cuffs, the shoulders, and the straps. The pants were a slightly lighter gray with black trim on the outside seams. Additionally, each man was issued two heavy dark blue woolen shirts, a sack coat, two pairs of drawers, two pairs of socks, a pair of cowhide shoes, and the linen and glaze cloth cap cover, which became a seemingly endless source of entertainment for the men. The carcass of the cap was constructed of haircloth, the frame and studding of wire and whalebone. Its front visor sat square with the front elevation, while the rear visor, or piazza, extended downward at a one-third pitch. With patent leather trimmings and an inside finish of black alpaca, it was a quality garment, finely constructed and more durable than anything else the men would be issued now or in the future. The boys used it as a toy, using it to play catch or substituting it for a football. Some played "hop, step, and jump" with it, the "jump" portion of the game always ending on someone's cap. To everyone's amazement, the cap would always return to normal with a little coaxing, the wire portion of the garment allowing for its flexibility.

The Sixth was a strong, full regiment of 1,045 men. Of this mass, Company K comprised of ninety-two strong souls. They'd lost a few for various reasons, and signed a couple in the interim. Although the Company K boys had been drilling since their arrival in camp, their real training had begun in earnest when they'd been absorbed into the regiment. The daily drilling was severe. Beginning at dawn with reveille and a roll call, they'd drill by company for an hour before being served breakfast. Following the meal, there'd be a sick call, a fatigue call, and then a guard mount, where the changing of the guard would occur before the men would be led in two and a half hours of company or squad-sized drill. Then came formation, followed by dinner, followed by a half hour of free time, followed by formation again. On most days, it would now be about 1:30 in the afternoon. All ten companies, A through K (excluding J, as there was no company designated with the letter J), would come together as a regiment and drill together for the next three hours, practicing anything and everything military. Upon completion, they'd be dismissed by company for supper. After another break, each man given to his own activity for a half hour, they'd form up again, this time for dress parade. Then, with darkness approaching, the commander would give the order for tattoo to commence, meaning that all disturbances and loud talking were to cease within fifteen minutes. Tattoo quickly became Arlis' favorite time of the day. He'd use it as a time for reflection, correction, self-education, and unwinding. Occasionally, he'd write a letter to his folks during this time. Following a nine o'clock final roll call, the men would prepare for bed, sleep usually coming within minutes of hitting the pillow, the soldiers being exhausted in mind and body. At dawn…reveille, followed by a roll call.

Upon arrival at Camp Randall, the Company K boys had spent the first couple of nights sleeping on wooden pallets inside wooden barracks. It hadn't taken long, however, for the men to realize that they weren't alone in their blankets. Fleas—thousands of them—consistently made the nights long and uncomfortable. So when the men were evicted and issued tents a few days later, they were thrilled to be leaving their quarters. Within a week though, the weather had turned unseasonably cold, and, due to a shortage of blankets, many of the men spoke of being willing to trade the cold, damp nights for the itchy ones. Some of them were truly serious.

Slowly, the men were becoming soldiers. They had a very long way to go yet, however. They were footsore, many having open blisters on their feet that required nightly attention. Many of the men weren't used to such arduous daily work. They were sore all over, their backs and shoulders aching from the heavy loads they carried on the drilling fields and parade grounds. Arlis, initially feeling overwhelmed by it all, was growing accustomed to the army way of life. He found much of the drill to be similar to barn dancing in that if you knew how to count and knew your right from your left you could figure the rest out fairly easily. The officers and NCOs of the company—and of the regiment, for that matter—were patient men, as most of them were learning too, sometimes openly reading from a training manual right in front of the men. Often, while other regiments were being screamed at, the men of the Sixth were having things calmly explained to them on the drilling ground. Arlis found this environment to be a much easier way to learn, as he had more difficulty focusing while being screamed at than when things were simply laid out for him. That said, he'd seen his share (and then some) of a shouting sergeant and a bellowing officer.

Now, sitting between Billy Harrison and Mickey Sullivan at the chow table as the boys bantered good naturedly about how each was the best in the company, Arlis realized that, although many of the men could take him in a fair fight, most didn't hold up to him in marching ability or on the drilling ground. He was as good as any on the firing line, too, being able to load and accurately fire as well as the rest of his comrades. He hadn't expected this, as his experiences with guns had been minimal, having only hunted a few times with his father. He'd taken down a few deer over the years, but the Jenkins family hadn't needed to hunt for their meals, as the farm and Mineral Point's butcher, Martin Tubbs, had provided well enough for them. Lost in thought about how Mama and he used to visit Mr. Tubbs' shop, Arlis was suddenly aware that Ira Butterfield was talking to him.

"What're ya thinkin' on there, Badger?" Ira asked, "yer mommy on yer mind again?" He laughed, looking around the table at the boys immediately around him. They were laughing, too.

"Actually, Butterfly," Arlis answered, chewing on a piece of bacon, "I was thinking of *your* mama, and how she could out-soldier the lot of you!" he said, pointing from man to man, in an arc: Mickey, Ira, Hugh, Albert, and Billy. Now it was Arlis' turn to laugh, and the boys continued laughing, only this time at Ira's expense.

"Whaddya think, Tall-T," Ira said to Hugh, "who's the better soldier, me or the Badger?"

Talty put a finger to his chin, acting like he was seriously considering the question. Then, he said, "Without any doubt, me arse!" and laughter erupted again.

Once the men quieted again, Tarbox turned to Mickey, said, "It's been a coupla days, Mick. Go on, give us one."

Mickey smiled, said "Ah, what am I, some kinda circus act? Ya think I kin just roll 'em off 'cause you boys think I oughta?" He frowned, feigning irritation.

"Come on, Mickey," Billy said. "You can do it."

"Ahh, shut up, Hairy One," Mickey said, using Harrison's nickname. Billy had light blue eyes that bordered on silver, and sported a bushy, chin-strap style beard with no moustache. His arms were nearly as hairy as his face. "Ima thinkin' here," Mickey snapped. He leaned back, looking upward at the ceiling of the hall. "Alright, boys, here goes." Drawing a deep breath, he paused for dramatic effect. Then he picked up his cup and held it high, as if making a toast. Loud enough to stop conversations and turn heads from all over the room, he said,

"All morning long, the boys of Company K
Be drillin' and marchin' and findin' their way
Wishin' an' hopin' that they're worth a lick
but alas there's no soldier quite as good as ol' Mick!"

Laughter and applause erupted, and Mickey rose to take a bow. As he sat down, Arlis patted his shoulder, impressed at Mickey's ability to rhyme under pressure. The room buzzed, and for a moment no one noticed the regimental commander, Colonel Lysander Cutler, walk in and stand by the door, searching the room with his eyes. Of small build and medium height, the colonel was a handsome man. He was in his mid-fifties, with soft eyes, a triangular nose, and a short, graying moustache complete with a matching beard, which gave him a distinguished look. Cutler had a reputation as a tough disciplinarian, and although Arlis knew little about him after only two weeks in the army, he held the man in high esteem.

"Attention...Company!" someone barked, and the men immediately rose to their feet, standing at attention.

"As you were, men," the colonel responded. "Return to your meal. Captain Dawes, a moment."

"Yes, sir," the captain said, quickly moving down the aisle. He and Cutler left the mess hall together.

Arlis finished his meal, one of the first to do so. He liked to finish well before the end of mealtime so that he could relax and allow the meal to settle before getting back to soldiering.

"Nice, Mickey," he said now. "Too bad you're a poor judge of soldiers, though."

"Heh. Yer jus' jealous, Badger. Even the colonel knows... you didn't hear him put up an argument, did ya?"

The rest finished their meals and sat, relaxing and talking as they waited for Dawes to come back and dismiss them. Those who smoked fired up their pipes and cigars, and soon the room was dank and foggy with tobacco smoke. The conversation at Arlis' table turned to drill.

"Rainin' hard out there," Tarbox said. "Westcott says we're gonna load an' fire in the rain. He says we're gonna get a lesson 'bout keepin' our powder an' percussion caps dry. He says those that fail ta do so will get extra marchin'."

"Damn," Mickey said adamantly, looking out the nearest window. "If he's right boys, best ta keep yer pouches covered." Though the window was constructed of fogged glass, it was easy to see the raindrops as they pelted off of it. It was pouring outside.

Suddenly, a loud and urgent voice said, "Men! Silence please!" It was the company's first sergeant, David Quaw. "The captain would like to say a piece."

Dawes was standing at the head of his table again, holding a piece of paper in his hand. He stood for a few moments, reading and re-reading the words before setting the paper down on the table in front of him. He looked around the room at the men, quietly collecting his words.

"Thank you, Sergeant," he said, nodding at Quaw, who returned the nod. "Men, I have in front of me a report given to me by Colonel Cutler. It details a terrible fight that took place in Virginia just yesterday. At a place called…" the captain paused, searching the paper in front of him for the information, and then continued, "At a place called Bull Run, the Rebel forces have achieved a decisive victory over General McDowell and our federal brethren. Apparently, the defeat of our forces is total, with the remnants of our army retreating into Washington. The threat of the Rebels marching on the Capitol is high."

The room was silent, each man absorbing what the captain was telling them. After a few moments, Dawes said, "The Sixth Regiment has orders to board a train to Milwaukee tomorrow, and then it'll be on to Washington after that." Dawes again looked around the room, making eye contact with many of the men.

"Men," he said, "we're going to war."

22
Camp opposite Fredericksburg, Virginia
June 28, 1862
Afternoon

"IT'S HOTTER THAN HADES IN HERE," THE SOLDIER FROM the Second Wisconsin said. He slumped on the bench until his body fell to the floor of the cell. Arlis, seated on the opposite bench, looked up from his work. He had been diligently digging the dirt out from under his thumbnail with his other thumbnail.

"You decide that sharing the floor with the earwigs and centipedes isn't so bad after all, Beasley?" he asked the man, who lay on his back in the darkened gloom of the room.

"The buggers be damned," came the answer.

They were sharing a ten-foot by ten-foot square room, built of solid wooden walls and floors, the door as solid and wooden as the rest of the room. Three wooden benches sat about two feet off of the floor along the walls that didn't harbor the door. The ceiling of their domain was nearly ten feet high. A small, one-foot square window was strategically placed near the ceiling above Arlis, serving as the only source of light. The light shining through the window was divided by a solid iron bar that ran vertically through the center of it, making escape impossible. The room was a wooden jail cell, one of maybe five or six like it, in the camp building known at the guardhouse. It was not built for comfort. The cell was oven hot, and the humidity added to the misery as the floor, walls, and benches felt wet to the touch. Those soldiers who had thought to commit a mild infraction in order to get out of drill or some other unwanted duty soon found the experience of the guardhouse to be far worse than anything that the army needed doing.

A third man, Private John Cook from Company D of Arlis' regiment, lay supine on the bench opposite the door, one knee raised and one arm draped over his eyes as he tried to sleep. Cook was a short, stocky, and muscular man who was a frequent visitor to the guardhouse. He wasn't a regular because he was a shirker or a criminal, but because he had a serious problem with authority, particularly that of his company commander, Captain John Marsh. Cook had a famous temperament that had earned him a reputation among the soldiers as a man not to be messed with. This reputation went far beyond his own company and the other companies of the

Sixth, extending to those of the entire brigade. Arlis didn't fear Cook, as he'd had few contacts with the man and even fewer reasons to anger him, but he respected the man's temper and his ability to take anyone in a fight.

Cook had come into the guardhouse yesterday morning, his face reddened with anger.

"That sonovabitch is the worst hypocrite of all of the bloody hypocrites," he'd said.

"Who?" George Beasley had asked, instantly regretting it.

"*WHO THE BLOODY HELL DO YA THINK?*" Cook had shouted into the man's face, and the room suddenly seemed smaller to Arlis.

Hours later, as the three men were eating their evening meal, Arlis had chanced the question, "What did you say to him, Cook?"

Cook, through a mouthful of corn, said, "I tol' the dumb fuck that if he wasn't gonna use his head fer soldierin,' then I knew a blacksmith in Tomah that could use an anvil."

Arlis erupted in laughter. Seeing that it was safe to do so, Beasley did, too.

"No shit?" Arlis asked.

"I'm in here with ya, ain't I?"

Now, as Private Beasley lay on the floor among the insects and Cook tried to nap on the bench, keys rattled outside and the door opened. A corporal that Arlis didn't recognize stood in the hall.

"Cook," he said, "on your feet. You're a free man. Before you return to your company though, the captain wants to have a talk with you."

Cook, who hadn't moved a muscle until now, slowly stood. Beasley rolled to his right, giving Cook some walking room, his body now under the bench. Cook stretched, reaching as high as he could while standing on his toes. Then he slowly sauntered out the door, saying nothing. The door closed and the keys jingled again.

Arlis looked up at the window. A single, white cloud was visible, moving fast in the sky. The wind was obviously blowing hard at the altitude of the cloud, but whether or not there was a breeze blowing at ground level, Arlis couldn't tell. No breeze whatsoever could be felt in this damnable place.

He sat down again on the bench. Then, suddenly feeling tired, he lay back on the hard wood. With the heat and humidity adding to his fatigue, he rolled onto his side and slid backward so his back contacted the wall. Within minutes, he was asleep.

Nearly a year had passed since the regiment had left Camp Randall and come east to Washington. They'd arrived in the nation's capital in the afternoon on the eighth of August and had slogged through the muddy streets to their muddy camp, the men disenchanted and disappointed that they wouldn't be receiving a visit from the Rebels after all. The army that had been so badly defeated at Bull Run had found some organization under a new general, a fellow named McClellan, who had wasted no time in fortifying Washington with the survivors of the disaster. Every day, fresh regiments were arriving in the city from all over the country, and McClellan was purging his command of those officers he felt were incompetent.

The Sixth Wisconsin was reassigned to a new division under the authority of Irvin McDowell, the very commander that had led the union forces in the disaster at Bull Run. They were brigaded with the Second Wisconsin, the Seventh Wisconsin, and the Nineteenth Indiana Regiments, a bonding that would remain for the rest of the war. The Second Wisconsin had been at Bull Run, causing Arlis and the others to behold them in awe and fascination. Their uniforms, although the same in design and construction as those of the Sixth, were already battle scarred and tattered. Their regimental colors had bullet holes in it, the ultimate feature of envy for troops that had yet to see a battlefield.

The brigade was put into action manning the defenses of the city. Since there was now little chance for a Rebel attack upon Washington, drill became the main order of the day. The boys of the Sixth were finally issued the blue federal frock coats, but the state-issued clothing underneath also remained. Most exciting for the boys were the brand new rifled muskets of various makes and origins the regiment had been issued. Many were issued the modern 1861 model Springfield rifled musket. Arlis, however, was given a .69 caliber model 1842 Belgian Liege rifled musket. Most of the men who were issued this weapon were quick to complain, criticizing it for its bulk and weight. Arlis didn't mind, however, figuring that as one of the taller men in the company he'd have an easier time wielding the Liege than the smaller men would. Soon, he'd taken to calling it "the mother-in-law," explaining to those who asked that "she was noisy, unstable, unpredictable, and heavier than she ought to be." Once armed, the boys of all of the regiments in the brigade began working again at becoming more skilled as soldiers.

Then, in October, Lieutenant Colonel Julius Atwood suddenly resigned after Company E's Captain Edward Bragg was promoted to major over Adjutant Haskell, triggering reverberating changes throughout the regiment. Soon, six lieutenants and four captains were purged from the regiment, and no one, especially privates like Arlis Jenkins, knew why. Rumors abounded. One of the lieutenants that found himself purged was John Crane, who had introduced Arlis to Captain Dawes and had gotten Mickey Sullivan into the company back in April when, according to Mickey, "others had deemed me too frail to be a soldier."

Arlis had been incredulous. "You? Too frail?" he'd asked, bewildered. "You may be small, Mick, but you're every bit as strong as me."

"Shhh," Mickey had said, winking and holding a finger to his lips. "I was jus' seventeen at the time. I turned eighteen on June the 21st. Crane knew I was too young and he stuck his neck out fer me."

"Damn," Arlis had said. "You're only a couple of weeks older than I am."

The purging of officers rocked the entire regiment, and Mickey, Arlis, and the boys had more than one discussion on the subject, trying to make sense of it all.

"You kin fit all ten of those officers into one of four categories," Mickey had said. "They're all either incompetent, they're incorrigible, they opposed Bragg fer major, or they're Irish." All four really were possibilities. It was widely known that Colonel Cutler was fond of giving his officers written examinations on everything that had to do with warfare. Some of those officers that had had the most difficulty on the drilling ground were still in the regiment. Some of the Irish officers were still in the regiment. Some of those who opposed Bragg for major were still in the regiment. The boys couldn't quite figure it out.

Life went on. The brigade continued to improve in the arts of maneuver and war, drilling and marching in the mud of the winter. In February, on Washington's birthday, a great celebration was held in camp. The men paraded before the high command to mark the occasion, and when volleys of blanks were fired by the men to celebrate the holiday, Mickey had been shot in the back with a ramrod that a soldier from the Seventh Wisconsin had failed to remove after loading his weapon. Arlis and the others were horrified, vowing to find the culprit and enact their revenge on the fellow, accident or not. They never did find out the offending soldier's name. Mickey spent a few days in the hospital and returned, beaming with pride, holding claim as the first man in Company K "to be wounded in the line of duty."

The drilling and the parading continued well into the spring, and when McClellan finally moved across the river, taking the Army of the Potomac with him, the boys in Mc-Dowell's Brigade stayed behind, feeling the war passing them by again. Most were certain McClellan would take Richmond before summer ended and they'd miss the fighting.

"Somebody's got it in their skull that we western men are ta sit out the whole scrap," Talty said. "If I ever find out who that is, Imma gonna show the bugger up close that we kin fight better 'an most, be gob!"

In early May the brigade commander, Rufus King, was promoted and General John Gibbon, a West-Pointer, took over. Gibbon had stayed loyal to the union despite the fact that three of his brothers had joined the Confederate army. He was a short man with long legs, a combination that the men found humorous when the general sat upon his equally small horse. His hair was short against his scalp, his moustache long but groomed, and he sported a short, trim beard. Known for having a short, sharp temper, Gibbon was reputed to have a knack for telling the truth no matter whom it might hurt. Though he was hard on the men they loved him for his candor, toughness, and obvious affection for discipline and drill, if only to better them in their jobs as soldiers. They knew their commander's chief priority was their own safety and well-being.

On the seventeenth day of May, the men under Gibbon received brand new uniforms. Every man in the brigade now matched, each wearing a woolen blue shirt underneath a blue federal frock coat, light blue trousers, and the black Hardee hats that would become the trademark of Gibbon's Brigade. Additionally, the soldiers were issued smart white gloves and matching white gaiters, accessories that the boys initially raved about, but soon found nearly impossible to keep clean in the muck and mud of army camp. Just the same, they were proud and happy to be dressed in the federally issued clothing for a few weeks, until the cheaply made woolen shirts began to fall apart. The men were forced to either resort back to their old state issued shirts or (as most men of the Sixth did) go back to wearing their home-spun clothing from their days at Camp Randall. So many men of the Sixth were wearing civilian shirts that the men of the Seventh began referring to them as the "Calicos," a nickname that would last for the duration of the war.

The men of the Sixth, in turn, began calling the men of the Seventh "Huckleberries." Someone claimed it was because the boys of the Seventh were fond of eating the fruit. Someone else said that a bunch of them had stolen a number of huckleberry pies from a Washington civilian. Arlis doubted both stories, thinking that the Seventh had earned the moniker because of their high and mighty attitude, acting like they were better than everyone else.

Now, with his men fully outfitted and fully armed, the new commander added strict discipline to the regimen of intense drilling, and the men felt an immediate disdain for the regular army officer, who had also added a daily review at 5 o'clock in the morning to the schedule. They drilled in the morning, in the afternoon, and in the evening. Arlis joked that the officers would interrupt a drill just so they could make the men drill. When they weren't drilling they either stood guard mount or they were on the parade ground.

The men of the Sixth Wisconsin began to move as one, and they soon distanced themselves from the other regiments on the drilling ground. In fact, it wasn't long before the Sixth became the best-drilled regiment of the four in the brigade, thanks to the efforts of Adjutant Frank Haskell, whose intense and obsessive drilling forced them to move easily and smartly under even the most difficult of circumstances.

Still, the men of Gibbon's Brigade grew restless and tired

of being the first line of defense for the capitol city, being placed just across the Potomac River from Fredericksburg, Virginia. Soldiers, when not entertained by the act of soldier-ing, will often look to mischief for entertainment when no such entertainment is provided for them. Two days ago, in the early morning hours of June 26th, Arlis had been on a grave-yard shift picket duty when a couple of the men got word of a barrel of beer being stored and chilled in the river, just one half mile from their current location.

"Soldiers are stupid," Arlis said in a whisper to Sullivan, Butterfield, Talty, and Tarbox. The five of them were standing in a circle, quietly discussing the prospect of acquiring the beer. "You boys hear a rumor and you go off half-cocked, be-lieving anything you want to believe, just 'cause you think that faith alone will make it true. Leave me out of this."

"We'll need someone on the picket line anyway," Mickey said, "all ya gotta do is keep watch, Badger."

Arlis, amazed at the absurdity of it all, said, "And what do I do when Lieutenant Kellogg comes poking his nose around, wondering why you boys aren't at your posts?"

"Only two of us'll go," Mickey said, his face barely visible in the dark night. The waning moon was a sliver in the clear sky. "Who's it gonna be?"

"I'll go, be gob." Talty said matter-of-factly.

Arlis grabbed the short Irishman by the arm and, in a whisper loud enough for all to hear, asked, "Talty, have you *ever* ended a sentence without saying 'be gob?'"

Talty, smiling, answered, "Of course I have...be gob."

"I'll go with him," Butterfield said, "The rest of ya, if any-one asks, me and Talty are in the sinks with the gripes and you boys thinned the line to cover fer us."

Arlis shook his head and turned away, watching the front again.

"Okay," Mickey said, "Go. But make sure you're back in

an hour, no longer. Any longer, you'll be at the mercy of the dawn. Don't forget…the sign is banner, the countersign, bunting."

Off they went, and Arlis checked his pocket watch. 3:40 A.M. One hour was a long way off. Mickey and Albert walked back to their posts and Arlis was alone, the river about seventy-five yards in front of him. After he'd checked his watch for the fourth time in nine minutes, he felt an urge to throw it in the river with the beer.

Time passed, and Arlis caught himself looking to his rear for an approaching officer more than watching his front for enemy activity, silently cursing his comrades for this stupidity. Every noise that came from behind him caused alarm… caused him to hold his breath, listening for the approaching lieutenant.

Then, Arlis saw two figures approaching directly at his front. He checked his watch. 4:31 A.M. He squinted, the two silhouettes of Butterfield and Talty were obvious, one tall, one short, even in the dim light of the predawn. Looking harder, Arlis saw no bounty, no prize, no barrel. No beer.

Later, Arlis would describe his actions as a spontaneous practical joke, something that even he hadn't really known he was capable of pulling. He blamed the army, and the boys of Company K, for the corruption that would cause him to do such a thing.

The men approached, reaching a distance of maybe ten yards, when Arlis raised his musket at them, aiming for the opening between them, his finger behind the trigger guard for safety. He ignored the protocol of giving the password and demanding the countersign, and instead, cocked the hammer back, the hard click audible in the quiet night.

"Who goes there," Arlis asked harshly, angrily.

The boys halted in their tracks. Then, "Abe Lincoln," in Talty's obvious voice.

All in one motion, Arlis raised the barrel of the musket and pulled the trigger, firing over the top of his friends. The gunshot was deafening, seeming louder than normal here in the quiet dawn. The knees of Talty and Butterfield buckled in unison, causing them to squat in the predawn light.

"Jesus Christ, Jenkins! It's us fer God's sake," Butterfield said in a harsh whisper.

Arlis ignored him. In a high, nasally voice, each word drawn out and distinct, he said, "I voted for Stephen Douglas."

He'd been given three days in the guardhouse for his "little mishap" while on picket duty. Three days was the going price for an accidental discharge of a loaded musket, an offense that Major Bragg said the army takes very seriously.

"You could have killed someone," he'd said at the court martial. "Three days in the guardhouse should give you plenty of time to think about keeping your musket under control."

Arlis had been grateful to the boys, especially Tall-T and the Butterfly, for keeping their mouths shut about the truth of the matter. They'd been good sports about the whole thing, and Arlis was certain that he would have been served a much harsher sentence if his superiors had known it was a practical joke.

Now, he woke from a fitful nap in the stagnant heat to the sound of keys jingling again. Sitting up, he rubbed his dry, irritated eyes as he anticipated the door opening. For a moment nothing happened. Arlis looked at Beasley, who was lying on his bench again, his eyes upon the door.

The door opened and the same corporal from earlier in the day appeared, holding the door open wide. Private John Cook, who'd been freed less than an hour before, stepped into the room.

"Good Lord, Cook," was all Arlis could muster.

"I know, I know," Cook said, "I can't keep my fuckin' mouth

shut around that asshole." He sat down hard on the open bench. "Ever since the bastard claimed we was a dirty and lousy company when he took over commandin' it and took the credit fer turnin' us clean an' neat. Fuckin' lies!" He slammed a balled fist down hard on the wooden bench. "We was all fine and right before he ever came." He rubbed his forehead vigorously, then violently unbuttoned his shirt and took it off, throwing it onto the floor.

"What did you say to him this time?" Arlis asked, lying back down on the bench.

"I tol' 'im I have enough vigor and bang ta follow a real soldier, such as his wife, all of the way ta Richmond. To hell for that matter, but listenin' to him drone on fer a matter of minutes makes my ass tired."

23 The Samuel Pry Mill, Keedysville, Maryland
November 6, 1862
Night

ARLIS STOOD ON THE RIVERBANK UNDER THE LIGHT OF THE full moon. The light bounced and danced off the river, reflecting a ghostly haze through the spotty fog that hovered low over the waves. Autumn being in full effect, the air was cool, the trees were bare, and the ground was littered with last summer's leaves. Cold enough to see one's breath as it exited the mouth, it wasn't cold enough to visualize nasal exhalations. Arlis inhaled deeply through his nose. He could smell a smokehouse and the distinct, sharp scent of pig shit; both welcoming odors compared to the mixture of blood, death, unwashed bodies, and human waste to which he'd become so accustomed.

The sound of the master face wheel, still in operation even with the mill acting as a hospital, was loud as it turned in the quiet, windless night, transferring its power to the lay shafts via the lantern pinions. The mill was pulling extra duty as the transformation from mill to hospital had occurred at the worst possible time—the harvest. Now, around-the-clock grinding was called for, with much of the produce being transformed into edible goods and consumed by those on the property.

Exactly fifty days had passed since Arlis had been wounded in the cornfield near Antietam Creek. It had been fifty days of surgery, pain, more surgery, more pain...and then more pain. The doctors hadn't been able to find all of the pieces, claiming that after removing nearly forty pieces of jagged metal from his torso in two surgeries, whatever metal remained inside him would stay there for the duration of his life. Arlis hadn't dwelled on it too much. As a patient at the makeshift hospital somewhere in the heart of Washington County, Maryland, he'd seen horrors innumerable, as the doctors had practiced their profession on the endless line of wounded men that had found their way to them via ambulance, wagon, caisson, carriage, stretcher, or by foot. He'd considered himself lucky, as most of the men still here were forever scarred by missing limbs. Arlis still had all of his. It turned out that Antietam had been the bloodiest day of the war overall, and Arlis felt fortunate that very little of the blood had come from him.

He knew nobody here. None of the men he'd seen come through here had been from his regiment. There were dozens of hospitals set up in every setting possible, such as government buildings in Washington, factories, churches, halls, and homes. A couple of weeks ago, a staff officer had come by to verify that Arlis was here and not dead, deserted, or misplaced by the Army of the Potomac. The company knew where they could find him.

He walked out onto the pier, the weathered, bleached wood visible in the light of the moon. He sat down at the end of it, dangling his bare feet off the end and allowing them to hover inches above the water. In his hand were two letters; one from home, and one from regimental headquarters. Neither correspondence had anything to do with the other...until Arlis had opened both of them.

He stared at the letter from Lt. Col. Bragg. It was readable in the bright light of the full moon, but Arlis wasn't really seeing it. It had arrived earlier in the day, a response to Arlis' week old request to be granted furlough, a much-needed getaway from the sights and smells of the hospital. Permission had been granted. Bragg would generously allow Arlis to finish his recovery far away from the hospital and the war. Smiling with relief and joy at his chance to live as a civilian again, at least for a full month, he'd moved on to the second envelope, which had been delivered to him by the same courier that afternoon.

Arlis had received roughly one letter for every four he'd sent. He wasn't sure if this was due to the mail or the lack of letters from home, but since he'd only sent about fifteen of them home, well, he hadn't received much mail at all. Two of them had been from his mother, one from Rachel, sent because Mama had given Rachel an assignment to do so, as she had stated in the letter. Arlis had received all three while in the Washington camp, the last coming nigh a year ago. In late September, he'd sent one home telling his family that he'd been in the great battle at Antietam, had been wounded, and that he had come out of it alive.

The letter that he'd received today had been in his father's handwriting, causing immediate alarm, as Arlis wasn't sure when the last time he'd known his father to write to anyone, let alone his son. It was dated August 27th, one day before the regiment had had its first general engagement with the Rebels. That fight had taken place on the Brawner Farm, not far from the city of Gainesville, Virginia, on the opening day of the 2nd battle of Bull Run. Written with no emotion, it provided news from home that Arlis would rather not have received.

Arlis, 27 August, 1862

Rachel has passed on to the next world. Doctor Kirkwood tells me she died of a broken heart. He says it was caused by a condition in the valves of the heart that induced her blood to percolate much like a coffee pot would. She died on the sixteenth. Your mother has been sent by train to Madison to the hospital for the insane they have there. I have been unable to get through to her here, as she has been so overcome with grief that she hadn't eaten for more than a week. Hopefully, the doctors there can return her to her prior state.

Regards,
Papa

Arlis scissor kicked his feet back and forth above the water. Had he thought about it, he might have been cold, as he was dressed only in a blanched cotton shirt and matching drawers that stopped above the knee. But he didn't think about it. His mind contained a whirlwind of anger, sorrow, blame, and guilt, all of which spun and twisted about Mama, Papa, and Rachel, like a violent storm, not allowing Arlis to focus on anything for long, his brain moving to the next emotion, the next person. He felt guilty for not being there for Rachel, for Mama, for both of them through this, wondering if Rachel had been in pain at the end or if she'd even known that something was amiss. He felt guilty for being 900 miles away at the time of her funeral, holding himself responsible for signing up to go to war. He felt guilty for not being there for Mama, even though he knew that he'd never have had the words to say to her to prevent her from collapsing into herself, as Papa's letter was insinuating had happened.

And, oh, the anger! He was angry at Papa for being so damn callous! He burned inside as he thought of how Papa had sent her away rather than try. What about this damn letter? How crass and heartless it was...how cold and tactless. Had his father gone insane as well, the only difference being that the man was able to eat and work and go on with his days? His anger extended to the army and the postal service, too. Two and a half months had passed since this letter had been stamped and mailed. Did nobody have the respect for the soldiers and their families to properly forward letters?

Arlis lay back on the pier and closed his eyes, grimacing through the pain caused by the movement. The tissue in and around his ribcage throbbed. He continued to scissor kick, attempting to force the anger to exit through the motions. He wanted to cry...he had tried to cry earlier after reading the letter for the first time, but no tears had come then, and none would come now, either. No amount of thinking about Rachel in the grave or Mama in an asylum could produce enough sorrow to push away the anger long enough for him to purge his sadness.

He opened his eyes and gazed upon the cloudless sky. The moon and stars were brilliant against the bruised, purple background, and Arlis found himself silently noting the constellations, tracing their patterns with his eyes. He folded his arms across his chest and thought about how complicated things had suddenly become, how much easier it would have been had he been the one killed by the cannon fire, and not Danny Cummings.

His thoughts shifted back to Rachel, how sweet and innocent she'd always been. *Mama's angel*, he thought, remembering his sister as she'd looked standing in the garden, watering the vegetables at age fourteen, the month before he'd left for

Camp Randall. She might have been fourteen, but she seemed younger, as the world had yet to mark her or cause her worry. Boys hadn't even been on her mind, yet. Now, he felt his eyes well up with unshed tears; ready for the explosion of emotion that he was sure would follow. A full minute later the sadness had dissipated, and his eyes blinked the tears away.

He thought of Violet. Next month would mark the fifth anniversary of her death. Arlis found it hard to believe that only five years had passed since he had lost her. It seemed like forever already, and with all of his life to think of her, remember her, and long for her, how long would forever feel like when five years already felt like eternity? He thought again about Mama and her inability to soothe his pain, knowing that he'd be no better at soothing hers. He could hold her, rock her—as she had done for him when he was younger, and he had a sudden longing to do so—but finding the words to say would not come easy.

He realized he would be going home, but he no longer had any desire to do so.

24 Madison, Wisconsin
November 13, 1862
12:45pm

ARLIS JENKINS HAD A REPUTATION. WELL, NOT ARLIS PER SE, but rather, the brigade in which he belonged to in the Army of the Potomac. The men of Gibbon's Brigade had received a moniker after the Battle of South Mountain, where they'd stormed up the rocky elevation under tremendous enemy fire. Word had it that the moniker had come from General McClellan himself during a conversation he'd had with General Hooker whilst the battle raged, during which he'd stated that the men in the black hats "must be made of iron." The name stuck, and in the following weeks the newly named "Iron Brigade" or "Iron Brigade of the West," received a lot of attention in the press. The Rebels had seen the mettle of the Iron Brigade before, at the Battle of Gainesville and at the 2nd Battle of Bull Run, and they'd lived up to their name before they'd even received it, earning the respect of their enemy, most notably those men in the Stonewall Brigade, who seemed to meet them at every turn. When the Rebels saw black hats on the battlefield, they knew they were facing a formidable opponent.

Before receiving his official leave from the army on the afternoon of November sixth, Arlis had received a visit from Major Dawes. Though in no mood for pageantry, he had been impressed and humbled by the attention from the major, who apologized to Arlis for Lt. Col. Bragg, who had wanted to make an appearance in person but had regimental business to attend to. Arlis had smiled politely and said that he understood.

"Can you stand without too much trouble?" Dawes said.

"Yes, sir," Arlis said, and stood up, grimacing less than the pain called for.

The major had brought along a brand new uniform, identical to the one that Arlis had worn at Antietam.

"Stand at attention, Private Jenkins," Dawes said, and then he promoted Arlis to corporal, which caused Arlis to wince and Dawes to laugh.

"Additionally," Dawes had said, "the commander of the Sixth Wisconsin Regiment would like you to know that you've been recognized for your actions at the Battle of South Mountain on September 14, 1862. For your extraordinary courage and commitment to duty—in causing great harm to the enemy and saving the life of a comrade while in the face of great danger—Lieutenant Colonel Bragg has made account of your actions in his official report of the battle." Dawes extended his right hand and Arlis took it. "Congratulations, Corporal Jenkins," the major said.

"Thank you, sir."

"You're welcome," Dawes said. "You've earned it."

"Sir," Arlis went on, "if I may ask, as long as we're on the subject of South Mountain, have you heard any word of Mickey?"

Dawes sniffed and looked at the ground. "Yes, he's home. Dr. Bartlett told me that Mickey lost most of his toes and half of his foot." His eyes found Arlis again, "He'll live, though."

"Thank you, sir."

Dawes nodded once. "I've got to get back now. The campaign has opened again, and we've been pushing the Rebels. They threw a few shells at us a few days back at a place called 'Snicker's Gap.' Such is war. Now, the regiment's at Warrenton, where we hear the weather's to turn cold and there's a possibility of snow. I should get back before that possibility becomes reality and hinders my efforts to do so."

Dawes left, bestowing his best wishes upon Arlis for a full recovery as the regiment needed soldiers like him. "Have yourself a grand time at home, Corporal Jenkins," he'd said, adding, "although no one envies your suffering, there are plenty who would like to be on that train with you." Arlis chose to remain closed mouthed on the subject of his family and his reluctance to go home. Instead, he told the major that he was thankful for the new uniform, complete with the corporal chevrons sewn onto the sleeves, as he hadn't been sure what he was going to wear on the train ride home. Clothing was going at a pretty stiff premium around the hospital.

Later he'd sat alone outside the hospital, waiting for the ride he'd procured to the train station. He had ample time to think on the citation he'd received. Guilt invaded again, the emotion seeming to be nesting inside his stomach lately, as he recalled how he'd helped Will Anderson to safety, dodging the intense Rebel gunfire to do so. Corporal Reuben Huntley and Private George Chamberlain had not been so fortunate, the latter having had his head blown off after Arlis had sworn to come back for him.

"Such is war," he said quietly, mimicking, though not mocking, the major.

That had been a full week ago. Now, Arlis stood before a large four-story, cream-colored brick building in Madison, surveying the layout of the grounds and the surrounding landscape. He was in a square courtyard containing many hard benches and lushly padded chairs; each strategically placed below large, brightly colored umbrellas which protected both the fabric and those seated from the sun and precipitation. The yard was bordered on two sides by a three-foot high, rectangular brick flower garden containing rose bushes on one side, and the stems and remnants of the previous summer's black-eyed susans, marigolds, forget-me-nots, and tulips on the other. Beyond the garden, a copse of bare, evenly spaced maples dated the grounds to perhaps three years. What leaves had fallen had been raked and removed by the staff, or perhaps the residents, if the hospital was so progressive. A large, yellow sign was lettered in light blue, identifying the grounds as belonging to the "Wisconsin Hospital for the Insane, Mendota."

The building sported identical floor to ceiling windows on all floors. The outside decorum contained fixed shutters and two solid iron bars that were molded into an elongated "S" shape, giving the observer an illusion of ornate opulence. Arlis wasn't fooled. He knew they were nothing more than barriers to keep the occupants from escaping or falling to their deaths. Whatever contents sat behind the windows lay obscured behind the glare of the sun, which was perched high in the early afternoon sky.

To the south of this building sat a large, two-story mansion. The signage identified it as the office and residence of the staff employed by the hospital. This building was constructed of the same brick as the other. Its windows, however, were not of the floor to ceiling variety, but of the type that sat square in their placements, three-feet by three-feet, many of them open in the mild November temperatures. Unlike the windows on the other building, these were not barred.

Arlis, looking resplendent in his new uniform, was in no hurry. Alone in the courtyard, he removed his Hardee hat, wiping his dry forehead as if it were damp with perspiration, and took a seat in a chair under one of the umbrellas. A squirrel, nervous and skittish, made its way through the courtyard. It stopped every few feet to reassess its safety before bounding up into the rose garden, stopping once more to stare at Arlis before disappearing behind the bushes, not to be seen again. Upon the disappearance of the squirrel, Arlis turned his attention to the sky as the sun ducked behind a feathery cloud. Farther west, steel blue storm clouds lingered on the horizon, though the threat of rain appeared to be more than an hour away.

It had been a long week coming home to Wisconsin. It had been made longer by Arlis, who had stepped away from the depots when his trains had stopped in Pittsburgh, Toledo, and Chicago. He had spent the night in inns on all three occasions, delaying the reunion with his mother he was dreading so much. By the time he'd reached Toledo, still searching for the perfect words to say to Mama, he realized that there was a distinct possibility that Mama wasn't even in the hospital anymore. By the time he'd reached Chicago, he realized that if she wasn't in the hospital it was because she was no longer among the living.

Walking down the unique streets of downtown Chicago, oblivious to where he was, he'd found a tavern in which to down a drink and eat a meal. Pushing through the front entrance, he'd found all of the tables taken, the patrons staring at the man in uniform out of curiosity. He'd decided to belly up to the bar and instead of a drink and a meal he'd settled for a drink and then another drink, slamming two shots of whiskey in a manner of minutes. After a third shot, another soldier appeared to the right of Arlis.

"That's a Hardee hat," the soldier said, pointing at Arlis' hat as it lay upon the bar. The man was swaying from alcohol consumption. Arlis looked at the man, who had sergeant's chevrons on his blue coat, the buttons showing that he was an Illinois man. The brass numeral on his kepi indicated he was in the 17th Regiment from that state. The sergeant was in his late twenties with shoulder length black hair and matching eyes. He had an elongated face, showing two or three days' worth of beard. He was dirty, his face and neck both in need of a good, hard scrubbing. Arlis ignored him, finding the saloonkeeper with his eyes, who refilled Arlis' glass.

"Who're you with, in your shiny new uniform?" the soldier said. "You look like yer fresh from the womb, boy." He laughed menacingly as he leaned over the bar. "More whiskey!" he said to the barkeep.

Arlis said nothing and turned away, facing the front of the tavern.

"Listen here, boy," the sergeant said, louder now. He spun Arlis around, who locked eyes with the man. "I was at Fredericktown and Donelson…I took a minie ball in the shoulder at Shiloh." He pointed to his right shoulder as if Arlis could see the wound through his clothing. "Yer gonna listen ta me when I'm a talkin' at ya, corporal."

Arlis, roused by the man's audacity, arrogance, ignorance, and by the whiskey, said, "Sixth Wisconsin, Sergeant. I've seen the elephant at South Mountain, Gainesville, Second Bull Run, and Antietam. This uniform's new because my old one was blown off me in Maryland, *Sergeant*." The last word came sarcastically, sardonically.

The sergeant's eyes grew wide in recognition. Perhaps he thought he'd been upstaged, perhaps he thought Arlis was full of it. Perhaps something else altogether was on his mind.

"Well, looky here," he announced loudly. Patrons of the tavern were growing uncomfortable. "We've got a western man in the Army of the Potomac." He laughed heartily. "Everyone knows there ain't a damn good thing goin' on in that shitty eastern army. All you boys ever do is turn yer backs on the Rebs an' run, skedaddlin' back to Washington." He punched Arlis in his right arm, the blow landing in the exact spot he'd taken the wound. Looking directly at Arlis, his smile vanished. In a harsh, monotone voice, he said, "When are you fellas gonna learn how ta fight?"

Arlis turned and faced the bar again, allowing the pain in his arm to subside while picking up his shot of whiskey. After downing it, he set the glass back on the bar and glanced sideways at the soldier, gauging the distance between the two of them. Then, without warning, he swung his right arm in a backhand motion, striking the man hard in the windpipe with the heel of his closed hand, a trick he'd seen a few years back in a fight between two miners. The sergeant dropped to the floor instantly, grasping his throat with both hands, gasping violently.

Arlis picked up his hat, placed it on his head and then flipped a few coins on the bar for the drinks. After muttering an apology for his behavior to the bartender, who smiled and gave him a nod, he squatted next to the struggling man.

In a low voice Arlis said, "Well, looky here…it looks like the boy that's fresh from the womb learned how to fight just in time to get the best of you, Sergeant." Then, without waiting to see if the man would ever breathe again, Arlis left the tavern, the eyes of everyone following him out the door.

The following afternoon he'd arrived in Milwaukee, where a much friendlier reception awaited him. He was doted on by anyone who read a newspaper, and Arlis had received the attention with almost the same amount of contempt as he did the behavior of the sergeant in Chicago. Two men nearly got into fisticuffs over offering him a ride to the hotel. He'd walked away from them to settle the argument, obtaining a ride in the back of an Empire Brewery wagon instead.

Now, as the sun peeked out from behind the cloud again, Arlis stood and stretched. Placing his hat on his head, he walked the short distance to the mansion and opened the door. The lobby smelled of cigars and was decorated with Victorian style furniture. A fancy brown davenport, upholstered with a pattern of red roses, sat along the opposite wall. It was cradled on either side by two high backed, matching chairs. The wood floor was covered by a large oval rug, immaculate in condition, offering a pattern of various flowers in a golden vase. The walls were paneled from floor to ceiling, with a six-inch border at the top containing an elegant hand-carved decorative pattern. To his right was a mirror, six feet in height, adorned at the top with two cherubs facing each other. Two portraits graced the wall behind the furniture, featuring prominent men in prominent poses. To Arlis' left was a large oaken desk, the top neat and tidy, containing few items. Just as Arlis noticed the man seated behind it, the man spoke to him.

"Good afternoon. How may I assist you?" he said, standing up. He was middle-aged with a full head of silver hair. He sported a matching tight, thin moustache that sat well above his upper lip. He was dressed in a well-tailored three-piece suit…black shirt, black pants, black vest.

"Ah, yes, uh," Arlis stuttered. He swallowed and started again. "My name is Arlis Jenkins. I'm here to see my mother, Mrs. Abigail Jenkins. Please accept my apology for coming here unannounced, sir. I'm just now returning from the war."

"That's no problem at all, Mr. Jenkins," the man said, offering a hand. Arlis shook it. "I'm Maxwell Roberts, hospital director." He pulled a watch from his pocket and glanced at it. "It's now after one o'clock and most of the residents are finishing their meals. If you'll have a seat over here," he gestured at the lobby furniture, "I'll find Dr. Hargrove." He offered a closed-mouth smile, walking with Arlis toward the davenport. "It is our policy that visitors meet with our medical staff before visiting our residents."

"Thank you, sir," Arlis said, taking a seat on one of the hard-backed chairs. The director retrieved a hat from behind the desk and passed through the door.

Arlis sat with his hat in his lap feeling out of place and uncomfortable on the stiff, high-backed chair. After a few minutes went by, he stood and moved to one of the portraits. A man with robust red hair on the flanks of his head stared back at him. Appearing to be in his fifties, his square face, pointed nose, and stark eyes emanated determination and backbone. The plate identified him as James Duane Doty, Wisconsin Territorial Governor, 1841.

"Mr. Jenkins," a voice said from behind.

Startled, Arlis spun around, a bit too quickly.

"I'm sorry to have frightened you, Mr. Jenkins. I'm Dr. Hargrove. Gideon Hargrove." He offered a hand to Arlis, who took it.

"Just a little jumpy is all, Doctor. I'm a bit apprehensive about my mother."

"That is certainly understandable, considering the circumstances."

Arlis studied the man. In his voice there was a hint of the East Coast. The accent, slight as it was, implicated Massachusetts or perhaps Rhode Island. With an oval face and soft hazel eyes, high cheekbones, and dark hair slicked with pomade, Arlis estimated him to be between fifty-five and sixty years of age. He wore gray trousers and a light blue frock coat with a high collar, similar to Arlis', but without the military splendor.

"I'm more than a little curious about what those circumstances are, Doctor. The last information I have is from late August, a vague note from my father stating my mother was sent here following the death of my younger sister."

The front door silently opened and Mr. Roberts stepped in. He walked around the desk, returning to his seat.

"Come with me to my office, Mr. Jenkins," the doctor said, gesturing with an open hand toward the left side of the room. "We have much to discuss there. Then I'll take you to your mother."

A few minutes later the doctor was seated behind his desk, which was similar in size and appearance to the one belonging to Mr. Roberts, and Arlis had taken a seat in an unstained, tan rocker, as uncomfortable as the chair in the lobby. Daylight shone through two square windows and was the office's source of lighting. A bookshelf, filled with literature of varying genres, mostly medical, was carved directly into the wall between the windows. An oil lamp, well used but unlit, sat next to a large tin ashtray on the corner of the desk. Paperwork was strewn about the desktop, the doctor being slightly less organized perhaps than the director of the hospital. A book authored by Amariah Brigham, entitled *Remarks on the Influence of Mental Cultivation on Health*, sat open upon the desk, its pages worn and oily from handling. To the doctor's left, in the corner of the room, stood a fully intact skeleton, bleached white, its eyeless sockets glaring at Arlis as he sat in the rocker.

"Mr. Jenkins," the doctor began, his hands folded on the desk before him. "Your mother's case has been," he hesitated, either considering his words or pausing for effect, "difficult. When she arrived at the hospital, she'd been nearly catatonic from the effects of laudanum. She'd evidently downed an entire bottle of the opiate on her way here." He pulled a drawer open on the right side of the desk and retrieved a large envelope, placing it on the desk before him. Looking hard into Arlis' eyes, he said, "When I say she was 'nearly catatonic,' I mean she was completely unresponsive, her breathing rate and pulse being slowed to critical levels. She was very near death. Her overdosing of the medicine seems to have been an attempt at suicide."

Arlis shifted in the rocker, saying nothing, waiting.

"We were able to give her small amounts of water for the first few days while she recovered. Food was another matter altogether." He opened the envelope and removed the contents, placing the first sheet in front of Arlis so that he could read it. "These are daily food consumption records, Mr. Jenkins."

Arlis interrupted, "Doctor, if I may? Please, call me Arlis."

"Arlis it is." He pointed at the first lines of the paper in front of Arlis with a stubby finger. "These records indicate the daily food and liquid intake of your mother. As you can see, getting any nourishment at all into her was a difficult endeavor."

Arlis scanned the paper, noticing marked improvement after two and a half weeks of residency at the hospital. Then, for three weeks, she'd consumed plenty of food and water on a daily basis. In mid-October, the records reverted to the way they'd been in September, showing little to no food consumption. The record ended on October 25th, there being no more room on the page.

"I'm not following this, Doctor," Arlis said, looking up from the record on the table. "This shows that she'd decided to eat and then, for some reason, she'd changed her mind."

"She hadn't *decided* to eat, Arlis," the doctor said. He opened his mouth to speak and closed it again, uncertain of the words. After a few moments, he said, "Are you familiar with a device known as a speculum orum?"

"No," Arlis said, his voice low and gruff. He was horrified.

"A speculum orum is used to—…"

"I know what it is, Doctor Hargrove," Arlis hissed. "When I said 'no,' I wasn't admitting ignorance. I was reacting adversely to what you were about to say." He paused, hoping the hostility he was feeling would creep back down where it had come from, rather than burst forth in angry words at the doctor. "You're telling me you used a mechanical device, like the type that's used on slaves, to force my mother to eat?"

"It's not nearly as bad as it seems now, Arlis. We have a—"

Arlis interrupted again, "It is *entirely* as bad as it seems, Doctor. Who gave you permission to do such a thing?"

Hargrove smiled spitefully. He spoke in a clear, soft voice. "Your father, in admitting your mother to our hospital, gave implied permission for us to do what it takes to provide what is best for her. Our responsibility, first and foremost, is the survival and well-being of our patients. Your mother, upon arrival, weighed ninety-three pounds. She was already underweight at that poundage. When we began the process of making her eat she was at eighty-two pounds and showing no change in her willingness to cooperate with any of the directives of the staff. There is more to her story than just her refusal to eat, Arlis. She refuses to do anything except sleep."

He fumbled through the paperwork on the desk, finding a page covered in handwritten notation. "This is what we call a 'summary log.' It records our daily observations of the patients. You'll find elucidations from all of our staff here, from Doctor Smith and me, the nurses, even housekeeping. Your mother, early on, became aggressive at our attempts to treat her. She violently attacked those that attempted to talk to her, bathe her, or feed her. At first, we countered these attacks with medicines, such as opiates. But we soon discovered that she was feeding off of this course of treatment, becoming violent again once the medicines wore off." He reached for another drawer, retrieving a box of cigars. "Care to smoke with me, Arlis?"

Arlis selected a cigar, noticing it was already pre-cut. The doctor sparked a match on the side of his desk and reached across, holding it in a manner so that Arlis could bring the cigar to the match. Once Arlis' cigar was flamed, he lit his own.

"You must've stopped force-feeding her," Arlis said, chewing on the end of the cigar. He'd taken to smoking earlier in the year, indulging when tobacco was available. He wasn't entirely fond of the act, finding the execution of it clumsy and unnatural. He'd only smoked one time since he'd been wounded at Antietam, sharing a pipe with a kind stranger outside the Toledo train depot.

"Yes. I'll speak on that in a moment," Hargrove said. He pulled a long drag on the cigar and inhaled deeply, something that would have caused a considerable coughing fit if it had been Arlis. Exhaling while speaking, he said, "After we'd ascertained she was assaulting the staff in order to be medicated, I sat down with her and had a one-sided conversation with her."

He paused to pull the ashtray into the center of the desk. "Your mother is receptive, Arlis. By this, I mean she can understand anything that is spoken to her. Occasionally, you can see the understanding in her eyes or in her face, but she remains mute. Other than a desultory scream or a yell in anger, I have yet to hear her utter a single intelligible word. During that one-sided talk, I told her that regardless of how aggressive she became, I'd no longer consider opiates an option. From here on out, I told her, any aggressiveness would be met with either leather or mechanical restraints."

Arlis leaned forward assertively, "Don't tell me that-..."

Hargrove raised a hand and interrupted, "This, Arlis, has been the only success story in the course of her treatment. She hasn't been aggressive since...and we've never needed to apply the restraints." He tapped the cigar on the ashtray, leaving a half-inch long ash behind. "As to the use of the speculum orum...we contacted your father via letter, mailing it the day after the first use of the device. Although we believe it to be the best course of action in the treatment of your mother, we understand that it is a somewhat controversial procedure. We asked your father to give us his opinion on the matter, and he responded in writing, giving us permission to continue the feedings. Evidently, the decision weighed heavily on him, because after a while he came to Madison by train, wishing to see a demonstration of the procedure, as he was having difficulty forming an image of it. I grew excited at the presence of Mr. Jenkins, as I hoped that his being here might jolt Mrs. Jenkins into, well, into something other than her trancelike state.

"Your father had little to say to your mother, not that I'm pushing any blame onto him. I understand this situation has been hard on him, as well. Your mother remained in her state for his entire visit, which lasted the greater part of one day. We went ahead with the demonstration of the speculum orum, and Mr. Jenkins objected to the use of it. He signed a waiver that shall relieve this hospital from all liability if she should die from starvation. That was the last time we forced your mother to eat. We still make her drink water, albeit through another, less invasive method."

The room grew quiet as Hargrove finished speaking. They sat in silence, smoking, the room darkening slightly as the sun again slid behind the clouds. Arlis sat in the chair, slowly rocking back and forth, creating no sound on the carpeted floor.

"Your mother isn't insane in the normal sense of the word," Hargrove said. "She is deeply depressed...deeply despondent...and a genuine danger only to herself. Even while acting out aggressively, she was never a true danger to anyone, especially at her reduced weight and strength. She's just given up on life, Arlis. There is no medical treatment for those who no longer wish to live."

Staring at a knot in the grain of the desk, Arlis, almost whispering, said, "I'm glad you're not using the speculum orum anymore."

Hargrove again dragged deeply on his cigar, inhaled, and blew the smoke out through his nose into his lap. Leaning forward, almost placing his head on the desk, he found Arlis' eyes and said, in an equally quiet voice, "I understand your issues with the device, Arlis. I understand the issues that your father had with the device, too. They're the same issues." He raised his head back to a normal angle, drawing the gaze of Arlis with him. "My perspective, though…my point of view, is this: Starvation is a very long, agonizing process, Arlis. Body tissue begins to discolor and contract as it tries to devour itself in a last ditch effort for survival. Your mother is really nothing more than skin over bone. Have you ever watched a human being, one that is otherwise healthy in body, starve to death? To me, the speculum orum is a much more humane treatment than allowing someone to starve. Your mother is going to die, Arlis. It's no longer a matter of 'if,' but 'when.' Unless there is some miracle at this late hour in her treatment…unless your presence here can spark her into a change of attitude…unless, *something* happens; you've arrived in time to say your final farewell to her."

Arlis reached for the ashtray and tapped the cigar out. Standing up, he winced as his ribcage stretched and he let out a minor groan.

"Dr. Hargrove, may I please see her now?"

25 Madison, Wisconsin
November 13, 1862
1:30pm

ARLIS STOOD IN THE OPEN DOORWAY OF HIS MOTHER'S ROOM, the doctor behind him, staring at the woman in the rocking chair. The room was larger than he'd thought it would be, based on his assessment from the view in the courtyard. The large, rectangular window allowed ample light, even as the sun sat behind an overcast curtain. A fairly large single bed was in the right, back corner, the side of the bed butting up against the wall. It was neatly made and featured a solid oak headboard, with a colorful patchwork quilt folded in half on the foot of the bed. A simple, six-drawer dresser stood by the wall to the left, adjacent to the door, a set of clean nightclothes folded on top. On the wall above the dresser was a painting of a lake scene, detailed with ducks, a goose in flight, a swan, and a pair of deer having a drink at the shoreline. Arlis noted that the painting was held in place by four nails that had been driven discreetly but directly through the canvas, making the removal of the painting without considerable effort impossible. It was the only decorative item, other than the quilt, in the room.

Having exited the mansion and returned to the courtyard with Doctor Hargrove, Arlis had thought about his father and the interaction he'd had with his mother when he'd made the trip here the prior month.

"Doctor," he'd said, "what exactly did my father say to my mother when he came here?" The courtyard was now buzzing with activity, as many of the residents were sitting outside after their dinners. An old, wrinkled man paced back and forth in front of the rose garden at a pretty quick clip. Arlis watched as a woman sat where he had earlier, speaking adamantly to some unseen person and wildly gesticulating with her hands.

"Not a lot, as I said before. I'd left them alone together, as he'd asked me to, and also because I feared that he wouldn't interact with her in the same way if I or Dr. Smith were in the room with them. I vividly remember him asking her if she was ready to come home, a strange question, I'd thought. Other than this, I only remember him imploring her to eat something, as he was here to watch us feed her. Arlis..." he trailed off, stopping his speech and his gait at the same time. Arlis stopped as well and turned to face him.

"I was going to wait until the end of your visit, but asking about your father has created a perfect segue. Your father had more to say to *you* than he did to your mother. He told me chances were high that you'd come to visit, as he was sure you'd have some leave coming. If you did come by, I was to pass this on to you." He held out a fat brown envelope, sealed with wax. Written upon the front, in his father's handwriting, was one word:

ARLIS

"Leave coming," Arlis said, surprised. He took the envelope from the doctor's hand. "How could he know I had some leave coming?"

"I don't know," Hargrove said. Pointing to the envelope, he added, "Perhaps the answer is in there?"

Arlis broke the seal and opened the envelope. Inside, he found a small leather pouch tied with a leather drawstring and one sheet of paper. He opened the pouch. It contained a fairly large sum of cash in various denominations. Without counting it, he placed it in his pocket and let his attention fall on the letter.

Arlis, 19 October, 1862

I hope this letter finds you well. I received your letter of late September on the day before I left for Madison. I hope you have not been hurt too badly. I am very relieved to find that you are still among the living after so terrible a day.

As you know by now, mother has been in a horrendous state. I've found her to be in the same condition here in hospital as she had been at home. Hopefully by the time this letter reaches you there will have been some change for the better.

I've heard rumors of soldiers not being paid for months on end. Just in case, I have enclosed 300 dollars to be used however you see fit.

I've returned home to sell the mine and the rest of the assets. Upon conclusion of such business, I'll return to remain by mother's side for the duration of her stay.

Regards, Papa

"Three weeks," Arlis whispered. To Doctor Hargrove, he said, "He left three weeks ago to make an attempt at selling the business. Did he tell you whether he intended to return or not, Doctor?"

Hargrove looked thoughtful, pursing his lips as he scanned his memory. "I don't recollect him saying anything about returning."

The woman in the courtyard chair stood, pointing a bony finger at an invisible subject in the rose bushes. She became louder now, angrily accusing someone of bringing mud inside the house and soiling her antique rug. Close by, a nurse clad in a white apron with shoulder straps and a belt about her midriff observed the woman. Arlis barely noticed.

"Tell me straight, Doctor…how long does she have?"

Hargrove frowned and sighed. Turning over his hands, palms up, he said, "Days…perhaps a week."

Minutes later, having climbed the stairs to the third floor, Arlis gasped at his mother, horrified by what he saw. The forty-year-old woman before him looked nearly twice that age, her forehead wrinkled, the eyes sunken, her normally full cheeks narrowed and gaunt. Her eyes, hollow and lifeless, looked without seeing. Her hands appeared smaller, tapered and bony; her emaciated wrists visible at the end of her bed-clothes. Arlis was certain he could wrap a hand around one of her shins, both of which were exposed below the knee-length housecoat and above her slippers, and be able to touch his fingers together. A quilt lay in a heap on the floor next to her feet, similar in size and pattern to the one on the bed.

Arlis entered the room, setting his knapsack against the wall next to the door, and walked to a spot between the door and his mother. Sitting near the window in the rocker, Mama faced the corner of the room to the right of the door, blankly staring at a spot on the floor. He watched as she breathed, the breaths numerous and shallow, coming at a much faster rate than they should be for a woman sitting so calmly. Arlis hoped that she'd realize he was there, perhaps find him with her gaze, and he crouched into a squat before her, more than an arm's length away, trying to place his frame into her line of sight. Finding her eyes with his, he realized that she either failed to see him, or she was ignoring him altogether.

"Mama," Arlis said. She didn't move. He shuffled closer, spider-walking across the wooden floor without standing up, and he placed his left hand on her right knee. It felt hard and cold, like a spindle on a staircase in winter, and he jerked his hand away in surprise, before forcing himself to place it upon her again, this time slightly higher, on her lower thigh.

"Mama," he said again with urgency, lightly shaking the hand upon her leg. Her eyes moved in their sockets, first up-ward and then revolving to the right and down, in the direction the sound had come from. In a moment she was looking directly into Arlis' eyes, but if there was recognition behind them, Arlis couldn't tell. He forced a smile, baring his teeth the best he could, realizing that the corners of his mouth were refusing to cooperate.

"Hi Mama," he said, rubbing her leg gently. His hand moved to hers, and he placed it over the top and held it. "I've come a long way to see you, Mama." He pulled her hand close to his face and kissed the back of it. It felt colder on his lips than in his hand. He retrieved the quilt from the floor and spread it on her lap, covering her from her hips to her feet. He reached under the quilt and took her hand again.

"I took the train here from Maryland," Arlis said. "The regiment won't need me back until you're well," he lied. "I've come to take care of you, Mama."

Mama's gaze slipped away, aiming somewhere around his navel. Arlis looked at Doctor Hargrove, who was still standing in the doorway.

Taking his cue, Hargrove said, "I'll take my leave now. I'll have someone bring a chair in for you. If you need anything else, there's always somebody close by." He left, pulling the door slowly closed.

Arlis looked at his mother. Her eyes remained fixed upon his midsection. He felt wholly helpless and speechless. He allowed his gaze to shift outside where the cloud cover continued to darken the sky, matching his mood. He stood, watching Mama's eyes remain fixed as he did so.

In the courtyard, hospital staff hurriedly escorted the residents into the building, as the wind had picked up and rain had begun to fall in large, intermittent droplets. It was obvious that not all of the patients were willing to go in just yet, the staff struggling verbally and physically to convince them. Arlis watched as two male employees picked a man up, one holding him from behind with his hands under the man's arms and wrapped around the torso while the other picked up the man's legs. As the man struggled, they quickly disappeared from view below the window. Arlis turned away and walked to his mother's bed. He sat down hard, the straw mattress hissing under the weight of his body. There, he put his head in his hands, wondering if anything would ever be normal or feel good again. A knock at the door caused him to raise his head and rise to his feet.

"Come," he said.

The door opened. A rather obese man grappled with a rocker similar to the one that Mama was sitting in. He pushed it through the door ahead of himself and then walked around it, dragging it the rest of the way into the room. He placed it a few feet away from the other one.

"Anything else, sir?" he panted.

"No, thank you." Arlis said.

"I'll be somewhere on the floor if you need anything," the man said, wiping his cheeks and neck with a handkerchief from his pocket. "The name's Yancey."

"Thank you, Yancey," Arlis said quickly. Wanting the man to leave, he didn't offer his name. Instead, he walked to the door and grasped the knob, waiting for the man to pass before closing it behind him. He stood there a moment and listened as Yancey's footsteps receded down the hallway and then turned quickly, trying to catch Mama looking at him or perhaps doing something else; secretly he was still hoping upon hope that all of this was just some kind of act or performance which she'd eventually come out of. She was in the exact same position that he'd last seen her.

He went to the chair, grabbing the arms with his hands and positioning it beneath him directly in front of Mama before sitting down hard, his eyes nearly in line with her gaze. She didn't move. She didn't flinch.

"Mama, this is horseshit!" he exclaimed, attempting to shock her. Mama would never tolerate her son using that kind of language. "I spent the whole trip thinking on what I could say to you, Mama. About the only thing I'm positive of is that there are no perfect words for things like this. In those penny novels you like to read the character always seems to know what to say. But that's not real life, Mama. Either that's the truth or I'm just not smart enough!"

He sat back in the chair and looked out the window once more. The sky appeared darker yet. Looking again at his mother, he leaned forward and found her hand. Loudly, but not shouting, he said, "Do you think that you're the only one that's hurting because Rachel died? You're selfish if you think you're the only one that feels sorrow." He found her eyes again, this time by gently touching her under her chin and raising her head. Her skin felt dangerously thin. It reminded him of wet parchment…if you rubbed it too hard, it would easily rip under the pressure of your hand.

"What about Papa, Mama? What about *me*?" Quieter now, just inches from her face, he said, "How can you do this to *us*, Mama? How can you be so damn selfish, Mama? How can you love Rachel so much that you'd die over her death but not live for your husband and your son?" His eyes welled up with tears now, and he continued, "Don't you love us enough to live? Can you not see what this is doing to me, Mama…what it's doing to *me*?" A tear fell from the corner of his eye, tracing the pattern of his nose, before getting hung up on his upper lip. "Mama," he said through a sob, "I need you to live…for me." He let his head fall forward and his lip released the tear, causing it to fall to the floor.

The tears fell freely now, and Arlis allowed his body to come forward out of his chair. He knelt on the hard floor and buried his head in his mother's lap, sobbing. Behind him, the empty chair rocked as if a restless spirit occupied it.

When it came, the voice sounded old. It was raspy and dry, obviously passing through vocal chords that hadn't seen enough use of late. It said, "You're already dead."

Arlis figured his imagination had taken over, but he raised

his head anyway. This time, as he looked into the eyes of his mother, he could see life in them. As he backed away to get a better look he saw those eyes following the movement of his, and a short, harsh laugh escaped his lips, though he found no humor in any of this.

"What, Mama?" he said, wiping his wet cheeks with a hand. Even her breathing had changed, as the rate had slowed and the depth of her breaths had increased. "What did you say, Mama?" he asked again, knowing full well what she'd said.

"You're already dead, Arlis," Mama said again, the voice still raspy but clearer than last time. "You're just a ghost before me."

Arlis waited for more but she offered nothing. After a moment, he said, "No, Mama. I'm not dead. This is me in the flesh." Taking her hand in his again, he said, "You feel me touching you, Mama? Can you feel my hand upon yours? I'm *alive*, Mama."

Mama's lips parted and closed as she tried in vain to swallow. She smacked her lips twice and then licked them in slow motion, causing Arlis to think about getting her a drink of water. He looked to the dresser in his periphery, remembering that he'd seen nothing upon it earlier. He didn't want to chance leaving her alone, lest she go mute again when he returned with the water. He waited patiently for her to continue. After nearly a minute, she did.

"I read the Tribune, Arlis…all last summer I read that paper. I couldn't not read it." Her eyes darted left and stayed there a moment. Arlis nearly panicked, thinking she was gone again, but within a few seconds her eyes came back to the right and found his again. "I just spoke in bad grammar, I'm afraid."

Arlis laughed, and he felt the tears coming again. "I know, Mama," he said. "Negation…you taught me well. You used a double negative, but I know what you meant." He smiled at her, his eyes glimmering through the unshed tears.

"Fair Oaks, Shiloh, Oak Grove, Mechanicsville," Mama said, slowly and deliberately. "Every fight was in print." She licked her lips again. "I watched them all in the newspaper, counting the dead and the wounded and the missing." She lifted a wrinkled hand and searched for his face. Arlis moved closer, allowing her to touch his cheek. "This is a different kind of war than the ones I taught you about, Arlis. This war has brought about killing unlike any killing ever seen. The dying is unprecedented. Every battle seems to leave more dead boys on the field than the last one." Her hand fell as her strength faltered. Arlis put it back on her lap, and held it with his own.

"I'm not dead though, Mama," he said. "I've come through safely and so have thousands of others like me." He thought about his combat experiences at South Mountain, the heavy gunfire he'd somehow survived. At Gainesville, his brigade had stood in an open field and traded gunfire with the Stonewall Brigade for nearly an hour and he'd somehow come out unscathed.

Then came Antietam. Arlis knew that his mother had no knowledge of his being wounded. He wasn't about to tell her now, either.

"Arlis, you didn't need to go to war to be taken," Mama said, tilting her head. "God would've come and taken you right in your bed at home just like the rest of my babies. Why you felt the need to rush things along, I don't know, but you did. You're the only one that's gone off looking for death. Perhaps the only reason you've been spared so far is because death has been lingering too long in Mineral Point. But he'll find you, Arlis. Death finds all my children."

Lightning flashed, causing Arlis to flinch. A few seconds later the thunder came in a long, angry roll. Arlis glanced out the window and saw the rain coming down in torrents. It occurred to Arlis that the reason the letters had stopped coming from home probably had nothing to do with the army or bad service from the post, but because Mama had stopped writing altogether, as she'd already given up hope.

"Mama, I've got a little over a year left on the term of my enlistment," he said, lying to her again. His enlistment would expire in July of 1864, a full twenty months from now. "And the army has allowed me enough leave to nurse you back to full health, too. That'll use up plenty of that time, won't it? I'll make it through this war, and then everything will go back to normal on the farm, Mama."

She looked at him with obvious patronage. "My boy," she said, "Wars like this one don't end. Wars like this one will go on indefinitely, forever, with the fighting and the dying continuing until the last man on one side or the other is killed. What other way is there for it to end?"

Arlis was stunned. He hadn't really thought about how all of this would end. He had no answer for her.

She sighed, saying, "Once the armies cease being armies, the losers will take to the hills. They'll fight as guerrillas. It won't *ever* end, Arlis, and I have no intention of being here when they come to tell me that you're among the dead. No mother should have to bury all four of her children."

Arlis pondered for a moment, "Then I won't go back. Maybe they'll *let* me come home with you, stay home with you. I've done enough fighting. I've even got some words of praise for my courage from the Major. They'll understand. When I tell them of the hardships you've faced, Mama, they'll *insist* I go home."

Mama raised the corners of her mouth in a half-hearted smile, the kind borne of pity. She raised her hand again to his face, softly caressing his cheek. It felt like lambskin that had been left to dry in the sun for weeks.

"Child," she said, softly, "You're not listening. God will find you wherever you are. He's made it clear that my children are more important in his world than they are in my own. I'm not angry about it anymore. It's just the way it is." She let her hand fall to her lap. "If you go home, it'll just be easier for death to find you."

"Mama, you're not talking sense," Arlis argued. "If God means to take me then why didn't the flu take me with Violet and the rest of them? And Mama, Papa needs you."

Mama's answer came quick and cold. "Your Papa hasn't needed anything for a very long time, Arlis. Your Papa's body has been void of his spirit for years, now. He died with Ezra."

"No, Mama," Arlis said, angry now. "*You* died with Ezra. Nothing's been right about you since the storm. Rachel dying gave you an excuse to give up. You're giving up on Papa and you're giving up on me. You're being selfish and hoggish and mean and narrow. Who the hell are you to give up like this, anyway? Do you think you're the only one who's lost their children? What about Mrs. Rhys? She lost her husband and all of her children." He paused to breathe. "What if everybody gave up when they were filled with sorrow? God wouldn't have room enough for all of them!"

Mama's eyes floated downward to the floor, either in an attempt to avoid consideration of Arlis' questions or because she could no longer keep them focused on him. Arlis, hesitating in anticipation of what she might do, went silent. The rain pelting against the window sounded angry and unforgiving. Lightning flashed.

Minutes went by. Arlis passed the time watching the water make patterns on the outside of the window, obscuring any view of the world beyond. Mama stared at his feet.

Finally, in a quiet, soothing voice, he said, "If God had plans for taking you, Mama, then he'd do it on his own accord. Who do you think you are starving yourself like this… attempting to take your own life?"

Her head wobbled left as her eyes rose from the floor again, finding his in the gloom of the room. She gave him a hard stare, the softness gone. "If God's decided that this is the way I should go, then nobody is making you stay and watch."

"Well," he said, the anger coming back. "I'll watch any-way...and we can watch each other suffer."

26 Madison, Wisconsin
November 14, 1862
Morning

ARLIS STARED AT HIS OWN EYES IN THE MIRROR WHILE USING his hands to smooth out the wrinkles in his uniform. In the mirror, a much older man gaped back, one with large, purple sacks under his eyes. This man looked as if he hadn't slept in weeks, and Arlis wondered when the last time he'd studied his own reflection in a mirror had been. Had the war aged him so? The wounds? The worry over his mother? He had no answers for the old man in the mirror.

He stood in the lobby of the mansion, opposite the director's desk, awaiting the appearance of Dr. Hargrove. Yesterday, when he'd stepped through the door of this building, he'd hoped to make a difference in his mother's care. He'd hoped that he'd be able to get through to her, perhaps enough to get her to go home with him. Now, as he stared at himself under the decorative cherubs on the lobby mirror, he wondered if he should be admitted to the hospital as a patient himself.

The previous night, after the conversation with his mother, Yancey had brought in a cot for Arlis to sleep on, setting it up next to his mother's bed. Bedtime for Mama and any others that could not be trusted with oil lamps was sundown, with the staff preparing her for bed around dusk, which came even earlier than usual tonight as the gale punished the Mendota landscape. Arlis had left the room to find a meal and collect his thoughts, consuming a bowl of broth in the commons as a female nurse had changed Mama into fresh nightclothes. With Mama tucked into bed, the nurse had made an exception and brought in an oil lamp, giving Arlis strict instructions to keep it out of the reach of his mother. Arlis had only nodded, placing the lamp on the dresser and choosing to sit in the rocker they'd provided for him.

He'd sat thinking for a long time, as Mama had gone back to whatever world she lived in. He thought of his parents and how the loss of his siblings had affected them, wondering just how he'd been changed himself. He could sense no real revisions within himself, any real changes coming either so slowly or so abruptly that he didn't recognize them as such. Mary, who had been born after Rachel but before Ezra, had died as an infant when Arlis was six. He hardly ever thought of her, but he knew that his mother still thought of her daily. Well, at least she had up until Arlis had left for Camp Randall. He thought of Ezra fairly often, usually out of pity for losing his life at such a tender age, never being able to grow up and experience life as an adult. Perhaps Ezra had been the lucky one after all, seeing as he wouldn't ever have to experience days like this one, conversing with a stubborn, suicidal parent. Arlis didn't *miss* Ezra, not in the sense that he'd miss Rachel or Violet, as he had barely known the two-year-old boy that had yet to develop a personality. This thought added to the feelings of pity he had for his brother. It occurred to him then that he had no such pity for Mary, and upon that realization, the notion that he felt no guilt or remorse for his lack of feelings weighed upon him in its own sense, causing him to further scrutinize himself. *What if God's only reason for taking the lives of my siblings has been to get a reaction out of me?* he thought.

The wind had continued to howl and whip, causing the

206 | Eric Schlehlein

building to moan as the air wormed its way through the gaps of the windows. The temperature dropped, changing the rain into sleet that rattled off the glass pane, reminding Arlis of the sound that chicken feed made when tossed onto the hardened gravel outside of the coop. He stood and went to the window, where he attempted to peer beyond his own orange and red silhouette, the spooky image appearing courtesy of the lamp behind him. Lightning flashed in the distance, confirming the hopelessness of trying to see anything outside. The image through the glass was much like gazing into a pond after disturbing the sediment on the bottom.

"Mama," he said, turning from the window back to his mother. She lay supine in bed with the covers drawn just above her small, depleted bosom, the knot of her bony collarbone vivid and revolting. Her eyes were open and staring at the ceiling, as if waiting for something, perhaps God, to materialize there. Arlis walked to the cot next to the bed, his footfalls alarming in the quietness of the room. Shuffling sideways through the one-foot gap between the bed and the cot, he sat on the cot facing his mother and watched her. Her breathing had returned to its quick and shallow pace as the body attempted to compensate for the lack of nutrients through the change in oxygenation. Arlis removed his boots, allowing them to fall solidly on the floor one at a time in an attempt to make her blink or flinch. She did neither.

"How do you just come and go like that?" he asked, scooting from the cot to the bed. He sat next to her with his hips at her waist, looking down on her in the scant light. "I'm not stupid, Mama. You know that." He smiled at her. "If you're not gonna talk, then I will. I know you can hear me." He pulled the envelope from his father out of his pocket and held it up so that, if she chose to, she could see his name in his father's script. "Papa left this with Dr. Hargrove for me." He left the letter inside the envelope and flipped it over repeatedly as he spoke.

"Dated October the nineteenth, it is. Papa tells me he's gone home to sell the mine so as to come back here to take care of you. Won't that be swell, having all of that time on his hands with all his worldly responsibilities in the past?" He glanced at her eyes, looking for reaction. She blinked involuntarily.

"It's been three weeks since he left here," Arlis continued, "and whether or not it takes that long to sell the mine, you and I both know he isn't coming back. You're starving to death and the man you married has abandoned you."

Thunder cracked outside as the sleet continued to batter the window. Showing no emotion or reaction, Mama stared at the ceiling.

"I'm a '*ghost before you*,' Mama?" Arlis said menacingly, watching the lamplight cast an orange glow over the gray pallor of her face. "You look who's talking, now." He paused, again looking for reaction. Finding none, he said, "I'm not planning on asking Papa about his reasoning, but I don't mind raising the question to you about what that might be. The mine, you think? Really? Is the business more important than you, or me, or Rachel? Maybe it's because he just can't face what you're doing. Is this just his way of dealing with his own pain? Or is it that he just doesn't give a shit, which might explain why he sent you to Madison in the first place."

He sat silently for a minute. The lamp on the dresser behind him cast light that flickered and danced off the walls. Arlis fixed his gaze on his own shadow on the wall in front of him, huge and intimidating compared to the tiny lump of a shadow that his mother threw. Looking again at his mother, he said, "Whatever his reasons, they're just that…reasons… and I'll find all of them outrageous and contemptible."

Silence pervaded the room, the sleet either tapering off or having converted back to rain. Arlis felt nauseous, all of his anxiety and worry knotting somewhere in his abdomen, leaving him sick, exhausted, and hopeless.

Arlis rubbed the side of his face with a hand and said, "When the doctor told me they were using a speculum orum to feed you, Mama, I nearly went mad. I was relieved when he said Papa came and made them stop. Now, watching you wither away like last summer's daisies, I'll sign the papers to let them force-feed you if I have the right. Sometimes just seeing something can change a man's mind. I won't let you do this."

He watched as her eyes darted left and down, toward the foot of the bed, and then back to where they'd been. He took her hand and gently squeezed, adjusting his position on the bed. "That's right, Mama. I'll take on the responsibility of feeding you myself." He leaned forward and furrowed his brow. "It doesn't have to be that way. I am in earnest, Mama, when I say that anything I can do to save you now I do only out of love. You're the only person I have left to love in this barren, hateful world. You and I, we can be each other's strength. We can be each other's rock. We can be each other's charity." He broke off, watching as a single tear fell from the corner of her right eye and made its way into her ear, causing his own emotional response. His eyes welled up with tears. "Mama...*please.*"

He stood and went to the end of the bed, removing his trousers and shirt, dressing down to his undergarments and socks. He stepped to the dresser and killed the lamp before returning to the bed and climbing under the covers alongside his mother. He grimaced quietly at the pain the maneuver caused his fragile side, glad that his wounds would face the ceiling rather than be stuck underneath the weight of his own body. Then, placing his head lightly upon her shoulder, he held his mother as she'd often held him in his youth, silently caressing her hair, her face, her arm. Minutes passed. Arlis attempted to match the speed and depth of his mother's breathing, but found it cumbersome and difficult. If he tried for too long, he knew, he'd actually have to speed his breathing rate up more to compensate. He returned his breathing to normal and stroked the bangs on her forehead.

He raised his head and held it with the palm of his left hand. Lightning flashed, and he borrowed its luminance to steal a glance at her face, ashen and smoky, her eyes still open. A memory of a distant bible study flared through him, and he softly quoted from the book of Daniel.

"Therefore I was left alone, and saw this great vision, and there remained no strength in me: for my comeliness was turned in me into corruption, and I retained no strength." He continued to stroke her forehead gingerly, lovingly. "We have a lot in common with Daniel, Mama. That one…Daniel, chapter ten, verse eight…it describes both of us. See, when you're dead and gone, Mama, I'll have lost the last person that means anything to me, and I'll not seek the affections of another." He swallowed hard. "With no one to love, I'll never have another to mourn."

As he went silent, he noticed her breathing slow, stop, and then resume its quick pace. He let go of his head and lay it upon his arm, which he stretched out beneath the pillow. Exhaustion took hold, hard and quick. He closed his eyes and allowed the fatigue to set in. He hadn't been aware of how tired he'd been, thinking now about the day's events and how they'd probably aided in his drowsiness. He was struck by how affected a body could be from emotional stress; how a few hours of strain could collapse a man's vitality more than a full day of army drill. This line of thinking caused him to slip back to Camp Randall and the company dressed in their grays, stumbling around like the rough recruits they'd been. Sergeant Westcott was yelling at somebody for turning right when they should have turned left, and Arlis snickered in his mind—and perhaps in the flesh, too—at the mistake so many had made in the early days of training.

Suddenly, Westcott was in his ear, screaming at him to

"get up that hill and bring back yer pards!" *Chamberlain*. Arlis tightened, looking at those around him…Talty, Sullivan, and the Hairy One. They offered no assistance, no judgment. They stared at him blankly, until Harrison gestured to the hill that had materialized in front of the company.

Arlis, in a panic, held his musket at the ready and bolted to the base of the hill. Here, he realized something wasn't right; he was still wearing the state issued gray uniform they'd worn so long ago. *We never fought in these*, he thought, recognizing the unmistakable outline ahead as that of Turner's Gap, the ground growing hard and rocky, as he made his way up the battlefield at South Mountain. The Rebs were firing at him now, the balls whizzing and buzzing past his head and ricocheting off of the rocky formations, which were larger and rockier than any he'd seen his first time here.

The elevation increased, and the vegetation transformed, changing from prairie grass to tall, winding weeds. Then, out of seemingly nowhere…*oh God, no*. Cornstalks. Arlis pressed onward, upward, searching for familiar ground—the ground he'd last seen George Chamberlain lying upon, bloodied and frightened. He saw him now, laying between the cornstalks… stalks that (at nearly twice the height of a grown man) were far taller than they had any business being.

"Badger," Chamberlain said as Arlis approached. "The corn's *alive*, Badger."

Of course it is, Arlis thought, squatting next to Chamberlain. "I'm gonna get you out this time, Maid," he said, calling him by the nickname the boys had given him. Chamberlain hated it.

"I ain't yer chambermaid," George said, frowning. "Careful of the leg, now." He reached out and grabbed Arlis by the front of his coat, gripping hard and pulling him close. With their faces just inches apart, George said, "This is your last shot, Badger. Don't fuck me this time."

Arlis pulled away and slid his arms beneath Chamberlain. "I couldn't even get to you last time, Maid. I'll save you
this time." He easily picked the man up, as one might pick
up a knapsack or a bushel. He weighed next to nothing, far
less than he should have, anyway. He turned to head down
the mountain and the gunfire increased. It was close, loud,
and chilling. Arlis took two steps and was forced to stop, as
something had caught on Chamberlain and was impeding
his movement. Arlis turned and watched as the cornstalks
moved and grabbed, collapsing around the man, taking hold
of Chamberlain's arms and wrapping around his neck.

"*NO!*" Arlis screeched, taking hold of his bayonet and slash-
ing at the leaves, cutting them at their origins on the stalks. He
quickly found that it was no use; as one was cut free, another
would take hold. Arlis increased his cutting speed, thrashing
wildly at the stalks while pulling. Finally both were free, the
sudden release from the bondage of the plants causing him to
fall to the ground, Chamberlain sprawling out next to Arlis.

"Hey," Chamberlain said, "I told ya ta watch the leg!"

Arlis gave a quick look behind them, expecting the corn
to try again. But the stalks were gone, allowing a full view
of the Rebel line, a fortified trench about seventy-five yards
to the front. Rebel heads poked up from behind the walls as
their owners fired muskets at the men, who seemed to be the
only Union soldiers on the battlefield. He felt his heart racing—beating as fast as his mother's had been—and now his
breathing rate matched hers as well. This time, he'd have no
problem keeping the respirations at that measure.

"Okay, once more," Arlis said to Chamberlain, picking him
up. He held him like the man was a toddler, with one arm
under his buttocks. As he started to the rear again the Rebels
fired a full volley, blowing Chamberlain's head clean off and
knocking Arlis to the ground again. Sitting up, Arlis settled
next to the headless corpse, the top of the neck cut clean,

bloodless, and looking like a round log that had been sawed in half. The firing ceased. Arlis looked toward the Rebel line, but the Rebs were gone, the terrain altered again. He realized he was no longer on the South Mountain battlefield, but in the courtyard of the hospital; the crazy old woman yelling at someone for getting blood all over her antique rug. He was abruptly surrounded by the familiar faces of Company K, who held their heads low in shame, disappointment, or plain old disapproval.

Then, Violet Rhys, fourteen years old and dressed in an elaborate red calico dress, resplendent with a repeating, white maple leaf pattern, pushed her way through the crowd of on-lookers to stand at the feet of the corpse on the ground. Arlis sat wide-eyed, his focus fixed on the girl.

"You stupid, stupid boy," said Violet, refusing to make eye contact with him. "Can't you save anybody?"

Arlis followed her gaze to the body on the ground, his eyes scanning it from the feet upward. The body was dressed in white bedclothes and slippers, wrapped in a quilt. *Mama!*

He awoke with a start, sitting bolt upright and breathing in a quick, labored manner. He'd been sleeping on his back with his mother next to him. He drew his knees up and hugged them, letting the nightmare dissipate, slowing his breathing. He glanced at his mother next to him in the light of the early morning, saw her legs as lumps under the covers, and wondered what time it was. He felt as if he'd just fallen asleep minutes before.

He looked to the window. Although the sky was blue and the sunlight brilliant, Arlis could feel the coldness of the room. Winter was coming. He turned back, looking at his mother. She lay on her left side, facing away from Arlis, and he wondered if maybe she was already awake, staring vacantly at the wall on the opposite side of the bed. *What kind of life is this?*

"Mama," he said quietly, so as not to scare her if she was still asleep. Achieving no reaction, he again said, "Mama!" louder this time. "It's morning, Mama." He waited a moment, listening for her breathing. He was hoping the rate of her breath would offer a clue as to whether or not she was awake. He heard nothing.

Alarmed, he reached for her shoulder and grasped it, turning her toward him. He felt the stiffness immediately, the body cold, congealed, petrified…lifeless. Her eyes remained open, the vacancy true, appropriate, and undeniable.

Arlis wept.

"I'm so very sorry, Mr. Jenkins," Hargrove said, causing Arlis to turn from the mirror. Arlis just looked at him. "Even I am surprised at the suddenness of her passing," the doctor continued, "I do pray that your final hours with her shall offer you some closure."

Arlis felt numb. He thought of telling Dr. Hargrove about the conversation that he'd had with his mother. The actuality of her talking to him last night would certainly cause the doctor to raise an eyebrow, leading him to interrogate Arlis about their discussion. If his mother had still been alive this morning, he surely would have discussed at length everything that had occurred the previous night with Hargrove, including the possibility of resuming the use of the speculum orum.

Now, he felt he had put Mama over the edge by bringing that subject up with her, that Mama had somehow forced an end upon herself in the night because he had threatened to coerce her into living. This brought a heavy dose of contrition and self-condemnation upon him. He was physically sick from shame and liability, and he had no stomach whatsoever for discussing any of it with anyone. In response to the doctor's statement regarding closure, he simply nodded, moving his eyes to the floor.

They briefly discussed the arrangements for Mama's transportation to Mineral Point for burial, something that had been worked out previously by Tom Jenkins and Dr. Hargrove. The doctor informed Arlis that he'd send a message to his father via telegram, and that it was his hope that Tom Jenkins wasn't already in transit back to Madison. Arlis chose not to tell Hargrove that his father would surely be in Mineral Point to accept it.

They parted, the doctor apologizing once more, and Arlis walked out into the sunshine and inhaled the crisp autumn air. Looking skyward, he saw pink, billowy wisps of narrow clouds passing near the sun, radiating shades of copper and lavender, sienna and peach in all directions. It was an image that might have caused him to gasp audibly on another, less painful, day. Gazing blankly at this natural tapestry, he wondered if he'd ever again be able to enjoy such a sight.

27 Belle Plain, Virginia
February 25, 1863
Night

MICKEY WAS BACK AND FULL OF STORIES FOR THE BOYS, WHO were all thrilled to see him. Having been discharged after losing his toes and part of a foot at South Mountain, he'd gone home to Mauston to find that, "there was nobody there worth a bugger ta talk ta. Take yer pick," he said to the men around the campfire, "invalids who claim ta have killed half the Rebel Army, cowards gripin' that congress might make 'em fight, or the women that were growlin' 'cause they had ta pay fifty cents a yard fer calico or twenty five cents fer a spool o' thread. I was gettin' downright morose, so...I signed up again!" The men howled.

The first to see him as he came into camp that afternoon, Arlis had greeted Mickey with a hug. He had had to tell him not to go at him so roughly because of his wounds.

"Mickey, what the hell happened to your face?" he asked, noticing what appeared to be small scratches and lacerations all over his face. On his nose was a deep cut, crescent moon shaped, the exact size of a man's thumbnail. It was scabbed over and oozing.

"Oh hell, some vet back home claimed the army in the west was better than our beloved Army o' the Potomac. I set him right. Gave the bugger a good ol' 'Iron Brigade' rap on the noggin. He marked my face up a bit first, though."

Arlis smiled, remembering the confrontation he'd had with the sergeant from Illinois. "There's a lot of that going around."

They spent a few minutes removing clothing to share their battle scars, and suddenly Arlis was aware of a new man, a private in a brand new uniform, standing eight feet away, watching the exchange between the two old vets.

"Who's your friend?" Arlis asked.

"Ah, that's Bath," Mickey said. "Come here, Davey," he said, wiggling a finger.

"Private David Bath, this here's..." Mickey recoiled, noticing chevrons on Arlis for the first time. "Damn, Badger, when did they put ya in charge o' soldiers?"

"Yep, call me 'Sergeant,'" Arlis said, "I made corporal in November, Mick, and they put another chevron on me last month. Nothing gets a man promoted faster than another man dying."

"Well then," Mickey said, grinning. "Bath, this is Sergeant Jenkins."

"Pleased to meet you, Sergeant," Bath said, extending his hand.

"You're a replacement?" asked Arlis flatly, ignoring the hand. "You're in Company K, then?"

"Yes, Sergeant," the private answered, retracting his hand nervously.

Looking at Mickey, Arlis nodded toward Bath and said, "He the only one you brought with you?"

"The pickings are slim in Juneau County, Badger. Anyone that's worth a damn is already in the field. Bath here just reached the ripe age o' eighteen at the beginnin' o' the month."

"Mmm," Arlis said, having nothing to add. He studied the boy, who appeared to be so young, so...green. Maybe five foot, six inches in height, Bath had a round baby face that was marred here and there by an occasional pimple. His eyes were light brown, and matched the tint of the freckles that were on his high cheekbones. His walnut hair had a hint of red in it. Although he wore the same blue suit as the others in Company K, he had yet to be issued a Hardee hat and musket.

"There's a Captain Otis from the Second Regiment that made the trip down here with me. He brought a doctor and three enlisted men with him, replenishin' the ranks o' his company."

"George Otis?" Arlis asked.

"Dunno," Mickey answered, "the man's a captain. Don't reckon I go around askin' the officers 'bout their first names."

"It's gotta be him," Arlis said, looking off in the distance. "Captain Otis is from the Point. My father and he..." he trailed off, remembering. "He and my father were close once."

"Yep," Mickey said, "I've been tellin' Bath 'bout how he'll be in the greatest company of the greatest regiment of the greatest brigade of the...well, that's about it, I guess, I'll not brag fer the rest of the army til they've gone and earned it."

Mickey told Arlis he had read the casualty reports from Antietam and had seen the names of Cummings and Harrison on the killed list. In return, Arlis told him about Abbott and a few of the officers from the other companies who had also been killed there.

"Shame," Mickey said. "Were ya'll engaged at Fredericksburg?"

"A bit. We took a few shells, nothing major. Six wounded."

Arlis had returned to the regiment shortly after leaving Madison, choosing to go back to the war rather than attend his mother's funeral and confront his father about how he'd handled the whole situation. He thought he'd feel better skipping Mama's funeral, abandoning her in death as she had abandoned him in life. He was wrong. Now, when he thought of her, he felt only remorse and shame. He had realized all too late that immaturity had gotten in the way of good judgment.

He'd arrived in plenty of time for the Battle of Fredericksburg. The Sixth Wisconsin lay alongside the Rappahannock River with the rest of the First Army Corps, engaged in minor combat with the Rebels. The real action went on to their right as the blue lines made assault after assault on a ridge called "Marye's Heights." It had been the worst one-sided defeat yet for the Army of the Potomac. The attack had been the brainstorm of General Ambrose Burnside, who had since resigned and been replaced by General Joseph Hooker.

"Emmons and DeJean got sick after Fredericksburg," Arlis said to Mickey, speaking of two Company K boys. "They went to a hospital in Washington and never came back. One died on Christmas Eve, the other on December thirtieth. I can't remember which was which."

"Shame," Mickey said again.

"Smitty died last week. Andy, that is. Lewis Smith is still here. Andy dropped dead during a formation. No one knows why." Looking at the recruit, Arlis said, "Don't even need to get shot at to end up in the ground, Bath."

"Yes, sir, uh, I mean…no, sir," Bath stammered.

"Don't call me 'sir,' Bath. I work for a living."

Confused, Bath responded, "Yes, Sergeant."

Addressing Mickey, Arlis said, "We've got a new regiment in the brigade, Mickey. The Twenty-Fourth Michigan joined us sometime last fall before I got out of the hospital."

Mickey grunted, his opinion of the Michiganders loud and clear.

"Gibbon requested them," Arlis continued, "Well, not *them* exactly, but a regiment, anyway. After Antietam, the brigade was thinning out pretty badly." He gave Mickey a soft punch on the shoulder. "You missed the best raid of the winter, Mick. Along about, oh, two weeks ago, whenever the twelfth was, half of us or so got on board a steamer and headed down the Potomac to a place called Heathsville. Colonel Fairchild from the Second led the raid. We came back with upwards of forty-five horses and mules, and enough bacon to feed us for the rest of the month. All without firing a shot." He pointed behind him with a thumb. "There's a few hundred Negroes that came back with us, too…they'll cook and clean and whatnot for you for cheap, if you're interested." He looked in the direction he'd pointed. "There's more than a thousand of them in the contraband camp. More and more seem to come in every day. I've grown fond of a family, four in all. Jesse and his wife, Sadie, and their young ones. Sadie is quite talented at getting the mud out of my uniform. I give them two bits a day to come around and do whatever I ask of 'em."

Mickey's mouth dropped open. "Jesus, Badger. That's about half of your pay!"

Annoyed, Arlis' response was short, "You think I'm doing this for the money?" He looked away, felt his vexation subside. "Oh hell, Mick, I don't need the money. I've got plenty to last until the Rebs kill me." He laughed, but it was a feeble attempt at humor.

Mickey stared at him, and Arlis knew he was being scrutinized. Seconds of silence followed.

Bath, oblivious to the awkwardness, said, "Sure is muddy around here."

"That's the first sign yer in an army camp, Davey," said Mickey. "Mud everywhere."

"Mickey, Lieutenant Ticknor's tent is over that way," Arlis said, pointing to a row of officer's tents. "Take the young buck with you and report to him. Jerkey will be glad to see you, I'm sure." Jerkey was the nickname the boys had given to Ticknor back at Camp Randall, before the company was officially mustered into the Sixth. Ticknor had been a sergeant then. "He'll assign Bath to a squad. Do what you can to make sure it isn't one of mine."

"Sure thing, Badger," Mickey said. He lingered a moment, watching Arlis with concern in his eyes, then turned and went slogging through the mud in the direction of Ticknor's tent. Bath tagged along.

Arlis watched them take a few steps, then called out, "Hey, Mick!"

Mickey stopped and turned, silently waiting.

"It's damn good to see you again."

Now, as Mickey was sitting on a campstool he'd brought from home and regaling the tale of his trip back to Virginia to the boys, Arlis sat in his underpants on an empty crate ten feet from the circle, working a piece of sewing thread through a needle. He balanced a three-inch by three-inch square mirror on his lap to reflect the firelight back toward its source, illuminating his hands before him. Having successfully threaded the needle, he began working on mending his torn trousers. This would be the third time he'd needed to fix this pair. Private David Bath stood nearby, repeatedly going through the manual of arms. To Arlis, the worst thing about new recruits was that nobody trained them before sending them to the company. They had to learn everything on-the-job. For the company, that meant that today you could receive a few replacements and then be expected to perform on the parade ground tomorrow in front of the commanding general, with no consideration for the newness of the recruits. All were expected to march in step and right wheel, left face, and salute when told to do so. For the replacements, it meant that if you were awake and not eating a meal, you were drilling.

"Stay at shoulder arms, Bath," Arlis said, without looking up from his work. "Now, salute!"

Bath, with his musket on his right shoulder, brought his left arm up and across his chest, striking the musket with his hand and holding it there.

"That's it," Arlis said. "Back at it now."

Bath complied. Arlis continued sewing up his pants, his tongue sticking out of the corner of his mouth. He'd been irritated but not surprised when Bath had come back to him that afternoon, outfitted with all the accoutrements necessary for soldiering, including a musket. Arlis was in charge of two squads, one of which was down from twelve to seven men, and he had been pretty sure that seven was the lowest of the eight squads in the company.

"So I've got these scars on my face from the fight, see," Mickey was saying, "and Captain Otis makes a remark 'bout how I look like I survived the pox,' and that gives him an idea. As we're boardin' the train in Chicago, he points at me and asks the doctor if it was determined ta be small pox or not. The doc says, 'Inconclusive,' and all at once the entire car emptied, leavin' the seven o' us soldiers ta have the whole car fer ourselves." The boys roared with laughter.

Arlis looked up and grinned. *Same old Mickey*, he thought.

"...took us through Dunkirk, Elmira," Mickey continued, "all the way ta Washington City. From there we caught a steamer, dropped us right at yer front door." He pointed toward the Potomac, which lay less than a mile to the east.

"Private Bath," Arlis said calmly, "Shoulder your weapon

and stand at attention." Bath complied. Arlis finished his last stitches and put his sewing kit away. After putting his trousers on, he stepped over to Bath.

"Present arms," he said, and Bath quickly went through the motions, extending the musket before him. "You learn quickly, Bath, but your left thumb should be against the stock, not wrapped around it, like this," he grabbed Bath's thumb and laid it against the rifle, "you get it quicker than a lot of the recruits do, though."

"Thank you, Sergeant."

Arlis patted him on the chest with his palm. "That's enough for your first night. Your time is yours until roll call. Use it wisely." He turned and went back to his crate. Reaching into the haversack, he found his clay pipe and tobacco pouch, both purchased from one of the many sutlers who set up shop in the camp, and packed the bowl. He struck a match and sparked the pipe, the practice of smoking becoming second nature to him. Suddenly Bath was standing to the left of him, setting up his own campstool and warily watching Arlis for his reaction. Arlis offered none as he turned his head and watched the boy sit, but raised an eyebrow as he turned his gaze back to the boys around the campfire.

"Why don't ya join the boys 'round the campfire, Private? Get to know 'em a little," Arlis said, staring at the back of Albert Tarbox.

"Well, if it's all the same ta you, Sergeant, I'd just as soon sit right here. Mickey's doin' all the talkin' and there ain't nothin' he can say that I ain't already heard on the ride down here."

Arlis looked at Bath blankly, the pipe clamped between his teeth. Then he erupted into laughter, drawing looks from the boys around the fire. He laughed hard for nearly ten seconds, the cackles morphing into giggles and finally dissipating into sniggers. He caught his breath.

"Damn, Bath," he said finally, holding the pipe in his hand.

"I haven't laughed like that in a long time." He held the pipe up as if toasting the private's remark. "I can empathize with you on the subject of riding cross country on a train with Mickey."

They went silent, sitting in the crisp, cool February air. The night was mostly still, the sky clear with an occasional cottony cloud passing by, looking like gray wood smoke against the black backdrop. The mud at their feet had hardened a bit as the temperature hovered around freezing. The fire felt warm even at this distance, but certainly wasn't necessary to the Wisconsin men, who were used to far colder temperatures in February. Arlis preferred the colder temperatures, which were the only alternative to ankle deep mud.

Mickey droned on, "…she says ta me 'yer Irish an' yer in the Iron Brigade?' And I says, 'Yeah, there's quite a few of us in that particular brigade, and she says, 'how come yer not in the Irish Brigade?'" He waited while his audience laughed, Talty enjoying the joke more than most. When the commotion subsided, Mickey said, "So I says, 'If they put every Irishman that's in the army in the Irish Brigade then it wouldn't be the 'Irish Brigade,' it'd be the 'Irish Corps.' She didn't get my meanin' by that, so I says, 'I'd rather be the only Irishman in the Iron Brigade than be the only iron man in the Irish Brigade.'"

Arlis offered a closed mouth smile and shook his head. "Are you Irish, Bath?" he said, turning toward the private.

"My family's Scottish, but I'm fourth-generation American," he answered. "My great-grandfather fought in the revolution in the Pennsylvania militia. He served under a colonel named Daniel Brodhead. I know little else about him. He died long before I was born."

Arlis nodded and dragged on the pipe. "This regiment is a mutt when it comes to ancestry. Company K has a lot of Irishmen, born here or in Ireland, but lots are English too, at least in ancestry, me included." He pointed at Mickey, "Mick was born in Ireland, but he left there by the age of five. His folks brought him through Canada and into Wisconsin by way of the Great Lakes. Company D is mostly Irish. Company C, or the "Jayhawkers" as they call themselves, is mixed much like us, but they've got a lot of French boys descended from trappers in Prairie Du Chien. Then there's Company F…the boys from Milwaukee. They're exclusively German. The boys call them 'Dutchmen,' but that's not really accurate. Many of those boys don't even speak English. Company H is mostly German too, but not completely."

Bath nodded, said, "How come they put such different groups together in the same regiment?"

Arlis pulled on the pipe and inhaled, blowing the smoke out through his nose. "When they called for volunteers, back in '61, companies were formed in groups of eighty-five to one hundred in towns all over the state. As they came into Camp Randall, the fellows in charge just mixed them up any old way, ten companies to a regiment. Company E, who call themselves 'Bragg's Rifles,' is from Appleton mostly. Company D was formed in Milwaukee. Company A was formed somewhere in Sauk County, just where I don't recollect. Company G is from Beloit. Company H calls themselves the 'Buffalo County Rifles,' and they were formed in Fountain City."

Arlis looked at Bath, who was staring at the moon. Arlis shifted his gaze to the half-moon overhead, thought *a fortnight away from full.* He said, "Is that a first-quarter moon or a last-quarter moon?"

"I'm not sure what the difference is," Bath admitted.

"Is that moon waxing or waning?"

"Waxing, Sergeant?" Bath said, confusion in his voice and on his face. "I reckon I don't know what that means?"

Arlis leaned forward and tapped the spent bowl out against the side of the crate. "Waxing means it's between the new and the full moon, that more of it'll be visible tomorrow. Waning's the opposite; the moon being between full and new and less of it being visible tomorrow. What I'm asking is this: If the clouds cooperate tomorrow night, allowing you to see the moon, will you be able to see more or less of it than you're seeing right now?"

"Uhh, more of it?" Bath said, wholly uncertain.

Arlis frowned. "Are you guessing or are you confident of that answer, Bath?"

"Yeah, I'm guessing. I don't pay much attention to the moon."

"Ayuh," Arlis said. He found his tobacco pouch and re-packed his pipe. Bath watched him, squirming in anticipation of further explanation for this line of questioning. Arlis sparked the bowl and gave it a few hard puffs.

At the campfire, Mickey was talking about the possibility of congress passing a draft law, something that the newspapers had been going on about for some time. He was saying that a vote was imminent, and since the Confederacy had passed a similar law last year, it was only a matter of time before drafts were being held in the North and their ranks were being re-filled by men who had no interest in becoming soldiers.

His pipe lit, Arlis shifted his attention to one of his brogans; drawing his foot up across his leg he inspected the frayed sole, which was caked with mud from the mire of the army camp.

"Well?" Bath asked, unable to take the suspense anymore.

"Well, what?" Arlis said, running a finger underneath the sole where the stitching should have been.

Bath straightened and said, "Well, Sergeant?"

Arlis looked up, baffled. When the private said nothing further, he said, "No, Bath," and chuckled. "I mean, what do you want? When we're sitting here like this you can quit the formality."

"Why're ya askin' me about the moon?" Bath asked. He was nervously examining his new, flawless Hardee hat, running his thumb around the brim and watching the firelight glint off of the metal "6."

"Damn brogans are rubbish," Arlis griped, inspecting his other foot. "I got these off a sutler's wagon outside camp. Paid a high price for 'em, too. The ones the army gave me lasted longer." He put both feet on the ground and pulled at the pipe. Turning his entire body and facing the young soldier, Arlis made eye contact. "You're not a farmer or a fisherman, by trade, Bath. You're not a miner or a mason or a brick maker or a carpenter. You didn't work on a riverboat. Nor were you a lawman or a sailor or a soldier or a night watchman—although I already knew you weren't any of these last four without asking you about the moon. A man's knowledge of the moon can tell another man a lot about him. Before all of this mess," Arlis said as he pulled the pipe from his mouth and opened his arms wide, gesturing at the camp as a whole, "I was a farmer *and* a miner. Both can be worked long after the sun goes down when the moon is up and close to full. Most of your work as a miner is done in the blackness of the underground, using artificial light, so when you come up to the surface any natural light seems a Godsend." He pointed at Bath, "If you weren't a student back home, Bath, then my gut, the moon, and those unseasoned hands of yours tell me that you're probably a clerk or shopkeeper." Arlis realized that Bath had the look of a scolded child on his face.

He softened his stare, tilted his head a little, and said, "There's no judgment in what I'm saying here, just truth. If I'm wrong about the clerking thing then I'll guarantee you that I'm right when I say that whatever you do, you do it by daylight. Now that you're a soldier, you'll be paying a lot more attention to the moon."

Arlis turned his attention back to the pipe, which he smoked vigorously until it was cashed. He emptied it and returned it to his haversack. Looking again at his footwear, he muttered, "Wish I had a decent pair of brogans."

Bath sat on his stool, silently studying his hat. A short spell later he said, "My Pa's a cobbler. He's teachin' me ta make shoes."

Arlis' head whipped in the direction of Bath and they stared at each other for a couple of seconds, then both burst out laughing.

"I don't suppose you can fix these buggers, can you?" Arlis said as the laughter subsided.

"Not a chance, Sergeant."

They sat in silence for a while, listening as Tall-T was telling Mickey a tall tale about how he'd earned the love and admiration of a "fine southern belle" during the Heathsville raid. Mickey was being a fine sport in going along with it.

A breeze began blowing lightly from the west, blasting the men with a rush of February air. Arlis tilted his hat to the left and covered his cheek until the wind abated. He looked at Bath out of one eye, who was staring at the ground as if something mesmerizing was happening there. On the boy's face, he saw worry, apprehension, uneasiness.

"What's on your mind, Bath?" Arlis asked. Bath looked up at Arlis, who held his gaze for a long while.

Bath shook his head slowly and said, "I'm not rightly sure I can put it into words, Sergeant." He was still fiddling with his hat. "I was sure excited when I found out that Mickey was gonna go back to the war and take me with him. I mean, I would've signed up with anyone who would've taken me, which was everyone, as the recruitment never seems to stop back home. But with Mickey…hmm, well I was signing up with the best, no doubt." He stopped, put the hat on his head, and went back to staring at the ground. Arlis was patient, sitting with his hands folded in his lap and his eyes on the recruit.

"I ain't even a soldier," Bath said suddenly, finding Arlis' eyes again. "I'm thinking that maybe I don't belong here. I mean, how can I even think about measuring up to all of you?"

Arlis considered this, slowly nodding his head. "We're in the same company as one another now, Bath," he said softly, "We're in the same regiment, same brigade, same corps, same army. From here on out, our experiences will be one and the same. It doesn't matter *how* you got here. All that matters is what you do on the march, on the parade ground, and on the battlefield. That might sound like a lot, but it's no more than is expected out of any of us." He coughed into a closed fist. "This brigade is the best drilled brigade in the Army of the Potomac. You're looking into my eyes, right? Do you see any bullshit behind these eyes?"

Bath, realizing Arlis was asking a real question, said, "No, Sergeant."

"That's right, Private. Soldiers love to bullshit. Ninety percent of what you'll hear in camp is bullshit. If you listen to what Talty is saying over there you'll discover you're knee deep in bullshit. But when I tell you that the 'Iron Brigade' is the best drilled brigade in all of the army, you can bet I'm not bullshitting you. We've never turned our backs to the enemy, but we've been outnumbered in every fight." Arlis paused to redirect his line of thinking. "Do you know the five regiments that make up our brigade?"

"Yes," said Bath. "Mickey told me. The Second, Sixth, and Seventh Wisconsin Regiments, the Nineteenth Indiana, and now the Twenty-Fourth Michigan, according to what you said this afternoon."

"That's right. Now, there's a lot of rivalry between these five regiments about who's the best and all, but there's no doubt that on the drilling ground, the Sixth Regiment will destroy any of the others in a straight up competition. We are the best-drilled regiment in the best drilled brigade in the entire army, Private. Am I bullshitting you?"

"No, Sergeant."

"That's right…and here's the clincher as to how you'll know that I'm not bullshitting you: Your company, my beloved Company K, is *not* the best drilled company in the Sixth. That honor can only be claimed by Company B, or the Prescott Guards, as they call themselves. Company K is pretty damn good, but Company B is the finest drilled company in the whole damn Army of the Potomac, period."

"Really?"

"Sure as I'm sitting here. Watch this." Arlis yelled to the boys around the campfire, "Hey boys, who's the best drilled company in the Sixth?"

Everyone yelled back, in unison, "Company K!"

Arlis shook his head. "See? That's army bullshit, Bath."

Bath laughed and said, "I'll take your word for it."

"Anyway," Arlis said, moving forward, "My point is this: We weren't this good when we signed up. We're this good because we've had excellent officers and excellent noncoms. We've had strong, competent leaders who cared about how we move, act, shoot, and march. It doesn't matter that you've never soldiered before, Bath, because we'll *make* you into a soldier. A damn fine one. I already told you that you're getting the movements down faster than most. In no time at all, you'll fit right in. You wait and see."

Bath nodded slowly. After a few seconds, he quietly said, "I sure hope so."

Arlis grabbed his watch and checked the time. "Fifteen minutes 'til roll call now. I think I'm gonna have one more smoke." He found his pipe and tobacco and had it blazing a minute later. "You wanna smoke?"

Bath waved him off and they sat in silence as Arlis smoked. Bath watched as Mickey gesticulated wildly with his hands as he told the boys a story about how General Burnside had tried to show him up by riding his horse over the top of him, and how Mickey had threatened the horse and rider with a loaded musket, forcing Burnside to back down.

"He was forcin' stragglers from his own corps along by ridin' over those that were layin' down and he ordered me ta get up an' get a move on," Mickey said. "I ignored the pompous ass, as he weren't my boss an' I wasn't stragglin' besides, just restin' a bit. He said he was gonna make me get up and get back in line an' then he spurred his big black horse towards me. Well, let me tell ya, I was right pissed. Nobody, not even a general, was gonna ride me down like a dog, so I rose up and brought my musket ta the ready and cocked it. It was still loaded from picket duty the previous night." He paused, staring into the sky, remembering. Shaking his head, he continued, "Not sure now if it was because he felt sorry fer me or because he read his own death in me eyes, but he pulled up and asked me which regiment I belonged ta. When I told him, he said, 'yer one of the western men,' and rode off, tellin' me ta hurry along as soon as I could." There was a mixture of awe and laughter from the men around the fire.

Bath leaned over toward Arlis, "More bullshit?"

Arlis scratched the stubble on his chin, said, "I wasn't there to see it, but I think this one might've really happened. Mickey's stories always have *some* truth in 'em."

The wind picked up again, scattering the glowing embers of the campfire among the men, who quickly inspected their clothing, ensuring no surprises later.

"Sergeant Jenkins," Bath said sheepishly, "Why'd you tell Mickey that you didn't want me in your squad today?"

Without hesitating, Arlis said, "Because I don't want to feel it when you go and get yourself killed."

The talk around the fire was dying. The men, paying attention to their pipes and cigars, had become lost in their own reflections and thoughts. Arlis looked at Bath, who'd gone back to staring at his own feet.

"Look Bath," Arlis said, "I know you weren't looking for me to go bragging about how great the Sixth is when you were confessing about your doubts on whether or not you belong here. I didn't lie to you, we *are* the best. But truth materializes in many schemes, and one of them you'll need to know is this: Being labeled as the 'Iron Brigade' is a nasty, double-edged sword. 'Iron' is just a moniker, nothing more. We're a disciplined, well-trained bundle of soldiers, but we bleed as much and as easily as anyone else. Other brigades, other corps, even civilians, thanks to the newspapers, have lofty, sometimes unrealistic expectations of this brigade. Because we're the 'Iron Brigade,' we're expected to be tougher, stronger, and more obstinate than everyone else. We're expected to be more seasoned and hardened than everyone else. We're expected to take hailstorms of lead and not flinch, but rather, to bleed and die as if it's why we joined up in the first place. We're expected to take the hill no matter the cost, and then hold it 'til the last man. We're not allowed to retreat or break or be beaten, *ever*, or God forbid, turn our backs to the enemy and run away. This brigade lost 1,750 men earning the name 'Iron Brigade.'" He looked at his watch. Four minutes until roll call. At the campfire, the men were stirring. Talty had already stood and was stretching.

"Leading up to our first battle," Arlis continued, "we were all scared. Few would have admitted it, but we all were. I had no idea how I'd handle seeing the elephant; if I'd be brave or run, or if I'd just freeze up and be useless. I know that's how you're feeling now. You are afraid of two very distinct unknowns. You're afraid that you're not going to be a good soldier, and you're afraid of the combat experience itself. Both are unknowns to you."

He drew on the dead pipe and exhaled audibly, blowing nothing through his pursed lips but air, which condensed upon respire in the cold night air. He tapped the spent bowl against the side of the crate. "When we fought at Gainesville last August, even the officers were unsure of their abilities as soldiers." Arlis marveled at how little time had passed since he'd first seen combat. He cocked his head as he calculated the months gone by. *Six. Only six long months*, he thought. "Seems like years ago now," he said.

"Anyway, the officers were afraid of the same unknowns that you are, but they had an additional one to fear. They didn't know how the men under their command would react to being under fire, and what their own reaction would be if those men failed to do their duty. As we marched into battle for the first time, a few of our officers threatened to shoot down any man who broke and ran or who failed to do their duty at that time. Looking at these men around us now, all of them, with their courage proven and their experience known far and wide, any order such as that being issued now would seem absurd. The men themselves would be extremely offended by such an order, as any shirkers or cowards that were in this brigade, this company, are all long gone. The next time we're preparing for a fight, no one will need to voice an order like that."

He pointed at Bath's face and shook his finger. "Being your sergeant, Bath, it'll be my duty while we're fighting to keep an eye on you to make sure that you don't run, but I already know that I won't need to deal with you personally. See, the veterans of this company have a reputation to protect. Even the privates will turn and shoot down a man who's running away or causing panic to spread within the ranks. That's the kind of responsibility and encumbrance that comes with being labeled as a member of the 'Iron Brigade.'"

Arlis stood and stretched, feeling the tight burn in his scarred ribcage as he reached his hands high above his head. "Now let's go. Time for roll call."

28 Gettysburg, Pennsylvania
July 1, 1863
10:30 am

THEY'D BEEN ORDERED BY LIEUTENANT COLONEL DAWES TO lie down in the field. Dawes was in command of the regiment, as Colonel Bragg had been kicked in the foot by a horse a few weeks back and was now recuperating in Washington. The regiment was being held in reserve as the rest of the brigade went into action against the Rebel line, currently invisible to the Sixth in the woods ahead of them. The regiment had hurried forward on the run, rushing to gain a position on the left flank of the brigade, where they had been halted. The men of the Sixth watched as the rest of the brigade hurried over a slight rise and into the trees, disappearing into the open woodlot beyond.

Suddenly, an aide galloped up to Dawes and spoke hurriedly to him, causing the commander to order the regiment to lie down in the field as they were now. Gunfire erupted in a tremendous crash from the woods as the rest of the brigade ran headlong into the Rebel line.

"Something's wrong." Arlis said, lying prone in the field.

Bath, who lay to the immediate right of Arlis, said, "Why?" His head flailed from side to side, frantically scanning the scene before them. He was wide-eyed. "What's going on?"

"That aide that rode up to the colonel is Lieutenant Marten, one of Doubleday's aides," Arlis said, loud enough for most of the men around him to hear. "Something must have happened to Reynolds if Doubleday is giving the orders." Reynolds, a very competent Pennsylvanian, commanded the First Corps. He was in charge of three divisions containing seven infantry brigades and a brigade of artillery.

Arlis watched as the commander of the brigade guard briefly met with Dawes, who then split the guard into two fifty man companies. Each company was ordered to lie down on the flanks of the Sixth, one company per side. This strengthened the regiment to 340 men and officers, which was still less than thirty-five percent of the strength that they'd mustered in at Camp Randall two years prior. The Sixth Wisconsin was now the only regiment that was not yet engaged in all of Wadsworth's division, consisting of the Iron Brigade and Cutler's Brigade, which was made up of four New York regiments, a Pennsylvania regiment, and an Indiana regiment. Cutler's Brigade was already in action on the right flank of the Iron Brigade.

"We're in reserve?" Bath asked, irritation in his voice. "Why the hell don't they let us in on the left of the Twenty-Fourth?"

"Relax, Tubber," Arlis said, using the nickname that the company had bestowed on Bath. He looked sideways at the replacement. "Usually they use the reserve regiments to plug the line where the action is hottest. Be careful what you wish for, Bath. You're gonna see action today. The whole damn Rebel Army is out there somewhere."

Another aide on horseback approached the mounted Dawes.

"That's Lieutenant Jones," Arlis said. "He belongs to Doubleday, too."

"How do ya know," Bath asked loudly, attempting to be heard over the gunfire.

Arlis spun his head wildly toward Bath and yelled angrily, "Because I pay attention, Bath. Open your eyes and shut your mouth now!"

Dawes turned and passed the order down the chain of command. Captain Ticknor, now the commander of Company K, passed it to his men.

"On your feet, men!"

July 1st, 1863 had dawned cloudy and rainy, just as it had for much of the march northward. The boys of the Sixth had cof-

234 | ERIC SCHLEHLEIN

fee and hardtack for breakfast, and had rushed through their morning routines in order to get back on the march. Rumors had passed through the ranks that a cavalry unit had engaged the Rebels a few miles north, and were in a desperate attempt to hold the high ground. After another Union debacle in May, (this time at Chancellorsville, Virginia), General Robert E. Lee had again taken his army north through Maryland, to invade the lush and fertile farmland of Southern Pennsylvania. The Army of the Potomac had pursued, but they always seemed to be a day's march behind the Confederates. The boys of the Sixth had left their encampment at South Mountain in great haste on the 28th of June to march northward in chase of the Rebels, stopping to camp in Frederick. Here, the men were informed that General Meade had replaced General Hooker as Commander of the Army of the Potomac. Come morning, they were on the march again, halting to camp in Emmitsburg, Maryland. Drizzle had fallen constantly since they'd left South Mountain, dampening the mood for much of the march. Last night they'd camped on the south side of Marsh Creek, signing the muster to receive their pay in the process.

Here, Dawes had read General Meade's address to the troops. Arlis had barely paid attention, the words seeming to be more bluster from another arrogant general, a man who was far from the reach of the enlisted men. Arlis didn't even know what Meade looked like, let alone what his competence level would turn out to be. He was utterly sick of generals, their boasts, their maneuvers, their blunders, and their miscalculations that resulted in fatal consequences for those under their command. First came McClellan, then Pope, then McClellan again, Burnside, Hooker, and now Meade. To Arlis, they were all the same: Bumbling fools.

Yesterday, as the boys of the Sixth made their way northward from Emmitsburg, they'd held the advance position of the entire army, and had been the very first to cross the Mason-Dixon Line into Pennsylvania. Civilians young and old had come out to greet them, offering milk and whiskey, bread and meat, water and wine. Boys and girls had welcomed them with tremendous enthusiasm, marching alongside the Wisconsinites and watching the movements of the advance guard and flankers. This morning, after receiving orders to pack up and be ready to march at the crack of dawn, the march had begun with more of the same. Once again, farmers offered the boys what they could, voicing their relief that they were able to give their produce to the boys in blue rather than having it taken by the boys in gray. Today, however, the Sixth was last in the order of march for the Iron Brigade, taking up position behind the four other regiments.

The drizzle had stopped and the sun came out, occasionally hiding behind the stratocumulus clouds that would remain in the sky for the rest of the day. The morning temperatures were cooler than normal, making the march more bearable than the others of late. The trees were still and the wind non-existent. The regimental band, arguably the worst of its type in the entire army, kept the cadence by playing "The Village Quickstep," and "Rory O'Moore." After the band had gone silent, the boys of Company K passed the time by singing:

On the distant prairie where the heifer wild,
stole into the cabbage in the midnight mild.
Everyone that knew her said she was a thief
and should be killed and quartered and issued out for beef.
On the distant prairie, hoop de dooden do
On the distant prairie, hoop de dooden do...

Spirits were high. Arlis found it a bit odd to see the company's morale at such a high level with a battle looming so closely, but he knew it had a lot more to do with the lush, beautiful landscape and the weather becoming brighter than with impending combat. The last time the Rebels ventured north, it had resulted in Antietam, the bloodiest battle of the war. Arlis knew that a severe fight was inevitable, as the Rebels had to be thrown back across the Potomac.

They marched northward, passing through rolling hills of rich farmland, where the wheat fields reflected the sunlight toward the sky in waves of gold and amber. They were all taken with the beauty of the land, which remained untouched by war, innocent and angelic in sharp contrast to the barren desert that was now Northern Virginia. They passed cornfields, apple orchards, peach orchards, and abundant gardens containing vegetables of every type. The idea of the Rebels raiding these farms made Arlis' ears burn with anger.

Now, rumors were passed through the ranks as truth. Robert E. Lee was dead, and Longstreet was now in command. The Rebels had taken Harrisburg and were holding the governor for ransom. Lincoln had fired General Meade, who'd only served as the commander for three days, and had replaced him with McClellan. This last one drew a mighty hurrah from the boys of the regiment, most of whom had always loved "Little Mac."

"Army bullshit," Bath said to Arlis, who grinned.

Someone in the company began a chant calling for the company commander, Captain Ticknor, to sing. He was by far the best singer in the company (and perhaps in the whole regiment), since Captain Edwin Brown of Company E had been killed at Antietam. After maybe a half a minute of cajoling, the captain complied, and soon the lyrics of "Benny Havens O" could be heard, resonant and soothing, coming from Ticknor, his voice mellifluous and dulcet. Four verses later, the boys were hushed and mellowed, remaining in this condition long after the captain went quiet. Now, each man was hidden inside his own mind, thinking, praying, longing, missing, planning, or worrying.

Cannon fire could be heard coming from ahead now. Although some claimed it was coming from the right and others from the left, all agreed that it was cannon fire. Arlis, realizing the time had come, turned to Hugh Talty on his left.

"Hold my musket for a minute please, Tall-T?"

"Alright then," Talty said, taking the weapon, asking no questions.

Arlis took his pack off, opened it, and pulled out the 1860 model Colt revolver he'd found while the brigade was covering the retreat of the army at Chancellorsville. He'd been on the march when he'd stepped on the weapon as it lay in the underbrush, flawless and pristine. It had still been fully loaded. Last week, while camped at South Mountain, Captain Ticknor had walked by as Arlis was inspecting the gun. Arlis had snapped to attention.

"At ease, Sergeant Jenkins," he'd said. "That's a fine revolver. It's exactly like mine." He pulled his own revolver from his holster and handed it to Arlis. Arlis held the guns alongside one another. Pointing to the one Arlis had found, Ticknor said, "Where'd you get it?"

Arlis told him, but added, "The caps were wet when I came across it. It won't fire."

"Oh?" Ticknor said, "That's no problem. I'll get you plenty of 'em. Balls too. You just make sure I'm the highest ranking man that sees you with that weapon, Jenkins. Officers get nervous when enlisted men have loaded revolvers."

"Yes, sir."

Ticknor had been true to his word, returning from the quartermaster with enough cartridges and caps to kill a whole company. Arlis had loaded the weapon with cartridges that very day. The gun holds six rounds, each in its own chamber. Arlis had held off on placing the percussion caps onto the raised apertures located at the back of the chambers until now, so the gun wouldn't accidentally discharge while he was on the march or in camp.

Now, as Talty held his musket, Arlis carefully placed a cap on each of the cones of the aperture. Then, with the hammer resting on one of the safety pins between two live chambers to prevent the gun from firing, he shoved the weapon into his belt at the front of his pants and then reclaimed his musket from Talty.

"Thanks," he said.

Ahead, Dawes ordered the national colors to be unfurled. The drum major, R.N. Smith, had begun to play "The Campbells are Coming," and soon the regimental band joined in. The regiment marched on, passing ordinary buildings that would become landmarks simply because they lay on the route taken by these boys on this very day. The landmarks included buildings such as the Snyder House, the Rose Farm, the Wentz House, and the Sherfy Farm. Reaching a farm with the name "Codori" written upon a shingle, they left the Emmitsburg Road, turning left and crossing through fields of prairie grass and wildflowers. Without haste, the men moved northwesterly toward a building in the distance that sported a round cupola. Prominent and conspicuous, the cupola was a fleeting image, disappearing and then reappearing as the elevation of the terrain rose and declined.

The town of Gettysburg was visible now as they advanced through farmland, passing close to a house where a man and his daughter had knocked down their own fences, allowing for easier passage through the terrain.

"Boys," yelled Talty, "We ain't in Virginia anymore, be gob!"

Passing a patch of short sweet grass, Arlis watched as a number of robins, perhaps a dozen of them, hopped and hunted earthworms, the scene reminding him of how his mother and he used to compete at finding the first robin of the spring.

His stomach tightened at the thought of his mother and the impossibility of any such competition ever occurring again. He felt anger at her unwillingness to live for him, even if only so that at this instant he could long to be with her, to run to her, to be swallowed up by the safety that her arms would offer, his head in her lap, her fingers running through his hair. Her death had cheated him even of this fantasy. As it always did, the anger turned to sorrow, and he turned his head to watch the robins eat until he could see them no more. At this moment, he envied the birds and their free will, their ability to fly away in any direction as soon as the shooting started.

The cannon fire, although intermittent, increased in volume now, and soon the order was passed down to form lines and to prepare for action.

"By companies into line!" Dawes yelled, "Forward into line! By Companies, left half wheel, double quick, march!" The men moved with all the precision and skill that two years of hard drilling had produced. Quickly, they formed the battle lines as ordered, ready to advance to a position on the left flank of the 24th Michigan.

Then the order to halt came down, followed by the order to lie down and wait in reserve. The men of the Sixth watched the rest of the brigade run into the wooded lot to their front as gunfire erupted along the entire line.

"Sergeant Jenkins!" It was Bath. Arlis ignored him, waiting for the order from Ticknor. Having just been ordered to stand up and face to the right, the company stood in column, facing north, with the rest of the brigade in furious combat in the woods on their left flank. Their time in reserve had been short, lasting no more than a couple of minutes.

"Sergeant!" Bath yelled again.

Arlis, impatient and irritated, rolled his eyes over to the

private, who stood to his immediate right. "What do you need, Tubber?"

"I lied about my age, Sergeant." Arlis watched as Bath's Adam's apple raised and lowered as he swallowed multiple times. "I'm just now sixteen."

"Why are you telling me now?" Arlis said, his eyes to the front again. "Are you trying to get out of this fight?"

"No, Sergeant. Uh, no. I just…I think God might be angry with me. I just thought I best come clean before we go into battle."

Arlis looked at Bath again, who actually appeared younger now that he'd made the confession. "Tubber, God knows your real age and I don't care how old you are as long as you do your duty." He flashed a smile at the boy. "The Rebels on the other hand…well, they might not be so forgiving."

Bath laughed nervously.

"Just stick with me, Tubber," Arlis said, patting the boy on the shoulder. "We'll get through this together."

The order came. The regiment was to advance at the double quick northward, moving from left to right behind the rest of the brigade. They moved quickly and methodically as the battle on their left continued. After moving northward for a hundred yards or so, they were ordered to "file right…march!" and they turned east, moving into a battle line that was perpendicular to the rest of the brigade's line. Facing north again, Arlis could see the guns of a union battery driving to the rear, with the men of Cutler's Brigade in full retreat, moving to the east.

Directly in front of the regiment, a stone's throw away, was a road situated between two rail fences, lying parallel to the battle line of the regiment. Many years later, Arlis would learn that this road was the Chambersburg Pike, but no one in the regiment had knowledge of this now. The men of Cutler's Brigade continued to retreat from left to right across the Sixth's field of vision, well on the other side of the pike.

Arlis suddenly realized what was happening, and understood why the regiment had been ordered to move to this location. The extreme right flank of the line had been overwhelmed, putting the entire corps in danger of being flanked and collapsing. The sixth was sent here to stop the collapse of the right flank and to check the Rebel advance.

We're one damn regiment, Arlis thought. *One damn regiment is supposed to save Cutler's entire brigade?*

Some of the Rebels were aware of the Wisconsinites on their flank and turned south, firing into the Sixth's line. Dawes, on horseback, moved out in front of the color guard, in full view of the entire regiment. Suddenly, his horse reared and plunged, sending the lieutenant colonel sprawling to the ground. Dawes immediately rose to his feet, raising his hands above his head in a gesture to the men, giving them the clear message that he wasn't shot.

"I'm alright, boys!" Dawes shouted. The regiment gave a mighty cheer, and then the horse was up too, bleeding from a bullet wound in her breast. She removed herself to the rear of the line, the men parting in haste to allow her through.

Dawes, on foot now, ordered the regiment to move to the first fence, south of the pike, and halt. Ahead, the Rebels were chasing and firing on the men of Cutler's Brigade, who were in full flight. Dawes ordered the regiment to fire into the flank of the advancing Rebels. The devastating fire from the flank checked the Rebel advance. The Rebels, unsure what to do, stopped in their tracks before reversing direction, then moved directly away from the Sixth and disappeared into a ravine.

"Looks like the ground just opened and swallowed 'em up," said Bath.

Arlis thought they'd jumped into a creek or a small river, but looking to his right, he saw the ditch continue for quite a distance and recognized it as a railroad cut, very much like the one he'd seen laid through Mineral Point years ago. The

Rebels raised their heads up and fired a volley, and some of the men fell as Dawes ordered the regiment to climb over both fences and advance.

Arlis, his musket reloaded, climbed the first fence and crossed the road to the second. There, he waited for Bath, Butterfield, and Talty, and he watched as Mickey was fussing over his musket, which apparently wouldn't fire. Mickey was yelling something to Adjutant Brooks who, finding a musket on the ground, gave it to Mickey, who then returned to the line and climbed the fence alongside the others.

The Rebels were firing at will now from the cut, creating gaps in the lines of the Sixth as the men struggled to reform on the north side of the second fence. Arlis watched as Captain Ticknor silently made his way back across the road, a bullet in his chest. The color was rapidly draining from his face. He collapsed as he reached the fence, never to move again.

"Quickly boys!" Arlis yelled to those around him. "Form up, quickly!"

Dawes ordered another volley, and the men obeyed, firing by company at the Rebels in the cut. Reloading, Arlis thought back on last summer's battle outside Gainesville on the Brawner Farm, where they had stood in line and exchanged gunfire with the Rebels for nearly an hour, neither side gaining nor losing ground, but both sides losing men. Now, even as his regiment had the high ground, the downward slope of a few degrees leading to the cut about 175 paces away, Arlis recognized that the Sixth was at a serious disadvantage. The Rebels in the cut had a significant defilade, allowing them to fire and reload under cover. If the Rebels fired only a few organized volleys from their position it might mean the destruction of the entire regiment.

Arlis rammed the ball into his musket and then returned the ramrod to the notch underneath the barrel. He looked behind the line to his left, searching for Dawes. He was hoping that Dawes would see the gravity of the situation. He was certain that if Colonel Bragg were here, they'd charge the cut.

He saw Dawes now. He was in the road on the far side of the regiment, talking with an officer that Arlis didn't know. Suddenly, both officers drew their swords and Arlis felt relief, knowing that the order would come soon. Anticipating the order, Arlis found his bayonet and pulled it from its scabbard. The order came.

"BAYONETS!" the officers ordered, one by one, down the entire line. The men attached the weapons to their muskets obediently.

"Charge, bayonets!" The officers yelled, causing the men to lower their muskets to their hips and let out a boisterous "Huzzah!"

The order to charge came down, the men of the color guard and those companies adjacent to it stepping off first. A slight delay between each company's advance came naturally, and because of this, the entire regiment charged in a giant "V" formation, the color guard at the point, with Dawes among them, and the brigade guard on the flanks.

Arlis ran, watching Bath in his periphery as he did so. The boy was next to him, charging with the rest of the company, and Arlis shifted his thoughts to his own legs, which were weak with fear and the realization that he might be hit at any moment. He had to will his legs to move because with each step forward they seemed to want to seize up. He felt the terror manifesting as a knot in his stomach. It rose rapidly, settling into his throat. Now, he felt as he always had when he was being shot at, like he'd swallowed a whole apple and had it lodged in the back of his throat. He felt the dryness in his mouth and lips and he licked them now, surprised by the coarseness of his tongue. The sweat beaded on his brow, his body in revolt against the madness of this charge, his subconscious perhaps showing more sense than his conscious self ever could. Aware of his fear, he remembered how he'd previously gritted his teeth while in combat, the results of which caused him pain for nearly a day afterward in his gums and teeth. He unclenched his jaws now, happy to have caught himself in the act and hoping that, if he survived the day, he'd be able to experience a pain-free sleep.

As the Rebels continued to pop their heads up and fire he fought the urge to return it, knowing that he had little chance of hitting a Rebel while on the run. Around him, and all down the line, men were falling and struggling to the rear, clutching wounds.

"Align on the colors!" Dawes yelled, "Close up on the colors!" He was repeating this order continuously. As holes opened in the line due to men falling out, the men to the right of the color guard moved left to fill the gaps, and those to the left of the color guard moved to the right.

Arlis ran on. Looking to his left, he saw that Talty was no longer there. He moved that way, filling the gap, and found himself running alongside a man he didn't know—a Company B man—who was abruptly hit and fell into Arlis, knocking him sideways as if he was attempting to tackle him. Arlis, staying on his feet, pushed the man off and ran on, stumbling as he attempted to control his footing in the shin-high prairie grass and uneven terrain. He was now directly behind Bath, trailing the recruit by about four steps, when suddenly the back of the boy's head exploded as a ball exited just above the base of his neck, showering Arlis' face with blood, bone, and brain matter.

"Jesus Christ!" Arlis yelled, spitting Bath's blood and tissue out of his mouth. He was horrified and repulsed, feeling like a hooked fish, as he slowed slightly to spit repeatedly. He stepped on the sprawled corpse of Private Bath, planting his foot firmly in the small of the dead boy's back. The guilt of this accidental step rose in his gut with the revulsion from the blood in his mouth. Although he knew he wasn't hit, he was blind in his right eye, which had received most of the splatter from Bath's terrible wound. He franticly wiped his eye with his hand, restoring his vision to a blurred murk.

"Align on the colors! Close up on the colors," Dawes screeched.

Arlis continued to run at a slower pace, the rest of the company ahead of him now. *There's something they don't put in the textbooks,* he thought, feeling a deranged laugh rise in his throat. *Always shut your mouth while on a charge, lest you get the blood of the man in front of you poured down your throat.* He was nauseous, the taste of Bath's blood on his tongue. He wiped his tongue repeatedly on his blouse. Blinking furiously, he cleansed his eye well enough to see clearly, and realized that he was just now a little more than halfway to the railroad cut.

He increased his speed to a sprint, dodging the dead and wounded as he ran by them. Being behind the charging company allowed him to see the carnage in a way that most couldn't, and he realized that only about half of Company K was going to make it to the cut. He tried to put this thought out of his head, instead concentrating on his footwork, being sure not to step on or collide with any of the wounded men. He passed Eugene Rose, who was attempting to stop the bleeding in a leg wound, and Chauncey Wilcox, who had a hole in his bicep. He hurdled over Billy Hancock, who was bleeding profusely from a chest wound.

"Close up on the colors!" creaked Dawes, his voice damaged from the constant yelling.

Arlis was amazed that Dawes was still on his feet, being among those in the color guard, who were always the most luscious targets of the enemy. He ran on, gaining on his own company, which continued to move ahead and left, filling the gaps as those around them fell.

The first men of the regiment reached the cut now and the

gunfire of both sides increased, the men firing point blank into each other's lines. Arlis watched as many of those in companies E and B reached the cut only to receive a hailstorm of buck and ball, falling away before getting off a shot. Now, as his own company approached the cut, he noticed some of the men dropping to one knee as soon as they reached the edge, causing the Rebels to fire over their heads. Arlis adopted that strategy for himself, and as he reached the edge and dropped to a knee, he was surprised that none of the Rebels in front of him fired, as many had already discharged their muskets and were in the process of reloading.

The cut, about six feet deep and nearly fifteen feet in width at the spot in front of Arlis, was sheltering hundreds of Rebels, of which maybe ten or twelve posed an immediate threat to Arlis. He was looking down the sight of his musket, moving the barrel from one man to the next, looking for the target that posed the greatest actual hazard, still amazed that none of these men had fired at him.

To the left, beyond the Sixth's colors, the gunfire increased again. Arlis chanced a quick glance in that direction, revealing a fight for the colors of the Rebel regiment going on just mere yards away. To the right of Arlis more gunfire erupted, and it was suddenly apparent that a number of Wisconsinites had entered the cut on the flank of the Rebels and were pouring fire directly into their ranks.

Shouts of "Throw down your muskets, put down your muskets," came from all down the line, the men of the Sixth imploring the Rebels to give up rather than be shot down like pigs in the cut. Arlis joined in the chorus, and soon, one by one, the Rebs were dropping their weapons.

Abruptly, a group of the Rebels to the right of Arlis broke and attempted to climb the other side, and more gunfire erupted. Some made it out of the cut and turned, pouring their fire into the Federal line on the other side. Arlis watched as Mickey jumped into the cut, maybe fifteen feet to the right of him, and threw a sword at a fleeing Rebel, before going down in a heap with a bullet in his shoulder. Arlis turned his musket on the Rebels that had climbed out, aimed at one and fired, and then he dropped the musket and pulled the Colt from his belt, cocking the hammer, and pointed it toward the men in front of him. One of them, a young boy with a square face and a wide, sunburned nose, held his musket at the ready, anger and disdain on his face, his butternut jacket in tatters on his dirty body. Arlis shot him in the face.

"Anyone else want one?" Arlis screamed. "I've got five more if you want 'em. Just hang onto those guns of yours and you'll earn one!"

The man directly in front of him, a sergeant, dropped his musket and raised his hands. In a deep, southern drawl, he said to the men around him, "Put 'em down, fellers." The muskets dropped.

Then, from the left, the distinct, cracking voice of Dawes, "Where is the colonel of this regiment?"

From the cut, not far from Dawes' location, came, "Here I am…who are you?"

Dawes jumped into the cut and pushed several startled Rebels out of his way, many of which were still armed. Arlis held his breath in fear for his commander's safety. He was surprised not only at the audacity of the lieutenant colonel, but also by his own proximity to him, which meant that the regiment had lost a great amount of men in the charge.

"I command this regiment," Dawes said, approaching the opposing commander, "Surrender or I will fire." The Rebel commander was a major. He said nothing, but promptly handed his sword to Dawes. Now the Rebel muskets were tossed down in droves, the officers handing over their swords and revolvers to the officers of the Sixth. To the left, a fierce fight was still going on for possession of the colors of the

Rebel regiment, which turned out to be the Second Mississippi. Thirty seconds later, the Rebel flag was in possession of a Company I man, Frank Wallar, and all firing ceased on the line. No more than twenty minutes had passed since the regiment had been ordered to lie down in the field.

Behind the Sixth and to the left, it became obvious that the rest of the Iron Brigade had driven off the Rebels in the woods, as the firing there had become sporadic and rare. To the immediate left of the Sixth, the 14th Brooklyn and 95th New York continued to mop up remnants of the railroad cut survivors, many of whom had attempted to escape out of the western end of the cut. Sporadic firing could be heard for a short time, then ceased altogether.

Dawes ordered Major Hauser and a detachment of men to march the prisoners to the provost guard. Lieutenant Goltermann volunteered his Company F (or what was left of them anyway) to deploy as skirmishers, north and west of the regiment's current position. Arlis found Mickey on the opposite side of the cut drinking milk from a canteen, a gift he'd received from a Dutch farmer earlier in the day. Mickey was staring at the body of Sergeant Albert Tarbox, lying supine on the ground next to him, a wound in his chest, the eyes open and vacant. Arlis sat down near the head of Tarbox and found his own canteen. He rinsed the blood out of his mouth and spat on the ground, away from the fallen man. Then, he drank.

"I took a ball in the shoulder," Mickey said, his eyes glued to the dead sergeant. "He came up next to me and said, 'They've got ya down, Mickey, have they?' and then he fell on his face, stone dead. I turned him over." He drank from the canteen. Arlis leaned over and closed Tarbox's eyes with a bloody hand.

A cavalry detachment rode up to help with the prisoners, and suddenly the division's commander, General Wadsworth, was ten feet away, mounted on a beautiful black horse. Arlis and Mickey rose and stood at attention, Mickey's boot filling with his own blood.

"My man," Wadsworth said, pointing to Mickey, "You are too badly hurt to be here." He signaled to a cavalry sergeant, who rode over. "Take this man into town. The courthouse is set up as a field hospital. Follow the road into Gettysburg."

"Yes, sir," the man said, holding out an arm for Mickey. Arlis pushed Mickey up on the horse, behind the cavalryman, and the two of them rode off to the east, toward the town. Arlis was aware that Wadsworth was staring at him.

"Sir!" he said, going to attention again.

"At ease, Sergeant. You're going to need to have that wound in your face sewn up, soldier."

"No, sir," replied Arlis, "The blood's not mine, sir."

Wadsworth turned his horse 180 degrees, then whirled his head around and glared hard at Arlis. "What's your name, Sergeant?"

"Jenkins, sir. Sixth Wisconsin."

"Well, Sergeant Jenkins, the Rebs have carved their own version of that railroad cut," he paused, pointing into the ravine, "into the side of your face. You're wounded, son. Now I'm ordering you to get into town and have your face looked at by a surgeon. I'll tell Colonel Dawes where you've gone."

"Yes, sir," Arlis said, and Wadsworth rode off. He put his fingers to his face and felt the groove, hot and wet, beginning just under his right eye and tracking to the middle of his ear, his tragus shot away. He felt his cheekbone, exposed just under the eye, and he was shocked that he had had no inkling of when this had happened. He wiped his cheek with the back of his hand, swiping downward to his neck, realizing that he had bled at a pretty good clip. He'd assumed that the fluid he'd felt seeping into his collar had been sweat, or possibly Bath's blood, which he could still taste in his mouth. With the realization that he was shot, the pain came sharp and intense, like someone was holding a hot poker to his cheek.

He made his way east, in the direction of the town, walking along the northern ridge of the railroad cut. He stopped briefly, thinking he should see if someone else might be in need of his help, but after gazing upon the carnage around him he thought differently. There were so very many that required help. He continued eastward toward the town of Gettysburg.

Up ahead, he could see the cliffs of the cut flatten slightly, the ridges appearing less intense and allowing him an easier opportunity to cross the cut. The brush here was thicker, the prairie grass augmented by sporadic appearances of pigweed, nettles, primrose, and sweet white violets. Carrying his black hat in his hand, he passed a number of dead Rebels. Crossing the cut, he saw a few Rebels on the other side that had been killed in the Sixth's initial volley, when the Rebels were still pursuing the men of Cutler's Brigade. Those from Cutler's Brigade lay scattered among them, having been shot down while in retreat, the wounds in their backs exposed as they lay prone on the ground.

He continued to walk alongside the cut with the ridge ten feet from his path, as it offered less resistance than the tall growth to his right. Now, approaching the high water mark of the Rebel advance, he became wary of a Rebel lying on his back to his left, near the edge of the cut. The Rebel, who was round in the belly and seemingly unhurt, appeared to Arlis as if only asleep, a hand still firmly gripping the musket that lay across his chest. Arlis pulled the pistol from his belt and held it at his side, glaring at the Rebel as he made his way past. The Rebel didn't move.

From Arlis' right came one low, harsh word: "Yank!" It was gruff and forced, sounding as if it had been spoken through liquid. Arlis whirled and cocked the hammer, sure that he'd be shot at any moment. He saw no one. He whirled around again, looking at the Rebel with the round belly, who still lay as if asleep. Turning in the direction from which the voice had come, Arlis advanced cautiously toward a patch of waist-high joe-pye weed. A hand slowly moved skyward from the brush. Arlis approached guardedly.

A stocky Rebel with an elongated head, hawk's nose, and a full, foot-long beard the color of sandalwood lay severely wounded in the brush. Blood trickled from the corners of his mouth. He wore a ragged waist-length gray coat that lay open, bearing no rank or insignia. The homespun shirt underneath his coat was pulled up to his chest, revealing multiple wounds in the man's abdomen. Initially, Arlis thought that someone else had opened the man's coat to rob him of valuables or baubles, but the multiple wounds made it obvious that the man had rifled through his own clothing in a desperate search for where he had been hit. The Rebel's smoothbore musket lay unloaded nearby, just out of the man's reach. His left leg lay fully extended, the knee of his trousers torn out, the foot bare, calloused, and dirty. His right leg lay underneath him, the foot pinned beneath the man's backside. It was this sight more than the gruesome wounds in the man's gut which most alarmed Arlis, the position obviously uncomfortable even under the best of circumstances. Standing over the badly wounded Rebel, Arlis put his hat on his head and, having gently placed the hammer against the firing pin again, tucked the revolver in his belt. The Rebel's eyes widened as he gaped at the black hat, recognition coming over his face.

"Black—" the Rebel said, forcing the word through as blood pooled in his airway. "Iron—" he tried again, pointing at Arlis' hat, the word garbled and moist, one syllable in the Mississippi accent. He lowered his shaking, pointed finger, aiming it at the Colt in Arlis' belt, and said, "Mercy," the word strained and guttural. He erupted into a coughing fit, blood and spittle spraying from his mouth onto Arlis' trousers.

His airway clear of blood for the moment, the Rebel swallowed and looked Arlis in the eyes. "Blessed are the merciful: for they shall obtain mercy," he said, quoting the Bible.

Arlis knelt down and lifted the man's right hip slightly, pulling the trapped foot from beneath him. Straightening the man's leg into a position of comfort, he said, "Matthew: Five, seven."

"Kill me, Yank," the Rebel said, blood filling his airway again. "Please!"

Arlis looked into the man's eyes, the dark brown irises silently pleading, the pupil's pinpoints in the bright sunlight. Large bags had formed under the man's eyes from months—perhaps years—of stress and sleep deprivation. The face was turning gray, matching the man's uniform in color. Arlis rose to his feet and sat down above the wounded man's head. Reaching beneath the shoulders, he pushed the Rebel up into an awkward three-quarter sitting position and propped the man's head upon his own chest, causing the Rebel to grimace and groan with the movement. He could smell the man's sweat, the odor dank and sweet, intermixed with blood and the effects of a ruptured, exposed bowel. He found the Rebel's canteen, opened it, and poured a little of the water into the man's mouth. The Reb drank, swallowing loudly, the liquid gurgling as it reached the man's abdomen, where it exited the body through one of the wounds, bubbling up as if coming from a spring. Arlis rolled his eyes skyward in a silent protest as the tears came. From his lips came a soft whimper. He closed his eyes.

"More," the Rebel said, and Arlis complied, the results being the same.

Arlis, sobbing now, quoted from the book of Revelation: "And God shall wipe away all tears from their eyes; and there shall be no more death, neither sorrow, nor crying, neither shall there be any more pain, for the former things are passed away."

He gave the Rebel another drink and then scooted backward, gently lowering the man's head to the ground. The Rebel, shaking from weakness and pain, struggled to breathe, swallowing uncontrollably. Arlis pulled the Colt revolver from his belt and rotated the chambers, ensuring that the hammer was in place over a live cylinder. Then, placing the weapon on the Rebel's chest, he found the man's hand and placed it in the firing position on the gun, cocking the hammer.

Arlis looked into the man's eyes, finding them alive with fear but dull with pain. "Second Corinthians reads," he said, the words forced passed hard sobs, "'we are confident, I say, and willing rather to be absent from the body, and to be present with the Lord.'" He squeezed the Rebel's hand firmly, forced a soft smile, and said, "I shall see you in Valhalla, my brother." Then he stood and walked in the direction of the town, not looking back. He counted his steps. When he reached nine, he heard the shot.

29 Gettysburg, Pennsylvania
July 1, 1863
Afternoon

HE FOUND THE COURTHOUSE BUZZING WITH THE ACTIVITY of surgeons taking limbs, stitching wounds, and saving lives. The civilians of Gettysburg had shown him the way, each of them offering their assistance, food, water, whiskey, affection, and thanks. Doctor John Hall, the bearded, wide-jowled surgeon of the Sixth Wisconsin, was in front of the building, triaging the wounded and sending the most serious cases to Doctor Bartlett, who was putting the bone saw to use in the makeshift hospital. As Arlis approached, Doctor Hall turned and assessed the damage, mistaking the blood of Bath and the dying Rebel as Arlis'. "Where are you wounded, Sergeant?" Hall said frantically, nearly tearing the coat off of Arlis. Finding no wounds under the woolen shirt and having received no response from Arlis, he stepped back, his eyes scanning, searching. He said, "How bad is it?"

Arlis, his mind clouded and distant, simply said, "It's not mine."

Hall scowled and took Arlis by the arms. Half helping and half tripping him, he lowered Arlis to the ground at the base of the steps. There, he rapidly assessed Arlis for wounds, going so far as to remove the shirt completely.

"It's just your face, then?" Hall asked, holding Arlis by the chin and looking into the wound.

Arlis moved his eyes to the doctor and, staring at the man's long slender nose, he simply nodded.

"We'll get ya stitched up soon enough," Hall said. "You can do yourself some good by finding some water and cleaning that wound."

Arlis moved his gaze from Hall's nose to his eyes. He said nothing.

Gripping Arlis' chin harder, Hall shook his face and said, "You listening to me, Sergeant?"

Arlis frowned, irritated by the movement that so abruptly forced him into clarity.

"Yes, sir. I'm listening," he said, his voice low, the tone indignant. "I'll clean it up."

"Good. Find a well behind one of these buildings," Hall said. Pointing to a bucket on the top step near the entrance of the courthouse, he said, "Take that bucket and dump it out, then refill it for me."

"Yes, sir," Arlis said. Without wasting another moment, Hall was gone, moving on to the next wounded soldier.

Arlis put his hat on, leaving his shirt and coat where they

lay. He lingered a moment, then climbed the five steps to the door of the courthouse and retrieved the wooden bucket. It was filled halfway with water that had been thickened and reddened by the blood of the wounded. Instantly, Arlis knew why Dr. Hall had asked for a refill. He descended the stairs again and turned left, passing the well-manicured shrubbery that lined the front of the courthouse. He passed two soldiers from the 19th Indiana Regiment, one helping the other to the steps of the courthouse, both nodding to Arlis in recognition of his black hat. Arlis didn't notice. Turning left again at the corner of the square building, he dumped the contents of the bucket, watching as the bloody mess foamed and bubbled in the dirt. Suddenly his stomach rose, causing him to turn and retch, his knees weakening to the point of giving out. He knelt and allowed the contents of his stomach to come up. He heaved four times, all that was required for purging the un-digested water in his system, the morning's breakfast having been digested on the march hours before.

Finished, he sat down with his back against the wall of the courthouse. He felt the exhaustion of the morning's combat hit him; his mind was fogged, hands numb, legs aching, feet sore. He was terribly thirsty. He found his canteen and drank down the last two or three swallows, but they were not nearly enough. He thought about getting up and going to the well as the doctor had asked him to do, but his fatigue transformed any motivation for doing so into apathy.

In the street, the walking wounded found their way to the courthouse, some with comrades acting as crutches, others with civilians tagging along, ensuring the men found the sur-geons before collapsing. Arlis watched them come one by one, each sporting wounds of varying degrees. Many of them were easily recognized as belonging to the Iron Brigade by the hats on their heads.

Now, in a voice that was boisterous and unmistakably Irish,

the lyrics to "The Battle Hymn of the Republic," albeit slightly modified, came bellowing down the street.

"In the beauty o' the lilies Hugh was born across the sea, with a glory in his bosom that'll surely fuck ya, see. As ya die 'cause yer a Rebel, I won't die 'cause I'm Talty, be 'gob, I'm marchin' on."

Arlis grinned. *Talty!* He struggled to stand, keeping a hand against the building for balance and watched the street, waiting for Talty to come into view.

"Glory, glory, hallelujah!" Talty shouted. "Glory, glory, Talty's comin'! Glory, glory, Talty shot ya, blew yer arse inta Hell, be gob!"

Talty rounded the corner. Seeing Arlis standing against the building, he halted, a dark glass bottle in his hand. He stood motionless, squinting at Arlis.

"Tall-T," Arlis exclaimed, pushing off the wall and walking toward the private.

"I'll be damned, Badger! How ya be?" Talty said, grinning.

"Ace high, Talty... Ace high."

Talty raised the bottle in a toast. "Here's to a live Lemonweir Minuteman," he brayed, and then tipped the bottle up, drawing a long drink. He swallowed and wiped his mouth with the back of his hand. Staggering slightly, he walked up and embraced Arlis, who was surprised by the gesture. "I was startin' ta think I was the only one left," said Talty.

"Nah," Arlis said, "There's at least a handful, Talty." He pointed to the courthouse. "Your nephew's in there. He took one in the shoulder."

"Thanks be ta God, be gob."

Arlis studied the older man. He was coatless, the left sleeve torn from his shirt at the shoulder. His arm was bandaged just above the elbow. Arlis said, "Ya hurt bad?"

"I reckon I ain't hurt *good*. I gotta hole or two in me, but I'll live." He held the bottle up, peering at it against the sun.

"Have a drink with me, Badger. I'm buyin'. Good 'ol Irish whiskey, be gob!" His words were slurring, the effects of the whiskey already obvious. He pointed in the direction he came from. "I love this town, Badger! People jus' givin' ya shit 'cause yer wearin' a blue suit. I say we stay up here an' fight the rest o' the war."

Arlis started to decline and changed his mind. "Sure, Talty," he said. Gesturing to where he'd been sitting, Arlis said, "Come sit with me. I might have a hunk of bacon left."

They collapsed to the ground together, Arlis from fatigue, Talty from the effects of the alcohol.

"Are you sure you aren't bleeding to death," Arlis asked, genuinely concerned.

"Nah, a Dutchman from Company F patched me up. Cost him his shirt ta do it. Mighty nice o' him. Couldn't understand a word he said." He drank and then offered the bottle to Arlis, who took a swallow.

Arlis dug through his pack and found the bacon, hard and dried like jerky. They took turns drinking from the bottle and gnawing at the hunk of bacon until both were used up.

"Helluva groove there in yer face, Badger," Talty said, smiling. "That'll scar up nicely. You'll have no problem linin' up the girls back home. Hah!"

"Yeah, I reckon not."

"Well, I think I'm drunk 'nough ta muster da courage ta see the doc, now," Talty slurred. He looked at Arlis, "Sure is good ta find ya among the livin', Badger."

"You too, Talty."

Arlis watched as Talty rose and staggered to the corner of the building, where he turned and made his way toward the entrance. He suddenly remembered the task that the doctor had given him, and found the bucket where he'd left it. He rose, dizzy from the whiskey, and grabbed the bucket, teetering as he made his way behind the courthouse to the well, where he drank and refilled his canteen. Then he rinsed the bucket before filling it with fresh water.

Turning back toward the courthouse, he felt the call of nature coming on and eyed a double-seated privy behind the building next door. Over one door, a shingle was nailed to the wood, the name "Oscar" carved into it. "Wilhelmina" was written above the other door. He made his way over there, aware of a commotion in the street, a woman screaming or crying or something, a man yelling at her to "get inside." Arlis ignored the noise, set down the bucket and his pack, and went inside the "Oscar," as his belly knotted in a cramp.

Suddenly, gunfire, and lots of it, erupted from the west. Now, a general volley, perhaps by an entire regiment, exploded, followed by the firing of cannon. More gunfire sounded, sporadic yet great in volume, the men obviously firing "at will." Arlis had difficulty determining the direction of its origin as the sound bounced and echoed off the walls of the buildings.

Another large volley exploded, this one sounding like it had come from the north. From the street, more commotion, as the voices of men yelling to each other became louder, causing Arlis to abandon his efforts at using the privy. Now, he heard a woman imploring someone to stop running, going so far as to call that person a coward, begging him to stay and fight. Arlis felt the hair on his neck raise up, his arms covered in gooseflesh, as he knew what he'd witness as he went back outside. Without having relieved himself, he buttoned his trousers and pulled his suspenders over his shoulders.

Bursting from the privy, he grabbed his knapsack and threw his arms through the straps. He ran around the side of the building and into the street, where a great many men in blue were running toward him, not in groups, but as individuals, retreating in disorder, fear upon their faces. These were not the men of the Iron Brigade, as they wore kepis on their heads rather than the familiar black hats. Arlis watched as a line of

Union soldiers, keeping their bearing and their unity together, halted in the street a few blocks away. There, they fired a volley in the direction from which they came, only to be fired upon in return, the results of which were devastating, with nearly half of them falling where they stood. The rest broke and ran. The Rebels fired into the backs of the fleeing Federals, the mass of falling bodies causing dust to rise up from the ground like smoke.

Now, men in blue were coming at him from the north as well. Two great masses of blue were converging on each other in the street—one from the west, one from the north—as the men continued to fall back in disarray through the town. Cannon fire erupted, sending solid shot bounding directly down the narrow street, tearing apart men as they tried to escape. Arlis watched, wide eyed, as a ball went through the courthouse above his head, showering the ground with damaged brick and mortar.

"Jesus," Arlis said. He was angry, realizing that all of the morning's efforts—the taking of the cut and the capture of the Mississippians—had gone for naught. If these boys in blue didn't rally, the Rebels would win the battle and the day.

"Stop!" Arlis yelled as a soldier ran by. He grabbed the man by the sleeve of his coat.

"Get off me," the man bellowed, pushing Arlis' hands away. Arlis spun with the movement, feeling the effect of the whiskey, and fell in the street. Two more men ran by him.

More solid shot came down the street, the balls busting through the walls of nearby buildings. Arlis, his eyes wide with fear and anger, knew it was time to leave.

Getting to his knees, he pushed himself to his feet with his hands. His pack felt like a hundred pounds on his back, his knees wobbling like a calf's when attempting to stand for the first time. Arlis heard the battery firing again, and then he was airborne, spinning and corkscrewing through the air, his pack going in one direction, he in the other. He landed on his head and shoulders, the base of his neck touching down on the ground first, before he somersaulted onto his front side, his mouth filling with dirt from the street. He shut his eyes as the pain in his head detonated, a thousand points of light shooting through his brain. He fought hard to hang on, mindful of his brain's desire to fall asleep, recognizing the danger of remaining in his current position, exposed in the openness of the street. He lifted his head, trying to spit the dirt out of his mouth, the action feeble and useless. Now, he aimed to push himself to his knees, but couldn't find the strength and his elbows buckled, causing him to fall on his face again.

"Ahh," was all he mustered in an attempt to scream. He rolled to his back, attempting to see down the street, but his vision was blurred by tears, dirt, and pain. He lay his head back down in the dirt.

The battery fired again...*boom, boom, boom, boom.* Four guns firing down the street, the trajectory slightly higher as they aimed at the mass of retreating men. Arlis listened as the balls found their marks, pounding through wood, brick, mortar, and men. Through the cobwebs in his head, he held onto a fleeting thought about finding shelter, perhaps pushing with his feet to the steps of the courthouse, which lay just mere feet away. Attempting to push off with his left foot, pain hit him like a live shell in his lower leg...a hot, searing sharpness forcing his eyes to open wide and his hands to clutch at the dirt in the road.

He lifted his head and looked at his leg. It was almost completely severed below the knee, at mid-shin, the trousers torn and bloodied, the leg dangling at a right angle and hanging on by the skin on the left side. Arlis tried to scream again and whimpered, the air escaping his lips in short, rapid bursts. He stared at the mess, his head shaking violently, no longer worried about getting out of the way or fighting the sleep, and he felt his bowels move as his bladder voided, the hot liquid pooling in the dirt between his legs. Laying his head back again, he felt the rest of his strength leaving him, the bright sky dimming rapidly, the world morphing, sable, lightless. He closed his eyes and saw Violet Rhys, fourteen years old and dressed in an elaborate red calico dress, resplendent with a repeating, white maple leaf pattern. She smiled at him, and he no longer fought the slumber, the dormancy. He welcomed it.

30 Gettysburg, Pennsylvania
July 4, 1863
Morning

ARLIS AWOKE TO THE SOUND OF RAIN FALLING. HE BLINKED at the ceiling above him, trying to focus on the wood slats and the ornate pattern that bordered the room. The face of Corporal William Campbell moved into his line of sight, startling Arlis and causing him to jerk his head to the left. Pain and grogginess met him, followed by nausea. Arlis needed a moment before he could open his eyes again.

"Good morning, Sergeant," Campbell said. He was seated to the right of Arlis, on the cot in which Arlis lay. "Try and stay with me, would ya, Badger? I can't stay long."

Arlis felt like he'd been hit by a carriage. His head and neck ached, his vision was blurred and murky. His left leg was on fire; his stomach felt like it would come up at any moment.

"What the hell?" he said, though not to Campbell. He put a hand to his eyes and rubbed them, breathing deeply through his nose. The smells, a mixture of sweat, feet, blood, shit, and piss hit him hard, sending him back to the mill in Maryland. For a moment, he thought he was there.

"You've been wounded badly, Sergeant," said Campbell.

"The Rebs took your leg with a shell." His words seemed distant, nonchalant, like he was telling Arlis that the Rebels had stolen his hardtack. "You gave your head a good bounce, too, Badger. Doc's been feedin' you chloroform and morphine for two days, so what you're feeling in your head is mostly medicinal."

Arlis had hazy memories of the previous few days. Everything prior to getting hit in the street was clear in his mind, including the charge on the cut, the encounter with the gutshot Rebel, and his drinking soiree with Talty. Two days ago, he'd found out about his leg...and then found out about it again, seemingly for the first time, yesterday. Now, the memory of that discovery came back, the shock of the loss gone, but the gloominess and mortification in full effect. He made no attempt to look at the leg, knowing it would be wrapped in a bloody bandage beneath the blanket that covered him.

"Where are we?" he managed, his voice cracking from dryness. "Can I get some water?"

"Gettysburg," Corporal Campbell said. Campbell had been in Company K since its inception. Having gone to a bucket near the door, he brought a dipper of water to Arlis. He said, "It's a small town in Southern Pennsylvania."

"Yeah, I remember," Arlis said, downing the water. He scanned the room, focusing the best he could on the people and things he could see. The room was square, the cots placed within a foot or two of each other, each containing a wounded man. More wounded lay on the floor in the center of the room, packed as tightly as possible, causing Arlis to wonder how the staff got around. Arlis' cot was in the corner of the room. He looked hard at the man in the next cot. He didn't know him.

"You're in a courthouse," Campbell said, gesturing upward with his eyes. "There's been a hell of a row here, worse even than Antietam, wouldn't ya know? The Rebels held the town 'til this morning, when they seem to have just picked up and skipped town. They took one hell of a lickin' yesterday, I tell ya. Looked like Fredericksburg all over again, 'cept our side did all the killin' this time."

"The boys are still fighting?" Arlis asked.

"No. Three days' worth of fightin'," Campbell said. "It's rainin' today…and neither side is much up for a fight. When I say it's been a hell of a row, I mean it. Multiply the railroad cut by the entire army and then again by three days, Badger. There's gotta be tens of thousands of dead out there. Anyway, after we retreated through the town, when you got hit, we dug in on the high ground south of here." He pointed with a dirty index finger. "They came at us yesterday and the day before… they tried to hit the other flank too but failed, and we held on …God damn, we held on! The Rebels have taken a lickin' unlike any we've given 'em before."

Arlis tried to sit up and failed. "Gimme a hand, Campy," he said, and this time as he pushed off on the cot, Campbell grabbed him and helped him sit up. The pain in his temples throbbed with his pulse. He shut his eyes for a moment, then opened them and scanned the room.

"Where's Mickey?" Arlis said.

"Ah, he and a bunch of others left this morning for a hospital in Littlestown, seven miles distant. Any who could walk were sent there. Billy and Wallace Hancock, Hugh Talty, Chauncey Wilcox. We've got more over at the railroad depot too, Badger. Lots of our boys are over there." Arlis nodded. "How bad was the company shot up, Campy?"

Campbell's face soured. "Bad. Everson took one in the thigh and he don't look good. Temple and Crawford are wounded, they're in the corner over there." He pointed diagonally across the room. Placing a hand on Arlis' chest, he said, "Badger… Ticknor's dead, and Tarbox, too."

"Yeah, I saw Tarbox," Arlis said, grimacing. He closed his eyes and rubbed them again. "He died at the cut."

Campbell nodded and then shook his head. "Fletcher's gone, and so is Scoville. Bath is missing."

Arlis opened his eyes and froze, his gaze on the face of Campbell. "Bath is dead. He was killed in the charge."

"You sure?" Campbell said, cocking his head.

"I'm sure, Campy. They shot him in the head."

"Damn."

"Yeah."

Campbell's eyes went wide. "Badger," he said, his voice revealing revelation. "General Reynolds is dead. Sharpshooter got 'im in the head before we even charged the cut."

Arlis' mind went back to the morning of July first. "*Something must have happened to Reynolds if Doubleday is giving the orders,*" he'd said to Bath. To Campbell, he managed, "Hmm."

They fell silent. Campbell rifled through his pockets, retrieving a dirty, wrinkled piece of parchment. Then, he said, "Reports say that of the 420 men of the Sixth who charged the cut, only 240 made it across the field. Of the 33 men in Company K to make the charge, only eight are fit for duty. I'm one of 'em. First Sergeant Smith is in command of the company, as all of our officers are either killed or wounded. It's the same for the other companies, too. Nobody has any officers left, it seems. Dawes is the only field officer that is fit for duty not only in the Sixth, but in the entire brigade."

Mama's words came back to him now, and Arlis shuddered. "*Wars like this one will go on indefinitely, forever, with the fighting and the dying continuing until the last man on one side or the other is killed. What other way is there for it to end?*"

In a voice barely above a whisper, Arlis said, "Mama was right."

"Beg pardon?" Campbell said, raising his eyebrows.

"Never mind."

The corporal let it go. "Anyway, I gotta report back. Sergeant Smith sent me here to see how many of our boys are still among us." He looked toward the door. "I don't think the Rebels are gonna charge today, but if they do, I should be there to whack 'em with a broom." He chuckled. Patting Arlis on his good leg, he said, "You take care now, pard."

Campbell stood and headed for the door.

"Campy," Arlis said weakly.

Campbell turned around, waited silently.

"Today's Independence Day, isn't it?"

"Yep, it sure is, Badger."

Arlis opened his eyes and said, "Two days back I turned twenty."

Campbell, smiling, said, "Is that right? Well then, happy birthday to ya, Badger." He nodded once and walked out the door.

31 Mineral Point, Wisconsin
August 31, 1863
Morning

HE FOUND OUT ABOUT HIS FATHER'S DEATH IN A MOST unusual way. Having arrived by train to Mineral Point in the morning, Arlis decided upon visiting the graves of his mother and siblings before going home. Looking at the family plot, he found not four headstones but five. All had been carved from sandstone, the two in the back complete with the birth and death dates of his mother *and* father. The newest one read:

FATHER
THOMAS JENKINS
1821—1863

He forgot about the others, his eyes falling upon Papa's

grave, the plot still rounded slightly, the grass short and sharp like the stubble on his face.

He stared at the stone, feeling nothing but emptiness and a vague curiosity about who might have handled the funeral and placed the marker. It didn't even occur to him to wonder how his father had died. If his father was in this grave, then Arlis was the last surviving member of his family. He didn't even have any cousins. Someone unrelated, perhaps an employee of the mine, would've handled the arrangements. Arlis, thinking hard on the subject, could find no obvious names that sprang to mind. His father had distanced himself from everyone, including his own family, long before Arlis had left for the war.

Gaping at the grave, he worried that perhaps he no longer had anything to come home to, his only possessions being the clothes on his body, the wooden stump attached to his leg below the knee, and the crutch under his armpit. His knapsack had vanished after he'd been wounded in the street, and with it, all of the money left in his possession. What if all of the money, the assets, and the property were gone?

Arlis felt a pang of guilt for thinking along these lines rather than contemplating the souls of his departed family. He thought about offering a prayer but no words came. When he tried to feel the presence of his mother, his brother, or his sisters, none of them showed themselves to him. He sniffed hard and rubbed his face with his free hand, lingering for a few moments in an attempt to feel something before admitting to himself that it wasn't going to happen.

He turned and hobbled away, relying heavily on the crutch. Passing through the gate, he made his way to the street and headed for home.

32 Mineral Point, Wisconsin
August 31, 1863
Noon

ARLIS FELT SURPRISE FOR THE SECOND TIME OF THE DAY AS he stared at the sign nailed to the door of the house.

KEEP OUT
PROPERTY OF
MR. ARLIS JENKINS

John T Harris, ESQ
Front Street
Mineral Point

Arlis tried the door, found it locked, and sat down on the wooden porch. He pulled the cuff of his left pants leg, crafted baggily just for such occasions, high over his kneecap, and loosened the leather strap that secured the wooden leg to the fleshy stump.

"Front Street," he said aloud, and sniggered. The Mineral Point Cemetery nearly butted up against Front Street on the north side. He'd walked right past it on his way down Commerce Street, limping and hobbling for the two-mile walk home, only to find out he'd need to go back there to get into his own house.

He unwound the bandage that shielded the stump from the strap. Underneath, the flesh was moist and tender, oozing from the scabs and painful to the touch. He sat staring off toward the road, his hand massaging the meat below his knee for some time. He looked around the front of the property; the farm was in obvious disuse, the chicken coop sat neglected and leaning to the east in need of serious maintenance and paint. The grasses, domestic and not, were growing long and wild; they had even popped up where Arlis had never before seen vegetation grow, such as in front of the steps and along the walkway to the barn, reminding him of a similar situation on a neighboring farm years before. He rose to a standing position, the crutch under his arm, and looked around the porch at the house and the deck surrounding it. It hadn't seemed to be in such a deplorable condition when he'd gone off to Madison two summers ago. Now, barren and untenanted, the property appeared spurned and lonely, needy and inconsolable. The porch was weathered and cheerless, the uneven boards posing a tripping threat to anyone who ascended. The siding was in need of repair and a coat of stain. The windows hadn't been cleaned for more than a year, sending Arlis' mind off on thoughts of Rachel and his mother, who by this time last year were already gone. Arlis saw the house and property as mirror images of his family…lost, wanton, neglected, and dead.

He turned the bandage upside-down and inside-out and then rewrapped the stump, ensuring a dry section be lain over the raw flesh. Then, having reattached the crude, pointy, prosthetic leg, he walked across the porch and down the steps, the metal tip of the leg clicking as if he were repeatedly slapping a nickel on a table. He'd intended on going to a window and peering inside, but had now lost all stomach for such a thing. He'd grown afraid of the ghosts of the past he'd see in there, the furniture mocking him in its dustiness, the floor begging him for attention.

Using the crutch for support, Arlis made his way down the drive, his concentration on the ground before him, beginning the long walk back to Front Street.

"A horse, a horse," he bellowed, "my desolate farm for a horse!" He was in earnest.

33 Wonewoc, Wisconsin
April 26, 1864
Morning

ARLIS STOOD AT THE GATE THAT LED TO HIS NEW PROPERTY, feeling refreshed and renewed. He was galvanized with hope and purpose for the first time in as long as he could remember. Just today, he'd purchased the sixty-three acre farmstead from a man named Gamble, who'd had enough of farming and had decided to move back east to wherever it was that he'd come from. Arlis, gazing upon the rolling hills of his new land, the backside of which butted up against the Baraboo River to the west, had no intention of farming the estate. He'd bought it only to escape the growing prison that his home in Mineral Point had become.

The money had still been there. In fact, there had been more money than Arlis had ever thought possible. His father, having left his mother at the hospital in Madison, had gone home to liquidate the family's assets just as his letter had stated. He'd been patient about selling the mine. By conducting shrewd business with the help of the attorney, John Harris, he had sold the business to a group of investors from the twin cities, more than 250 miles to the northwest. The paperwork had been completed late in the evening on Christmas Eve of 1862, the principals signing the documents on a sawhorse in the dark of the moon. According to Mr. Harris, all of the individuals involved had left with smiles on their faces. Mr. Jenkins had voiced his relief for having unburdened himself of the mine, while the investors were looking forward to making a killing through selling lead to the Union war effort.

"Your father had me convinced he was looking forward to living a contented life in retirement," Harris had told Arlis, who'd sat across from him in his office last August. "Once the sale was handled, we turned to liquidating his stocks and

drawing up a new will. I never dreamed your father was planning anything other than a secure future for himself and you."

Tom Jenkins had sold nearly everything the family owned,
including the livestock, and put the cash neatly away in Washburn's Mineral Point Bank. Then, so as to raise no eyebrows
in his hometown, he'd taken a trip to Dodgeville eight miles
north, where he had his own gravestone engraved. Returning to Mineral Point, he'd set up another meeting with Mr.
Harris, this one at the lawyer's office. When Harris arrived
for the appointment, he'd discovered the gravestone propped
against the wall a few feet from the corpse of Thomas Jenkins,
who had shot himself in the head with a Dreyse 1850 Model
Needle Fire Revolver.

Tom had left everything to his son. He'd handled the end
of his own life like he'd handled the business...efficiently.
There had only been one detail that hadn't been communi-
cated to Harris: How to get in touch with Arlis. Harris didn't
know if Arlis was in the Sixth Wisconsin or the Fiftieth, and
had petitioned Madison for any records they had on the soldier. He'd still been waiting for a reply when Arlis hobbled
into his office.

At a time when there were only three millionaires in the
entire nation, twenty year old Arlis Jenkins was worth more
than half a million dollars. As a result, everybody wanted a
piece of him. Every day, seemingly, another invitation would
come asking for his appearance at this event or that event,
requests coming for him to speak to a group of veterans, children, doctors, lawyers, etc. Many would use the war and his
experiences as an excuse to open a conversation, only to get to
their real motivation later...money.

Some wanted to bathe him in pity, pouring out their sympathy, real or not, for the loss of his parents and siblings. Arlis
didn't want to talk about any of it. He spent most of the winter cooped up in the mother-in-law cabin behind the main

house, as there were far fewer memories behind those walls to haunt him.

Not all social occasions were bad. He enjoyed the flirtations of the young ladies of the town, whatever their motivations may have truly been. He had no intention of following up any such consorting, choosing to leave any further experiments in affection to his own imagination, always rejecting any real advances from those who were bold enough to do so. He was wary not only of the intentions of the females, but also of the emotions in himself. He had no intentions of caring for any-body, as all who had ever held his heart or his import had left him prematurely.

And then there was Johann Stabelfeldt, the clockmaker. Herr Stabelfeldt had apprenticed under the master clockmak-er, Vinzenz Beha of Eisenbach, Germany, before immigrating to America in 1845. Stabelfeldt met Arlis at the "Welcome Home" gathering put on by the town in Arlis' honor, and had taken a rather strange interest in his peg leg, finding it to be crude, bulky, and not nearly up to the task for which it had been designed. Not fully understanding what the German was up to, Arlis had allowed Stabelfeldt to take measurements of the prosthesis and his kneecap, moving on to his good leg, gauging the circumference of the shin and ankle, pausing to record his findings each time.

Then he measured the length of Arlis' foot, being so bold as to remove Arlis' shoe in the process, recording the num-bers on parchment as he placed his finger alongside his own cheek, mumbling calculations to himself. Arlis sat silently in discomfiture throughout the odd encounter, though he had nearly forgotten it entirely within a matter of days. It was the appearance of the quirky artisan at the door of his house almost two months later that brought the memory of their meeting back to Arlis.

"I'm zorry for ze intruzion," Stabelfeldt had said, standing on the porch. He held a small wooden crate in his arms. "If you'll excuze the impozizion, I've brought a gift for you."

Arlis had led him into the kitchen, where Stabelfeldt explained his reasons for all the fuss at their previous meeting.

"I'm not zertain, but I zink I've created an appendage zat shall eliminate much of your dizcomfort und mozt of your limp," he said, his accent heavy and representative of the Black Forest. From the crate he removed a wooden foot and placed it upon the table. Hand carved and finely sanded, it was almost completely accurate in the anatomical sense from the knob of the ankle down, with rounded ridges separated by subtle lines designed to mimic toes and the gaps between them. The arch was delicate and concave, a nearly perfect reproduction of Arlis' remaining foot in mirrored form. From the crate, the clockmaker then took a series of metal hinges and a spring, silently demonstrating to Arlis the procedure for assembly. Then Stabelfeldt removed the final piece from the crate. It was a hand-crafted replica of Arlis' lower leg, complete with the curves of the lower calf muscle and a slightly protruding shin bone. A leather strap was attached at the top for fitting the device to the knee. Pointing to the three small holes that were drilled through the bottom, the artisan quickly attached the top hinge to the shin piece and held the entire prosthesis up for viewing.

Stabelfeldt pushed his chair back and stood. Then, he tenderly walked the foot across the table, tilting the shin piece forward slightly as he did so. As he lifted and moved the top piece forward, the hinges obliged the joints to move like a real ankle, allowing the heel of the foot to drop to the table before the toes. He walked the foot across the table and then back again, and Arlis was enthralled and amazed at how real the action looked.

"Now," Stabelfeldt said, laying the prosthetic leg on the table. He looked into Arlis' eyes with a hard stare. "I have no idea if zis vill verk or not, Arliz." He stoked the pointed goatee on his chin. "I've never created anyzing like zis before und I only got ze idea after having too many glazzez of beer at your party. I zink it vill vork, az gravity iz all it requirez." He picked up the leg and began walking it back and forth upon the table again, reminding Arlis of a puppet show he'd seen as a child. "I've had no vay of tezting it vor real. Zo, let'z be careful. Let'z take it zlow. But let'z give it a go now, shall ve?"

"Yes, sir," Arlis had said, sliding the chair back to allow room for Stabelfeldt to attach the leg.

Within an hour, Arlis would be walking about his kitchen, the pain greatly reduced, pacing back and forth like an expectant father, marveling at the ingenious invention as if it were the greatest thing since the wheel.

"You should make these for a living, Mr. Stabelfeldt," Arlis had beamed, "there are thousands of men who are in need of these."

Stabelfeldt waved a boney hand at him. "I make clockz."

"Well, at least allow me to pay you for it," Arlis said. "This isn't just a wooden leg, sir…it's art…it's craftsmanship. It's wonderful!"

Again Stabelfeldt waved him off. "Nah," he said, "Conzider it my contribution to ze var effuht." He pointed at the leg. "Wiz time und uze, ze spring may vear out." He reached into a pocket and pulled out a handful of hardware, spilling it onto the table. "Hopefully, zez vill lazt you a lifetime."

Arlis, humbled and grateful by the magnanimity of the German man, had chosen to repay him through the purchase of clocks, instead. Within a month of receiving the prosthesis, he'd nearly cleaned out the clockmaker's shop, donating most of the purchases to local organizations. He gave one to each of the churches in town, most of which raffled them off in fundraising ventures. The Town Hall sported one, received in memory of Thomas Jenkins, on the wall just beyond the meeting place of the town board, where for years it would judge the decisions made there with its own political verdict, "Cuckoo, cuckoo."

Winter settled in, and the visits from well-wishers, admirers, beggars, and pseudo-friends declined to a trickle before ceasing altogether in early January as the snow piled up. Arlis, having enough firewood and food to last the winter, did nothing to clear the drive of the foot deep snow, securing his home from all but only the most eager visitors, of which there were few.

Without warning, the nightmares started. At first, he'd have one or two a week. They were impossibly mixed realities of childhood and rejection, drilling and hatred, killing and regret, parades and denial, mining and contempt, bleeding and death. By the time the snow had stopped falling and the earth began purging itself of its white blanket, he was experiencing nightmares at the rate of one or two per night, waking from each covered in sweat, often times lashing out violently at the participants in the nightmares, swinging and shouting at them as they disappeared beyond the curtain of reality. He became fearful of sleep itself, often times lying awake for hours, afraid of the phantoms and visitants that would surely come as soon as slumber took hold.

With the snow melted and the temperatures mild, the well-wishers and activists returned. So did the preachers, all hoping for the chance to save Arlis' soul. By mid-March, Arlis had had enough and began making plans to escape the only town he'd ever called home.

John Harris, Esq. was his only consort. Like his father, Arlis had lied to his lawyer about his true intentions, feigning a move to somewhere east out of political aspirations when he really had no plans other than to pull up stakes and find a quiet corner in which to hide. Knowing how people talk, he told the lawyer to draw up the paperwork that would allow him to donate the farm to the town to be used as they saw fit, winking at the man as he added some bullshit about using the good deed to gain political notoriety. Arlis felt adventurous in telling the lie, then wondered slightly why he was trying so hard to cover his trail. He'd be leaving in early May, he'd told Harris, and the town could take possession of the farm on the eighth. This was another lie, told only so that he could avoid the townspeople showing up in droves to say their goodbyes.

Now, on the 26th of April, Arlis stood on his newly purchased property in Wonewoc, Wisconsin. The parcel sat opposite the stem of a "T" intersection, with his nearly quarter mile long driveway leading to the front gate and the modest house beyond. Here, he'd decided, he'd find purpose and tranquility in caring for animals that would have no other purpose than to be cared for by him.

Arlis sniffed and looked skyward. The smell of the pines lining the river to the west was sharp and sweet in his nostrils. Above, the sky was a mixture of pewter and peach as the sun gained a foothold in poking through a thick cloud. Arlis climbed into the driver's seat of the wagon and urged the team forward through the gate to their final destination. Finally, he was home.

34
Wonewoc, Wisconsin
June 30, 1872
Noon

TUCKER FREEMAN WAS THE BEST NATURAL HORSEMAN ARLIS had ever met, and yet he was only nine years old. The only son of Wonewoc's only black family, Tucker had been born into slavery on an Arkansas plantation in November of '62.

Unlike many slave children, he had no memory whatsoever of belonging to anyone other than his parents. Arlis had taken to paying the boy a handsome wage for performing various tasks, such as sweeping out the stables and feeding the horses. Today, he had Tucker combing his acreage on horseback, seeking out the free grazing livestock that was spread out over the sixty-three acre parcel, ensuring that nothing was amiss with any of his animals. It was a rare day indeed when something was.

Two hours ago Arlis stood in the doorway of the stable watching as Tucker rode up, beginning his dismount before the mare had even stopped. Handing the reins to Arlis, the boy smiled brightly and removed his cap.

"I ran her like ya axed me ta, Mista Jenkins. She runs real good."

"Thank you, Tucker," Arlis said. He actually hadn't needed Tucker to run the horse, he just wanted to watch the boy ride. "Anything going on out there?"

"No, suh. Nothin' a'tall. Sure is a fine day fer ridin', afta' all dat rain las' week." He turned and looked toward the river. "Da ground's good an' soft...but not too soft." He looked at Arlis again. "Do ya need anythin' else, Mista Jenkins?"

Arlis reached into a pocket and pulled out a coin, placing it in the boy's hand. "No, Tucker. If you can come back tomorrow I'd like some help cleaning up the stables. Maybe we'll groom the oxen, too, if you're up to it."

"Yes, suh."

"Thanks for coming by," Arlis said. "You can go on home now."

"Yes, suh, uh, thank ya, suh." He put his hat on and walked away. Arlis led the horse, a mare named Dolly, toward the stable.

"Mista Jenkins," Tucker called from twenty feet away. Arlis turned and looked at the boy, raising his eyebrows.

"I's almos' forget, Mista Jenkins." He ran to where Arlis

stood. "Da widow Boyd tol' me ta tells ya dat she'd be right by here at noon today. Says she's got's some bidness or sumptin' ta talk on wit ya."

"Really," Arlis said. It wasn't a question.

"Yes, suh. She says she'll be callin' on ya afta church." said Tucker. He kicked at the ground, waiting for a reply.

"Did she say what her business was with me, Tucker?"

"No, suh, but she says she's gonna bring a roast beef wit her and dat I's should tells ya ta be hungry when she gets here."

"Really," Arlis said. Again, it wasn't a question.

"Yes, suh."

"Thank you, Tucker."

"Welcome, suh."

Now, as noon approached, Arlis sat facing the town in his front courtyard, having set the wooden table with his finest dishes and cutlery, nervously anticipating the arrival of Mrs. Boyd. Then, after pulling up the tall weeds that grew along the picket fence bordering the courtyard, he'd brought another chair outside and raised the sun umbrella. Not sure what to do next, he walked the length of his driveway and opened the gate leading to the road, allowing the widow easy access to the property. He checked his watch again: 11:48 A.M. Having checked the street again to see if she was approaching, something he hadn't done in nearly thirty seconds, he walked back to the fenced-in courtyard to make sure that everything was as tidy as it had been three whole minutes ago.

"You stupid, stupid boy," he muttered.

Madeline Boyd, nee Hoard, had been born and raised in upstate New York. Her father, a lawyer and congressman, was progressive enough to send his daughter to Elmira College, an all-female school, where she became a member of the very first graduating class of 1859. Shortly after graduation, she'd married Robert Boyd, a Presbyterian minister who'd been employed by the college. When the war began, Robert had gained a captain's commission, serving as chaplain in a New York regiment, where he'd contracted measles and died before the regiment had even left its home state. Madeline, either because of her pain or in spite of it, had moved south, offering her services as a nurse in one of the many hospitals in Washington. There, she performed exemplary work, receiving a letter of commendation from Dorothea Dix, the Superintendent of Army Nurses, who had initially refused to employ the young widow based on her tender age and striking beauty. After nearly a year and a half in Washington, Boyd had felt her sanity slipping as a result of the death and gore, and had gone back to her home in New York where she taught school for the rest of the war.

In 1866, Mrs. Boyd had found an advertisement in a newspaper asking for experienced teachers to come to Wisconsin. Deciding that she'd had enough of the constant prying from her always curious in-laws, former or not, she'd packed up and headed west, settling in Wonewoc. Her arrival caused more than a little commotion in the small town, with the mystique of her beauty mingling with her charm, education, social status, and a past that many were in a rush to discover. Having nothing to hide, Madeline understood the dangers of a secretive past and the idleness of a gossiper's tongue. She circulated quickly, ensuring the stories that made the rounds of the town were cemented in truth rather than conjecture. Soon, she'd been hired on as the school mistress, teaching the seventeen children of the town during the winter months. Beginning the following summer, she'd taken to laundering the linens of those bachelors in town that were wanting of such services. This was how Arlis had come to know her. This summer marked the fourth season that the widow Boyd was providing this service for Arlis. But today was Sunday. Laundry day fell on Wednesday.

Being the introvert that he was, Arlis seldom allowed his

curiosities about women to pass beyond superficial. Having little interest in any social contacts beyond the care of his livery, most in Wonewoc thought Arlis to be shy or aloof, if not a straight up brooder. Although some shunned contact with him, as awkwardness would often rule any conversation, nobody could accuse Arlis of ever having been intentionally mean or nasty. As time moved on, Arlis could sense himself foundering more and more when engaging his neighbors, and his inability to hold an adequate conversation only led to him withdrawing more. In a sense, Arlis was becoming his father, and he knew it.

His attitude toward Mrs. Boyd was an exception, however. Although he had never really minded being alone, those times that he'd think about the widow were the only occasions he'd actually feel lonely. She was the only living woman that made him feel a sensation of longing. Since he'd first met her nearly six years before, Arlis had felt an unwilling eagerness to seek her out and interact with her, finding a way to merge the life of a man who boards and cares for livestock with the life of a schoolmarm. Every time he'd gotten serious about such scheming, through making plans to attend the widow's church or some other venture, the reality of his past would slam into him, and he'd remind himself that everyone he'd ever cared for had been taken from him. It was easier to live in anticipation of a romance that would never be than to risk losing that romance to a God that ripped all those he loved from his life.

Having checked the street again and finding it empty, Arlis retrieved a pitcher of tea punch from the kitchen, dropping in several chunks of ice he chipped from the ice box, and brought it outside along with a couple of tall glasses. As he prepared to pour himself a glass, he looked up to find a Concord buggy parked just inside the fence, with Mrs. Boyd swinging the gate closed behind her. His mouth went instantly dry. Without hesitating, he took a long drink directly from the pitcher.

What business might this woman have with me? he wondered. *Perhaps she's going out of town and needs her horse looked after?*

The buggy, pulled by a single horse, stopped near the gate of the picket fence. This time, Arlis was there to help the lady from the carriage.

"Good afternoon, Mrs. Boyd," Arlis said, taking her gloved hand in his as she stepped from the buggy. "I hope that you are feeling well today." He said, already feeling awkward.

"I am, Arlis, thank you. How are you faring?"

"I'm well as well, ma'am," he said. "I must admit that it was a most pleasant surprise when Tucker announced you'd be paying me a visit today." He looked at her basket, covered with cheesecloth and placed neatly on the bench of her buggy. "May I help you with your basket, please?"

"Certainly. Thank you."

He took the basket, pushed open the gate, and followed her through. He was pleased the conversation had gone well. He was struck by her beauty. She wore a light blue prairie dress so pale in color it was almost white. It was as fine a garment as any in Wonewoc, the back protruding slightly from either a bustle or a crinoline. Arlis reminded himself that she was still dressed for church and most likely not fussing so much over this encounter. Her skin shone mildly, beaming her fair complexion, the texture smooth and faultless. Her eyes were a deep green and noticeable from yards away. To Arlis, she was ethereal, airy, almost spiritual. When she walked, her upper body made no vertical motion whatsoever, conveying an illusion of floating. She seemed to hover just above the ground, as if a slight breeze controlled her speed and direction, a phenomenon that had long fascinated Arlis.

Petite and delicate in bearing and presence, Arlis found the widow to be a contradiction on many levels. To him, she was larger than life, strong and soft, sturdy and tender, quiet and engaging. He was sure that she was fragile. He was equally sure that nothing could break her. Nothing except God, that is.

"I've brought some roasted beef and some trimmings, Arlis," she said, taking the basket. "If you'll see to unhitching Greeley, I'll set up dinner here."

"Yes, ma'am."

She nodded toward the gelding. "Just turn him loose. He won't go far."

"Yes, ma'am," Arlis said again, turning toward the buggy.

Arlis watched the widow with one eye as he went through the motions of unhitching Greeley from the buggy. Using cutlery she'd brought along, she sliced thin slivers of beef from the mass, still hot despite the half-mile ride. Then she fluttered around the table, buttering bread and serving a green vegetable, seemingly disinterested in anything other than that which was right in front of her.

"God, help me," muttered Arlis, turning the horse loose. He returned to the courtyard, where Mrs. Boyd had finished filling the glasses with the tea punch.

"Let's eat it while it's still hot," she said, smiling. They sat across from each other at the table. Instantly, the widow bowed her head and waited. Arlis, nearly missing the cue, clumsily offered up grace, bowing his head only so far as to be able to still see the widow's face through stolen glances.

They ate. Much of the meal passed in silence, the quietude interrupted by talk of weather and non-invasive town gossip, such as the death of Mr. Newley, who had owned the general store in town. The verdict on what would become of the store was still in question. Arlis, having complimented Mrs. Boyd several times on her cooking, made a few attempts at fishing for the reason of her visit, even going so far as to comment about not deserving such lavish treatment. After receiving nothing more than a "thank you" and a wave of a hand, he resigned himself to patiently waiting her out. With each passing minute, he could feel his pulse increase.

"This tea is wonderful," Mrs. Boyd said, emptying her glass. "What's in it?"

Arlis poured her another. "It's a sweet tea punch, ma'am. My mother used to brew it. It's always been my favorite summer beverage. It's strained tea, boiled and poured over a sugar loaf. Add some sweet cream and boil it again. The real recipe calls for a bottle of claret or champagne. This version has neither, so calling it 'punch' isn't accurate. Instead of the claret, I add cherry juice."

"I may ask you for the recipe later."

"And I shall give it willingly. It's no secret. It comes from a book called "The Kentucky Housewife." He instantly blushed, adding, "It was my mother's cookbook, published before you and I were born. I still have the copy, ma'am."

She stiffened slightly and pursed her lips. "Arlis," she said, the tone flat. "I've been calling you by your first name since you first insisted upon it years ago. I think it's about time you started calling me 'Maddie.'"

"Yes, ma'am," he said.

A quarter hour later, the dishes cleaned and set aside and the remaining food hidden away beneath cheesecloth again, Mrs. Boyd withdrew a letter from the basket.

"I've had some big news from a town called 'Sun Prairie,' just east of Madison," she said, handing Arlis the letter. "As you can see, I've been offered a teaching position."

Arlis read the letter, written in fine calligraphy by a man named Samuel Weston. In it, he commended Mrs. Boyd on her laudable education and sterling reputation as an educator, offering her not only a teaching position, but also control over the curriculum of a small private school. He closed by asking that she respond to the offer in kind by the end of July. Arlis felt his stomach tighten. He had to concentrate hard to keep disappointment from contorting his face.

"The salary they're offering is generous," she said. "It's four dollars more per month than I'm earning now."

"That's wonderful, Mrs. Boyd. When are you leaving Wonewoc?"

She sipped her tea. "I haven't decided if I'm going to take the job yet."

Arlis looked at her blankly. This was getting peculiar. "Mrs. Boyd, that's an annual increase of forty-eight dollars *and* full control over the studies. Opportunities like this don't come by very often. What could possibly be holding you back?"

She put her glass down and looked at Greeley, who was grazing on the tall grass south of the courtyard. Taking her time, Arlis thought she appeared to be steeling herself in preparation of something. He waited anxiously.

"Mr. Harvey has gotten engaged to the Bailey girl," she said finally. "Did you hear about that?"

Arlis shook his head.

"This is a small town, Arlis. Having come from a bustling city in New York, and having lived in Washington for a while, I had worried I wouldn't be happy here. There was always a possibility that the natives wouldn't accept me like one of their own." She paused, adjusting the bun in her hair. "I've found that I've been happier here in this little town than I could ever be in a large city. There are good people here. I have *friends* here. And I have a job here that I find rewarding."

"It's rewarding to wash a man's britches?" Arlis quipped.

She laughed. "I don't miss the noise and the smells of the city…and I've found that I can obtain any item I want through the general stores here in Wonewoc, or up in Elroy just by paging through catalogs. I've been left wanting of nothing, materially speaking, since I moved here…well, except for oysters. I grew awfully fond of oysters back east."

Silence ensued. Arlis, sensing her discomfort, allowed her

to take her time. He sat with his hands folded in his lap, feeling the coolness of a northerly breeze on his neck.

"Alright…forgive me for being so forward, but here it is," she said, her eyes locking on his. "If you'll take to courting me, Arlis Jenkins, I'll have reason to turn down this job offer and remain here in Wonewoc, plain and simple."

Arlis was stunned. He felt a laugh rising in his throat and stifled it. Speechless, he said the only thing that came to mind. "Ma'am?"

Mrs. Boyd rolled her eyes. "I'd be a lot more comfortable if you called me 'Maddie,' Arlis."

"Yes, ma'am."

"Look," she said, cupping her glass in her hands, "I'm widowed, but I'm still a young woman. I spend my winters teaching other people's children, all the while wishing I had my own. As happy as I am, I'll never be fulfilled until I've got a family. It's really all I've ever wanted. I've watched the men in this town, most of them anyway, marry themselves off to the other young ladies, never really having given me a thought." She took a drink. "I think I know why, though. They're intimidated by my education or by my job. Some stay away because I was married to a preacher, thinking they can never live up to some sort of imaginary expectation I must hold. The veterans know that my husband was an officer, but his title was honorary, as he knew nothing of soldiering before signing up. And the rest…well…" She tapered off.

Arlis leaned forward and refilled his glass. "I'm not sure that your lack of offers has had anything to do with any of those things." He cleared his throat. "As long as we're being forward here, I'll offer up my own opinion. You, ma'am, are a beautiful, smart, graceful lady that carries herself with an air of elegance and dignity that I've found unmatched in my adult life. Your education certainly has something to do with it, but who your husband was or what he did is irrelevant. It's *you*,

Mrs. Boyd, that carries an aura of excellence...of purity...of virtue. There is nothing in this town more sterling than your image. If men don't approach you, it's not because they're not interested, but rather, because nothing in this frontier town could possibly present itself as cleaner or more polished than *you*. These farmers and blacksmiths and shopkeepers see you as untouchable."

She was blushing and staring into her lap. "Thank you, Arlis. That may be the nicest thing anyone's ever said to me. I am just a woman, though."

"No. You're a *lady*," he corrected.

"Okay, then. But this lady finds herself longing for the company of a man, Arlis. School teaching has given me ample occasions for socializing with people, but not for spending time in the company of men. Church offered some, but for that whole piety thing again. My entire reason for taking up laundering was to have an opportunity to socialize with the bachelors of this town, yourself included. I've been fixating on you for a long time now, Arlis. I'd have talked to you about this a lot sooner if you were a church going man."

"Just because a man doesn't go to church doesn't mean he's not a believer," Arlis said.

Her eyes grew big. "I didn't mean it like that. I meant if we had more reason to socialize I'd have had more opportunities to talk to you like this, instead of asking questions like, 'Am I using enough starch?'"

He laughed, causing her to laugh as well. After a moment, he grew serious again.

"I'm not sure if you know what you'd be getting into, being courted by me." He stopped and looked out over his land, searching his mind for words. The day was getting hot. He was grateful for the slow breeze that cooled his forehead, allowing his body to remain virtually sweat-free.

"I'm much like a shipwreck," he said, "On the inside and

out. You can see me lying on the floor of the ocean but it's hard to see the reasons I'm down here. I'm visible, but unreachable, and I'm full of holes, real and imagined. This scar here on my face isn't the only wound I've got. I'm still carrying metal in my side and my left leg is made of wood from the knee down." He poured the rest of the tea punch into their glasses. "I've got another pitcher in the kitchen."

"I don't care about your scars, Arlis. I find you to be a handsome man. I always have."

He smiled a closed mouth smile. "Thank you. But it's the scars you can't see that are the ugliest. I can be woefully melancholic. I'll go days, sometimes weeks, avoiding people. I can be reticent and taciturn to a fault. I avoid getting close to people simply because I can no longer bear having them taken away from me. Everyone I've ever loved is dead."

He paused, allowing those words to linger a moment. "I'm constantly being invited to veteran's affairs and gatherings, and can think of nothing I loathe more than sitting around listening to a bunch of old soldiers bragging and reminiscing about a past that I'd just as soon forget. I avoid all major public functions, including weddings and funerals, because the only subject that seems to come up is the war."

The words were coming faster now. "Fireworks scare the hell out of me, so I stay home on the fourth of July. I'm horribly afraid of cornfields and won't go near them once the corn is waist high. I seldom sleep through a full night because I have nightmares that are so vivid I wake up screaming."

He stood up, succumbing to the urge to flee, and walked rapidly to the fence, stopping only because the barrier allowed him to go no further. His heart felt as if it would palpate right out of his chest. He placed his hands on the fence and stared into the town, watching the movement, seeing nothing. Sweat beaded on his forehead now, and he could feel the shame and embarrassment wash over him as he felt her hand on his shoulder.

Speaking quietly, slowly, he said, "I've said more to you just now than I've said to anyone in eight years." His eyes were still on the road. "During the day, I can control the memories. I can put them down if I need to. But at night, there are no rules. Anything can happen when you're asleep. I tried to be a drunk once. The whiskey just made the dreams worse and I woke up feeling ill in the morning."

"I have the dreams too, Arlis."

He turned his head and found her eyes. The emerald irises emanated fire, reflecting the light of the sun's rays. He struggled to keep the eye contact, feeling as if looking too long at something that beautiful would constitute staring.

"I nursed the wounded boys in Washington for nearly two years, Arlis. I'm trying to forget the war, too."

Arlis closed his eyes and hung his head. *Of course,* he thought.

"Forgive me," he said. "One of the chief symptoms of being antisocial is selfishness. I tend to think only of myself."

She said, "The expectation is that we move on, living our lives like nothing out of the ordinary happened. For years, we were surrounded by anger, and death, and blood, and the sights of things that nobody should ever have to see, doing things that nobody should ever have to do. We're all shipwrecks, Arlis. We're all broken and nobody knows how to fix us."

Arlis, his head still hung, said, "I reckon I'm not looking to be fixed."

She grabbed his shoulder and turned him to face her, toe to toe. Lifting his chin with a gloved hand to force eye contact, she said, "I am."

He smiled and allowed a chuckle to escape his lips. Feeling his eyes welling up with tears, he turned back to the table, said, "More tea punch, then?" and led her back to her chair. "I'll get some more."

He went into the house and came back with the other pitcher, topped off with ice. They sat quietly for a few minutes, enjoying the shade and the breeze while drinking their beverages as Arlis continued to swim in uncomfortable embarrassment.

After a while, he said, "I can't fix you."

She set her glass down and looked at him. "I know. That was unfair of me to insinuate such a thing. We'll always be broken, Arlis. What you can give me, for certain, is a man to take care of...babies to nurse and diaper, and a warm lap to put my bare feet in as we read to each other on cool autumn nights."

Arlis, feeling a mild burn in his loins, shifted in his chair.

"I'll be thirty-one this October," she said. "You're about the same age, I'm sure." She paused, anticipating he'd take the bait.

"I'll be twenty-nine on Tuesday."

"Well, happy birthday, then."

He nodded his thanks. From behind the house, a dog barked.

"I can't wait any longer, Arlis. Every day I feel myself drying up a little more. If I'm to have a family, things will need to get moving soon. You've been my first choice as a husband for years, and now that Roger Harvey has asked for the Bailey girl's hand, you're my last as well. I can't lay it out there any plainer than that. If you'll court me, I'll stay. If not, I'll take the job in Sun Prairie."

Arlis pointed to the pitcher. "More tea?"

"No, thank you. I'd be spending the rest of the day in the privy." She swirled her finger around the rim of her glass. "Do you *want* a family, Arlis?"

He felt his chest tighten. Now, for the first time since his mother had given up he felt an intense craving for affection. Suddenly, he realized how hollow he was on the inside. *I'm starving to death*, he thought.

"I…I don't think I could be a very good father."

She smiled. As she did, her eyes lit up again. "Arlis Jenkins, you are perhaps the gentlest man I've ever known. The way you care for and groom your animals and the animals that others put under your care is most admirable. I've seen you with Tucker and Johnny, how genially you treat them and how they've never had anything but kind words to say about you."

Arlis chuckled. "That's because I pay them so well."

"Maybe," she went on, "And that's another thing. You're the most generous man in Wonewoc. You pay those boys a higher wage than many men earn in the trades. Last summer, during the drought, you loaned out your horses and mules to the Lindsay family after theirs died, and then you refused payment."

"How do you know about that?" Arlis snapped, a little too harshly. Lowering his tone, he said, "I asked them not to say anything to anybody."

She cocked her head to one side. With a sorrowful look, she said, "Arlis, *everybody* knows about that. Someone always says something in a small town. It's not even the first time you've been so benevolent." She smiled again. "The O'Learys and the Tylers own horses that you've gifted them."

Arlis sniffed and rolled his eyes, saying nothing.

"You've been here for a long time now, Arlis. You undercharge for your services and you overpay for the services of others, including my laundering. Everybody in Wonewoc knows you're sitting on something. You couldn't possibly have made a profit since you've been here."

Arlis raised an eyebrow. "I reckon I don't hide it well."

"Some say you're the richest man in all of Juneau County."

"I wouldn't know about that," he said. "I reckon I'll never be hurting for a nickel, though."

"Are you worried that I'm after your money, Arlis?"

Arlis shook his head. "Quite a ruse you'd be up to, looking to Sun Prairie for work."

From behind the house, the dog barked again. Arlis put his fingers in his mouth and let a sharp whistle loose. A moment later, a yellow lab ran around the house, appearing at the gate.

"Simon," Arlis said.

"Oh, he's lovely!" She stood and went to the gate, letting the dog through. "Oh my, he's all wet."

"Heh! Yeah, he spends most of his days tormenting the ducks in the river. Feel free to turn him loose again. I'd hate to see him ruin your dress."

"No, he's not *that* wet." She turned her attention to the dog. "Oh, you're a good boy, aren't you? Stay down, now." She removed a white glove and stroked his ears. After a moment, she returned to the table, removing her other glove. She reached into the basket and pulled a hunk of beef out. Using her knife, she carved the beef up and threw it on the ground. Simon ate.

"I'm not looking for riches, Arlis, just a loving family."

"I know. Besides, there are men with less money who live much more lavishly than I do. I don't spend a lot of money. I've had hand pumps installed in the house, the barn, and in the stables so I don't ever have to go far for water. I've got an icehouse out back and an ice box in the house. I like to sit close to the rain but not in it. Last month I hatched a plan to attach an awning to the house for that purpose. Don't know when I'll get around to acting on it. It's the simplest things that give me the most pleasure. A lap cat…a hot fire…this tea punch." He took a sip from his glass. "I've given money to several Negro charities, including almshouses and schools. Helping the Negroes gives me a sense of purpose, I suppose, beyond feeding and watering these beasts."

"It's pretty obvious you're fond of Tucker Freeman," she said. "I come from a long line of abolitionists. My folk's house was a safe house for a while. Escaped slaves would follow the Underground Railroad to our cellar, and then board a vessel on Lake Ontario, taking them to Canada. I was too young to know what was going on." She laughed. "My folks didn't tell me until after John Brown's raid, and by then I'd already been through college. How about you, Arlis? What's your story... before the war?"

Arlis looked at her. A breeze teased a loose tuft of hair above her eyebrow. Falling in love with the widow would be so damn easy. Losing her before her time on the other hand...

"What?" she said, uncertainty in her voice.

"I apologize for staring, madam, but it seems to me that you must be a character in a Shakespearean play that I've yet to read."

She smiled brightly and shook her head. "I surely hope it's a comedy, then."

"Me too," he agreed.

"Now tell me. Were you and your family abolitionists?"

He frowned. "Nobody in my family ever talked about the Negroes, except matter-of-factly. Truth is, I didn't care one way or another about slavery. Even now, I have no real affection for the Negroes. I knew that obtaining their freedom didn't mean that life got any easier on them. In many ways, it became more difficult. They were suddenly without a home or shelter, with no way to buy food or to clothe their young. That's why I help them. Nobody should have to go without."

"You're a good man, Arlis Jenkins," she said.

"It's easy to put myself in their shoes, is all."

She reached across the table and took his hand. It was the first skin on skin contact he'd had with her. He thought about pulling away, and then didn't.

She said, "Not a lot of men would try those shoes on."

They sat quietly for a while, holding hands. Simon fell asleep at Maddie's feet. Overhead, cottony clouds floated by effortlessly, the only witnesses to the affection going on in the courtyard below.

"Maddie, if you say you'll come by here next Sunday after services, I'll do my best to have fresh oysters on hand for you."

Maddie's eyes nearly doubled in size. "Arlis Jenkins! I'm astonished!"

"What?" he asked defensively. "I'm inviting you to dinner is all."

She laughed. "No, silly…you just called me 'Maddie.'"

35 Hillsboro, Wisconsin
July 16, 1881
Morning

"YER SURE YA DON'T WANNA STAY AROUND TODAY, HELP ME dig some more rocks outta the ground?" Mickey said.

Arlis leaned forward in the saddle and laughed. "Sounds like a good time, Mick, but I've gotta get back. I told Maddie I'd be home around noon. She'd be one to worry."

"Meh, worth a shot. There's a post office in town, Badger. If ya get there soon it'll still go out today." He spat on the ground.

Arlis sniffed, catching the dank smell of the pigs in the sultry morning air. It was going to be hot again today. "It's a good letter, Mickey. It might not stop him outright, but it'll make him think. He'll reconsider his next book topic."

"Mebbe."

The door of the house slammed. Angeline approached, carrying something wrapped in white linen. "Take these for the road, Arlis. Blackberry muffins, just come from my oven."

"Thank you, ma'am. They smell wonderful."

"You're most welcome. Please give our love to your family."

Arlis smiled and tipped his cap. "Certainly. Thank you for receiving me with such fine hospitality without notice. I promise not to make a habit of it."

She returned to the house, leaving Mickey and Arlis alone between the house and the barn, where Johnny was following Fannie with a bucket of water. It was almost too heavy for him to carry.

"Have a safe trip home, Badger. I'm gonna start my writin' campaign tonight. Oughta be right fun, I reckon, mixin' sarcasm an' prose."

"It's your specialty, Mick," said Arlis. Nearby, a cicada buzzed noisily, camouflaged high in a tree.

"So long, Badger."

"So long." Arlis looked at Nelda, who waited patiently. He needn't give her a spur. Gently, he said, "Home, Nelly," and off they went.

36 Letter to Mr. M.W. Taylor July 15, 1881

15 July, 1881
Mr. M.W. Taylor
Care of the Oswego Daily Palladium

Dear Mr. Taylor,

Your esteemed speaking tour, being so renowned in New York,

has nevertheless found great notoriety outside of the Empire State. Word of it has traveled as far as the western states, where many people here in Wisconsin, most notably the veterans of the "Iron Brigade," are taking great interest.

We must apologize for being ignorant of the great exploits of the 147th NY Regiment at the great and terrible Battle of Gettysburg. Unlike many regiments that fought and bled on the battlefield that day and the days that followed, the reputation of that regiment has not preceded your tour. We were aware of the presence of this regiment as we arrived on the field that day, but we had assumed that they had fled the field with their backs to the enemy as the great majority of Cutler's Brigade had done, assuring the necessity of the famed charge of the 6th Wisconsin on the railroad cut, thus saving General Cutler from the embarrassment of having his entire brigade cut to pieces. Understand, we mean the 147th no disrespect. Truth is: The boys of that fine regiment got themselves caught in a spot that was just too hot to handle. It could've happened to anyone, we suppose.

Now, we members of the Iron Brigade understand that you are not, and have not, ever been a soldier in the Grand Army of the Republic. We have done our research on the subject of YOU, Mr. Taylor, and have discovered that you have made your adult living by recording in writing and speaking of the tales and stories of others, most notably those who have marched to the drum and fife, and who have bled upon the battlefield for their country and the freedom of others. Perhaps your current topic has been fed to you by someone who has been less than truthful in their history of the events at Gettysburg; perhaps your topic is a work of fiction created by yourself, strictly for profit.

Some veterans, being hard-headed and stubborn as warriors often tend to be, refuse to open their minds to even consider that the events of 1 July, 1863 happened in a completely different manner than their memories recollect. Such men would consider demanding their satisfaction in the form of a duel, should the old way of settling minor disputes such as this one still be in common practice. Others would forgo the formality altogether, choosing instead to emasculate you by leaving you in a bloodied heap on the front lawn of your property.

We the undersigned, however, have a different perspective on the latitude. Seeing how boldly you make your case for the glory of the 147th New York Regiment, even among veterans of that state that stood idly by and watched as we charged singly and alone on the railroad cut that day, we'd like to invite you to make the journey to our state capital, where we'll welcome you and encourage you to speak before our veterans and dignitaries alike. We'll personally vouch for your safety while you're here, and you can set all of these veterans of the "Black Hat Brigade" straight on how the events of the day in question really unfolded.

We shall be anxiously awaiting your response, sir. In the meantime, we'll be hastily contacting as many veterans of the Iron Brigade and Cutler's Brigade as we can, assisting you in publicizing your book and speaking tour.

We are
Your humble and obedient servants,

Arlis Jenkins,
Sergeant, CO K, 6th WIS Vols

James P "Mickey" Sullivan
Sergeant, CO K, Sixth WIS

EPILOGUE

Gettysburg, Pennsylvania
May 18, 1921
Afternoon

THE CAR WAS A 1921 LEXINGTON TOURING MODEL, PAINTED cherry red with black trim. Rhys Jenkins had rented it from a dealership in Harrisburg after the four of them, Arlis, Maddie, Rhys, and Rhys' seventeen-year-old son, Teddy, had made the trip by rail two days prior. Except for Arlis, who had spent nearly two months of his life in Gettysburg nearly fifty-eight years before, this was the first visit to the battlefield for all of them.

They'd watched it rain all morning from their hotel room. The water had come down in torrents, leaving Arlis and the rest of the party feeling sure that today's trip would be postponed until tomorrow. But the rain had stopped by 11:30 A.M., the sun had come out, and the group voted to go on with the plan of touring the battlefield after all. Rhys, being in the driver's seat, felt it best to do the battlefield in reverse, visiting the Round Tops and the site of Pickett's Charge before moving on to the railroad cut. This would allow the terrain that mattered most to his father to dry in the sun, hopefully allowing for a safer walk for both of the elderly tourists.

Maddie, five months away from turning eighty, was as spry as she'd been at fifty. This she attributed to God and a nearly salt-free diet, having had little need of the mineral since they had the icehouse to preserve their meat instead. Arlis, slightly less ambulatory than his wife, was nevertheless healthy as he approached seventy-eight. His prosthetic leg, crafted by the canny clockmaker more than half a century ago, was still functioning like new, its spring having to be replaced only once since its creation.

Arlis, having had little to no interest in reading about the war other than in correcting what had been improperly reported, knew less about the battlefield than the others. He wasn't interested in gaining an education on the matter, either. As the car stopped at the different landmarks, at places with unusual names like "Little Round Top," "Devil's Den," etc., Arlis would remain in the car as the others stepped out to read the monuments. To Arlis, all of the granite seemed excessive.

When the car stopped on Cemetery Ridge, at "The Angle," Arlis joined the others in viewing the low, stone wall and the field beyond. Even he wanted to see the ground that held those troops that had annihilated Pickett's command. There, he stood silently with his spectacles on, looking at a monument to a Rebel named Armistead, whom he had never heard of before. Then, shaking his head slowly, he returned to the car, his weight on his oaken cane.

"Damn fool, that General Lee," Arlis said to Maddie. "How he could order that charge so soon after Fredericksburg I'll never know."

The car moved northward along the Taneytown Road. With the town just ahead, Rhys turned right on Emmitsburg Road, and they slowly rode into the town. As the car passed Middle Street, Arlis stared silently at the courthouse where he'd spent the better part of two months. He said nothing, lest Rhys decide to stop the car and linger. Two blocks up, they turned west onto Chambersburg Street, which eventually became Buford Avenue, the road that Arlis remembered as the Chambersburg Pike.

"About a mile now," Arlis said quietly.

The car bounced and rolled along the gravel road as Arlis half-heartedly looked for landmarks denoting locations he'd passed on his walk from the cut into the town. He found none. For more than half a century now he'd avoided coming back here, ignoring the invitations for the 25th and 50th anniversaries, passing on opportunities to hear presidents and former generals speak about the glory and blood expended on these fields so many years ago. He had long felt that those who'd bear witness to the ground that the Sixth had covered that day would somehow know, through clairvoyance or some other higher perception, exactly what had transpired on this ground in July of '63, instantly becoming aware of everything Arlis had done and experienced.

As little as half an hour ago, Arlis had found himself bracing against having to explain his actions to his family, as if there'd be markers along the route denoting the exact spots where Bath's head had exploded, where Arlis had shot the Rebel in the face, and where he'd given his Colt revolver to the dying Mississippian. Now, he saw how ludicrous those notions had been. As the car gained on the Macpherson Woods, the trees growing larger as the car approached, Arlis realized that he could say as much or as little as he wanted and the group would leave the battlefield with only that knowledge which he wished to share. He felt a pang of regret for not having realized this sooner. Maybe this trip could have happened long ago, instead.

"Stop here," Arlis said. "This is it."

The car rolled to a stop and Rhys cut the engine. The Jenkins family stepped out, each member gazing off in a different direction, trying to make sense of the battlefield and what had happened here.

"Doesn't look like much," Teddy said, looking in the direction of the railroad cut.

"Didn't then, either," said Arlis. With his cane in one hand

and Maddie's arm supporting the other, he limped south across the road, stopping at the rail fence. The rails had long ago been replaced, the fence showing no damage from the gunfire that it had endured fifty-eight years before. Arlis ran his hand along the top, carefully caressing the top rail, consciously avoiding slivers.

"Right about here's where Captain Ticknor fell," Arlis observed. "Give or take ten feet. We came from over there," he said, pointing with his cane to the slight swale between Seminary and McPherson's Ridges. "The rest of the brigade was in the woods off to our left, in a hot firefight with the Rebels. Those trees are a lot taller now." He swung the cane around behind him, aiming it in the direction of the railroad cut. "Cutler's men were over here, getting their tails whipped, and we gave the Johnnies a volley from this fence. Then, across the pike we went, charging 'em Iron Brigade style." Still holding Maddie's arm, he turned and crossed the pike, toward the cut. He squinted hard, looking at the land near the cut. Tall granite monuments stood adjacent to it, one every twenty feet or so.

"Let's figure on a way to get on the other side of this fence," Arlis said.

"I've got this, Grandpa," said Teddy. He approached the fence and took hold of a post, trying to jar it loose. Having no luck, he moved to the next one, and then the next, until he found a post that gave under the immense weight of the large boy. Having pushed it forward a few inches, the top two rails slid easily from the slats. Teddy pulled on the third rail, which came out with a groan, and he tossed it on the ground next to the others, leaving just two rails left.

"Do you want me to take these last two out, Grandpa? I'd have to push on the post some more."

"No, Teddy. Just help me over it, please. Your grandma, too. We're gonna need to fix it before we leave."

"Yes, sir."

Once on the other side, the four of them locked arms, Rhys on the left, Teddy on the right, Arlis and Maddie between them. Slowly, methodically, they traversed the terrain, the ground soft and pliable beneath the shin high grass. Arlis, looking ahead, felt his legs weaken as the memory of the fear washed over him. For a few steps, he had to force his muscles to propel himself forward, and he sensed his wife picking up on his uneasiness as she glanced sideways at him. He turned his head and offered a smile.

Looking forward again, Arlis could see the edge of the cut much clearer this time around, as there was no smoke to obscure the ground where the Mississippians had been hiding. The angle they were taking to the cut was slightly left of the original, he figured, as the monument ahead of them appeared to have been placed where the colors of the Sixth had reached the cut. Step by careful step, they made their way across the former killing ground. No one spoke, no one asked questions. None of them needed an explanation as to what had happened here.

"Hold up," Arlis said, letting go of the arms that were holding him. Looking to the right, he eyed the ground, studying it from the cut to the fence and back again. Then, his gaze shifting to a spot a few feet in front of him, his eyes glassed over with tears as sorrow took hold, and he wept. Maddie took his arm, and Rhys, fearing the sobbing would weaken his father's knees, steadied his old man from the other side. Teddy, uncomfortable in not knowing what he should do, hung his head, staring at the ground near his feet in the tall grass. There, a metallic object gained his attention by reflecting the sun. Soon, he was staring at a corroded letter "B" in his palm, which he fiddled with for a few moments before returning it to its rightful place in the field. For several minutes, nobody said anything.

"I've spoken sparingly over the years," Arlis said, wiping his eyes, "about David Bath, who was killed here." He pointed to the right. "I reckon that he fell right about there. He was only sixteen when..." his voice failed, and he began sobbing softly again. Maddie gently squeezed his arm. Somewhere nearby, a bird was singing. Arlis, his composure regained, said, "Not a day goes by I don't think about him."

They linked arms again and resumed the hike across the field. In the sky, citrine rays burst forth from behind the high cirrus clouds, resonating an angelic glow over the fields to the west. Ahead, the Iron Brigade symbol on the eleven foot, red granite monument to the Sixth Wisconsin Regiment became visible. As they approached, Arlis, glasses on, realized that the four-sided monument was blank on the side facing him. In a moment of panic, he worried that maybe they'd come all this way for nothing.

Teddy, having stepped to the east side of the monument, read the words he found there out loud. "On July second and third, this regiment lay on Culp's Hill. On the evening of the second, it moved to support Greene's Brigade and assisted to repulse Johnson's Division. Number who lost their lives in the Sixth Wisconsin Regiment during the war: Killed 163; died of wounds 71; total 234."

Again, Arlis felt panic. *Culp's Hill,* he thought. *Why would the monument at the cut be inscribed with "Culp's Hill?"*

Teddy moved to the back of the monument. Reading, he said, "Sixth Wisconsin Volunteers...First Brigade, First Division, First Corps, July first, 1863. It lists the other regiments of the Iron Brigade at the top, Grandpa."

Arlis and Teddy moved to the west side of the monument, Arlis from the south, Maddie on his arm, and Teddy from the north. Here, Arlis stared at an eagle engraved above an etching of the flag, as Teddy read the words inscribed below.

"In the charge made on this railroad cut, the Second Mississippi Regiment's officers, men and battle flag surrendered to the Sixth Wisconsin. Loss in the Sixth Regiment: Killed 30; wounded 116; missing 22; Aggregate 168."

Maddie, patting Arlis on the arm, said simply, "It's nice."

Arlis sighed audibly, puffing his cheeks as he blew the air from his mouth. Aware of his own relief and validation, he acutely felt his age and the accompanying exhaustion, the debility caused equally through physical and emotional means. Looking at Maddie, who lovingly met his gaze, he smiled feebly.

"Let's go home," he said.

ERIC SCHLEHLEIN
is a freelance writer and historian,
with a deep appreciation for all
things Americana. He has served
his community the last fourteen
years as a member of the Hartland
Fire Department and has served
as president of the Hartland
Firefighters Association, Inc.,
where he is now well into his
third term. He lives in Hartland,
Wisconsin with his wife and
three children.

Photo By David A. Ried, St. Louis, Missouri

www.EricSchlehlein.com

CPSIA information can be obtained
at www.ICGtesting.com
Printed in the USA
FFOW04n1732090816
26578FF